A PERNICIOUS FABRICATION

BEATRICE HYDE-CLARE MYSTERIES
BOOK XIII

LYNN MESSINA

potatoworks press · greenwich village

Title Production by The Book Whisperer

Never miss a new release! Join Lynn's mailing list.

To Mandi Bierly, who rolled up her sleeves and jumped in.
Thank you!

Chapter One

To be sure, Beatrice, Duchess of Kesgrave, knew better than to argue with a man holding a gun. As offended as she was by Gerald Prosser's characterization of her facial expression as a wince when it had very clearly been an annoyed scowl, she nevertheless responded with a cool nod and promised to do better next time. Then she held out her hand to indicate she was ready to make a second attempt at hitting the target with the loaded pistol.

Rather than cede the weapon, the famed marksman tightened his grip on the firearm and confessed to having made a slight miscalculation. "You are not yet accustomed to the recoil, your grace, and I progressed to gunpowder too quickly. You must not allow this development to discourage you! It is I who am to blame. As a gently bred female, you have no natural proclivity for shooting, which is as it should be, but I allowed my enthusiasm for the sport to overcome my judgment. Of course we must proceed at a more measured pace to suit your skills and abilities. I trust you will be kind enough to forgive me."

As he spoke, Prosser wrapped the gun in a cloth and

returned it to his case, from which he retrieved a smaller pistol with an ivory handle. "Let us return to the Holster, your grace, so that we may practice until the movement is familiar to you."

Bea bared her teeth.

Prosser, either unable to recognize the sneer or determined to ignore it, regarded her cheerfully and urged her to take the firearm. "Your caution is commendable, but you must not permit past failures to impede future successes. I promise you, there is nothing wrong here that cannot be fixed with diligence and patience. I am determined to work with you as long as necessary."

Smothering an intense desire to clobber the condescending instructor over the head with the proffered weapon, she accepted the pistol calmly, then proceeded to set up her shot and pull the trigger. The gun rebounded and she held steady—as she had been doing for four weeks before they had advanced to gunpowder.

At long last, progress!

But now she was losing ground.

To some extent, it was her own fault, for she knew Prosser's low opinion of women and should have plastered a bland smile on her face the moment he had begun to lament the coarse female mind's inability to rationally assess threats. Incapable of conceiving of someone with the natural constraints of her gender having the intellectual heft to recognize the insult, let alone bristling with offense at it, he attributed her tightened expression to the only logical explanation: surprise at the gun's recoil. Even after weeks of his expert tutelage, the feeble duchess had still yet to gain control of her response.

'Twas discouraging, of course, but no matter!

He would persevere even if it meant returning to the very

first step of her instruction and reviewing the components of the pistol.

Gerald Prosser never shirked his duty.

Bea, who had been excited to finally have the opportunity to prove herself worthy of ammunition, could not believe she was actually regressing. She had mastered her response to the recoil in late May—by the end of the third session, in fact—and even Prosser had noted that the display of control was unusual for someone of her ilk.

At the time, she had naively assumed he meant a beginner.

Without a doubt, she appreciated the absurdity.

Her sense of humor was too finely honed for her not to find it highly amusing that her instruction was now going in the reverse direction, and she could imagine Kesgrave's laughter as she recounted how she had managed to backslide. Even so, the situation was intolerable and could not be allowed to continue. A new teacher was in order, and if Verity Lark decided against taking on the mantle, then Bea would find someone else.

As it had been only three days since the duke's illegitimate half sister had been released from Newgate, Bea knew it was too soon to draw any conclusions regarding her intentions. The former inmate was probably still recovering from the depredations she had endured during her stay in the squalid prison, and between returning her affairs to order and soothing her friends, who had been highly distressed by her internment, she probably had not had a chance yet to think about the lessons she had agreed to conduct in exchange for accepting Bea's help in proving her innocence.

Miss Lark would send a note soon enough.

In a day or two most likely.

As eager to advance her relationship with La Reina's daughter as she was to gain proficiency with a gun, Bea found the wait interminable, but having deferred to Kesgrave's request to allow Miss Lark to set the pace, she could not contact her now to inquire about her intentions. Even a missive releasing her from the obligation could be construed as coercive.

All she could do was bide her time.

Bea would give it one more week.

If Miss Lark had not sent word by next Wednesday, she would find another shooting instructor.

Her impatience would be tempered if her other lessons were proceeding with the same plodding caution, but she had made great strides in her other disciplines. Just last week, Carlo observed that her footwork, most notably her advance-lunge, had improved significantly, and when apprehending Miss Lloyd's killer earlier in the month, she had employed one of Zimmer's brawling maneuvers to great success.

No, Prosser was the problem, not her ability to acquire new skills.

Unaware of these thoughts, the accomplished marksman congratulated his student on her progress for the day, noting that her willingness to accept her limitations rather than rail against them argued for her ultimate triumph. "Perseverance, your grace! If you continue to give your all to the process despite a lack of aptitude, you will eventually acquire a semblance of control, perhaps even as early as Christmas."

Bea, offering a tight smile, thanked him for his encouragement.

"Of course, your grace," he replied smoothly as he accepted the Holster from her with tepid caution even though it presented no threat. "You may assure your husband of your steady progress. He is certain to be proud."

Escorting him inside the house, Bea promised she would relay the pertinent details to the duke at the earliest opportunity. She would have accompanied him to the entry hall, but

Marlow waylaid her as she passed the conservatory to announce she had a guest. "Miss Hyde-Clare is waiting for you in the drawing room. Mrs. Wallace is preparing a tray."

Having expected a call from her cousin for several days, Bea was not surprised by her appearance, and leaving Prosser in the butler's capable hands, she went to find out what argument Flora would use to try to convince her to spend a week at Red Oaks, the Holcroft family estate, after they left London at the end of July. Aunt Vera had proposed the stay on Sunday, insisting that the Duke and Duchess of Kesgrave's presence was required if Flora was to have any hope of making a positive impression on her beau's relatives.

As unappealing as the prospect of spending a week in the country as a guest of people she had never met was to her, the sojourn would delay her arrival to Haverill Hall by several days, which was not without its allure. Highly anxious about earning the respect of the sixty-plus servants who staffed the large ancestral home, she welcomed any legitimate excuse to put off the inevitable.

Lending her consequence to the Hyde-Clares' stay achieved that goal without the implication of cowardice. Indeed, it suggested its opposite, for it was an act of heroism to voluntarily subject herself to a full week of Aunt Vera's rambling digressions and Uncle Horace's disdainful glares. Far from being allowed to enjoy the comforts of a pastoral retreat, she would be called upon to soothe her aunt's anxieties and coax her uncle back to good humor.

The very thought exhausted Bea.

And yet if she were not there to help keep the ship steady, the responsibility would fall entirely to Flora, who wanted above all things to make a good impression on the Holcrofts. Forcing the girl to endure the mortification of her parents without support seemed cruel.

Kesgrave, she knew, would agree.

Entering the drawing room, Bea found Mrs. Wallace laying a plate of rout cakes and strawberries next to the teapot on the table, an indication that her cousin had been waiting for some time. "This is lovely. As thoughtful as ever, Mrs. Wallace. Thank you."

Flora signaled her agreement with this assessment by raising her chin several inches and calling the housekeeper a treasure. "Her grace is fortunate to have you," she added, employing the avuncular tone with which she frequently addressed her cousin in an effort to convey a sort of world-weary wisdom.

If Mrs. Wallace noticed anything amiss in the odd stiffness in Miss Hyde-Clare's remarks, she did not reveal it as she smiled politely and left the room.

As soon as she disappeared into the hallway, Flora lowered her chin, rounded her shoulders, and grinned at her cousin. "Well, what do you think? Too much gravitas, too little gravitas, just the right amount of gravitas? And you must be unsparing in your verdict. Do not worry about hurting my feelings."

As Bea did not know the context of the question, she was uncertain how to respond and after a moment's hesitation settled on the kindest option. "Just the right amount."

Unsatisfied with the answer, Flora scrunched her nose doubtfully and asked if she was certain. "You do not think the tilt of my head was too imperious? Here, look again," she said, mimicking her earlier pose. "Do I seem frightfully digni-fied? Like a gracious young woman who exudes respect and confidence? As I said, you must be brutally honest with me. No critique is too minor."

Thoroughly baffled, Bea begged her cousin to explain. "Perhaps if I knew to what this was in reference, I would be able to provide a more useful response."

"My stay at Red Oaks," Flora replied as though stating the

obvious. "I am practicing my manner so that I can appear ingratiating, kind, and wise. That is why I am here. I have spent the past week honing my approach on the staff in Portman Square and am now ready to test it with your servants. Did Marlow comment on my demeanor? Did he happen to mention how mature I seem for my age? Dawson swore he was much impressed, but you know he is too fond of me to say anything cutting. Plus, he would not want to upset Mama, for the household is already too chaotic for his liking."

Deeply amused by these antics, Bea kept her expression impassive as she reiterated her original opinion. "It is just the right amount of gravitas."

And still Flora was not appeased as she pressed for more information. "Does that mean Marlow said nothing?"

"Not a word," Bea revealed with unvarnished honesty.

Bravely, her cousin struggled to appear untroubled by this revelation, but the brightness in her expression dimmed as she said, "Yes, I see."

"Marlow is not particularly effusive," Bea rushed to add. "I have had only a few conversations with himself myself and I live here. But Mrs. Wallace is much more forthcoming and will probably comment on your new maturity to me later."

Clinging to this glimmer of hope, Flora said, "Do you really think so?"

"I am positive," Bea replied, resolving to raise the issue with the housekeeper herself so that she could not be accused of telling her relative a bald-faced lie.

Delighted, Flora asked if she should try giving a command to Bea's lady's maid. "Or maybe the groom? He is intimidating too. What is his name? Dinkins?"

"Jenkins," Bea supplied.

"Yes, Jenkins! Shall we go for a drive, and I can direct Jenkins on where to take us?" Flora asked, eagerly sliding forward in her seat. "We could go to Harding Howell, as I am in need of new hair ribbons. And you will see how graciously I issue orders—gently but firmly. It is a difficult balance to strike. I know I will have to issue many requests at Red Oaks, and I want Holcroft's family to see how ably I wield my authority."

Astonished by her cousin's sanguine attitude toward the impending stay, Bea confessed that she had suspected an entirely different reason for the visit. "I assumed you were going to echo your mother's plea that Kesgrave and I join your party."

Flora trilled lightly as she waved a dismissive hand in the air and said with blithe assurance, "Goodness, no. You know how Mama is, always worrying herself to a sliver about something or other! She is terrified the Holcrofts will consider us grasping provincials, as they are so very rich and live in a house almost as old as Haverill Hall. But I am confident there is nothing to worry about. Holcroft is everything that is honest and good, so I have to assume his family are just as lovely. He speaks so fondly of his parents and siblings, they cannot be beastly people. Reinforcements are not necessary, and you and Kesgrave have your own affairs to attend to. There is the nursery to prepare, for one thing, and of course you must discover everything there is to know about the hammam. I trust you will have the whole matter sorted by the time I arrive for my visit in September."

Bea flinched.

Unsettled by all thoughts of her imminent removal to the massive Matlock ancestral estate, she found it best not to look so far into the future.

First, she had to get through August.

Then she would begin to contemplate September and its hosting obligations.

It was always possible that her family's trip would be

delayed for one reason or another. A highly strung soul, Aunt Vera was subject to strange fits and might decide that the journey from Sussex to Cambridgeshire was simply too difficult to manage in the heat of the summer. Or she could realize that the grandeur of Haverill Hall, with its hundreds of rooms appointed in lavish detail by skilled artisans, was more splendor than her nervous disposition could withstand. She must know in some timid corner of her mind how readily such magnificence would devastate her into silence.

Or, rather, Bea dearly hoped that would be the case.

The contrary outcome—that Aunt Vera spewed an endless stream of nonsense—was too painful to contemplate. Regardless of where it started, her relative's rambling discourse always seemed to descend into a cutting critique of her niece, and Bea could all too easily imagine the damage it would do to her standing with the servants.

And the local gentry!

They would think the duke had married a mutton-faced slowtop by the time Aunt Vera was finished unintentionally maligning her in a desperate bid to correct a minor misstatement.

Her relative had done it a dozen times before.

As there was nothing to be gained by entertaining these dreary thoughts, Bea reminded herself to focus on the present and resolved to adopt Flora's cheerful outlook. The girl had much greater cause to fear the damage her mother could do, and she displayed no apprehension about it.

"Will Russell join you or is he staying in London?" she asked.

"He is coming with us," Flora replied smoothly, adding that he had originally announced his intention to remain in the city, but his father overruled the decision, insisting that the boy could not be trusted to conduct himself favorably. "He says Russell will bumble from one scrape to the other, disgracing the family and running up debts, which I think is horribly unfair."

Bea agreed, as in recent weeks her scapegrace cousin had shown a new maturity. While all the other spectators at the *Bright Benny* demonstration had responded to the steam engine's explosion with either shock or panic, Russell kept a cool head, matter-of-factly assessing the situation and proposing a reasonable course of action. "He is still a puppy and bound to make some mistakes, but he deserves an opportunity to prove himself. Undercutting his independence will yield the opposite of the desired effect."

"No, no, not to him, to *me*!" Flora said on a wild shriek as she flung her body forward to grasp her cousin by the shoulders and clench her fingers, revealing the limits of her composure. "You have to come. You just have to! Mama, Papa, *and* Russell? It will be a massacre, Bea. You know it is true! After one day with my family, the Holcrofts will think we are all bedlamites and sweep us out the door. I blame Sebastian. This is all his fault. Why did he have to be handsome, rich, *and* charming? Any decent man would have stopped at handsome and rich. But no, he has to be charming as well, so that everyone likes and respects him and wants the best for him. It is intolerable! His family will never accept me and why should they when he can look anywhere for a bride? Attractive, well-bred, wealthy, and adored—he could marry Princess Charlotte if he were so inclined."

Indeed, he could not, as the prince regent's daughter had married Leopold of Saxe-Coburg-Saalfeld at Carlton House only the month before. But even if there had been a royal hand available for the courting, Sebastian Holcroft would not have been able to secure it. He was an upstanding gentleman and a worthy suitor, but only someone as smitten as Flora could believe he might ascend to prince consort.

It was an endearing quality, Bea thought, only slightly

taken aback by the outburst, for her cousin frequently adopted poses she could not sustain. Less appealing was the insecurity underpinning the frantic plea, for she knew from painful experience how easy it was to doubt oneself. There she was, wringing her hands over her reception at Haverill Hall while Flora displayed the same lack of confidence.

Freeing herself from her relative's tight grip, Bea grimaced sympathetically and chided her for being needlessly harsh on herself and her family. "Your parents have their quirks and peculiarities, but they generally know how to comport themselves in polite society. Aunt Vera has even committed to memory several books on etiquette. They will behave themselves, I am sure of it."

"Humbug!" Flora said with a roll of her eyes that was as contemptuous as it was comical. "Granted, my mother knows the correct way to behave, but all sense deserts her the moment she becomes flustered, which happens more often when Russell is nearby, and you know how quickly my father grows impatient with her nervous babble. We will be there scarcely an hour before Russell challenges one of Holcroft's brothers to a duel over an absurd trifle, which will throw Mama into a dither, causing Papa to snap acerbically at her, and Holcroft's family will recoil in horror. And that is why you and Kesgrave *must* come. Your presence will add a weightiness to the proceedings and dampen Russell's high spirits and keep Mama in check and bolster my spirits. You are like ... like ... ballast!"

"Ballast?" Bea repeated, amused by the unlikely comparison.

Flora was almost as taken aback by the term as her cousin. "You see what is happening? I have been driven to using nautical metaphors. That is an indication of how dire it is! I mean, how do I even know what ballast is? Does it figure prominently in the plot of a Shakespeare play?" she asked herself softly, as if puzzled by a consuming riddle, then added with renewed vigor, "You will steady the ship, providing stability and control! You must do it. Please say you will do it! And Kesgrave as well. Dukes are so impressive."

"I think you overestimate the power of a duchy," Bea murmured.

Her cousin swore she did not, at least not one belonging to the sixth duke. "Kesgrave is frightfully imperious and haughty when he sets his mind to it. Remember him at Lakeview Hall? He was so erudite and severe! I was afraid to speak in case I got something wrong, even my own health. What if he asked me how I was and I said I was well when I was actually fatigued or hungry or chilled?" Flora asked, shivering dramatically. "I still cannot fathom how you had the audacity to openly question his expertise in the drawing room after Mr. Otley's body had been found. It was astounding. Of course, you must understand, I was horribly embarrassed by your brazenness and wished you to perdition, but I was also in awe of your daring."

Naturally, she was.

There had been no evidence of courage or pluck in the eighteen years Flora had known her cousin. It was only when Bea looked up from the spice trader's bludgeoned corpse into what she thought were the eyes of his ruthless killer that she had found the necessary mettle to speak up. Even with her decades of docility, the drab Miss Hyde-Clare categorically refused to submit to her own brutal slaying without issuing a word of protest.

She had been speaking her mind ever since.

And yet somehow she trembled at the thought of overseeing a mansion as majestic and sprawling as Haverill Hall. All those great strides forward, all those murderers identified and restrained—a dozen at last count—and she was still a timid miss at her introduction to society, hoping everyone would like her.

Keenly aware of the limitations of her own bravery, she could not deny Flora the solace of her presence and agreed to accompany the family to Red Oaks, pending the duke's agreement. "You may rely upon my consequence and support, although I must warn you that I do not possess your degree of gravitas when addressing the servants."

Whooping with delight, Flora threw her arms around her cousin in an exuberant hug and swore she did not deserve such kindness. "If there was any justice in the world, you would glare at me with the same pomposity as Kesgrave and allow me to sink into obscurity. But you are too benevolent for that. Mama will be beside herself with relief! She also thinks we need ballast. Russell told us to leave off pestering you, but nobody is pestering you. Indeed, I came here with the express purpose of allowing *you* to pester *me* into coming. You were to be so impressed with my maturity that you would feel compelled to witness it firsthand. But that is all beside the point now. Come, let us celebrate this happy occasion with a purchase of hair ribbons," she said, rising to her feet, then immediately dropping back onto the settee. "No! First I shall teach you gravitas."

Alarmed by what such tuition would entail, Bea begged off, insisting she could not consider taking instruction on an empty stomach, especially not after an hour of shooting lessons.

Immediately contrite, Flora apologized for her lack of consideration and held up the plate of rout cakes for her cousin's selection. "Sustenance is vital," she enthused, insisting that her training could wait until after they had eaten. "And do not feel as though you must rush on my account. I have all day, and there is nothing more important than helping you."

Well, yes, that was precisely what Bea was afraid of.

Chapter Two

❧❧❧

F lora's tutelage was worse than Bea had imagined, for she insisted with ardent sincerity that her cousin must begin her training with Marlow. If the lesson in gravitas was to have any hope of succeeding, then she absolutely had to start with the most terrifying member of her staff.

"It is daunting, I know!" Flora said sympathetically. "But you must trust me, as I have been practicing for two weeks and have refined the process. It works best if you can find a servant who is so frightening he muddles your thoughts. As you may suppose, this was a challenge for me in Portman Square, as Mama oversees an undisciplined household. But here it is easy because you have Marlow, who meets all our requirements. Now, the important thing is for you to remember that you do not wish to be harsh. A harsh affect implies a weak hand. Keep a loose grip on the reins. But do not think of him as a horse or a farmyard animal. Bear in mind the staff's fundamental humanity at all times."

Appalled at the notion of using Marlow in any fashion, let alone as a whetstone on which to hone her authority, Bea could not resist a faint smile at the stern command in her cousin's tone.

Readily, she agreed to hold in esteem the basic dignity of all people—and as such she could not take Marlow away from his duties for her own selfish purposes. "It would be an act of disrespect."

"But it is the highest compliment," Flora replied. "I would be hugely flattered if someone ... anyone ... was intimidated by me."

As if summoned by the conversation, Marlow appeared in the doorway, and Bea darted an anxious glance at her cousin, deeply worried that the girl would thank him for his timely arrival before explaining his part in the exercise. Fortunately, the butler was too imposing to elicit such a disclosure even in the newly emboldened Flora, who gasped awkwardly and pressed her back against the seat cushion, as if to increase the distance between them.

"Viscount Nuneaton to see you, your grace," Marlow said with his customary impassivity. If he had noticed Flora's antics, he would most certainly keep it to himself. "Shall I tell him you are home to visitors or ask him to leave his card?"

Bea was tempted to advise the latter, as she assumed his lordship had come with the same purpose as most of her recent callers: to discuss her removal to Haverill Hall. Lady Abercrombie had no doubt enlisted him in her campaign to compel the new duchess to host a house party to establish herself in the country.

But refusing him would be cravenly and she was not so fainthearted that she would evade one of the beautiful widow's emissaries. "You may show him in. And please ask Mrs. Wallace to bring another teacup. Thank you."

Soberly, he murmured, "Very good," and left the room.

As soon as he crossed the threshold, Flora let out the breath she had been holding and cried, "Goodness me! For a second there, I thought I had conjured him with my mind, which is a wildly distressing power to have and I want nothing to do with it. Can you imagine if my mother suddenly popped into the room every time I thought of her?"

"I would rather not," Bea said, sharing her cousin's dismay as she lifted the teapot to refill their drinks. She had just finished pouring when Nuneaton entered the room. As impeccable as ever, he wore imperial blue silk pantaloons and a cutaway coat in a lighter shade with elaborate embroidery and brass buttons. A newspaper was tucked under his arm, and noting the presence of the unlikely accessory, she followed her greeting with a question regarding the state of his health. "Are you feeling unwell, my lord?"

The viscount's well-shaped lips tightened into a frown as he came to an abrupt halt in the middle of the room. "You are a beast, your grace. I have come running all the way here to impart important information, upending my entire morning routine out of concern for your welfare, and you have the temerity to make fun of my appearance. I will have you know that I rarely leave my house before eleven in the morning and if this is the treatment to which I can expect to be subjected, then I shall never do it again. Having said that, please tell me what is discordant. I know it is not this color because Arctic blue suits both my austere chin line and chilly disposition. Is it the embroidery on the hem of my coat? I will confess now that you have broached the topic that I am unconvinced by the paisley. It is a dour note, more teardrop than feather. Nevertheless, my tailor's rendering of it is sublime. I will admit no criticism."

Rising to her feet, Bea hailed his sartorial choices as unimpeachable and acknowledged the validity of his opinion. The paisley was indeed lugubrious!

His lordship's frown deepened as he accused her of mockery. "I do not mean to cast stones, your grace, but it is very shabby of you when I dashed to Berkeley Square at the expense of my own high standards. I am certain two or three hairs are out of place, and it has taken all my self-control to resist the urge to return to my valet to finish grooming. I might as well be showing my ankles for my state of deshabille."

Bea laughed as she offered him a rout cake and invited him to sit down. "You are correct, my lord. It is cruel of me to tease. Please accept my apology for implying your presentation is anything less than flawless. I asked about your well-being only because you are carrying a newspaper, which is an accoutrement I have never seen you sport before. But do be assured, it shows your form to perfection."

Settling into the armchair, Nuneaton shook his head—which, it must be noted, was as pristine as the rest of him, with not a single hair out of place, much less two or three—and chastised her for continuing to taunt him after he had pleaded for mercy. "You *are* the murder duchess, though not quite in the way they mean."

Dismayed by the term, which she had heard for the first time only the week before, when it was used by one of the suspects in her investigation into Miss Wraithe's death, Bea wondered if several members of the beau monde had gathered at one of their clubs to discuss assigning her a new sobriquet. Her Outrageousness, for all its insulting excess, was perhaps a little too subtle for their liking.

Pensively, Flora repeated the description under her breath, as though assessing how it felt on the tongue. "It is rather stark, is it not, leaving nothing to the imagination. But I think I like it for that reason. 'Her Outrageousness' is so broad it applies to everything Bea does. Putting too much sugar on her rout cakes—outrageous. Investing in a steam engine concern—outrageous. Showing an interest in politics —outrageous. 'Murder duchess' is direct and focuses on her strengths without drawing other talents or interests into the conversation. Perhaps we should send a note to Mr. Twaddle-Thum informing him of your preference. I know he is a salacious gossip, but he cannot be bereft of all decency. In any event, abiding by someone's chosen moniker is a minor concession. It will cost him nothing and gain your goodwill.'"

Even knowing—well, strongly suspecting—that the notorious prattle was in fact Lord Colson Hardwicke, Bea had no intention of begging favors. Furthermore, she disagreed with her cousin's assessment: The murder duchess sounded infinitely worse than Her Outrageousness because it eliminated the distinction between identifying a killer and being one.

Regardless, it was all beside the point, as Mr. Twaddle-Thum had ceased tormenting her almost a month ago, which she reminded her cousin at the same time Nuneaton announced that the term had already been claimed by ... by ...

Bea did not catch the end of his statement because she had been speaking, and she looked at the viscount now for clarity. "Claimed by whom?"

"Mrs. Flimmer-Flam," he said.

But that was a nonsensical reply and Bea shook her head. "Flimmer what?"

"Flimmer-Flam," he repeated, opening the newspaper, which he had laid on the table next to his tea. "It is the reason I am here. I do not think it is cause for alarm because she is an aficionado of your work. All her reports so far have been complimentary, and she has yet to display the level of detail for which Twaddle is famous. But this is the third item devoted to your exploits in five days, and as the *Cheapside Advertiser* is not widely read, I thought I should bring it to your attention."

Bea, who had tensed at the caveat *so far,* reminded herself that Lord Colson's specific qualifications had made him uniquely suited for his vocation. As a master spy, he had spent much of the war with France undermining Napolean's forces, and he had readily applied those skills to gathering information about her life and movements.

Mrs. Flimmer-Flam could not be cut from the same cloth.

The data simply did not support it: England had a finite number of top-tier agents and the likelihood that two of them—which, conceivably, could be *all* of them—had decided to devote their talents to chronicling the exploits of the new Duchess of Kesgrave was vanishingly small. Bea had to believe the other spy, if he existed, had his own set of interests to pursue.

In that case, Mrs. Flimmer-Flam would rise only to the level of mild irritant, and she was already off to an excellent start by dubbing Bea the murder duchess.

Hopefully, that would be the worst of it.

Regardless, it was some relief to know the *ton* had not gathered in a quiet corner at Almack's and arrived collectively at a new designation.

And still, the fact that Mrs. Beveridge, who could not be a regular reader of the *Cheapside Advertiser,* had employed the term indicated that the new gossip's reach already extended further than Bea would like.

Flora, scoffing at the undue optimism of Nuneaton's observation, echoed the sentiment that served as the Hyde-Clare family's unofficial motto, insisting, "There is always cause for alarm."

But sliding to the edge of the cushion to improve her vantage, she read the first few lines of the article and allowed that his lordship's initial understanding appeared to be correct. "The text is highly flattering. Here, she describes you as 'valiant,' and it seems to be sincere. Twaddle undermines his compliments by citing examples that demonstrate the opposite, such as the time he called you 'a modest female' for examining Mr. Réjane's grotesque head, which had been severed from his body. Do you remember that, Bea?"

As the inaccurate description of her brash appraisal of the decapitated corpse appeared in Mr. Twaddle-Thum's first account of her exploits, Bea remembered it quite well.

Three months later, she still endeavored to disavow it.

Turning to Nuneaton now, she thanked him for his consideration in bringing Mrs. Flimmer-Flam to her attention, as the prattler had escaped her notice. "Presumably, Kesgrave's as well. You say this is the third item in five days to mention me. Have there been many?"

"Indeed, no. This is only the sixth item in three weeks," he replied, adding that its tone matched earlier stories. "As Miss Hyde-Clare noted, Mrs. Flimmer-Flam identifies herself as a devotee of your investigations and seeks to bring your good works to the attention of the wider public now that Mr. Twaddle-Thum appears to have lost interest. As the *Cheapside Advertiser* is a small newspaper with limited distribution, I would hazard that the editor saw an opportunity to gain from the *London Daily Gazette*'s loss. As you yourself have stated upon occasion, Her Outrageousness sells newspapers."

"As does the murder duchess," Bea said dryly.

Nuneaton did not deny it.

Determined to be cheerful, Flora reminded her cousin that she would soon depart from London, thus depriving the gossips of all news of her activities. "Mrs. Flimmer-Flam, whomever she or he is, will not follow you to the country, and by the time you return for the season next year, everyone will have forgotten about your remarkable inclination, especially if the weather continues to be so unpleasant. You know how people love to complain about cold and rainy summers."

It was, Bea realized with grim amusement, the first point in Haverill Hall's favor, but before she could appreciate the bright side of leaving the city, the viscount confirmed that he would be able to join her house party. He had initially considered his attendance unlikely, as the dates conflicted with his plans to visit his mother, but after some persuading by her recently widowed sister, the dowager viscountess had decided to go to Bath instead, to take the waters.

Having received no such invitation herself, Flora reared back in surprise as she looked at her cousin with an expression of utter devastation. Softly, pain seeping from every syllable, she said, "A house party? You and Kesgrave are hosting a house party, and I am not invited? Is that what is happening?"

Nuneaton, who appeared genuinely distressed by her response, apologized for speaking out of turn and even dared to suggest that Miss Hyde-Clare's presence was taken for granted to such an extent that an invitation itself was superfluous. "It would be like asking the sun to shine."

Struck by his kindness, which was at odds with the aggressive insouciance he strove to project at all times, Bea darted him a grateful look as she grasped her cousin's hand. "Lord Nuneaton is correct. Well, mostly correct. If Kesgrave and I were hosting a house party, you would be dragooned into helping ensure everything ran smoothly, so you would not quite be a guest. But we are not having a party."

The viscount begged to differ, as he had received a card announcing that very thing two days before. "You settled on the second week in September."

She did not, no.

When Lady Abercrombie called on Sunday to discuss guests and a date, Bea had adamantly refused to entertain either, and although the countess had left with a promise to resume the conversation later, she had apparently decided to proceed without the hosts' consent.

It was a shocking development and yet entirely predictable.

Bea had warned Kesgrave her ladyship had no respect for his authority.

He had scoffed.

Knowing she had been right was the only consolation to be had in the predicament.

Alas, it was cold comfort.

Firmly, she told Nuneaton that there was no party, only Lady Abercrombie's machinations. "She is trying to will the affair into being, but it is nonsense. You may join your mother and aunt in Bath."

The viscount shuddered and said he would rather spend a month in scuffed Hessians than take the waters for a single hour. "But I do not think it shall come to that, as I am not the only one who was sent an invitation. My sister received one as well, and I can assure you she is looking forward to it very much. She has already begun to plan her wardrobe."

Naturally, Bea felt a frisson of alarm at these words but told herself the situation was still manageable. Mrs. Palmer was her friend. She would understand.

Smoothly, Nuneaton agreed. "Katie is well familiar with scheming society matrons and will be entertained by the deft if ultimately unsuccessful maneuver. I wonder, however, how your other ... excuse me, I mean, Lady Abercrombie's ... other's guests will respond. One does not typically have invitations rescinded, especially not to house parties at famously lavish ancestral estates. Whatever will Mrs. Flimmer-Flam think?"

He posed the question in earnest.

Despite the lilting note in his voice, the hint of frivolity, his point was deadly serious, and Bea conceded that untangling herself from her ladyship's devices would not be simple. If she declared that the affair was all a hum on the part of the countess, then she would be opening herself up to derision—and that was only if people believed her. They were more likely to assume she had planned the party herself, then realized she had no idea what she was doing, panicked, and changed course.

Mrs. Flimmer-Flam would call her hen-hearted.

The caricatures of her trembling in a cupboard or with the covers pulled over her head in bed would appear in Mrs. Humphrey's window.

Any attempt to quietly take back the invitations would meet with the same fate, with Rowlandson depicting her locked in a tug of war with one of her guests, who refused to relinquish his hold on the precious card.

And why would he?

An invitation to the Duke and Duchess of Kesgrave's first party was a feather in the cap, and recipients boasted about feathers, did they not? They told everyone they knew.

No, damn it, she would not allow it.

Lady Abercrombie would not satisfy her monstrous ambition at Bea's expense.

And yet she was squarely boxed in.

Kesgrave, she knew, would be no more pleased than she by the countess's manipulations and might have an idea for how to extricate them. As a leader of the *ton*, he had more experience bending it to his will and was generally indifferent to its ridicule. As he was fond of saying, the moment the Duke of Kesgrave began issuing and rescinding invitations was the moment all of society began issuing and rescinding invitations.

The chaos that would ensue—it was amusing to imagine, but Bea knew it would not answer.

Flora, interpreting the look on her cousin's face as defeat, clapped her hands and solemnly swore to uphold her hosting duties. "You must not worry that I will let you down. I shall do whatever is necessary to make your debut event such a stunning success that diamonds of the first water like Miss

Petworth will launch themselves off cliff tops in their desolation at not being in attendance."

Nuneaton clucked and said one did not measure the success of a house party in corpses of Incomparables. "It is the number of letters sent. Happy guests who are well entertained have no time for their correspondence."

"Well, then, we better pray for sunshine, for Mama wrote six letters during our soggy week at Lakeview Hall, and those were before Mr. Otley got himself bashed to death in the library," Flora said with a thoughtful moue.

As the weather felt as out of her control as the party itself, Bea wanted to lay her head on the table in defeat. She did not, of course, for it was horrible behavior for a hostess, and she needed to sharpen those skills. But a moment later, when Marlow returned with the third teacup and announced that she had another visitor, she gratefully accepted the excuse to leave the room for a few minutes. She did not even ask who the new caller was, merely followed him down the corridor to the right.

To the right?

"Are they not waiting in the entry hall?" she asked.

They were not, no.

His grace had instructed him to show the guest to the ugly room.

"The ugly room?" she repeated with a hint of confusion at the unusual choice.

Mistaking her perplexity for unfamiliarity, he clarified, "The back parlor."

As it was Bea herself who had given the unwelcoming space, with its jarring brown and green color scheme and lack of natural light, its unfavorable designation, she knew precisely which room he meant. What she found confounding was why Kesgrave would direct a guest to it, as it had previously been reserved for unpleasant encounters. It was where she had met with Bentham after he had tried to strangle her and with Mr. Tyne, who had smelled as though his pockets were stuffed with a dozen rotting fish carcasses.

Patently, then, she could not expect a pleasant exchange, she thought as they passed the music room and she spotted Kesgrave standing in the doorway of the back parlor, just slightly on the other side of the threshold and behind him their caller, a tall, willowy man with black hair and broad cheekbones.

Hell and Fury Hawes.

Chapter Three

If Beatrice was startled to find the King of Saffron Hill in her home, she was even more taken aback by the blandly welcoming smile with which the duke regarded him. When they last encountered the overlord of the underworld—while investigating the murder of Kesgrave's uncle, who had formed a partnership with the blackguard—the duke had warned her in the strongest possible terms against making the error of underestimating Phineas Hawes, who presented himself well. His manners were ingratiating, his demeanor was mild, and he displayed a keen intelligence. He had all the address of a Bond Street beau begging an introduction to the brightest star of the season, and employing it to great effect, he had professed his admiration for Bea. To bolster the claim, he had even produced a caricature of her holding Mr. Réjane's severed head aloft, which he pleaded with her to sign.

Although lulled to some degree by his cordiality, she had never allowed herself to forget he was a dyed-in-the-wool villain. Even so, Kesgrave's reminder had been well taken, and she had complied with his prohibition against future dealings with only a minor caveat regarding Hawes's relevance to the investigation already underway. And yet there Hawes was, in her ugly back parlor, welcomed into their home by the duke himself, according to all indications.

As far as she knew, there was no business between the two men. Matters pertaining to the Duke's Brother, a gin parlor owned jointly by Hawes and Lord Myles, were to be handled by the deceased's son, Mortimer, whose interest consisted solely of ensuring all evidence of his father's involvement in the establishment was eradicated. He could not conceive what his sire had been thinking, linking the ancient and esteemed Matlock name with Hawes's sullied one. A refined man of good birth enjoying the many pursuits found in the capital, including fencing and driving, he wanted to be associated with neither hell nor fury.

Bea had met Mortimer only twice—and once fleetingly as he comforted his grandmother on the loss of her younger son —but he had impressed her as earnest and kind, traits that would place him at a disadvantage in a negotiation with Hawes. Perhaps he had requested Kesgrave's assistance in extricating the Matlock name from the agreement struck by his father. Six weeks after Lord Myles's death, the tavern continued to operate under the same sign, the word *duke's* elided by a black X. Thin and faint, the intersecting lines disguised nothing.

Another possible explanation for Hawes's presence was the remarkable still invention Kesgrave was shepherding through the labyrinthine patent process on behalf of its creator. The apparatus, which increased the speed at which gin could be made, would ultimately be worth a fortune, and Hell and Fury might feel entitled to a share of the wealth. He had absolutely nothing to do with the device's design or fabrication, but that would be of minor concern to a man who was accustomed to taking what he wanted.

No doubt he felt he deserved a share of every promising innovation in existence.

Contemplating these thoughts as she entered the inhospitable room, Bea realized that even if her speculations were accurate, they would still not account for Hell and Fury Hawes's presence in her home. Kesgrave had at least a dozen solicitors at his beck and call who could easily take charge of the issue for him, and then there was Stephens. Regardless of the difficulty, the highly competent steward would have it resolved by nuncheon and calmly return to his main duty: grumbling about the state of the roofs on the northernmost property.

If the King of Saffron Hill was in Kesgrave House, then it was because the duke had deemed it necessary for the King of Saffron Hill to be in Kesgrave House.

How very curious.

Bea smoothed all interest from her expression as she greeted Kesgrave, who returned her blank stare with a look of contrition. Then he apologized for taking her away from her guests, adding that the exchange would be short. "Mr. Hawes has promised to keep it brief. I trust you remember Mr. Hawes?" he asked mildly, turning his shoulders to the right as he conducted the introduction. "He was in business with my uncle."

It was a slight, the implication that she would not recognize the notorious criminal on sight, and she tilted her head as if summoning a vague memory. "Ah, yes, the investigation into Lord Myles's bludgeoning."

Delighted by the treatment, Hawes, who considered her something of a colleague, as violent untimely death featured prominently in both their vocations, stepped forward with his hand held out and owned himself pleased to see her looking so well. "Although aware of your condition, I would never be so gauche as to make reference to its discomforts.

But I know how trying it can be, especially in the morning. That you have managed to continue with your work at an unrelenting pace is remarkable, and I remain your most ardent admirer, your grace."

Next to her, Kesgrave bristled at these gallantries.

Bea could feel his annoyance rippling outward like waves, which was the purpose of Hawes's lavish praise. He had a way of exuding charm that seemed sincere despite its calculation, and she could almost believe he found the notion of a lady Runner as intriguing and amusing as the vast majority of Mr. Twaddle-Thum's readers.

Contemplating how to respond, she was tempted to curl her fingers into her palm rather than consent to the hand-shake. Ostensibly, it was a sign of respect, an indication that he considered her an equal, and yet it felt oddly like subjuga-tion. The overlord of the underworld regarded her as a curiosity—a strange and wondrous novelty.

As refusing to conduct the basic courtesy would call too much attention to itself, she grasped his hand lightly, then gestured to the quartet of chairs beneath a gaudy chandelier, its severe treelike branches darting at jarring angles. Deter-mined to match his insouciance, she thanked him for his discretion before asking him to explain the reason for his visit.

Hawes lowered his tall frame onto the seat and crossed one buckskin-clad leg over his knee. His Hessians gleamed in the dim light from a pair of sconces on the northern wall, and Bea, marveling at the care he took with his boots, wondered if he polished the leather with champagne as Brummell had instructed. "First, I would like to thank the duke for consenting to this meeting. I understand my presence here is a gross violation of etiquette and would not have begged entrance if I felt I had any other option. As I know your time is valuable, I will cease wasting it and jump straight to my purpose: One of my associates has been murdered and I need your help in identifying his killer, your grace."

Although she reclined as if settling in for an extended conversation, Bea had no intention of giving Hell and Fury Hawes anything he wanted. Firmly, she refused and indicated that the discussion was over by advising him to seek out the magistrate. "I assume that is all? Very good. I bid you good day."

Hawes smiled, introducing a note of levity, and said, "Come now, your grace. I know you have as much contempt for the magistrates as I, for they are incompetent bunglers who cannot solve a crime to save their lives. All they know how to do is post a reward in exchange for information and twiddle their thumbs until someone gives them a spurious lead that they may or may not choose to pursue. On the whole, I value their ineptitude because it allows me to conduct my business with a minimum of fuss, but now I require competence. I cannot permit a killer to murder a member of my organization with impunity. It undermines my authority and damages morale."

Bea imagined it did.

The King of Saffron Hill ruled by fear, and if his subjects did not feel safer within the castle walls than without, then his grasp on his kingdom would begin to slip. Given the extent of his realm, however, she could not believe he lacked the necessary tools to find the perpetrator himself.

He wanted her involved for a reason, which was all the incentive she needed to deny him.

But even if she did not suspect a nefarious secret motive, she would never assist him in any endeavor, especially not one that would help him tighten his grip on his illicit enterprise.

Coolly, she reiterated her lack of interest.

Untroubled, Hawes continued as though she had not spoken, adding that he had found the body himself that morning. "It was about an hour ago, and I came directly here because I knew you were my best hope for justice, your grace. I did not touch anything, not even the body. I knew from a glance that he was dead. There was too much blood for it to be otherwise. He was stabbed in the stomach with one of his work implements. I believe there was a struggle because chairs in the workroom were overturned, but you can make your own determination about that when you examine the scene."

Bea did not like his confidence.

Despite her repeated refusals, Hawes seemed convinced that if he simply kept speaking long enough she would relent and agree. It was a facile strategy, for she was not a governess to be worn down by her charge's repeated request, which the crime lord very well knew. If he would not accept defeat graciously it was because he had a reason to expect success.

His secret motive, she thought again.

"Take the case to Bow Street and ask for it to be assigned to a Runner," she suggested, leaning forward in her seat with a glance at Kesgrave to indicate to him that her patience was at an end. "Recently, we had cause to work with a man named Rusk. He was capable and trustworthy. Seek his help. You may tell him that the Duchess of Kesgrave made the referral. Now I believe we are done here."

Although she rose to her feet, Hawes remained firmly ensconced in the chair. "The victim is an associate of long-standing who has been working with me on a venture for almost three years. Although it has been turning a profit for the past eighteen months, the project has just entered its second phase that promises to bring the highest return on my investment. As you can see, the victim was valuable to me, and even if his murder did not upset the delicate balance of my organization, I am personally offended by it. I want the killer brought to justice. But if you refuse, your grace, I will have no choice but to make the body disappear. I cannot let word spread that I am so weak that one of my men was killed right under my nose and I did nothing about it. If I am forced to go that route, nobody will ever know what happened to him, not his friends or family or associates. He will simply cease to exist."

Ah, so that was how he hoped to persuade her, Bea thought. He intended to make her believe the pain of the victim's family was her responsibility. It was not an irrational approach to take, as she was capable of feeling empathy for the unknowing strangers, and yet she could not permit him to place the blame for his decision on her shoulders. Hell and Fury was a powerful man with a hoard of resources at his disposal. If a magistrate's only recourse was to publish an ad in the newspaper promising a reward in exchange for information, then he could stand to ensure the sum was convincing.

He was only playing at helplessness.

"As I said, Mr. Hawes, I believe we are done here," she added flatly, hoping he would concede graciously. If he continued to resist, then she would seek Marlow's help in encouraging him to leave. The butler, she suspected, was just outside the door waiting to be of service. "My condolences on your loss."

"Thank you, your grace," Hawes replied with an amiable nod as he rose. "I am disappointed that we could not arrive at an agreement that was mutually beneficial, but I should not be surprised at your resolve. Only someone with tenacity can take the path you have chosen, and I suspect you are wise to allow your prejudices against me to stand in the way of justice for the victim. I probably would wind up manipulating you to my own ends. Before I go, please let me extend my sympathies as well. I am sorry for *your* loss."

Bea thought it was a stratagem.

The first tactic had failed to achieve the result he desired, so he switched to another, implying the victim was known to her. Engaging her interest under a false pretense in hopes that it would sustain after she discovered the truth was a bold if ultimately misguided ploy.

Irritated, she looked at Kesgrave to see if he was as annoyed by Hawes's persistence as she and saw that he was staring at the other man intently.

Too intently, she realized, her stomach lurching with dread as she tried to figure out what Kesgrave found so compelling about the statement.

Only one explanation came to mind.

Of course it did, she thought, just as the duke supplied the answer.

"Mortimer," he said without inflection. "The victim is my cousin Mortimer Matlock."

Hawes arranged his features into a sympathetic moue, his lips drawing together as his brows tightened, and he shook his head regretfully. "This is not how I had hoped to tell you the news, your grace. I had thought to break it to you gently."

It rang hollow, his regret, for there was a lilting air to his reply, a gloating triumph that made it clear to his listeners that he had gotten exactly what he had wanted.

And it was not their assistance.

That had been inevitable.

Kesgrave was never going to allow the murder of his cousin to remain unsolved.

No, what Hawes had sought and received was the upper hand in the conversation. He had allowed them to believe they had a measure of control over the situation, that they were free to accept or decline as they saw fit, when in fact there were no options.

Although Bea wondered why he had bothered with the pretense, she already knew the answer: to display his power.

Men who had power wielded power.

It was as simple as that.

The more confounding question was how long Kesgrave had known Mortimer was the victim. If he had not realized it at the very beginning, he presumably had some inkling that the purpose of Hawes's visit cut close to home. It was the reason he had admitted him to the house in the first place. Only something truly dire could bring the King of Saffron Hill to Berkeley Square, for he knew the rules as well as they did: Members of the criminal elite did not make house calls to members of the aristocracy.

"It was through Mortimer that you met Lord Myles," Kesgrave said pensively, knitting together random events as he understood them to create a sort of cohesive whole. "The gin parlor is a recent development, whereas your association with Mortimer extends into years. The moneylenders to whom my uncle was in debt—that was your work. You arranged the play to ensure his losses were so steep he would require your assistance."

Indulging a faint smile, Hawes said that he had seen an opportunity and wasted no time in exploiting it. "But the play was always fair. I may cheat, but I do not *cheat*. If Lord Myles had had any skill with cards—or even a modicum of common sense—I would not have been able to gain control of him so easily. When his son found out about our arrangement, he was beside himself with fury. His one condition when he agreed to work with my organization was that nobody would know about the connection, and I had readily made the concession. But I considered the bargain null and void because Mr. Matlock withheld vital information. He failed to mention that his father was the opposite of a captain sharp. He was a lieutenant dull, and to make no effort to use his ineptitude to my advantage would have been a dereliction of duty on my part. Hundreds of people rely on me for their welfare, and I must do right by them. The Duke's Brother provides many of my constituents with good incomes, and it was wrong of Mr. Matlock to try to deprive them of some of the wealth and comfort he had always known."

He spoke well, Bea thought, which was unsurprising, as one did not rise to his level of success without possessing a few oratorical gifts. The power to persuade was just as important as the ability to bully.

The crime lord profession required brawn *and* brains.

Hawes's account also explained the falling out Mortimer had had with his father a few days before the latter's murder, when he discovered that the improvement in Lord Myles's living situation was attributable to his new business venture. Utterly appalled, he could not conceive of the sheer depravity of opening a gin parlor with Hell and Fury Hawes.

Bea, who had assumed the objection was to his father partnering with a well-known reprobate, realized now it was the public nature of the enterprise that Mortimer abhorred.

A quiet endeavor nobody knew about was unexceptional.

It was, she decided, a rational position to take if one's overriding concerns were money and reputation. Lord Myles cared only about accruing the former; sullying the latter was actually a large part of the appeal of the Duke's Brother.

Impassively, Kesgrave listed the pursuits at which Mortimer excelled: fencing, driving, pugilism, hunting. All familiar pastimes of the Corinthian set, none seemed to lend itself to the needs of a vast criminal network. And then he recalled that his cousin had been a skilled artist. "He demonstrated an impressive proficiency for drawing as a young boy and quickly progressed to watercolors and oils. He took private lessons after he was sent down from Oxford and developed his talent. He even started sculpting. He excelled at a variety of mediums, which appalled his father, who considered artists no better than tradesmen.

Mortimer made many futile attempts to have his work accepted in the Royal Academy's annual exhibition, and gave up four or five years ago after almost a decade of trying. Is that what he contributed to your organization?" Kesgrave asked flatly, almost as though he were bored by his own speculation. "Did he create credible copies of Da Vinci and Rembrandt paintings for you to sell to cits in Spitalfields?"

If Hawes was impressed by these deductions, he did not reveal it, instead noting how very deeply Mortimer resented being subjected to years of jibes from his father only for his tormenter to wind up as a tavern keeper. "I did not get along with my own papa—he was short-tempered and vicious—but I still think we rubbed together better than those two. When Lord Myles was battered to death with a candlestick, I thought for sure Mr. Matlock was the killer. You could have knocked me over with a feather when I heard the name of the real culprit. And that is why I am here," he said, turning beseechingly to Bea. "My instincts about these matters are terrible. I require your expertise, your grace. If we could just sit down and discuss it reasonably? Then I shall leave and allow you to go about your business. As I said, I want only to ensure that the person who murdered the duke's cousin is brought to justice. I have no other motive in seeking your help."

Bea complied, duly retaking her seat, as there was no point in delaying the inevitable. The faster Hawes relayed the facts as he understood them, the more quickly she could discuss the bewildering turn with Kesgrave, who could not be unmoved by the brutal murder.

And then there was the dowager.

Someone had to inform her of this latest tragedy.

First her son, now her beloved grandson, all in a matter of weeks.

Bea could not conceive how the septuagenarian could bear so much grief.

Hawes, as he sat down again, observed with amusement that he had never thought of selling copies of old masters to cits and commended the duke on his business acumen. "I would add that I could use someone with your instinctive sense of cunning in my organization, but I do not think the duchess would like your chances of survival. Every member of your family who has worked for me has come to a violent end. Regardless, Mr. Matlock was a highly accomplished sculptor and carved wonderfully authentic-seeming Assyrian reliefs. My operation will have to pause while I find someone to take his place," he added, raising his gaze until it met Bea's. "I hope you will keep that in mind, your grace, when you are conducting your investigation. You will understandably consider me among your chief suspects, and I want you to know Mr. Matlock's death is a great inconvenience to me. I think the fact that I am seeking your help is also exculpatory, but you must arrive at your own conclusions."

Bea would, yes, and she would accept nothing the crime lord said as fact. There were layers to his dealings, and what appeared at first glance to disadvantage him could end up working to his benefit. It seemed unlikely that he would ask her to find the culprit when he was the guilty party, but that held only if he actually allowed her to conduct a free and unimpeded investigation. Perhaps he planned to aim her toward a competitor or make sure she failed. She had only his word that he admired her skills and could be recruiting her in an elaborate show to appease his followers.

It was impossible to know.

In regard to his second claim, she did not believe it for a minute. A man of Hawes's experience would have a contingency plan in place in the event that something happened to his prized forger, especially if the scheme was as profitable as he had implied. Even if Mortimer had not been brutally stabbed, he could have walked in front of a carriage or been thrown from his horse.

Human beings were too fragile for Hawes to store all his eggs on one shelf.

To that point, she said, "How long a pause? I assume Mortimer's replacement is waiting in the wings. Does he know yet what you want from him, or does he still think he has been incredibly fortunate to have found a patron happy to support the arts? Did the Council of Academicians crush his hopes as well?"

Hawes marveled at her shrewdness before confirming the accuracy of the supposition: He *had* found Mr. Matlock among the cohort of artists whose work had been rejected by the Royal Academy. "It is a fertile hunting ground, as they say, and where I will look for a painter to carry out the duke's devious old masters scheme," he said, then darted a cautious glance at Kesgrave. "That is, assuming you do not plan to assert ownership of the idea. You will tell me, your grace, if you choose to pursue it, for I have no desire to be in competition with so powerful an adversary. The secret to overseeing a thriving enterprise is avoiding unnecessary strife."

Kesgrave thanked him for his consideration, and Bea watched as annoyance flitted across Hell and Fury's features at his failure to incite a waspish response.

Apparently, provoking the duke to anger was *necessary* strife.

As the peevishness passed, Hawes continued, noting that he did not yet have a replacement for the deceased. "I have my eye on several promising candidates and will approach one of them when the time is right. It behooves me to clear up this ugliness before returning to business as usual. It is always best to keep a scheme as uncomplicated as possible, your grace, a principle that applies to forged paintings as well. I advise you to bear that in mind should you decide to move forward."

His determined taunting of the duke struck Bea as a tactical mistake. Rather than exuding strength, it indicated weakness by revealing how deeply it irked him not to get the response he sought. She would have assumed a man with Hawes's experience would know better than to return to the same well when it had already shown itself to be dry.

There was, she thought, an advantage to be exploited from his frustration.

She just had to figure out how.

Earmarking that idea for deeper consideration later, she asked him to outline the specifics of his counterfeiting ring: how long had Mortimer been making copies of Assyrian reliefs, who purchased them, how many forgeries were in circulation.

Hawes smiled faintly and shook his head. "Oh, but you see, Mr. Matlock wasn't *copying* them. He was *creating* them. He made original reliefs that looked for all intents and purposes as though they were from Assyria in the ninth century b.c. They were masterful, and I think if he had shown any one of them to his father, Lord Myles would have bestowed his approval at long last—they are *that* good. Even so, I am taking a cautious approach and avoiding noted experts such as Lord Haysbert. No reason to tempt fate when the delightfully ignorant can be led down the garden path without protest."

Although Bea had never met the viscount, she had flipped through the first entry in his highly regarded and influential three-volume series on ancient pottery and found the engravings to be excellent. The writing, however, was a little overwrought for her taste. Every vase was a precious relic of a lost people; every urn whispered of an unknown history.

Wryly, she said, "I am sure his lordship appreciates your circumspection."

"Oh, but that is precisely the point—that he does not appreciate it," Hawes replied with languid amusement. "I suspect we will have to add more names to that list now that Mr. Matlock is no longer with us. I cannot believe his replacement will bring the same originality to the endeavor. One out of ten sculptors rejected by the Royal Academy would be able to faithfully reproduce an Assyrian relief. But how many of them can create a convincing original work? One in a hundred? One in a thousand? I know you doubt my sincerity, your grace, but Mr. Matlock was worth his weight in gold to me. Killing him would have been a terrible business decision, and I do not have the luxury of making terrible business decisions. Too many people rely on me."

Oh, yes, Hell and Fury Hawes, hero of the people, Bea thought cynically, observing that it was the second time he had credited himself with noble motives. Whether he said it in an effort to bait her or genuinely believed it seemed largely irrelevant.

Adopting Kesgrave's approach, she thanked him for the clarification, then reiterated her queries: How long had he been selling the forgeries and who bought them?

Hawes leaned back in the chair as he flicked an imaginary speck of dust from his lapel, an action Bea recalled from their first meeting. She had been taken aback then by the incongruity of the elegant sweep and the brutish subject. Now it seemed in keeping with his entire demeanor, the way he presented insouciance while retaining a firm grip.

"Two and a half years. It will be three in November," he said. "In contrast to the duke's proposed business model, our clients are established families looking to augment their antiquities collections. As anyone who has paid attention to Lord Elgin's ordeal knows, the cost of excavating authentic artifacts is high. His lordship spent upwards of seventy-five thousand pounds on removing the marbles from Greece only to recoup less than half of that from the British government. It is an untenable system, which is why I offer an alternative: a sense of authenticity at a fraction of the price. Dear old pater gets the pleasure of showing off his own treasured metope from an ancient temple without having to mortgage the estates. In practice, it is more of a service than a swindle."

To be fair, Hawes had a point: The former ambassador to the Ottoman Empire had spent a great deal of money on acquiring and transporting the relief panels, figures, and friezes from the Parthenon. A large part of those expenses were bribes and gifts to local officials to ensure the work of removing the marble continued unimpeded, which underscored the questionable morality of removing historical artifacts from their country of origin. Considered statesmanship by some, it looked like looting to Bea.

And yet she could not endorse the crime lord's scheme. It was fraud, pure and simple, and even if it created less demand for foreign treasures, it did not eradicate it. If anything, in providing an alternate market, he had most likely made the antiquities cheaper to acquire, thereby accelerating their removal.

When neither Bea nor the duke complimented him on his munificence, the crime lord continued to explain the scope of his operation. "As I was unfamiliar with the antiquities market, we approached it prudently, starting in Newcastle, as I was advised that its distance from London reduced the likelihood of an expert recognizing deficiencies in the reliefs. When no questions were raised, we slowly expanded southward and just made our first sale in London."

"The fraught time in your business," Bea murmured.

"You understand, your grace," he said with a nod of affirmation. "I knew you would. After years of careful planning, we have finally reached the most lucrative stage in our operation and now this setback. The timing is interesting, to say the least."

Taking note of the cadence, she asked if he meant to imply that Mortimer had been killed by a competitor in the counterfeit antiquities trade.

Hawes laughed.

Like everything else he did, it was calculated to elicit a particular response, but it also contained a note of actual humor.

"Your grace, I have no competitors," he said as his mirth began to subside and he regarded her with amusement tempered by fond condescension, as if examining a family pet. "I have irritants, nuisances, and one excessively persistent source of vexation, but competitors were eliminated long ago."

Bea did not doubt it.

The only question was how many were routed openly and how many simply ceased to exist.

"What about one of your buyers?" she asked, wondering if that could be the motive. "It is possible one of them discovered they had been swindled and killed Mortimer to strike back at your operation?"

Although further entertained by this suggestion, Hawes indulged only a smile as he chastised her for underestimating the complexity of the scheme. "It is not as though I have hung a notice on the door of my shop that says, 'Purchase your sham artifacts here.' The reliefs are sold through an intricate network of dealers and experts. If a customer suspected he had been gulled, there are half a dozen people to whom he would point his finger who have nothing to do with me. I rely on intermediaries. Mr. Matlock was even further removed. Nobody would have cause to suspect him. He was in every way the admired sporting buck he purported to be, pursing all the interests of a devout Corinthian, as the duke himself observed."

Bea thought his confidence was a trifle overdone. Anyone who spoke in absolutes was either fooling himself or lying to her. As thorough as Hawes was, he could not account for every factor, which meant a threat could come from any direction. It was a fact the crime lord understood well, for it was why he had dared the very great presumption of calling at Kesgrave House. Saffron Hill was a bustling district as was St. Giles and the other rookeries of London. Cellars and alleys were brimming with ambitious young men seeking to make their mark—and was that not the very definition of a competitor: an irritant you did not notice until it was too late?

And still, Bea was inclined to trust Hawes's understanding of the situation because it constrained the field of suspects. "Who do you think did it, then?"

"If I knew who the culprit was, then I would not be here, would I?" Hawes asked blandly. "Do you think this is a pleasant experience for me? I would rather drive spikes under my fingernails than sit in your parlor, but I swallowed my pride and knocked on your door because I have no idea who killed Mr. Matlock. The fact that I am willing to lay my counterfeit antiquities scheme bare for your examination should give you an inkling of how seriously I take this matter. You may bid me goodbye, then run to the magistrate and tell him all that you know. I have no claim to your discretion and can only request that you do the decent thing and use the information to find Mr. Matlock's killer."

Until he made the suggestion, it had not occurred to Bea to report his dealings to the authorities. Focused on the more pressing crime, she had considered them only in the context of the murder, and contemplating the possibility now, she wondered how useful the information would be. Hawes had been deliberately vague in his description, and all she knew was the supposed provenance of the reliefs. Possibly, an investigation could be conducted in reverse if one identified all the collectors of Assyrian reliefs in Newcastle, then found at least one who had purchased a forgery.

As the process would require a significant amount of time and attention, she doubted a magistrate would bother to make the effort, especially as there was little hope of legal action being taken against Hawes. A man did not rise to prominence by gaining control of a rookery without having a few law enforcement officials in his pocket.

With that vagueness in mind, she decided against pressing Hawes for the names of the men in his organization with whom Mortimer had routine business. Either he spoke the truth when he claimed to have no suspects in mind, or he was prevaricating freely. In both circumstances, the wiser option seemed to be to proceed without his influence. Unable to trust his motivations, she could not be certain he would not deliberately muddy the waters with irrelevant names or facts.

Consequently, they would investigate Mortimer's death the same way they would anyone else's: by scrutinizing his life. That meant starting with an examination of the crime's location.

It was, Bea believed, safe to assume that the stabbing pertained to the victim's illegal activities. For one thing, corruption frequently begat violence and vice versa. For another, the site of the murder implied a deep familiarity with Mortimer's sideline, of which society appeared ignorant. If the *ton* suspected the top of the tree Corinthian was producing forgeries for London's most notorious lawbreaker, then Mr. Twaddle-Thum would have mentioned it by now.

There was no way something so shocking and illicit would have escaped Lord Colson's notice.

Bea knew, of course, that these suppositions could prove

wildly inaccurate. Mortimer might have confided his secret to a trusted friend or blabbed about it while in his cups. She could think of a dozen ways the information might have spread beyond a tight circle and resolved to turn her attention to Mortimer's intimates if the first line of inquiry revealed nothing.

A collector who pieced together the truth about a recent fraudulent purchase based on whispers presented an appealing option, as he would stand at the intersection of Mortimer's two lives.

Kesgrave cautioned their caller against offering lectures on decency, and it was a sign of Hell and Fury's earnestness that he did not cavil at the criticism. He simply murmured in assent.

"We will start at the studio," she said.

Hawes immediately supplied the address and reiterated that he had disturbed nothing. "The room is exactly the way the killer left it. I am sure you will find it rife with clues."

It sounded like mockery to Bea.

And yet what did he have to gain from sending them on a wild goose chase?

Ah, but that was the aim of a pointless pursuit—to confound and divert its participants.

Hawes rose to his feet and announced his departure. "I think we can all agree I have stayed long enough. Thank you for your hospitality. It was both more and less than I expected. And you will alert the proper authorities, won't you? It is only right, as you are family and highly distressed over your cousin's violent murder. You will want the coroner to initiate an inquiry at once."

As the duke said, they would take all appropriate measures.

"Of course you will," Hawes said softly, a faint smile curving his lips.

Seeing it, Bea wondered again what they had been duped into doing.

The desire for justice—she could think of no cause less credible for the overlord of the underworld.

Hawes bowed over her hand and insisted he was in her debt. He knew how little she wished to assist him and advised her to think of it as helping the dowager make sense of a senseless act. "That I might benefit is a minor consequence that I hope you will not consider too deeply. It is best for your investigation if you do not spend time worrying about me, but I expect you will not be able to stop yourself. To that end, I look forward to seeing you soon, your grace, for the inevitable interrogation. Your last visit was delightful. And do not worry: I shall have those prints on hand for you to sign so you will not have to wait."

Although tempted to reply to this sardonic comment with a derisive one of her own, she allowed only a noncommittal nod and summoned Marlow to show him out.

Chapter Four

Bea waited until the count of ten.

Even knowing Marlow's curt efficiency, the way he bustled callers out of the house without allowing them to linger under one pretense or another, she paused a few seconds to make sure Hell and Fury was well beyond earshot before offering her sympathies. Reaching out to clasp the duke's hands in her own, she said, "Oh, Damien, how wretched. I am so sorry about Mortimer. I did not know him well, but he struck me as kind and sincere."

Kesgrave, thanking her for the sentiment, pressed a gentle kiss against her forehead and admitted that he was ill acquainted with his cousin as well. "We did not spend time together as children, as he was older by several years, and later, when we were adults, my uncle was always between us. Mortimer knew his father tormented me as a young boy, but desperately craving his sire's approval, he could not bring himself to say anything to his discredit, an act of cowardice that mortified him and colored our every interaction. Our exchanges were amiable enough, and we readily discussed our grandmother with mutual regard and concern. But the distance between us could not be bridged, and once we exhausted the topic of the dowager, we defaulted to cursory observations about Gentleman Jackson's left hook or the running conditions at Newmarket before hastily bidding each other adieu. Having decided to give up his art to appease his father, Mortimer devoted himself to becoming a proper Corinthian and had become quite an excellent shot. At Swithwick's shooting party in Devonshire, he bagged three grouse in a single afternoon. That is according to my grandmother. Mortimer was not in the habit of sharing his kills with me, as it hewed a little too close to home."

He spoke coolly, dispassionately, and yet a solemn note entered his voice as he tightened his grip. Emitting a hefty sigh, he said, "The damnable thing will be telling my grandmother. It has not even been two months."

It had not, no, Bea thought, recalling the scene scarcely six weeks before in the drawing room at Kesgrave House: the duke insisting he would accompany the dowager to the family seat in Cambridgeshire, the latter adamantly refusing to consider it. Although she had held herself in check during the quarrel, the effort it had required was readily apparent in the rigidity of the septuagenarian's pose, her spine as stiff and unyielding as a wooden floorboard. Having failed to protect Kesgrave from her own son's murderous rage, she could not bear any attempt to lessen her guilt, which felt well deserved, and Bea feared that Mortimer's murder would make the burden intolerable.

Despite her considerable resources, the Dowager Duchess of Kesgrave could no more save her grandson from the consequences of his folly than she could her son from the cruelty of his inclinations.

As Bea shared his reluctance, she suggested they postpone the unavoidable for the moment, deeming it less pressing than inspecting Mortimer's studio and alerting the authorities of his murder. "Every word Hawes uttered was chosen to persuade us to do his bidding, but his point regarding the crime scene is nevertheless true. The longer we wait, the more likely it will be disrupted. We must go there at once."

Kesgrave, readily agreeing on all points, wondered what they would find when they arrived at the studio: the room as it was left by the killer or a mise-en-scène carefully constructed to lead them to a particular conclusion. "As I cannot believe Hawes's interest in justice is sincere, I can only assume he has a desired outcome in mind. The thought of aiding him in that endeavor appalls me."

"Well, then, we shall not," Bea replied with bracing surety. "For all his determined fawning of my skills and accomplishments, Hawes thinks he is smarter than us, which gives us the advantage. Indeed, I wager he considers himself more clever than the vast majority of London, which is an almost unavoidable outcome of his success. As the feared head of a violent organization, he must rarely if ever hear dissent or criticism. Whatever dissatisfaction his management has engendered, it is whispered about behind his back."

The duke regarded her pensively for a moment before giving form to the implication. "You think his hold on the rookery has begun to slip."

She did not, no.

Rather, she thought Hell and Fury knew an empire was a slippery thing. "He cannot allow one display of disrespect for his authority to stand because it might lead to a second and a third. It must be handled swiftly and firmly. Otherwise, it reveals the limitations of his power. That is why he is taking the murder as a personal attack against himself, but it might be unrelated to Mortimer's work."

Kesgrave considered it unlikely, as his cousin was not generally known to keep a studio in St. Luke's to conduct his illicit business. "If it was, it would have reached my ears, as people love to run to me with tales. The only people who know about it are involved in the forgery trade. Obviously, we must treat everything Hawes tell us with suspicion, but I am inclined to believe him when he says the scheme is known to a select few. That will keep the pool of suspects small, and if the pool proves too small, we can expand the scope and look for the culprit among his friends and acquaintance."

As this notion echoed Bea's own thoughts, she nodded briskly before reminding him that they were not bound by some moral code to investigate all murders. "If the prospect of helping Hawes strengthen his position is too abhorrent, we can refer the matter to the magistrate and allow the authorities to handle it. They cannot *all* be inept buffoons like Piddlehinton, and the Runners are savvier than a country constable who would accept suicide as a rational explanation for a blow to the back of the head," she said, unable to quell her disgust at the memory of the rustic's enthusiastic adoption of Kesgrave's nonsensical account of Otley's death. Although the murder happened almost a year ago, the constable's instinctive obsequiousness still irked her. Having lived with the Hyde-Clares for more than twenty years, she knew well the habit of modifying one's own opinions to appease the vanity of illustrious members of the *ton,* but watching a man abandon all sense of logic had introduced her to a new nadir of servility.

Naturally, Kesgrave considered it his due.

Indeed, he did, yes, as his inviolate respect for the truth compelled him to point out that the constable's acceptance was in fact highly rational. "I had rendered a verdict, and he had nothing to gain by setting himself against me."

The offhand comment was delivered with the imperious ease of a grandiloquent pronouncement, and Bea found herself grateful for the reflexive pomposity, which replaced his earlier sadness. For the moment, he was thinking of neither his grandmother nor his dead cousin, and seeking to prolong the interval, she said, "On the contrary, he had the truth to gain."

Now the duke's lips twitched in a display of seemingly genuine amusement. "Yes, as I said, nothing. The only gain that has any significance to the landed gentry is of the material variety, and challenging a duke might have harmed his standing in the community, especially if I took a pet at having my word contradicted by a provincial bumpkin. Additionally, he knew nothing of my motive. I might have been a fop who imagined himself clever or the murderer diverting attention elsewhere. If it was the latter, he certainly did not want the obligation of arresting me."

These were, she thought, among the truest words ever spoken, for the constable would have been delighted to compliment the Duke of Kesgrave on how masterfully he had brandished the candlestick if given half a chance.

"The most sensible course was to bow to power and do nothing to upset the cart," he continued, releasing her hand as he turned toward the door. "That is why I cannot leave it to the magistrates. I do not know what sway Hawes has over the legal system, but as he struts about London with impunity, it is clear he has some. Despite his many crimes, nobody has ever tried to hold him to account. That is not by chance."

It was always revelatory for her to hear him discuss power, in both manner and substance. An orphan foisted on relatives who had accepted her out of begrudging obligation, she had known only its opposite and could not conceive of being at ease with the comforts it conferred. Kesgrave wielded it nonchalantly, and Hawes enjoyed the ineffable peace of not having to fret about enduring the consequences of his actions.

Contemplating the King of Saffron Hill's many crimes,

she asked if the duke believed Hawes had a hand in the murder. "At first glance, it would appear not to make sense, his recruiting us to solve the murder and subjecting himself to possible exposure for no reason. But perhaps he is laying a trail for us to follow," she said softly, then shook her head at the notion that Hell and Fury assumed they would be so easily led. "As you have noted on several occasions, Bentham made that wager and lost."

Kesgrave could draw no conclusion either way, which was why they would begin their investigation posthaste. "I would like to have some useful information before we call on my grandmother. I am not so deluded as to imagine it will render Mortimer's death any less painful for her, but I hope knowing the context of it will make it seem less senseless."

With this statement, the despondent look returned to his face, and Bea decided there was no time to lose. Action was always better than inaction.

Even so, she hesitated briefly, as she recalled Flora and Nuneaton, whom she had left in the drawing room. She had no desire to meet them and explain the strange and discomfiting circumstance in which she and the duke currently found themselves.

Gesturing to the time, which was approaching eleven, Kesgrave assured her that Marlow had long ago made her excuses. "He is too efficient to allow them to linger and possibly catch a glimpse of Hawes."

Bea dearly hoped so—or Aunt Vera would arrive within the hour to wring her hands over her niece's propensity to associate with blackguards and villains and apologize to the duke for saddling him with a wife who kept such low company. Then she would own herself baffled by the atrocious tendency, note that it had become a problem only in the past few months, and gasp with mortification as she realized she had implicated Kesgrave in the development.

The duke, pressing a hand on her lower back to escort her from the room, could not believe either visitor would recognize Hell and Fury if he strolled past them in the corridor at Kesgrave House. "*La Belle Assemblée* has yet to publish his portrait, and Nuneaton only flips through *Ackermann's Repository* at his club to discourage conversation about politics or sports."

Despite the conviction with which he stated the latter, Bea was forced to issue a correction. "His illiteracy is all for show. As he is a regular reader of the *Cheapside Advertiser,* I think it is safe to assume he subscribes to a variety of periodicals across a wide spectrum of perspectives. I would not be surprised to discover he is as erudite as Samuel Johnson."

Recounting the various services the viscount had performed for her, including reviving the Barrington Feint so that he could draw close enough to a suspect to smell his breath, Kesgrave marveled at her willingness to malign a man who had proven to be a staunch ally. "I am sure he has done nothing to earn the abuse."

It was, she thought as they crossed the threshold, precisely the charge Nuneaton would level at her if he had overheard the comment. Outside, Jenkins waited for them with the carriage, a turn that could also be attributed to Marlow's efficiency. Boarding the conveyance, she contemplated how much she should tell Kesgrave about his lordship's visit. Naturally, she wanted to complain about Lady Abercrombie's high-handed machinations and demand that he put a stop to the devious woman's unsanctioned house party at Haverill Hall at once. He would, she knew, be as outraged as she at the countess's inconceivable presumption and would not bow to a dictate that said an invitation could not be rescinded.

An invitation issued under false pretenses was not an invitation but an act of subterfuge.

Surely, the beau monde recognized the difference.

As she settled on the bench, however, she found she could not bring herself to say the words. With his cousin's murder and the dowager's grief, he had more than enough on his mind, and compared to those weighty matters, the problem seemed trivial.

And then of course there was her panic—no, terror—at the prospect of hosting illustrious members of the *ton* in a centuries-old monstrosity attended to by a large staff who knew nothing about her save she routinely mortified their dignified employer by compelling him to conduct murder investigations.

Indeed, it was the stuff of nightmares, for she had a particularly vicious one that kept repeating, and there she always stood, shivering in the cold in her nightrail in front of the house as a parade of carriages as far as the eye could see clattered up the drive and a mob of servants clamored around her saying, "What shall I do, your grace? What shall I do?"

She would not expose Kesgrave to her apprehension.

In recent weeks she had come to understand that he perceived her lack of confidence in herself also to be a lack of confidence in him, and while she did not entirely share the perspective, she could see how the emotional turmoil of her insecurities could begin to pall after so many months.

Bea would rout Lady Abercrombie herself.

How precisely she had no idea and resolved to send Mrs. Palmer a letter explaining the problem as soon as they returned home. The society hostess was level-headed, intelligent, and sly. With her help, Bea felt confident she would come up with a solution.

Kesgrave need never have an inkling.

Contemplating the things she could tell him, Bea urged him to congratulate her. "I have a new chronicler: a gossip-monger who calls herself Mrs. Flimmer-Flam. She has written only a few stories so far, and all have been complimentary. Nuneaton discovered her while reading the *Cheapside Advertiser*. That is how I know. He does not think her reach will be as extensive as Twaddle's, as the newspaper enjoys a limited distribution. But he thought I should be warned in any case. It is she who calls me the murder duchess, which lacks the subtlety of Her Outrageousness."

The duke's lips quivered as her examined her in the dim light of the carriage. "Is that a hint of regret I hear for Mr. Twaddle-Thum's light touch?"

"Light?" she echoed with a faint derision. "The three hundred words he wrote describing each crystal of sugar strewn on my rout cakes were heavier than an anvil."

"I think they have a certain poetic charm," he confessed.

Bea dropped her head against the cushion as she admitted that she did as well. "Lord Colson is an excellent writer in addition to being an exceptional spy. I find the excessiveness of his talents to be in poor taste. He should excel at one or the other, not both."

As Kesgrave remained doubtful of her theory, he consoled her with the possibility that Hardwicke might not be as gifted as she believed.

The vehicle turned onto Banner Street and slowed to a stop in front of number eight. A scowling Jenkins opened the door and offered his arm to help Beatrice descend. Although he said nothing about their errand, she could tell he heartily disapproved of it, for he knew it was connected in some way to Hell and Fury Hawes's visit. The timing was too coincidental for it to be otherwise.

The poor groom, subjected to so many unpleasant experiences by his employer.

No doubt, he was looking forward to the quiet pace of country life.

As Kesgrave did not know what they would find once they

entered the studio, he was unable to tell the groom how long they would be. Instead, he instructed him to walk the horses, which was unnecessary, as Jenkins knew well enough how to wait in a street.

Taking the duke's superfluous remark as an indication of his anxiety, Bea brushed her arm against his as they approached the edifice, a single-story structure squeezed between two much taller buildings. Both soared twenty feet above the small dwelling, severely constraining its access to natural light. The obvious limitation made it a strange choice for a studio, but she supposed the space had other advantages to recommend it. The location, for one thing, was well suited to an illegal enterprise, as the street was leafy and quiet, its inhabitants tucked behind drapes and shutters. Only one house among the dozens had an uncovered window, and Bea watched the curtain flutter across the road as Kesgrave attended to the lock.

It took him only a few moments.

Then he opened the door and stepped inside.

The interior was dark, as Bea expected, with thin tendrils of light creeping into the hallways from the room at the far end, and she passed one doorway as she strode toward the back.

Ah, now that was more like it, she thought as she entered the space, which was wide and airy, with a large skylight admitting rays of sunshine and a bank of windows providing a southern exposure. Although only about fifteen feet wide, the room was long, which allowed for the creation of a variety of work areas. Toward the entrance was a table, solid and thick and dusted with sand. Tools were scattered across the surface —chisels, cogues, scrapers—and next to it, against the wall to the left, was a cabinet, its shelves piled high with books and papers. The top drawer, open halfway, was draped with a canvas that grazed the floor.

Stepping deeper into the room, she saw the chairs Hawes had mentioned. They were both knocked over, one laying on its side, the other resting on its back. A few feet beyond them was Mortimer. He, too, was on his back, his blank eyes aimed at the ceiling, one of his carving implements sticking out of his stomach.

Bea lurched forward to take a closer look, then immediately pulled back to allow Kesgrave to decide how he wanted to handle the scene. The slain body of a murder victim was always ghastly, but there was something especially gruesome about the mangled corpse of an acquaintance. The familiarity of their form mixed with the unremitting emptiness of their expression combined with the grisliness of their final moments made them something new and disturbing.

And the blood—there was so much of it.

It had spread outward, oozing onto the floor and soaking the planks, and if there was one fact to be gathered at a glance it was that death had not come quickly. For several minutes, Mortimer had lain amid the splatter, life seeping out of him, and Bea flinched as she imagined the pain he had endured, both mental and physical.

And the killer, she wondered.

Did he flinch?

She supposed the answer depended on his objective. If he had arrived at the studio with the intention of killing the artist, then he would have steeled himself for the grisly consequences of his actions. There were dozens, if not hundreds, of ways to murder a man, and choosing to ram a sculpting instrument into his belly indicated a profound lack of squeamishness.

Hawes, she thought.

Surely, the overlord of the underworld had driven a knife into an adversary's stomach on at least one occasion. Brutality was how one retained control over one's underlings, and he would not hesitate to strike out in the most ruthless way possible if he felt it would strengthen his position.

But then why invite Her Outrageousness to inspect his handiwork?

Perhaps to ensure word of it reached the widest audience possible, she thought. Once Twaddle published his customarily thorough account of her investigation, the whole of London would know that no one was safe from Hawes's wrath.

Not even Mortimer's rank and august connections could save him.

No, that was nonsense, she decided, for the investigation could end in only one of two ways: Either she identified Hawes as the killer, in which case he would suffer the consequences of being a killer, or she failed to identify Hawes as the killer, in which case his reputation would not be burnished.

Or was the latter beside the point?

Would the people whom Hawes wanted to impress know without further evidence who was responsible for Mortimer's slaying?

Bea shook her head, confident the plot she was weaving was too complicated.

The simplest explanation was usually the correct one.

Finding the murderer benefited Hawes as he had claimed.

With that in mind, she returned her focus to the killer's intention. Had he called on Mortimer with the express purpose of murdering him or had their conversation devolved into a lethal argument? The convenience of the tool argued in favor of spontaneity. It was always preferable to bring one's favored weapon than to rely on the random assortment of options on hand. If a genial meeting had gone horribly wrong, then it was likely the victim knew his assailant. He had welcomed him into his studio.

As she wondered how many people knew about Mortimer's work, Kesgrave lowered beside the body, gripped the exposed end of the instrument, and tugged it free.

It was a chisel.

Six inches long, its tip was designed for carving a half-inch-wide hollow in stone.

Among the instruments on the table were sharper ones that would have accomplished the goal more cleanly, including a gouge that was as deadly as any dagger. A killer grabbing a tool at random, however, would not have the opportunity to make that assessment.

The duke remained silent as he examined the dull edge of the chisel before wrapping it in a handkerchief and returning to his full height. He placed the cotton square on the table and said it was strange to see his cousin looking so disheveled.

"Years ago, when he styled himself as an artist, he had an informal way about his dress, as if he was always too distracted by his work or the search for beauty to take pains with his appearance. But once he gave that up, he never left home looking less than flawless. His shirt points were always pristinely starched, and his pantaloons were always ruthlessly straight. And now he looks as though he tumbled down from a hayloft, and I do not know if that is the result of the attack or his work."

"His work, I think," Bea murmured, calling attention to the cuffs of his sleeves, which were rolled up to reveal fore-arms covered in splatters of paint. Struck by it, she turned to examine the other half of the room and realized it was lined with stacks of canvasses. Leaning against the back wall, anchored by bricks on the floor, was a massive painting of a pretty blond woman holding her seat as her horse reared, her easy command of the creature expertly conveyed in her light grasp of the reins.

It was gorgeous, she thought, approaching it with

measured steps, the vibrant expression on the subject's glowing face slowly coming into focus as she drew nearer. Given the victim's repeated failures, she had assumed he was a mediocre painter at best.

But this work—it was astonishing.

"I did not know he was this good," Kesgrave said as he stopped beside her. "My grandmother always said he was outrageously gifted, but I do not think I actually believed her because like many small-minded people, I equate talent with success."

Although spoken matter-of-factly, the statement was a mix of rebuke and regret, and Bea grasped his hand in her own. "Not small-minded, never small-minded," she insisted gently. "Maybe a little rigid and set. But it is understandable. The annual exhibition is considered the yardstick against which all artists are measured. I cannot conceive why the Royal Academy withheld its imprimatur."

The duke tightened his fingers gratefully, then raised her hand to his lips to press a gentle kiss. "I imagine the criteria are not absolute. Consideration each year most likely depends on the entries. Perhaps he had the misfortune of entering during years with exceptionally good submissions," he said, swiveling around to look at his cousin again. "I suppose this is bad luck too."

Turning away from the canvas, she examined the victim and committed to memory as many details as possible. Even in his shirtsleeves and crinkled trousers, he presented a respectable picture, with his blond curls cut à la Titus and patrician nose. He resembled his father sharply, sharing his considerable height and athletic build, but bore none of the ravages of dissipation that bedeviled Lord Myles. More than halfway through his fourth decade, he looked barely a day over thirty.

Nothing was strange.

Well, aside from the gaping wound in his belly, nothing was strange, she thought. If there had been a fight, then Mortimer had lost it pretty quickly, as there was no evidence of a struggle in his appearance. At the very least, part of his shirt would have become untucked from his pants or one of his cuffs would have unraveled.

Turning away, she studied the canvases against the wall. They were mostly still lifes grouped by subjects, and flipping through them, she realized they were studies. Mortimer had been working on his technique. In one series—an apple beside a jug of water and a daybook on a rough-hewn table— he appeared to be refining his ability to render texture. Another series focused on capturing the play of candlelight on a pitcher of water. At some point, he had switched to using a model, for there was a sextet of paintings of the blond woman from the portrait, all small and contained, depicting her in the modest setting of the studio.

Again, she was taken aback by his skill, how easily he evoked a mood with a few brushstrokes.

Finishing with the canvases, she rose and spotted a pair of unfinished reliefs against the opposite wall. As she knew little about antiquities, she found their appearance convincing. The slabs were not huge—only two feet by three feet—but there was a grandeur to the images, and they felt historically momentous even though they had been made weeks or even days before. Hanging above them, nailed to the wall, was a sketch of a woman in a boat, her hand trailing lazily in the water.

It was the same woman as in the paintings, she thought, turning next to the cupboard. Opening it, she sifted through the drawings on the shelf. They were early drafts of the other works in the room, depicting the progression of the artist's ideas as they evolved. In the first sketch of the accomplished rider, the woman sat calmly astride her steed, the reins in one hand as she stared off in the distance. The studies for the reliefs showed the images growing increasingly complex. A simple scene of a man crossing a river ultimately included dozens of fish and hundreds of swirls. Comparing the drawing to its counterpart against the wall, she noticed the final product was more complicated still, with the muscles of the swimming figure clearly and accurately defined.

"There are two more reliefs in the other room," Kesgrave announced.

Bea, who had not noticed his absence, glanced up in surprise.

"It is a storeroom, I think," he explained as he crossed the floor. "There are a dozen unused canvases, paints, brushes, more tools, several stone slabs. He was well stocked with supplies."

Returning to sketches to the cabinet, she picked up one of the books on the bottom shelf. A history of northern Mesopotamia, it contained a multitude of images, and if she did not find the specific elements used in the reliefs, she recognized the style that rendered shapes sparely. In the next tome, she found several of the motifs, including the conical hat and lavish beard the figure wore. Having researched his subject thoroughly, Mortimer cleverly created reliefs that credibly echoed the originals without copying them outright. The approach gave the forgeries an air of familiarity, which lessened the likelihood that an expert would identify them as such.

No wonder Hawes considered him a valuable asset.

Returning the books to a neat pile, she removed the cloth from the partially opened drawer and examined its contents. The compartment contained more supplies: chisels, gouges, plaster molds, charcoals, pen knives, pigments, scrapers, paints, brushes, sealing wax, nails, several pairs of leather gloves. Smocks were kept in the drawer below, as were hairpins, shoelaces, and a discarded sketch of a Roman coin, on the opposite side of which he recorded notes to himself, such as "fetch more lead" and "deepen the corner."

Bea folded the cloth and placed it in the top drawer.

Kesgrave, closing the cabinet's glass doors, noted that the studio was remarkably tidy. "There is some carving debris on the table, but it is a negligible amount. The floor is freshly swept, and the fireplace is empty of ashes. Whoever looked after it for him has been here recently. He or she might be a good source of information."

"If they were here yesterday, they might be able to help us narrow the time frame of the murder," she said before adding that his cousin might have attended to the space himself.

Kesgrave smiled faintly at the notion of a man of Mortimer's stamp cleaning his own hearth but conceded that it was possible. "I cannot imagine it, but I also could not imagine this either," he said, gesturing to the painting in the back and the reliefs against the wall and the sketches on the shelf. "It makes me wonder what he might have accomplished if his father had not pushed him to renounce art and adopt the conventional pursuits of a gentleman. If nothing else, he would not have wound up slaughtered on the floor of his own studio."

Spoken without inflection, the words nevertheless carried a dismaying bitterness, and Bea, feeling helpless to mitigate it, suggested he show her the storeroom.

Action was palliative.

"He might have had his footman attend to him here," she said as they entered the hallway. "If that is the case, then his secret was most likely not a secret at all. The murderer could be anyone. The best place to start is by interviewing the neighbors. I noticed the occupant across the street peering out when we arrived. He might be able to tell us something about Mortimer's habits and visitors."

The duke hoped so, as the thought of going door to door questioning every resident in the road held no appeal for him. They had done that during their previous investigation, and he had found it exceedingly tedious.

Gasping with deliberate theatricality, she replied, "Never say it was too thorough even for you!"

Gravely, he acknowledged he had limits and that they typically involved interactions with the general public. "And, yes, brat, I am happy to impose my sparkling pontifications on other people without any concern for their time or level of interest. The court recognizes the hypocrisy."

It was an encouraging sign, the rallying response, and she felt some of her own dread lessen as she followed him into the other room, which was precisely as he described. Aside from the three feet of floor directly in front of the fireplace, the space was brimming with furniture and supplies, so much so, she had to turn sideways to slip between a cabinet and a cupboard to examine the slabs of uncut stone. And behind them, leaning against the back wall, were large blank canvases, three in total.

Mortimer had plans.

Finishing her inspection, she returned to the hallway, where Kesgrave was waiting, and said she was ready to leave. "Jenkins can fetch the coroner while we talk to the neighbor across the street."

The duke hailed this suggestion as practical and stepped back to allow her to exit first. They were halfway to the front door when he stopped suddenly in the corridor, spun on his heels, marched back to the studio, and opened the top drawer of the cabinet. Withdrawing the cloth she had recently folded, he unfurled it with a determined flick of his wrists, the white cotton fluttering in the air before settling gently over the deceased.

Chapter Five

Once outside, they were greeted by Jenkins, whose relief at seeing them emerge from the shabby building was immediately undermined by the duke's request that he fetch the coroner. Raising a clenched fist in front of his scowling face, he cried, "I knew it! Didn't I say it? A visit from Hell and Fury Hawes could mean only one thing! Another murder! I told Johnny in the stables. I said to him, 'Her grace is off to look at another corpse.' But I'd hoped I was wrong because it is the devil's business, doing anything for that miscreant, even finding a killer. No good could come from this, mark my words. He's the culprit and he is using her grace to blame someone else. It is a diabolical plan, and I won't hear a word to the contrary!"

Naturally, he would not, no, for he continued to register his disapproval for another full minute before folding his arms across his chest and stomping away.

Although Bea was uncertain how to proceed, she felt confident that running after one's groom to soothe his jangled nerves was not the most appropriately ducal option. Kesgrave, seemingly untroubled by the outburst, insisted that

Jenkins would return soon enough to take command of the horses and fetch the coroner.

"I do hate to see him so worked up, especially when I share his cynical assessment," Bea murmured as she looked across the street at the house directly opposite. A figure seated in the window was intently observing their actions, and realizing he had been spotted, abruptly swiveled his shoulders and raised a newspaper to obscure his face.

Amused by the lack of subtlety in his movements, she pointed out the man to Kesgrave and suggested they interview their most promising witness before the man became too engrossed in *The Times* to answer their questions.

"Promising indeed," the duke said as Jenkins reached the end of the pavement and turned around, his glare just as pronounced even as his gait lightened. "Let us see what he has to say. And for the sake of accuracy, I am compelled to note that he is in fact reading the *Dairy Farmer Daily,* which ceased publishing daily more than a year ago. Now it prints once a week, on Saturday. If the gentleman in the window wishes to keep his surveillance habit a secret from his neighbors, then he should invest in a new prop."

Oh, yes, of course he recognized the newspaper and could recite its publication history down to the day.

Delighted by him despite the misery of the circumstance, Bea darted an amused glance at him as she knocked on the door and suggested he start a club devoted to obscure periodicals with Nuneaton. "You could meet on the first Monday of every month to discuss the most arcane newspapers in the country. You could even draft lists ranking them from extremely dull to highly tedious. It is riveting, I am sure."

Despite the mocking edge to this raillery, Kesgrave's expression remained smooth as he described the *Dairy Farmer Daily* as a vital resource. "It is where I learned that cows undergo emotional strain if they are subjected to too many changes at once—just as people are wont to do—and that leads to a decrease in milk production. Stephens reads the journal religiously and brings all relevant articles to my attention."

Considering how seriously the steward took his responsibilities, she expected nothing less and congratulated the duke on identifying another aspirant for his fledging club. "Membership has increased fifty percent in a matter of minutes. At this rate, you will be in the triple digits by the end of the week. If it grows much larger, you shall have to come up with a name for your new organization. And it will need an insignia as well, I should think. For the stationary."

"No, it will not, brat," Kesgrave said firmly as the door opened to reveal a woman in a dark blue dress and a light-colored mob cap.

Clutching a splattered cloth in one hand, she seemed out of breath, and when she spoke, it was to apologize for keeping them waiting so long. "I called to my father to answer the door, but his periodic hearing problem seems to have reemerged. Strange how that always happens when I am up to my elbows in boiling pots and he's just sitting in his chair," she said, looking over her shoulder and raising her voice. "Now how may I help you?"

"We wish to speak to your father," Bea announced.

The woman rolled her eyes. "Of course you do. His answering the door when it pertains to him would be too much trouble, wouldn't it? Do come in, then, but please wipe your shoes. I just scrubbed the floor this morning and would hate for mud to be trailed in so quickly. It will happen quickly enough regardless. My sons are at the market with their father and will make a mess as soon as they set foot in the house."

Casting a remorseful look at the back of the house, where her dinner pots simmered, the woman escorted them to the parlor. It was a cramped room, with too much furniture. Armchairs flanked a sofa, which pressed against a rolltop desk and a pedestal table. A screen blocked the fireplace, whose mantel was cracked in three places and appeared ready to crash on the floor at any moment. On the other side of the room, the *Dairy Farmer Daily* still resolutely before his eyes, sat their prospective witness.

On an inelegant scoff, the woman marched across the room and grabbed the periodical out of her father's hands. "The paper is months old, you do not care one lick about farming, and you have guests. Judging by their appearance, they are of an important sort. What they could want with you is beyond me. After they leave, I'll thank you to clean the privy. You promised you would do it before noon, and it is after one."

The color rose in his cheeks, either at the scathing reminder of his responsibility or the brutal removal of his ruse, but he managed to acknowledge her remarks with a dignified nod. "Of course, my dear. Thank you. You may leave us now."

His daughter huffed again, and crushing the newspaper against the dirty cloth, she swept from the room. As soon as she was gone, the man grumbled about their vanity and swore he had been watching the birds, not them. "You flatter yourself if you think you are as interesting as the magpies."

"Ah, you are an ornithologist," Bea said with a flash of understanding. No wonder he looked outside the window so much.

"I am!" he replied, adding that he had the binoculars to prove it.

But when he reached behind himself to retrieve the viewing device, he found only the cushion of his chair. "I must have left the blasted thing upstairs. Dorothy can fetch it. *Dorothy!*"

Flinching as he bellowed for his daughter, Bea rushed to assure him it was not necessary to disturb the other woman while she was cooking. "We do not require evidence."

"That is all well and good, but you won't be able to see the magpie nest without the binoculars," he explained before shrieking her name yet again.

"Nor do we need to see the nest," she added helpfully.

Despite her intentions, their host took great offense to her seemingly benign assertion and his expression turned belligerent. Hoping to repair the damage, although she could not fathom what had caused it, she sought an amiable comment pertaining to the nesting habits of English birds to offer.

Alas, all she could think of were facts about squirrels.

They were similar to birds in that they liked to occupy trees.

Their nests were called dreys.

As she opened her mouth to note the clever woodland creatures were able to smell food buried under a foot of snow, Kesgrave rose to look out the window and said he could see the nest plainly without binoculars. "What kind of twigs are those? Are they greasewood or hawthorn?"

Their host, who glanced at the duke with burgeoning respect, said he could not be certain, but they looked like birch to him. Then he pointed to the tree and described the structure of the nest, with its impressive dome top, marveling at the ingenuity of the magpie. He continued in his admiration for several minutes before seeming to remember himself and on an awkward laugh, apologized for his inordinate enthusiasm. "I tend to run on at length about the subject whenever I find someone who shares an interest. Dorothy thinks ornithology is a waste of time, her husband believes birds are only for eating, and my grandsons think I am addled. But that is neither here nor there. As my daughter observed, you are Quality, sir, and must want something very particular from me. I am Foster, by the bye. Joseph Foster. I did not recognize the insignia on your carriage, but it was a very fine vehicle and the horses are magnificent. I expect you will now tell me you are a lord of some sort."

Duly, yes, Kesgrave introduced himself and Bea.

Delighted to have his suspicion confirmed, Foster promised not to summon his daughter, for that would take them even farther away from the purpose of their visit. "But she would be beside herself to meet you, your grace," he said to Bea. "Dorothy has followed your exploits in the newspaper and thinks you are astute. She has been disappointed of late to see no new stories, but I told her that as a duchess you have other responsibilities than solving murders. And yet here you are! You want to know about the house across the way, don't you? I saw you enter without waiting for an invitation. Something is afoot!"

Having made this weighty pronouncement, however, he leaned back in his chair without asking the natural corollary, and Bea paused for several heartbeats before confirming that they were indeed gathering information about the house across the street.

It would be foolhardy not to take advantage of the tailor-made transition.

"Did your neighbor get other visitors this morning?" she asked.

Frowning, Foster admitted that he had been at his post for only the past two hours. "Dorothy's mother-in-law is coming for dinner, and the gel is up in arms about everything. She had me scrubbing floors at nine. I did it for as long as I could stand—almost a full two hours—and then retired to my office, if you will. I have been here ever since, and you are the first callers I have seen. Mrs. Frome next door got a wood delivery at 11:17. At least I think it was 11:17," he muttered uncertainly, reaching into the cushion and withdrawing a book. "I wrote it down. Technically, my journal is reserved for ornithological observations, but I tend to record everything I see. It is a habit, and it helps keep my brain sharp. Here, let us see. Yes, a delivery of wood to the Frome residence at 11:17. But that is all the activity I have seen. A quiet day so far."

Delighted by the existence of the journal—a fount of information, no doubt!—she asked if the road was usually more lively.

"Keep in mind that I do not sit in this chair all day," Foster warned sternly. "Dorothy makes me go to the kitchen to take meals with the family, and then there's the chores she continually asks me to do, from folding my counterpane to cleaning the privy. I also try to take a walk every day, even if I can't get very far on my tired legs, and of course I sleep at night. My bedroom windows overlook the back of the house, which is a less interesting view. There are hardly any trees, so fewer birds to watch, and almost no passersby. That said, there is typically a fair bit of comings and goings on the block, but you want to know about Louis Rousseau."

Although he stated it firmly, his tone ticked upward, making it more like a question, and she unhesitatingly confirmed that they were interested in Rousseau.

Mortimer, it seemed, had adopted a French identity for his artist alter ego.

Flipping to the previous page, Foster announced that the neighbor in question had welcomed two callers the day before during the hours he kept watch. "At 3:26, he received a shipment of painting supplies from Ackerman's, including three canvasses. The deliverer helped Rousseau carry everything inside, then drove off. The interaction lasted less than ten minutes."

Bea, who assumed the victim was visited frequently by the printshop, which also sold paint blocks, brushes, and pencils, considered the time notable because it provided them with their first parameter. The murder occurred after three-thirty in the afternoon.

"Was the other caller also a delivery?" she asked.

The lines on Foster's face deepened into censure as he announced with tart displeasure, "It was his doxy. He has a parade of them, at least a dozen, the damned Frenchie! I can only imagine what depravity was celebrated and encouraged in the iniquitous den in which he was raised, but this is a respectable neighborhood, and the idea that my grandsons have to live across the street from such disreputable goings-on—it is very upsetting."

Not wishing to appear unduly insensitive, she arranged her features into a sympathetic frown and tsked kindly for a few seconds before asking when the woman arrived.

"Four forty-six," he said, his antipathy deepening as he recited the time. "Broad daylight!"

It was another parameter.

"When did she leave?"

Foster could not say. His daughter called him into dinner at six-thirty, and after the meal he played chess with his son-in-law. "I did not get back to my chair until eight-thirty at the earliest. I kept my eyes on the magpies until it grew too dark to see them and went up to bed, around nine-fifteen, I'd say. Based on her previous visits, I would assume she left a little before eight. She rarely stays for more than three hours."

Although unverifiable, the information suggested a third parameter and a first suspect. A lover's inconstancy was an abiding motive for murder, and Mortimer, in the guise of Rousseau, appeared to be an exceedingly faithless beau.

But that was only Foster's interpretation of events. He had no idea what actually happened inside the little house, and recalling the freshly cleaned grate in the fireplace, she asked if it was possible he had misunderstood the situation.

"Could the young woman have been there to clean the house for Mr. Rousseau?"

Foster cackled as he said with harsh amusement, "Susie Brewer, cleaning house? I don't think so, your grace!"

Taken aback by the implied familiarity, she said, "You know her?"

"Everyone in the road knows her," he announced peevishly. "Susanah Brewer lives on this block, four houses down, at number three. You drove past it yourself on your way here. It is the one with black shutters and pink window boxes."

It was surprising, the notion that the doxy in question—one in a so-called parade of them—resided on the same block as Mortimer's studio, although not unheard of. The English gentleman had a marked disinhibition toward sullying the place where he slept, frequently regarding the female staff as his own personal harem. It was a proclivity to which one of Miss Brewer's family members might have taken exception if they knew about it.

And if Foster's understanding of the situation was accurate.

Given Mortimer's vocation and the works in his studio, it seemed just as likely that the girl served as his model, which, Bea reminded herself, did not preclude a warmer relationship. Artists were notorious for trysting with the female subjects of their paintings.

Her family's objections would stand.

According to Foster, however, the arrangement had the girl's mother's full support. "She has done nothing to remove her daughter from Rousseau's influence. In the beginning I assumed she did not know what was going on, for she is a widow with two young children to raise, but then the chit's visits grew longer and more frequent. Now she's there three times a week for up to three hours, which is impossible to overlook! Mrs. Brewer knows and has chosen not to care.

That is a decision I understand from a practical standpoint, for as a widow she has limited options, but it is morally repugnant. I used to greet her respectfully when we passed on the pavement, but now I look away and pretend she is not there. Mrs. Brewer might not care about the moral rectitude of the neighborhood, but I have my grandchildren to consider. I can't stand by and allow a rapacious hussy to corrupt them."

"Of course not," Bea replied sympathetically before glancing at the journal, with all its inviting tidbits of information. "Do you recall when the affair began?"

"March!" he snapped, turning to the appropriate page and perusing it quickly. "March third. You can see it here. I was so shocked, I put three exclamation marks next to her name. I even called out for Dorothy to come look, but she told me to stop spying on the neighbors. The visits increased in frequency, as I said, and that started on April twenty-ninth. And it has been Gomorrah ever since."

As for the retinue of women who proceeded Miss Brewer's tenure, Foster swore he did not know a single thing about them. "They are not from around here. At least not as far as I could tell. It is hard to be sure, as they came and went so quickly."

And yet he spoke with certainty!

Wondering if he had noticed more than he had realized about them, Bea asked him to check his notes for additional details and was immediately rebuffed. All he recorded were comings and goings.

"I am an ornithologist," he added stiffly, "not a peeping Tom."

Kesgrave, perhaps observing the intensity with which Bea stared at the journal, asked if there were other visitors who called frequently. "Does Ackerman's make regular deliveries?"

"Every four weeks or so," he replied without consulting

his records. "It is usually toward the end of the month like now. The collier comes twice a week, which is a lot of coal for a house that small, but I figure that's because Rousseau does not have the scratch to buy more than a few pieces at a time. Sometimes the postman brings a letter. A clerk comes by every few weeks and stays for about twenty minutes. But mostly it is just Miss Brewer."

Bea pressed for a description of the collier, as a twice weekly delivery of coal did not make sense in the context of Mortimer's arrangement with Hawes. Presumably, the tradesman was there for another purpose. Foster, alas, could tell them nothing other than the man was in every way unremarkable: average height, average frame, average features.

"You can keep asking me, but the answer will not change," he said snippily.

Accepting the rebuke, Bea switched the topic to Rousseau's schedule. "Does he arrive and leave at the same time every day, or does it vary?"

Now that was information Foster was happy to share, as he had been documenting the damned Frenchie's behavior for more than a year to his family's great indifference. Not a single one of them cared, not even his youngest grandson, who liked watching the magpies. "Up until January he kept the same hours almost from the day he took possession. He would arrive around eleven and leave at three. He started staying a little later, until four-thirty, sometimes five. Then in May it changed again, and you know why."

"Susie Brewer?" Bea asked.

"Susie Brewer!" he growled with a menacing scowl. "Now he stays until eight at the earliest, at least he has for the past two weeks. One night my son-in-law saw him leave around midnight. It requires no great leap of the imagination to conceive what he is doing. Disgusting!"

Indeed, it did not, she thought, picturing the painting

against the back wall of his studio. A work of that scale and magnitude would consume most of the artist's waking hours for at least a month. That he managed to also produce the required number of reliefs for Hawes as well as keep up his sporting activities was a marvel.

"Did he ever stay overnight?" she asked.

Smirking, he said no. "Susie Brewer is not *that* tempting. Sooner or later, he leaves, then returns in the morning at eleven like I said."

Grateful for the information, which allowed them to set an upper limit for the time of the murder, she was about to ask which days Miss Brewer visited the studio when Foster's irate daughter stomped into the room and ordered him to the privy. "You have dallied long enough! Martin will be home within the hour, and his mother will be with him. You know how she loves to criticize everything I do, especially in front of my children."

With an apologetic glance first at Bea, then the duke, Foster sighed and rose to his feet, promising his daughter he would attend to the matter as soon as he showed his guests out. Appeased, she darted from the room, and watching her leave, he shook his head. "She is going to be beside herself when she finds out she discussed the privy in front of the Duke and Duchess of Kesgrave," he said with a smile as he dropped the notebook onto the cushion.

Bea stared at it, just sitting there, ripe for the snatching.

It would be so easy.

Foster had already turned away from the window, presenting his back to the chair, and she was a mere two steps away. Smoothly, discreetly, she could sidle up to the seat, reach down, and snag the book without his noticing at all. He probably would not even realize it was gone until after dinner or maybe even the morning, depending on his son-in-law's keenness for chess.

LYNN MESSINA

But of course she did not take it.

A fine way to repay a man for his assistance—stealing his possessions.

Indulging one last look of regret, she tore her eyes from the journal and toward Foster, who was slowly making his way to the door. He led them into the narrow corridor, and when they arrived at the entrance, she thanked him for providing so much information. "Your ornithology notes are a lifesaver."

Foster, beaming with pleasure, swore he was happy to help, then begged her to be honest with him. "Rousseau is dead, isn't he? That's why you are here asking so many questions—someone murdered him, and you are investigating. You would be wise to start with Miss Brewer. A scorned woman is a dangerous thing, and Rousseau was not what you would call a constant lover."

Here, Bea hesitated before replying because she did not want to provide him with more fodder to malign Miss Brewer. He had already consigned her to harlotry, and adding murderess to her list of accomplishments would put her beyond the pale. And yet denying it completely or giving a vague answer would only put off the inevitable. As soon as the coroner arrived to remove the body, Foster would leap to the same conclusion.

Consequently, she admitted that the artist had been killed and that they would be questioning Miss Brewer next. "But I have no reason to assume her guilt, and as an investigator, I must withhold judgment until evidence suggests otherwise."

Foster shook his head at her tactful reply but made no further comment other than to encourage them to return to see the magpies later in the season.

"Thank you, Mr. Foster, we will bear that in mind," she said before stepping outside into the late-June air, which bristled with an unseasonable chill. She fastened the buttons on her spencer, and as they stepped onto the pavement, she complimented the duke on his comprehensive knowledge of twigs. "Did you learn the difference between greasewood and hawthorn at Eton or was that part of your study at Oxford?"

"As there are more than a thousand types of trees and shrubs native to England, one cannot describe the awareness of two in particular as 'comprehensive,'" he explained with intent sobriety. "A full study would take years, with courses in coniferae, cycadaceae, taxaceae, and monkey puzzle, and that would not begin to address plants and grasses. Regardless, I learned about greasewood and hawthorn from many brutal encounters in my childhood: Both are thorny bushes on the grounds of Haverill Hall, and I frequently found myself scraped by them as I explored the parkland."

Bea felt a frisson of delight at this answer, not only because it contained his customary pedantry, which she found irresistible, but also because it hinted at a lightening of his spirit. The heavy grief that had followed him out of his cousin's studio had lessened somewhat, and although she knew he would never play fast and loose with taxonomical classification, she accused him of inventing the last one on the spot. "There is no such thing as monkey puzzle."

Oh, but there was, and as they proceeded to number four to ask Miss Brewer about her relationship with the deceased, he patiently lectured her on its pertinent details, including appearance (spiky leaves, stout trunk), Latin name (*Araucaria araucana*), and ideal growing environment (porous soil, temperate climate).

Chapter Six

ﬂ

L ike the Foster residence, the Brewer house was a
three-story, redbrick edifice with small rooms, and
as Mrs. Brewer led Bea and Kesgrave to the parlor
to await her daughter, she apologized repeatedly for the mess
they encountered.

She had not been expecting visitors!

"We get so few, you see, just my late husband's brother and
his wife and my nieces," she said with a tight smile as she
kicked a basket of knitting needles to the side with her foot to
clear a path. Gesturing toward the settee, she invited them to
make themselves comfortable, then darted forward to remove
a skipping rope from the cushion before Bea could sit on it.
Thrusting it into her pocket, which fit only half its length, she
cast her eyes around the room and settled on a wooden chair
at the game table in the corner. She carried it over and sat
down. "I am sure Susie will be down any second now."

Bea assured her they did not mind the wait. "We are not
in a rush."

"Of course, of course," Mrs. Brewer murmured as she

tried to stuff the rest of the skipping rope into her pocket. Realizing it was futile, she ceased her efforts and allowed her hand to drop at her side, where it lingered for several seconds before settling on her lap. "May I ask what this pertains to? I do not want to seem nosy, but Susie is my daughter and it is so rare for her to receive callers. And aristocratic callers—that is unheard of!"

Although Bea was not impervious to the awkwardness of the situation, she could see no way around it. The nature of her daughter's relationship with the so-called Mr. Rousseau was the entire reason they were there. Consequently, she stated it plainly.

Far from displaying discomfort with the topic, Mrs. Brewer smiled beatifically and said, "He has been a godsend to our family, so much so I do not even mind the neighbors' malicious chatter. I cannot imagine what we would have done without him—and I do not mean only the additional income. It is a joy to see my Susie so occupied and happy. After her father died, I did not expect. ... And he is kind to the children! He has never once sent Susie home without treats for her little siblings. The dears have developed a taste for lemon drops. He has thoroughly corrupted them!"

Noting the benign pleasure with which Mrs. Brewer discussed the perversion of her younger children, Bea decided that Foster's understanding was wrong. Susie was not Mortimer's lover.

Consequently, she must have been his model.

"I have always been fond of lemon drops myself, so I expect they get the inclination from me," Mrs. Brewer added with an anxious look at the doorway. "The budget does not stretch to buying confections often, but I do try to get a little something extra whenever we have the money. I do not know what is keeping her. Susie is usually so prompt. But she was not expecting visitors. As I explained, we get few visitors, just family really."

"It is not a problem," Bea said.

Although clearly unconvinced, Mrs. Brewer nodded abstractedly and folded her hands in her lap. With one eye focused on the door, she thanked her guests for their graciousness and heaved a sigh of relief when her daughter finally appeared.

As Miss Brewer was wearing an azure silk gown more suited to a dinner party than a quiet day at home and her chestnut hair was styled à la Grecque with a knot on the left side, it was obvious to everyone in the room what had caused the delay.

Smiling widely, revealing a pair of charming dimples, she apologized for making her esteemed guests wait, but there was nothing to be done. She could not meet the prominent members of the Royal Academy in her everyday frock. "It is an honor, your grace," she said to Kesgrave, dropping into a deep curtsy, before raising, looking at Bea, and lowering again. "And your grace."

It was she, the girl from the painting, and as Miss Brewer rose to her full height, her chin held at a flattering angle as though she were still posing, Bea realized that Mortimer's hopes had been revived. Perhaps he had been inspired by the warm reception his forgeries had received among England's collecting elite or he simply desired to produce work that could be properly attributed to him. Either way, he had intended to submit the canvas for consideration by the Royal Academy and seemed convinced it would be accepted into the annual exhibition.

Knowing of her employer's ambition, Miss Brewer could fathom no reason why the illustrious Duke of Kesgrave would call on her other than to discuss her inclusion in the prestigious event.

The frown that had etched itself into Mrs. Brewer's forehead at her daughter's strange greeting deepened as the girl apologized for the unbecoming mess of the parlor. "I fear my mother's standards of cleanliness are not as stringent as my own. But we must not dwell on dreary things. Instead, let us talk about *The Huntress*. I assume you have come directly from the studio to meet the muse who posed for the magnificent painting. I know it is not the thing to lavish praise on a work that features myself, but it is only Mr. Rousseau's mastery that makes me appear so splendid, as I know I am plain."

In fact, she knew nothing of the sort. The woman sparkling in her blue dress and silky curls was fully cognizant of her extraordinary appeal. Miss Petworth, whose position as society's reigning Incomparable had gone unchallenged for two seasons, would kill for those dimples.

Kesgrave suggested they sit down.

Miss Brewer complied eagerly, taking the seat recently vacated by her mother, who did not display the same level of enthusiasm. Perhaps sensing that Susie had not accurately judged the purpose of the visit, the matriarch placed herself at the game table, several feet away, in the corner.

Continuing with the straightforward approach, Bea said, "I am sorry to disappoint you, Miss Brewer, but we are not here as representatives of the Royal Academy. We are here to investigate the murder of the duke's cousin Mortimer Matlock, who was known to you as Louis Rousseau."

Miss Brewer received this news calmly, her gorgeous brow furling only slightly as she looked at her mother, as if seeking clarity. Then she shook her head. "No, I am sure that cannot be right. Mr. Rousseau would not lie to me. He treated me with respect and swore I was the best model he had ever worked with. He called me his muse. Is that not so, Mama? When he came here to assure you everything would be aboveboard and decent, that is how he described me—his muse. And an artist does not lie to his muse. Therefore, you must be confused, your grace. Maybe the duke has lots of cousins and you find it difficult to keep up with them all? I know Mr. Rousseau is not dead because when I saw him yesterday he was alive. He sketched me for three hours before sending me home for dinner. And just like always, he gave me a handful of lemon drops to pass along to the children. Why would he do that if he was planning on being killed later in the evening?"

Her mother, whose sense of foreboding had not stretched to murder, jumped to her feet in palpable distress and enveloped the poor girl in a hug.

Well, she tried to.

Miss Brewer lowered her shoulders, evading the other woman's grasp, which she deemed a nuisance. "I do wish you would not do that, Mama, when I am trying to have a conversation with the duke and duchess. It is not right that they are going about telling people that Mr. Rousseau is dead. He would not die before his work was accepted in the Royal Academy exhibition. It was his life's grand ambition. He cannot die before achieving his life's grand ambition to see *The Huntress* on the wall in Somerset House. And what about me? If Mr. Rousseau is dead, then I will no longer have the pleasure of being his muse, and I am such an excellent muse. You know it is true, Mama. I muse beautifully, everyone says so, and if I can't do the thing I do best, I will have to find other work or marry an odious old man who doesn't know how to paint or draw or render my beauty in some other way."

Murmuring softly, Mrs. Brewer sought to console her child, whose eyes filled with tears at the prospect of this bleak future. "It's all right, my dear. Everything will be all right. You'll see, I promise."

But her words sounded hollow to Miss Brewer, who began to weep in earnest, and watching the drops fall down her exquisite cheeks, Bea tried to imagine her stabbing Mortimer in the stomach. With the girl's delicate beauty conferring an air of fragility, it was difficult to picture. Her narrow wrists hardly seemed strong enough to wield a sewing needle, let alone a chisel.

And what did she have to gain in murdering him?

If anything, she stood only to lose, as her success was tied to his.

That would all change if Mortimer had found a new model, which Bea allowed was possible. If he had grown tired of Miss Brewer and dispensed with her services, she might have struck out in fury at the prospect of losing the well-paying position. But finding a model was no easy task—at least not for Mortimer, who had auditioned a dozen women before settling on Susie—and Foster had not reported a second parade of women.

Miss Brewer dabbed her tears on the fine silk of her gown, causing her mother to wince and beg her to pull herself together. "Remember, you have company, and the duke and duchess are waiting to ask you questions about Mr. Rousseau ... I mean, Mr. Matlock. They have been very patient. And you do not want your face to get all blotchy from crying now, do you? That is not how a muse behaves."

Reminded of what she owed to her art, the girl brushed aside her tears once more and then lifted her head with firm resolve. "You are right, Mama. I owe it to Mr. Rousseau to conduct myself in a way that befits his high opinion of me, and I know he would want me to help find his killer," she said, turning to look at Bea and the duke, her lovely chocolate eyes translucent in their grief. "Please ask me whatever you wish to know, and I pledge to answer to the best of my ability."

Moved by the bravery on display, Mrs. Brewer grasped her daughter's shoulder and pressed it encouragingly. "You are a good girl, Susie."

Miss Brewer accepted the tribute stoically.

Bea, her voice gentle and smooth, said, "If I understand it correctly, you posed for Mr. Matlock yesterday?"

"That is correct," Miss Brewer confirmed.

"What time did you arrive?" Bea asked.

With an uncertain look at her mother, Miss Brewer replied, "It was around four-thirty? Joshua was yelling at Ginny because she hid his toy soldier after he poked out her doll's eye, and Ginny pulled his hair, and he started crying. I wasn't supposed to leave until five, but I went early because I could not stand all the shouting."

Judging by Mrs. Brewer's pained expression, she had found the ruckus difficult to withstand as well. "Yes, that sounds right."

"And how did you find him?" Bea asked.

Miss Brewer closed her eyes as though making a particular effort to recall his demeanor, and a stray tear slipped out. As it trickled mournfully down her cheek, she replied, "Mr. Rousseau was as eager as always to work with me. Earlier in the day he had received delivery of several large canvases. He had been waiting for them for almost a week and was eager to begin a new project. He had just finished *The Huntress.* If you have been to his studio, then you know the work: I am seated on a horse in a fine riding habit holding fast to the reins as the mighty creature rears."

Bea confirmed that they had seen the work.

Gleefully, the girl clapped. "Do I not look majestic? Like I was born on a horse and have a retinue of royal guards behind me? Here's something very shocking: I have never been on a horse. Isn't that right, Mama?" she asked, looking to her mother, who gave prompt confirmation. "I have never been on a horse in my entire life, and yet in Mr. Rousseau's depiction, I look as if I have been riding for years. That is the product of his talent but also my excellent musing. I allow him to see impossible things. He is convinced *The Huntress* will be accepted in the exhibition. He does not have a single doubt, and he told me to prepare myself for the unparalleled honor of seeing myself in the Royal Academy. He was so excited and full of life."

As she switched back to the past tense, tears welled in her eyes again, and she brushed them away with increasing desperation. "You must not fear that I will descend into another fit of weeping because I won't. I am in control of myself now. It is just that I had made such great strides in preparing myself as instructed and I could really *see* the majestic painting hanging on the wall of a very grand salon. And now I have to unprepare myself!"

It was, she confessed forlornly, the more challenging assignment by far.

Even so, Miss Brewer was determined to be helpful and reiterated that the victim's spirits had been high when she left him. "The last thing he did before showing me out was settle on the painting he was going to work on next. I am in a boat this time, lazily trailing my hand in the water on a lovely spring day as red-necked phalaropes paddle by. You might have seen it. He pinned the sketch to the wall. He planned to begin the first study for it tomorrow."

Indeed, Bea had. The sketch hung above the forged reliefs. "What time did you leave?"

Miss Brewer glanced again at her mother before replying. "About seven, I believe. Mama was trying to convince Joshua to wash his teeth before going to sleep. I remember because I had a lemon drop for him from Mr. Rousseau in my pocket and realized I should wait till morning to give it to him. Then I was hungry, so I had bread and cheese for dinner. It was a lovely evening. I did not have a single tinge of foreboding of what was to come."

"It was closer to eight," her mother amended.

"You are probably right," Miss Brewer said, noting that Mr. Rousseau had been reluctant to let her leave. "He kept bidding me good day and then thinking of another thing he wanted to show me. I was halfway out the door when he called me back to ask what the subject of his next painting should be. I said the boating scene because I could see myself looking particularly lovely beneath a pink parasol. Then he showed me some ideas he had for one of his reliefs and asked my opinion."

As she had been about to raise the issue of the forgeries herself, Bea appreciated the topic's timely introduction and asked the girl if she knew the true nature of the works.

The question momentarily stymied Miss Brewer, who furrowed her brow and repeated the query quietly to herself. "Oh, I see, you are asking if I knew Mr. Rousseau was a coun-terfeiter. I did know. He made no attempt to hide it from me. I don't think he could because the reliefs were so large, and it is not as though he could tuck them into a drawer when I came over. But he never discussed them with me other than to ask my opinion on how a work looked, and I have no idea what happened to them once they left the studio. I assume they were taken in hand by a large network."

Intrigued by both the girl's nonchalant acknowledgment of the crime and her insightful assumption, Bea glanced at Mrs. Brewer to gauge her reaction to the information.

None of it was revelatory, which was far from surprising.

As Foster had noted, a widow has limited options.

Bea asked Miss Brewer why she had drawn that conclusion.

"The profits were not huge," the girl explained. "Above his regular living expenses, Mr. Rousseau could afford to pay me and he rented the studio and he was able to buy handfuls of lemon drops whenever he wanted, but that was really all the scratch he had. Considering how much work he did each month, he should have had much more money. That makes me think the network was larger than just him and Mr. Kerrich."

Miss Brewer, in arriving at this impeccably reasoned conclusion, had accurately surmised the existence of Hell and Fury Hawes's organization.

Duly impressed, Bea asked the girl if she knew how Rousseau could afford to increase her number of weekly modeling sessions from one to three in May.

"Musing sessions," Miss Brewer corrected. "I muse, not model, and I do not know the answer. I assume he sacrificed other pleasures to make up the difference. Perhaps he took smaller quarters?"

"And yet he continued to buy the lemon drops," Bea said.

"Of course!" Miss Brewer replied tartly. "They were a necessity. Mr. Rousseau knew how important it is for me to get a proper night's sleep—a muse needs her rest. The lemon drops keep my fiendish siblings quiet, so I do not lie awake at all hours listening to their squabbling."

Unable to refute the logic, Bea asked about Kerrich.

"He is Mr. Rousseau's friend," Miss Brewer replied. "He helped him sell his reliefs by telling people they were authentic. Mr. Rousseau was skilled at making fraudulent antiquities, and I couldn't tell the difference by looking at them. But a collector with lots of money who bought things all the time? He is harder to fool. That is when Mr. Kerrich would step in to assure the collector the relief was real."

Another link in the chain, Bea thought, wondering how many there would be in the end. The more people engaged in the secretive illegal enterprise, the more people who might want Mortimer dead. "Is Mr. Kerrich a member of the Royal Antiquaries Society?"

Miss Brewer's lovely bow lips formed an O in surprise. "He is, your grace! Do you know him? I have met him only a handful of times because Mr. Rousseau said it was not prudent for them to appear to know each other. But from what I could tell, he is a nice man even if he is given to anxious fits."

As the Royal Antiquaries Society had been the seat of antiquarian study for more than two hundred years, it was the most obvious guess Bea could make. Over the centuries, it had counted some of the most respected scholars in England among its fellows, with several earning the highest commendation from the king. That one of its numbers would exploit the institution's venerable reputation for his own gain was not particularly shocking, as most men were venal, and yet she was taken aback to discover Kerrich would consent to associate with someone of Hawes's ilk. Most people would bend their principles if it would benefit them financially, but working for the infamous crime lord was to snap them in half.

No wonder Kerrich was frequently in a state of high agitation.

His life was unmoored from morality.

"He was highly distressed the last time he called, on Friday," Miss Brewer continued, noting that he had pounded on the door furiously until Mr. Rousseau answered. "He was up in arms about something, insisting he had been betrayed, and Mr. Rousseau told him it was a bad time and asked if he could he come back later. I didn't hear Mr. Kerrich's reply, but he refused to leave, so after more muffled yelling, Mr. Rousseau let him inside."

It was, Bea thought, an intriguing description, for if the antiquarian imagined himself deceived by a trusted associate, then he was perhaps more angry than anxious.

Especially if his assessment was accurate.

Depending on how egregiously he had been cheated or tricked by Mortimer, he might seek the ultimate revenge. "Why was Mr. Kerrich so unsettled?"

With a shake of her head, Miss Brewer raised her slim shoulders and then promptly dropped them again. "They spoke in the hallway, and I was in the studio, and they endeavored to keep their voices low. I busied myself by looking through the sketches I had posed for that afternoon. They were very good, but it was hard to pay attention with the pair of them just outside the door. I tried not to listen."

A bright flush suffused the girl's cheeks as she sent an apologetic look at her mother, whose lips tightened with disapproval.

Ah, so that was what Mrs. Brewer found beyond the pale —not widespread corruption but eavesdropping.

Defensively, Miss Brewer added that she made no attempt to monitor the private conversation. "I did not draw my chair closer to the door or press my ear against it. I stayed exactly where I was, at the table with the drawings."

"Nevertheless, you heard some of it," Bea said encouragingly.

The girl tilted her eyes down and admitted that she had. "But only stray words or phrases and mostly Mr. Kerrich's odd howls and screeches. As I said, he was very upset, and Mr. Rousseau tried to calm him down. He told the other man that he was overwrought and that it was not so bad. Mr. Kerrich screeched again and then lowered his voice to a murmur."

Although meager, the information was enough for Bea to begin to construct a theory, and she wondered at the source of the deception. If Mortimer had betrayed Kerrich, then it was not implausible that the latter struck back violently.

Mortimer's efforts to minimize the impact of his own actions would have only deepened the other man's fury.

Hoping to learn more about the source of the argument, she asked if Miss Brewer knew what Mortimer meant by *it*. "When he said, 'It was not so bad,' to what was he referring?"

Alas, Miss Brewer was at a loss to explain. "I don't know. They lowered their voices, and I heard little else. I think a project they were working on together went wrong because I heard Mr. Rousseau say something about having to stay the course. That upset Kerrich because he howled. He left a few minutes later, and I don't think his conversation with Mr. Rousseau calmed his nerves at all because he slammed the door so hard the jars in the studio rattled."

"And Mr. Rousseau?" Bea ventured pensively. "When he returned to the studio, did he seem upset as well?"

"Not in the least," she replied. "He apologized for the interruption, then picked up his pencil as if nothing had happened. I resumed my pose, and we worked in silence for another hour. I don't believe he thought twice about Mr. Kerrich's visit."

And perhaps that was the source of the problem.

Having sold his soul to Hell and Fury, Kerrich might resent the artist's divided attention. He wanted Mortimer to produce more reliefs to provide him with additional opportunities to make money from the corrupt scheme.

If Mortimer had decided to devote all his energy to painting portraits of Miss Brewer for the Royal Academy's exhibition, the antiquarian might consider that a betrayal.

As would Hawes, Bea thought.

Extricating himself from the bargain he had made with the infamous criminal would be no easy task, and Hawes could not allow him to simply walk away from their agreement, not when his skills were still required. It would set a bad example that could ultimately weaken his position. Better to slay the disloyal artist with one of his own implements to send a message to the rest of the organization.

The notion of Hawes as the killer, however, was undermined yet again by the fact that he had sought out the murder duchess's help. As always, yes, Bea allowed for the possibility that the play was too deep for her to understand the game. Having tangled previously with Kesgrave in the gin parlor affair, Hawes might nurture a resentment against the peer for pursuing the matter after he had warned him off and arranged Mortimer's murder as the instrument of his revenge.

But that was silly.

A man of Hawes's standing devising an elaborate scheme to retaliate for an imagined slight—it was too petty to consider. Only a child would strike back over something so minor, and the King of Saffron Hill had not ascended to his throne by wasting his resources on trivial vendettas.

And then of course there was the truth long known by her and reaffirmed by the recent investigation into Miss Wraithe's murder: The simplest explanation was typically the correct one.

Reaching for the less complicated explanation now, she settled on Kerrich as a satisfying suspect. He resented the victim and knew where to find him.

To identify the source of the betrayal, she asked Miss Brewer if she thought Mortimer had grown tired of carving the reliefs. "Did he begrudge the time they took away from his real art?"

"Not at all," the girl replied confidently before raising her chin as she considered the question more deeply. "At least, he did not give that impression because he took pride in everything he made, down to the smallest piece. I think he loved that he could support himself as an artist. He did not talk about his upbringing often, but from the few things he said, I got the sense that he was pursuing his art in defiance of his family."

It was, Bea thought, another astute observation.

"It is unfair because Mr. Rousseau was so talented and maybe if his family had supported him, he would still be alive," Miss Brewer added morosely, a teardrop forming in the corner of her eye. "And then I would still be able to do the work at which I excel rather than returning to the fishmonger, where everything smells rotten and nobody appreciates the elegant line of my jaw, much less captures it in a few graceful strokes of charcoal."

Equally saddened by the dark vision, her mother placed a soothing arm over her shoulder and assured her it was not as bad as all that. "You can take in sewing like me."

Sadly, this consoling promise did little to alleviate the girl's misery, and a second tear formed in the corner of her eye. As it hovered tremulously over her lashes, she lifted her hands to show how pristine they were, free of cuts and calluses and slim and straight. Plying a needle would leave her fingers as mangled as her mother's.

Having no rebuttal for this, Mrs. Brewer slipped her hands into the folds of her skirt, as if to hide the damage the trade had wrought to her own body. Miss Brewer rounded her shoulders, the tears starting to fall in earnest, and before her witness dissolved entirely into a fit of weeping, Bea asked if Mortimer employed someone to keep the studio tidy or if he attended to its upkeep himself.

"He did it. As far as I know, he did it. Sometimes I did the sweeping, which is all I am good for now," she said, her words barely comprehensible as the sobs overtook her.

Watching the girl shudder with grief, Bea tried to imagine her driving the chisel into the victim's stomach with the force of a Fury—because that was what it would have required for someone with her slight frame to stab Mortimer. She would have had to have acted with unrelenting speed and vigor, her hand steady, her mind fixed as she thrust through linen and skin, incapacitating him before he even knew what was happening. Anything less, and he would have easily overpowered her.

Bea simply could not see it.

Even if Miss Brewer somehow managed to plunge the chisel into Mortimer's belly, evidence of the kill would have been splattered on her arms and dress, which Mrs. Brewer would have spotted the second the girl entered the house. That meant they were either both lying or both telling the truth. The former required a remarkable amount of self-control in the face of her and the duke's questions, and it simply seemed too unlikely to Bea that a pair of novice criminal conspirators would be able to maintain such a composed response.

Furthermore, Bea could not identify a motive. Mortimer's death appeared to leave Miss Brewer and her family significantly worse off, and nothing in the studio indicated he planned to replace her soon. The sketch of the boat was pinned to the wall as Miss Brewer said, indicating his satisfaction with her work, and Miss Brewer's determined musing argued convincingly in favor of a professional relationship only. Her affect bore none of the signs of a scorned or heartbroken lover.

Assuming she had left her employer in good health as she stated, Bea figured the interval for the murder was likely between eight and midnight, which was not ideal. A four-hour span was unwieldy, and there was always the possibility that Mortimer had stayed later than was his habit, making the window even wider.

Having garnered all the information she could from the women, she thanked them for their time, and Mrs. Brewer, managing a polite reply, owned herself deeply gratified by their attention. It was all very wretched, to be sure, but it was not every day one had the honor of receiving a duke and a duchess. Her daughter tried to echo this sentiment, but all that emerged from her pretty bow lips was a despondent squeak. Mrs. Brewer patted the girl sympathetically on the back several times before leaving her to cry quietly on the sofa as she escorted her distinguished visitors to the door.

"She will be fine," Mrs. Brewer said softly as she led them to the entry, her tone thoughtful and introspective, as though she were trying to convince herself more than her guests. "She just needs a few days to get used to the idea that everything has changed again. It all happened so quickly. Mr. Rousseau spotted her as she was walking by his studio and within days she was making a good salary for something she did well and enjoyed. None of us expected it."

Intimately acquainted with sudden twists of fate, Bea murmured sympathetically and bid goodbye to Mrs. Brewer, who stood in the doorway, lamenting how easy it was to grow accustomed to a steady stream of lemon drops.

Chapter Seven

The dowager was delighted to see them.

Trapped in conversation with a female cousin—which one Bea could not say, as there were so many of them rattling around London and they all had the same general appearance: wrinkled skin, gray hair, rouged cheeks—she rose to her feet the moment she spied her grandson and his wife in the doorway. "Come in, come in, my darlings, please join us," she said with an eager smile, her hand waving in the air as she urged them forward. "Do not be shy. Eloise is imparting fascinating information about the medicinal uses of pleurisy root, and you will not want to miss a minute of it. No doubt you are familiar with it as a treatment for catarrh and indigestion, but apparently it excels at removing warts from the bottom of one's foot. Who could have imagined?"

Her guest, whose narrow lips and faded blue eyes marked her as one of her grace's Clairmont relatives, nodded soberly at this giddy announcement and explained that it was the plant's white sap that contained healing properties. "But it requires a diligent application. You cannot put it on only when you happen to remember and leave it off the rest of the time. It must be used every day. Otherwise, the offending protuberance will remain, and you will have stained the bedclothes for nothing."

"Eloise recommends keeping a note on the dressing table as a reminder," the dowager said as she lowered to the cushion with care. Her ability to sit down was not as agile as her capacity to rise up, a development that was unsurprising, given her age and physical condition. Well into her eighth decade, she suffered from a variety of ailments, many of which pained her daily and none of which included warts.

"Only a few words," Eloise hastily added to Kesgrave, who took the bergère next to her while Bea joined the dowager on the settee. On the occasional table were a pair of brightly decorated porcelain cups filled to the edge with cool tea and a plate of apple slices, equally untouched. "It does not have to be elaborate. Mine says *pleurisy root salve,* and it sits next to my hairbrush because I have to brush my hair every morning or I get intractable knots. It is also vital that you make the ointment every week. It dries out if you let it sit out too long."

The dowager, regarding her new visitors with arch amusement, congratulated them on the propitious timing of their arrival. "Eloise was just about to tell me how I might make the formulation myself."

Cautiously, the other woman raised the teacup to her lips as she confirmed the accuracy of the statement. Even so, the information was not urgent and could hold for another time. "Your guests do not want to listen to me dole out measurements of milkweed sap and beeswax. I am sure they have a more pleasant topic they wish to discuss."

At this wildly erroneous observation, Bea grasped her hands together, forcefully restraining herself from begging Eloise to recite the recipe. She welcomed anything that would put off the inevitable.

But it was not for her to decide how and when they informed the dowager of her grandson's murder. That prerogative belonged to Kesgrave, and Bea could not imagine him drawing out the scene. He was too pragmatic for delaying tactics, and she expected him to politely ask his cousin to allow him to have a private word with his grandmother.

If that was his plan, however, he did not implement it quickly enough, for the dowager immediately pleaded with Eloise to continue. "If I am to be gifted with the knowledge of how to make wart-removal cream, then I must insist on everyone being likewise blessed. It would be selfish of me to hoard the knowledge. One never does know when arcana could prove useful. The butler at Kesgrave House might develop a wart on the bottom of his foot and require immediate relief."

Taking no pleasure in the contemplation of a round, dry excrescence on the sole of an unknown male servant, Eloise grimaced in distaste and said they would resume the conversation at a later date. Then she shifted in her seat, returned the teacup to the table, and rose gingerly to her feet. "It is time for me to be on my way regardless. Sitting too long is bad for my hip, which grows stiff with inactivity, and you will want to enjoy a coze with Damien and his wife. I must say, Gertrude, I envy you your grandchildren. They are so thoughtful and attentive. Mine never call on me. The only way I can wrangle an invitation to dinner is by threatening to cut them out of my will."

The dowager tutted lightly at this wanton disregard of an elder and stood up to escort her cousin to the entrance hall, but Eloise would not hear of it. "No, no, please sit. I can find my way around, and if I dared to get lost, Sutton would promptly take me in hand," she said, making her goodbyes to Kesgrave and Bea. "It is a pleasure to see you both looking so well. When I return next week, Gertrude, I shall bring the journal article on pleurisy root, so you may read it for your-self. It is quite engrossing."

Decidedly unconvinced by the audacity of the proclama-tion, the dowager urged her cousin not to put herself out. "I will muddle through without it."

"It is no trouble at all," Eloise replied, carefully avoiding the edge of the rug with her cane as she began to cross the drawing room. The distance to the door was not especially great, but at her pace it felt like an epic journey.

Even a snail moved faster.

And yet Bea felt no impatience.

Her heart had squeezed quite painfully when Eloise expressed her envy of the dowager's grandchildren, and all she could feel now was intolerable dread.

Following that lovely tribute with the gut-wrenching news of Mortimer's death—she could not fathom how anyone could do it. If left to her own devices, she would launch into a lecture on the many uses of pleurisy root that would rival Eloise's in length and depth. Only the night before she had finished reading Nicholas Culpeper's extensive compendium on medicinal herbs and could hold forth on more than three hundred flowers and plants in stultifying detail.

Like Eloise, she could recite recipes by heart.

But the duke was different.

Unable to perceive the advantage of putting off the vile business, he resolved to dispense with the horrible duty immediately. He moved to the settee next to his grandmother and took her hands in his own.

And that was it—she knew everything.

The peculiarity of the action, the strange display of affec-tion, revealed the truth, and her entire body stiffened so quickly Bea thought she heard her spine snap.

A shattered look swept across the dowager's face, and she almost said no.

Her lips parted and formed the word, but she either held herself in check or found herself incapable of speech, and she nodded at Kesgrave, as if to give him permission. So he said it simply and gently, his own unhappiness at the deed so evident and pronounced that Bea had to glance away, compelled by their misery to give them the illusion of privacy. Having met Mortimer only twice, she felt like an interloper, and she stared at the door, wondering if she should leave.

Perhaps the decent thing was to give them a few moments alone. Last time, with Lord Myles, Kesgrave had made the visit without her, possibly for this very reason, as death was an intimate thing between grandson and grandmother. But as Bea leaned forward to stand, her hand was clutched by the dowager's bony one, her grasp surprisingly strong for the fraught frailty of her frame.

Still, she did not speak.

Her body, already rigid, seemed to constrict even more as she tightened her grip on her emotions, lashing everything inside.

Even her face was impassive now.

The inhumanity of the discipline was excruciating to behold, and Bea wondered how the duke could bear it. Surely, he would do something to break the unsettling control: speak her name, kiss her forehead, squeeze her hand.

But he did nothing.

Seconds passed, then minutes, and Kesgrave continued to regard the dowager as though she were a house of cards. If he made the slightest movement, she would crumble.

Of course he did.

He loved his grandmother too well to expose her to the raw pain of death when she was determined to freeze it out.

But the ice could not endure, not indefinitely. Sooner or later the dowager's heart would crack from the pressure, and it was better all around if the duke was next to her to catch the pieces.

It fell to Bea, then, to make the first fissure, and she cast about for something to say.

There was the Culpeper.

Adder's tongue (*Ophioglossum vulgatum*): a fern whose tall stalk resembled a snake's tongue, good for treating wounds and skin ulcers.

Yellow looseleaf (*Lysimachia vulgaris*): a perennial plant with yellow flowers, used to curtail bleeding and diarrhea.

Alehoof (*Glechoma hederacea*): an evergreen creeper of the mint family, known for reducing swelling and pain caused by excessive exposure to the sun.

No, not herbs.

An assortment of facts was too dry and pedantic.

Perhaps she should explain how the author organized his subject by planetary association—alehoof, for example, was filed under Venus. The dowager might find the attempt to establish order by an arbitrary metric as absurd as Bea did.

Oh, but order, she thought, settling on a strategy.

Softly, Bea brushed her free hand against the dowager's back, keenly aware of the pointy bumps of her spine, and said, "Here, your grace, do you wish to see a neat trick? Watch this: HMS *Majestic,* HMS *Goliath,* HMS *Audacious.*"

The dowager did not react.

Not a muscle moved.

But Kesgrave replied on cue, revealing no discomfort with the determined frivolity of her remark: "HMS *Goliath,* HMS *Audacious,* HMS *Majestic.*"

Having started down the path, Bea could only continue, smothering the niggling fear that she was making the horrible situation immeasurably worse. "And it can be any three ships in the Battle of the Nile. You can say HMS *Defence,* HMS

Vanguard, HMS *Ariadne,* and he will return them to the proper order."

Now Kesgrave lifted his eyes from his grandmother's form and regarded Bea with an expressive mix of gratitude and grief. Gently, he chided her for playing fast and loose with the truth. "The HMS *Ariadne* does not exist."

Injecting a note of cajolery into her tone, Bea said, "You see, your grace, you cannot fool him. I expect it works with other naval battles as well, but I have not had the pleasure yet of being bored to flinders by them. Perhaps if Kesgrave and I are fortunate enough to be invited to another soggy house party in the Lake District, I will be able to learn the name of the entire Spanish Armada."

She was prepared to say more.

Bea had discovered during her courtship of the duke and the early days of their marriage that she possessed a deep well of nonsense and raillery. She could talk coherently about inconsequentialities for hours on end.

It was not necessary, however, for the dowager replied, noting that Damien had always applied himself to his studies. "Mortimer as well. Both my grandsons were excellent students. They were not afraid to admit there were things they did not know and take steps to learn them. I was so proud."

And then she shuddered, her entire body rattling like a rickety fence, and she pitched forward into the duke's arms. Momentarily stunned, Kesgrave stared at Bea with bewilderment in his eyes before enclosing his grandmother in his embrace and lowering his head to whisper soothingly in her ear.

The storm lasted five minutes.

Overwhelmed by sorrow, the dowager allowed herself the luxury of indulging her anguish for five whole minutes, her head resting against her grandson's shoulder as sobs wracked her body, seemingly of their own volition.

And Kesgrave—holding her steady, so grateful that there was something he could do to alleviate her suffering and yet so troubled by the tumult of emotion. In all the years he had known her, he had never seen her as anything but calm and assured.

Even in May, when her surviving son was murdered in cold blood, she had maintained her composure.

And now this uncontrolled tempest.

Moved by the look of utter confoundment on his dear face, Bea reached up and swept a blond curl from his forehead. It was silky and smooth.

Then suddenly, it was over.

As if hearing the gong of a clock, the dowager straightened her back, pulled away from the duke, and withdrew a handkerchief from her sleeve. Dabbing at her eyes, she asked in a voice still gravelly with tears how Bea's investigation was proceeding. "I assume there *is* an investigation. If there is not, I expect you to begin one at once."

Bea did not know how to answer.

Yes, there was an investigation.

No, she did not think it was prudent to discuss it with her grace.

The duke, sharing none of her reluctance, confirmed that he and Bea were looking into the matter and would share their conclusions as soon as they arrived at them. "At the moment, there is nothing to know other than what I have already told you."

Alas, this statement rang hollow to the dowager duchess, who insisted they must know more than the sliver of information she had been given. "You said he was found stabbed to death this morning. Very well, then, *who* found him? *What* was he stabbed with? *Where* was he found? Your account lacks particulars, and as my granddaughter just demonstrated with aplomb, Damien, you adore particulars. Please stop treating me like a child in leading strings and tell me all that you know."

Kesgrave wanted to argue.

An obstinate look entered his eyes, and he pressed his lips together in tart annoyance. Nevertheless, he complied, starting with Hawes.

But not with the Hawes of that morning.

No, he went back years, to the Hawes who lured Mortimer into iniquity with the promise of earning his keep as a professional artist.

Siren song Hawes.

As misery had done little to dull her grace's sharpness, she readily drew the connection to her son and supposed it was Mortimer's association with the crime lord that led to Lord Myles's.

There was nothing for Kesgrave to do but confirm it.

The dowager's posture remained straight, her bearing almost regal, and yet Bea thought she detected a slight lowering of her shoulders, as if absorbing a blow.

When the duke had shared all the details he deemed pertinent—he would not, for instance, describe the murder weapon or how Mortimer appeared with one end of the chisel protruding from his gut—his grandmother thanked him for his candor, then fell silent as she digested the events. After a few minutes she said, "I should like to have a piece of his work for myself. You said the reliefs are very good. How do I acquire one? Do I purchase it?"

Obviously not, no, for the Matlock family would not be handing a single shilling to the man who had overseen the destruction of two of its members.

Authoritatively, Kesgrave said he would arrange it.

Nodding with gratitude, his grandmother thanked him

and said, "Art was always so important to Mortimer. He was drawing before he could walk. I am sure I have some of his earliest scribbles in the attics at Haverill Hall. I told Myles to leave the boy alone. Art was a harmless pursuit, and it made him happy. He was not hurting anyone."

As she spoke, the dowager tucked the damp handkerchief back under the silk sleeve of her gown. She would not give rein to her grief again.

"But Myles could not leave it alone," she said, continuing softly. "Something about the notion infuriated him. Perhaps it was the prospect of raising a dilettante. What would his friends at White's think of his son's amateurish daubs? Or maybe it was too close to being a tradesman. Once again, what would his friends think? Or maybe it was simply that he could not bear for anyone to be happy when he himself was so miserable. I suspect it was a little of all three combined with a small-minded pettiness he could never overcome. There is probably poetical justice in the fact that he ended life as a shopkeeper himself."

Distressed by the harsh grimace on the elderly woman's face, Bea knew there was nothing she could say to lessen her misery and settled for a banal comment about Mortimer's talent as an artist. "It is a shame he never found the acceptance he sought from the Royal Academy."

"I think his father did it," her grace announced abruptly. "I think Myles ensured Mortimer was rejected year after year. I have never said the words aloud before but have long believed he used either threats or inducements. I can think of no other explanation. His paintings were as good as or better than anything I have ever seen in the hallowed halls of the academy."

A shocking charge, it nevertheless comported with everything Bea knew about the man, and if it was true, then it added another layer of irony to Lord Myles's demise, for it was only through his intervention that Mortimer met Hell and Fury Hawes in the first place. Had he simply allowed his son to present his work in the showcase, he would still be alive to ridicule the boy for his talent.

Her grace, either unaware of this incongruity or inured to it, owned herself glad that Mortimer had gotten joy out of his vocation. "Despite how it ended, I am truly happy to know he had a chance to do the thing he loved and feel valued for it. There was always something disconcertingly desperate about his determination to fly with the Corinthians, as though he were trying to convince himself that he belonged. It never seemed like a comfortable fit, and I was terrified he would break his neck riding hell for leather against Hartlepool or another reckless buck."

Bea could think of no useful reply to this observation, for bleeding to death from a stomach wound did not strike her as a more satisfying end. Both options were equally awful, and rather than compare the two, she changed the topic, noting that Kesgrave had failed to mention the more significant work on display in the studio: a monumental painting of a beautiful young lady skillfully holding her seat on a rearing horse. "He called it *The Huntress* and I think you should have it as well."

The duke accepted the rebuke, adding that he would not allow the painting to go anywhere but Clarges Street. Then he strode to the door, where he conversed with the footman who hovered in the corridor outside. His grandmother eyed him suspiciously and asked what he was doing.

"I have requested dinner be served within the hour," he replied, returning to the settee. "It is just after five now and you will be hungry soon if all you have eaten this afternoon is a few slices of apples. I wager Bea is famished herself, since it has been several hours for her as well."

"As I am almost always ravenous, that is a safe bet to make," Bea added, deprecatingly.

"That is the product of your condition," the dowager said. "I was the same when I was increasing. But you cannot stay for dinner. You must resume your investigation. There is no time to spare."

In fact, there was plenty of time.

Kerrich would not be available for an interview until ten o'clock the next morning, when he would arrive at the Royal Antiquaries Society to perform his duties. Bea knew that information because she and Kesgrave had called on the building in Beak Street before continuing onward to the dowager's residence in Clarges. Apparently, they had only just missed him, which would not have happened if the coroner had made a timelier appearance. As it was, they had to wait another forty-five minutes for the pleasure of being treated with obsequious condescension: *Yes, yes, your graces, I am certain you are the true experts here, but I have been charged by the crown to do my duty and must muddle through as best I can. Now step aside and mind you do not step in the blood! Your clothes are far too nice for a stabbing death. Did you perhaps dress for a strangulation?*

Unconvinced by the cogent explanation, the dowager accused them of coddling her. "You think I am devastated by Mortimer's death and do not want me to sit by myself, stewing in my own gravy. You are trying to watch over me like a ninny."

"You *are* devastated," Kesgrave said mildly.

Her grace harumphed rudely.

Ignoring the guttural reply, he continued, "But we are not watching over you like a ninny. We are here to derive comfort from your presence and hope you derive comfort from ours in return. Now, your cousin Maria will be here to watch over you like an infant, but she cannot come until eight because she is playing whist with her cronies this afternoon."

Glaring at him thunderously, his grandmother said, "You could not be so cruel as to saddle me with that cantankerous old fool. I am a woman in mourning, overcome with grief."

"Precisely," Kesgrave said with an approving nod. "Nothing lifts your spirits like an argument and Maria is always happy to oblige. It is only for the night. You may toss her out on her ear as soon as the sun rises."

"And have the pleasure of listening to her daughter protest the abuse for the better part of an afternoon?" the dowager asked snidely. "No, I will not make *that* mistake again. I will have Sutton deny her entry. She can knock on the door all night to no avail."

Kesgrave smiled with genuine mirth. "An excellent plan. I am sure that treatment will not elicit a lengthy rebuke from Daphne."

Her grace's scowl deepened. "You think you are very clever, don't you?"

"No, just very concerned," he said soberly.

The dowager shook her head at this sentimental reply. "I am *fine*."

But even as she issued the ardent assurance, she clasped his hand again.

Having initiated physical contact with her grandson only a handful of times in the past dozen years, she had reached for him twice in one hour.

Clearly, she was not fine.

The duke, appearing to consider the matter settled, introduced a new topic in a bid to distract his grandmother from arguing further. "I would be grateful for your assistance with Lady Abercrombie. She is strongly of the opinion that Bea should host a party at Haverill Hall to establish herself in the country, and although I know Tilly is only teasing, Bea is worried she will issue invitations behind our backs to force our hand. To that end, I would be grateful if you could add your refusal to our own."

It was mortifying and infuriating, the way he framed Bea's concern, as though her insecurities were so acute she even invented things to fret about. Her anxieties were pronounced, to be sure, but each and every one was hard-earned. She did not jump at shadows, as evidenced by the fact that Lady Abercrombie *had* issued invitations behind their backs to force their hand!

Narrowing her eyes in a suspicious glower, his grandmother swore she had rarely been so insulted in her entire life. "I cannot believe you think I am so weak and feeble from grief as to accept that squeaker. All that is necessary to quell the countess is one of your imperious looks, Damien."

As word traveled quickly among the beau monde, Bea was surprised the dowager knew nothing about the affair. A determined gossip such as Mrs. Ralston would be eager to know who made the cut and would not hesitate to press the older woman for a complete list of names. The fact that she had not yet pestered the septuagenarian for information indicated that the countess had kept the gathering small.

At least, Bea hoped that was what it meant.

Finding the look of irritation infinitely preferable to grief, she decided to follow the duke's lead. "That is precisely the problem, your grace. Kesgrave shares your assessment of his imperious look and believes Lady Abercrombie has been sufficiently quelled. But I am convinced she is merely placating him. She is telling him what he wishes to hear because she knows he is too full of himself to doubt it. Nobody would dare lie to the Duke of Kesgrave!"

His lips twitching in reply, he said, "Or perhaps, brat, the notion that Tilly will pick a date, draw up a guest list, and send out invitations without our permission is too outlandish to even consider."

"Oh, but is it?" she murmured, thoroughly tickled by his certainty. He had no idea what was in store if she could not devise a way to counter Lady Abercrombie's machinations. The hit to his vanity would be ferocious if he discovered how blithely the countess had ignored his command.

"Damien is correct," the dowager added firmly. "Even Tilly recognizes that it is an intolerable violation. Nevertheless, I will do as you ask and give her a stern talking to on your behalf. I do fear you are overestimating the power of my disapproval, as I directed it to you and your wife only a few minutes ago and here you both remain. *And* Maria is coming in a few hours to my very great chagrin. I am quite, *quite* powerless. Never mind! Since you are resolved to join me for dinner, you may tell me about your plan to establish yourself in the country in a way that does not involve a large house party filled with high-flying intimates from London. I am sure it is twice as clever as Tilly's."

As Bea could not contemplate any part of her pending removal to the country with equanimity, she mentioned their plan to first join her family at the Holcroft estate in Bedfordshire.

The dowager managed a theatrical shudder at the prospect but otherwise refrained from comment.

Chapter Eight

With a bow window overlooking Beak Lane, the home of the Royal Antiquaries Society bore a startling resemblance to White's. Situated on a quiet road of elegant residences and one public house of middling repute, the vista offered none of the liveliness of St. James, with its modistes and jewelers and print shops and gambling hells. As a consequence, the thoroughfare received few passersby, and members who chose to avail themselves of the pleasant aspect were provided little in terms of entertainment.

Indeed, the most interesting foot traffic in recent months involved a scuffle between a harried postman and a gray-haired Scottish terrier, the latter of which clamped his teeth onto the hem of the mail deliverer's trousers and refused to let go. A crowd gathered as the man struggled with increasing fury to extricate himself, and Hollis Addleton, observing the tussle from the comfort of a leather armchair, tsked quietly to himself as none of the onlookers rushed to the aggrieved victim's assistance.

As these events had happened only the day before, they

remained fresh in Addleton's memory, and although the story could be relayed as a concise two-minute anecdote, its narrator seized the opportunity to rail against tangentially related bugaboos, such as the high price of the two-penny post, lax dog ownership, and a general lack of public spiritedness among the London populace.

"It will only be another minute," Couch said hearteningly to Bea and the duke.

And yet he held up the teapot and waved it enticingly before them.

Previously, he had advised them against accepting his offer of refreshment, as the brew was all but certain to be tepid because it had been sitting on the sideboard for over an hour. But that was before he had realized the member to whom they wished to speak was engaged in conversation with Addle the Prattle. In light of that revelation, he handed them each a teacup and urged them to settle in for a long wait while simultaneously assuring them there would be no wait at all.

"He will go on," Couch said with a tight, apologetic smile. "Mr. Addleton is something of the office gossip. It is his eye for detail. He misses nothing and considers it an obligation to make sure nobody else does either. It tends to make for a decidedly one-sided conversation and is why we call him Addle the Prattle. Make no mistake: He is an excellent antiquarian and I am honored to count him among my colleagues, but he can be long-winded. We have all learned the hard way not to call on him during a lecture. If you give him the opportunity to ask a question, the library in Alexandria will be rebuilt and destroyed again before he works his way to an actual query. He is chock-full of observations! Still, I can tell that he is almost finished now. It won't be another minute."

Even so, he filled a cup with tea and placed it on the table next to Bea.

A scholarly institution unburdened by the obligation to

appear fashionable, the Royal Antiquaries Society nevertheless sought to emulate the finest gentlemen's clubs, and the
parlor to which Bea and the duke had been shown was decorated with restrained masculine elegance, its comfortable
chairs upholstered in the finest leather and its mirrors gilded
in gold leaf. On the walls hung gloomy portraits of past presi-
dents, each one determined to appear more austere than the
last. Glowering above them was Hubert Millet, the eighth
member to hold the position, and it was thanks to his intervention that they were able to secure the building after the
passing of one of the organization's founders.

Across the room, seated in a corner beneath the surly-
eyed Reginald Bagford, president number twelve, Addleton
said, "I am not implying that Mr. Thurman stole the letter
from the postbox, but I do not know how else he could have
gained possession of it because I had slipped it into the pillar
myself."

It was, without question, a new topic.

Couch, his color rising, apologized to his guests for the
scene he was about to make, rose stiffly to his feet, and
stomped across the floor to interrupt the new diatribe. Tartly,
he said, "The Duke and Duchess of Kesgrave have done Mr.
Addleton the very great courtesy of allowing him to finish his
tale about the feral terrier despite requiring the attention of
Mr. Kerrich. Patiently, they have waited while he decried the
postmaster general and unruly curs and the widespread indifference to suffering in the capital, but they shall not twiddle
their thumbs while you mount your next hobby horse
without any consideration for their time and importance."

If Addleton was startled to find himself the target of his
colleague's vitriol, it was nothing compared to Kerrich's shock
at learning of the duke and duchess's interest. He leaped to
his feet with alacrity and bounded across the room to greet
his august callers with breathless wonder. Bowing to

Kesgrave, he said, "Your grace! I am so sorry you have been forced to wait. If your presence had been communicated to me"—here, he glared at Couch for withholding the important news—"I would have received you immediately. There was nothing Mr. Addleton and I were discussing that could not hold until later. Regardless, it is an honor! I am sure whatever you wish to say to me is of a private nature, and if you will kindly follow me to the first floor, we shall find somewhere quiet."

The confusion on Addleton's face was supplanted by naked curiosity, and Bea allowed that Kerrich's preference for a quiet room could be nothing more than a rational precaution against the prying interest of a colleague. All members of the Royal Antiquaries Society might routinely conduct their business on the upper floors to avoid public scrutiny, lest their dealings become fodder for one of Addleton's extended anecdotes.

And yet Bea could not believe that Kerrich was unaware of the connection. Even if he resolutely ignored the *ton* and its antics, the brutal slaying of Lord Myles at the hands of his business partner had created a furor in the press, and he would have to shun newspapers entirely not to have read something about it. Those reports made the relationship between the Matlock cousins plain.

Presumably, the real reason Kerrich led them to the secretary's office in the back of the building was he did not wish to discuss his corrupt business practices in the presence of his fellow antiquarians. The exploitation of one's reputation to swindle collectors was better suited for dark alleyways and deserted cellars.

Although not as bleak as either of those locations, the room was shabby and cramped, with smudged windows looking out onto the mews, threadbare bergères, and a large water stain on one wall.

Following the direction of her gaze, Kerrich grimaced and said, "The setting is not ideal, but it guarantees we will not be interrupted. Please sit down and make yourselves comfortable. I would offer tea, but I know you are eager to be on your way. Thank you again for your patience, your graces. Mr. Addleton is a rackety old prattle. Most of us know not to be alone with him or he will hold you prisoner, but he caught me unawares this morning as I was reading the *Post*."

The mention of Prinny's favorite newspaper settled the matter for Bea, for it had devoted copious amounts of attention to Lord Myles's slaying. The antiquarian knew why they were there, although perhaps only to an extent. If Kerrich was not the murderer, then at the very least he anticipated having to endure several probing questions into his and Mortimer's illicit activities. If he was the killer, then he expected be subjected to a lengthy interrogation by the murder duchess.

Kerrich's demeanor suggested the former.

A large man in thick spectacles and a mauve waistcoat, he smiled without a hint of self-consciousness as he lowered his bulk smoothly into the chair. It squeaked lightly as it accommodated his weight, and he crossed one leg left over his knee as he regarded them avidly. "Allow me to say again how gratified I am by your attention. I am certainly not worthy of it but will endeavor to provide whatever service is required."

Kesgrave, wasting no time on pleasantries, stated the situation plainly. "The duchess and I are looking into the murder of my cousin Mortimer Matlock, with whom you partnered in a plot to defraud collectors by selling counterfeit antiquities as though they were genuine. Mortimer produced the forgeries, and you authenticated them."

Kerrich's equanimity deserted him.

His jaw dropped, he gaped, he inhaled sharply, he snapped his mouth shut, and then he repeated the cycle twice. Whatever confidence he had felt in his ability to endure the interview without succumbing to panic left him in an instant, and he seemed literally to flail, his arms darting outward as though to steady his balance. Then, gripping the arms of the chair, he said, "I do not understand. Matlock was murdered? As in killed?"

Brutally, the duke said, "As in stabbed in the stomach with a chisel."

Kerrich blanched and wrapped his arms around his own considerable middle, either to protect it from an invisible threat or to stanch a sudden queasiness. Foundering for a reply, he said, "That is ... that is ... that is horrible. It is ... it is ... I do not know what to say. Are you sure? I mean, are you certain there has not been a mistake? I simply cannot believe anyone would want to hurt him."

"Can you not?" the duke asked mildly.

The antiquarian grew paler at the implication, his grasp on his belly tightening, but he retained enough of his wits to offer his sympathies. "Your grace, I am sorry for your loss. I did not know Matlock very well, but what I did know, I liked and respected. He was a diligent and hardworking man who treated me with respect and courtesy. He will be sorely missed."

If the scheme was as lucrative as Hawes said, then Bea imagined the deceased would indeed be missed. Kerrich's own income would drop in the absence of forgeries to authenticate, something she imagined he would have kept in mind if driven into a murderous rage by something Mortimer had done.

Kesgrave, accepting his condolences with a dip of his head, asked about his visit to the studio on Friday. "You arrived in a state of extreme agitation."

Although his color had yet to return, Kerrich seemed calmer as he contemplated the question before refuting the claim. "I did not call on Mortimer on Friday or any day last week or this week or the week before. I am been busy with my duties here. I am giving a talk on a paper on the uses of lapis lazuli in ancient Egypt, which was published in this month's edition of the Royal Antiquarian Society's newsletter. It is a prestigious honor, and I want to be prepared."

"You arrived at Mortimer's studio in Banner Street in a state of extreme agitation," the duke repeated calmly, undeterred by the denial. "What was the source of your anxiety?"

Typically, when Bea pressed a murder suspect on a subject he did not feel comfortable addressing, he typically accused her of being too distraught to think clearly. He would cite the gruesome spectacle of death, the delicate nature of her sensibilities, and the female mind's inadequate capacity to digest facts as evidence of her hysterical response.

With Kesgrave as questioner, that option was not available to Kerrich.

Consequently, the antiquarian continued with his original tactic, reiterating that the information was inaccurate. "I do not know who told you that, but their motives are not to be trusted. I have not seen your cousin in months."

It was, Bea thought, the wrong approach to take when the information provided by the duke was so specific. If he had referenced the visit in vague terms, then it would be reasonable for Kerrich to conclude Kesgrave was speculating in an attempt to discover new details. In that circumstance, Kerrich's determination to brazen it out was not entirely a losing gambit.

Kesgrave, responding to the request for information, explained that Mortimer had had company at the time of Kerrich's visit. "The witness recognized you from your voice."

Kerrich, darting forward, shook his head furiously as he swore, "Goddamn it! That girl! That blasted girl with the pretty dimples! She was there and spying on me. Matlock should have said something. Goddamn it!"

But having confirmed one aspect of his visit, he immediately contested the other and insisted he had not been extremely agitated when he called. "I was abrupt. A little abrupt maybe because it had been a busy afternoon and I still had several things to do. As I mentioned, I am presenting a paper in a few days. It is just like a girl to embellish! A little brusqueness becomes extreme agitation. I am sorry, your grace, that she sent you here on a fool's mission. I can only assume she is grief-stricken by Mortimer's passing. A girl with her limited opportunities getting a chance to model for an artist of his skill and talent—she will not be so lucky twice. I suppose we must forgive her for elaborating."

Ah, there it was, she thought, the misogyny she knew so well.

It would not be a murder investigation without a healthy dose of male contempt.

"I think Miss Brewer's assessment of your mental state was accurate," Bea said mildly, speaking for the first time. "But if you would like to continue to debate the matter, we can present the facts to Mr. Addleton and see what he thinks."

The chair creaked as Kerrich recoiled in his seat, and although an ornery look crossed his face, he forced a smile and admitted he was without recourse. "Touché, your grace, for outmaneuvering me. You are clever. I was agitated when I called on Matlock because I had just found out that a relief I had authenticated had been sold to the British Museum. That was in violation of our agreement!"

Bea was stunned.

Despite the cynicism with which she regarded Hell and Fury, she had still managed to underestimate the scope of his ambition. There was no higher place to aim than Montague House.

With that one sale, Hawes had defrauded the British government out of hundreds of pounds.

If that was the second phase, she could not conceive of what came next.

Fleecing the prince regent himself?

Still trying to grasp the immensity of the scheme, she said, "You put a prohibition on sales to the British Museum in your compact with Mortimer and he agreed?"

"Of course not!" he snapped impatiently. "The notion that he would sell one of his forgeries to the British Museum never occurred to me! Who would do such a thing? It is reckless and stupid! I demanded a southern border of Birmingham. *That* was our agreement—no sales to collectors south of Birmingham. Rubes in the north do not know an Assyrian tablet from an Asian tapestry. If a so-called collector in Berwick-upon-Tweed wants to puff up himself for the locals with one of Matlock's stone slabs, then I am happy to validate his ignorance and pocket some coins. There are not enough authentic antiquities in circulation for everyone who wants one to have one, so it is almost an act of kindness to increase the supply. Mr. and Mrs. Happy Rustic can show off their piece in the stable or the shed, wherever they would hang it, and impress the neighbors. Good for them, I say. But London collectors are—"

Kerrich broke off with a shudder, the fury seeping out of him as he pressed his forehead against the surface of the desk. "London collectors are intelligent and shrewd. They know enough to be suspicious. That is why I set the boundary at Birmingham. I could not risk someone calling into question my judgment. I am a member of the Royal Antiquarian Society, and as such I stake my reputation on every determination I make. I would not imperil my standing for any amount of money."

Oh, but he had, and as he raised his head back up, he acknowledged how deeply he had miscalculated the risk he had taken. "I thought I could trust Matlock. It turns out, I could not."

"He agreed to no sales south of Birmingham?" she asked.

"Without hesitation," he replied with a weary sigh. "He said it was a reasonable provision and that he shared the same concern. He *claimed* he was no more eager to be unmasked as a fraud than I was. It was a lie to appease me. Matlock admitted it, then mocked me for even believing him in the first place. A successful scheme was never going to abide by an arbitrary boundary. It was always going to grow in the direction that promised the greatest return."

"The betrayal cut deeply," she said, recalling Miss Brewer's description of the confrontation.

He laughed bitter as he said, "To the bone. He would not have dared if he considered me an equal. No, I was his subordinate, and he did not bear enough respect for me to listen to my opinion. To him, I served a function and that was all."

Bea asked how they had met.

"A society event," he said. "A lecture on Herculaneum. He was interested in the topic, making many insightful comments and asking so many questions. Everyone was impressed. He came to several functions after that and befriended half the membership."

Naturally, he did. It was the only way to assess who would be most useful.

"How long ago was that?" she asked.

Briefly, he furrowed his brow before responding, "Two years this past January."

"And how long until he asked you to authenticate counterfeit antiquities?"

He flinched at the description. "Three months. He was sly about it, very subtle, proposing it first as hypothetical and speculating whether it could be done. He knew provenance was central to its success and came up with outlandish ideas for how to manufacture it, allowing me to correct him. That was how he reeled me in, and before I knew it he was offering more money than I make in a month for a single certificate of authentication. I said I would do it on the condition we already discussed, and we moved forward with the sale. It was safe and easy, so we moved forward with more. We've sold two a month for a little more than two years. It was going swimmingly until I found out about the British Museum."

"That is why you called on him Friday in a state of intense agitation," she said.

He took issue with the description. "I was angry, not agitated. On balance, however, you are correct. That *was* the reason I called. I wanted to impress upon him the danger because it was unlikely his reliefs would pass muster with the properly trained experts at Montague House. I assumed it was not too late. He could withdraw from the deal, and everything could go back to the way it was. He refused."

Kerrich's affect changed as he recalled the scale of Mortimer's treachery. His cheeks darkened, his voice roughened, and his eyes flashed hotly. Bea pictured this version of the antiquarian pounding on Mortimer's door on Friday, demanding retribution for the abuse. "If the truth came out, your reputation would be in tatters, your life ruined."

"Everything I had worked for—gone!" he said, seething with resentment.

"And burning with fury and unable to stand the wanton callousness with which he imperiled your very existence, you returned a few days later and drove the chisel into Mortimer's stomach," she said with calculated softness.

Seemingly on the verge of agreeing, he pulled back in his chair and stared at her aghast before issuing a strident denial. "Never! I would never resort to violence. I told him I would not lend my imprimatur again and did not care how much money he offered me. I was done!"

As Miss Brewer had described a heated exchange that had gone on for several minutes, Bea knew the conversation did not end there, with Mortimer accepting the antiquarian's withdrawal from the scheme. "Did he offer you more money?"

Kerrich barked out an unamused cackle. "Why bribe my compliance when he could coerce it? Unbeknownst to me, I had actually been employed the whole time by a man called Rennie Rumpus, and if I did not live up to my end of the bargain, then Mr. Rumpus would step in to ensure my cooperation."

Next to her, Kesgrave stiffened. "Rennie Rumpus!"

Confounded by his recognition of a name she had never heard before, she looked at the duke for clarification, which he promptly provided: Edmund Renfield, Hell and Fury's chief lieutenant.

"Chief lieutenant," Kerrich repeated bitterly. "How benign you make it sound! He is a man with a long and varied career but is most famously known for pummeling his enemies to within an inch of their lives with his bare fists. He enjoys causing pain, which is how he got his nickname: Rennie Rumpus, ready to thump us. Of course you do not know him, your grace. A genteel lady such as yourself should have nothing to do with that dark underworld and its inhabitants. I was equally ignorant of his existence until Mortimer explained that it was to him that I owed my loyalty—him and Hawes. I could not walk away without upsetting Hawes, and it was Rumpus's job to make sure nothing upset his boss. The threat of violence was unmistakable. I had no choice but to back down."

Kesgrave pointed out that the forgeries scheme was a vast and complex undertaking.

Unhesitatingly, Kerrich agreed.

But Bea perceived the implication. "Who did you think was funding it if not a disreputable organization with ties to the criminal class?"

"Matlock," Kerrich said simply.

The duke smiled fleetingly. "You thought Mortimer had enough scratch to cover the investment costs of setting up an illegal antiquities trade that extends as far north as Scotland? To pay for materials, transport, and men?"

"Of course I did!" Kerrich retorted irritably. "His father was a lord! His cousin is a duke! Everyone knows the family has gold coming out of its ears. I thought it was a lark. I knew he had been repeatedly rebuffed by the Royal Academy and assumed he considered it appropriately ironical to have his work in some of the finest homes in England when he could not get even a toe in the academy. I figured he liked having a laugh at the expense of rich provincials. Why would I ever think otherwise? I had no idea of the true state of his financial affairs until after his father was killed and I read all those articles about his lordship owning a gin parlor. And even then, I assumed Matlock's inheritance was secure."

Although Kesgrave found this explanation dubious, Bea could not refute its logic. The Matlock family *was* obscenely wealthy, and only someone who had followed Lord Myles's career closely would realize how exuberantly he had squandered his money and estates. A casual bystander could be forgiven for assuming his pockets were infinitely deep.

"It seems obvious *now* that the plot was too complicated for him, but prior to our conversation on Friday, he never gave me a reason to think he was not in charge. Furthermore, it is not as though I sat at my worktable contemplating the size of the operation. All I did was provide paperwork validating the authenticity of the reliefs. Everything else was beyond my purview as an antiquarian," he said defensively.

Bea found it all a little too convenient, his claim of total ignorance, and she pointed out that he had worked with the deceased for more than two years. "You must be able to name at least one other member of the network. How did you know when to provide verification? Mortimer must have had a messenger he used regularly. Or what about the dealers who sold the reliefs to the collectors up north? Or even the name of one of the collectors you hoodwinked?"

Staunchly, Kerrich swore he could not. "There was no messenger or go-between. I would bring the certificates of authenticity to Matlock's studio at the beginning of every month myself. As the reliefs were his invention, there was no need for me to see or examine them. In the beginning, I insisted on inspecting each one closely to make sure the iconography was correct. To the uninitiated, one crown or scepter looks like any other. But after a while it became clear to me, he knew what he was doing, and my role became primarily researcher. For each relief, I identified a plausible site of discovery and created a believable history of possession. I specified whose hands it has passed through and when. It is detailed work and requires detailed records but allows me a great deal of freedom and independence. I swear on my life I cannot name a single person who is involved in the scheme except Matlock."

But he looked away as he made this ardent disavowal, and Bea, convinced the evasion was meaningful, insisted he did know someone.

The antiquarian mumbled in reply.

Leaning forward, as if to improve her hearing, Bea said, "I am sorry? What was that?"

"A dealer," Kerrich repeated churlishly. "I know the name of a dealer. *One* dealer. But Matlock did not introduce me to him. I happened to be in the shop when the proprietor received delivery of an Assyrian relief, and it looked like Matlock's handiwork. It disappeared into a storeroom, but I snuck in to get a better look. Once I confirmed it was his, I called on him to find out why one of his forgeries was with a London dealer, and he explained that Higgins was his conduit to the north. He kept them briefly before passing them to a dealer in Manchester, who distributed the reliefs to other dealers or sold them to collectors. That made sense, as the reliefs had to get to the north via an exchange of hands, so I did not doubt it. But I still made a point of returning often to the shop to make sure the reliefs did not appear on his shelves. To my relief, they did not. But those stupid, shabby trinkets *did* appear, which was almost worse. They were obviously fake and would expose everything if Higgins did not remove them."

Confused by the new direction, she asked him to identify who and what.

"Higgins," he spat with tart disapproval. "That is who. He is a fool and created a display of shabby trinkets masquerading as meaningful Roman artifacts: medallions, ampullae, et cetera. And the blasted cretin had gathered them in a large grouping, which made them look even more like playthings. I went immediately to Matlock and told him to have Higgins remove them. They would draw unwanted attention to his business practices, revealing him to be a cheat, casting suspicion on every sale he had ever made, and ultimately destroying my reputation."

It was, she decided, a reasonable sequence of events.

Revelations tended to come in rapid succession. "When was this?"

"I saw the relief in Higgins' shop in December. The abominable trinkets appeared soon after, either in late January or early February. And they are still there, only now it is worse because there are even more of them," he said heatedly, his color rising. "Higgins is delighted because they are popular with his customers. He is an asinine lackwit, but I expected better from Matlock. He insisted I was worrying about nothing, which is why I was in a lather by the time I arrived at the studio on Friday to discuss the sale to the British Museum. I knew his judgment was not always the best and feared he had allowed himself to be influenced by Higgins or someone equally disreputable. I called on him at his studio to remind him of our agreement, confident he would stop the sale and all would be well. Instead, he informed me that he had no control over the placement of the reliefs because it was not his scheme, but Hell and Fury Hawes's, and if I had a problem with Hawes's business decision, I could take it up with Rennie Rumpus. I left there furious, as you already know. But that is all. I returned to my home and contemplated my options before realizing I had none. I was in deep with the roughest of men and would continue to be in business with them until the moment Matlock released me or I was exposed for my illegal activities and drummed out of the Royal Antiquarian Society."

"But now you are free," Kesgrave noted without inflection.

Kerrich twisted his lips into an unamused smile. "Am I? Or am I merely in service to a new master? To be honest, I have no idea what happens next. I assume Mr. Rumpus will get in touch with me soon to resume my authentications. I hope that is not the case, but I think it is too simplistic to think Matlock's death changes anything."

Well, he would say that, would he not?

Anything else would be admitting to a motive.

A second motive, she amended, noting that fury at the deception was sufficient in and of itself.

"None of it matters anyway," Kerrich said on a heavy sigh, throwing his head against the back of the chair. "My signature is on the paperwork submitted to the British Museum, so I will soon be on the hook for defrauding the government."

And there was a third motive—revenge, Bea thought.

She asked how Kerrich had found out about the sale to Montague House, as the institution's acquisitions were not widely known.

"Maybe not in your circle," he replied with a faint sneer. "But additions to the British Museum's collections are enthusiastically discussed among the membership of the Royal Antiquaries Society, and I believe it was Addle the Prattle who told me about the relief. As soon as I heard it was Assyrian from ninth century b.c., I knew it was one of Matlock's. I *hoped* otherwise but knew in my heart. On the journey to his studio, I told myself all was not lost. I could be mistaken, and if I was not, Matlock could withdraw from the sale. I had no idea the terrible reality that lay in store for me."

Bea asked him where he was on Tuesday night from eight to midnight.

Kerrich flinched but conceded the necessity. "You cannot take my word for it, as you know I am a scoundrel who is willing to sell out his life's work for a few hundred pounds. I am despicable."

And yet he provided only a partial alibi, citing the men with whom he had dined until nine o'clock and his wife, to whom he returned at ten-thirty. He refused to account for the two hours in between as a matter of discretion, for he was not a cad to subject a young gentlewoman to charges of adultery.

Bea pressed, explaining that it was the only way to remove

him from the list of suspects, but he remained adamant. Having done no harm to Matlock, he had nothing to fear from their investigation and would only reveal the identity of his companion if it meant the difference between life and death. And riding on that high horse, he thanked Bea and the duke for their time and instructed them to leave.

Chapter Nine

Rennie Rumpus was not an easy man to find.

Unlike Hell and Fury, whose notoriety ensured that his location was widely known, Edmund Renfield did not figure prominently in drawing room banter, newspaper reporting, or conversation among serious men over glasses of port. He performed his duties quietly, diligently, providing whatever service his employer needed to support his illegal enterprise, and although he was often called upon to convince mushroomy upstarts that encroaching on Hawes's territory was detrimental to their well-being, he spent the vast majority of his time explaining to local shopkeepers the benefits of making a donation to Hawes's safe business fund. A modest contribution was the most reliable way to attain peace of mind and security in an uncertain world.

A former bare-knuckle boxer, he had none of the grace or nimble footwork of Gentleman Jackson, relying instead on brute force to overwhelm his opponent. His only advantage was size, but as he was tall and wide and thick and strong, it was all he needed. Even at his slightly lumbering pace, he could level an opponent with a single punishing blow.

As for how he had earned his nickname, nobody could say and the general assumption was he had given it to himself. It had rooted itself in the popular imagination, however, when spectators discovered how satisfying it was to chant, "Rennie Rumpus, ready to thump us" during a bout.

Renfield withdrew from the sporting scene after half a decade to join Hawes, who had defeated his last rival only a few years before to take command of Saffron Hill. Like any ambitious crime lord, he needed a strapping young man to protect him and intimidate his competitors. Renfield excelled at both, his success with the latter being so great he rarely had the pleasure of pummeling anyone anymore. His reputation combined with his powerful frame all but guaranteed that most comers backed down the second they caught sight of him. It was a rare day when he had to remove his tailcoat in anticipation of a brawl to cow an adversary, and the simple act of revealing his muscles was usually enough to send an adversary into retreat. Unfortunately, by that time, it was too late, for Renfield had gone through the bother of removing the garment and meted out a good thrashing as due compensation for his trouble.

If anything about the information Kesgrave had compiled on Edmund Renfield surprised Bea, it was the fact that he had gathered it at all. Previous to Hawes's visit yesterday, they had had only two encounters with him and the first had gone more or less according to plan. They called on him at his home, asked probing questions about his dealings with Lord Myles Matlock, endured several discreet threats about interfering with his criminal empire, and returned to their carriage unmolested. The duke had found the interview galling, infuriated by the subtle threats to Bea, but as soon as his uncle's murderer had been taken off to Newgate, he appeared to have forgotten about him altogether.

But he had not.

Rather, he had tasked his very capable steward with assembling a comprehensive report on the King of Saffron Hill and perused it thoroughly.

No, not perused.

Committed it to memory.

He would have been unable to spout the date of Renfield's last boxing match if he had not spent a significant amount of time with the material.

And with all that information at his fingertips, he still did not have an address.

Bea could scarcely credit the oversight. "The man who was able to find out in a matter of hours how many marriage proposals Mrs. Beveridge refused during her season eleven years ago could not identify where Rennie Rumpus lives?"

"The number of suitors Mrs. Beveridge rejected was not a secret," Kesgrave explained with a daunting stiffness to his tone, readily offended by the slight to his steward's competence. "She discussed it openly, as it added to her prestige. Renfield has not been similarly inclined, as it makes him vulnerable to malefactors."

"Bah!" she replied, unimpressed with this defense. "Surely, the estimable Stephens has more resources than just hearsay."

Kesgrave's lips twitched as he reminded her of the steward's responsibilities, which focused on matters pertaining to the estate. "He calculates the rents, estimates crop yields, and allocates funds for repairs. He does not don elaborate disguises à la Miss Lark to ask prying questions. I believe his most efficacious tactic is sending queries to his brothers and waiting for them to respond."

Although it was almost certainly a distraction from the pressing matter of identifying Mortimer Matlock's killer, Bea could not withstand the provocation. "Stephens has brothers?"

"Six," the duke affirmed.

Bea raised her chin in astonishment as she contemplated Kesgrave across the space of the carriage. "Six!"

"All stewards, all working for men of wealth and standing, all currently in London," he added with a grin. "Presumably, his parents are very proud."

At once, an image formed in her head of seven Stephens in a line, red hair neatly parted in the center, beady eyes intent and serious, impatient frowns as they tolerated yet another interruption to their day.

Bea could not help it—she shivered.

And yet she was utterly fascinated.

She wanted to press for more information but restrained herself because it was indeed a digression. They had yet to settle on an approach for finding Renfield and were driving to Saffron Hill on the expectation they would come up with an idea before they arrived, which she pointed out again.

"On the contrary, we do have a plan," Kesgrave asserted.

"Ah, yes," Bea said, resisting the urge to roll her eyes at the vague outline of a plot he had promoted. "We are going to a tavern with a sign that may or may not have a horse's head on it—"

"It resembles a horse but could be a donkey," he replied with some asperity. "It is not as though it might be a pig or a goat."

Graciously, she amended her description. "Very well, an equine of some extraction. Once inside the tavern, we are to find the man with the straw hat and bring a glass of cider to his table."

"A pint of cider," he corrected meaningfully.

"Thank you, yes, a pint, because the particulars are vital to success," she replied. "As we give him the *pint* of cider, we say,

'Tis a fine day for cards,' and he will invite us to sit down. He will then deal vingt-et-un, and after several rounds, he will give us Renfield's address."

"We have to lose the hands," he reminded her.

She nodded affirmatively. "Right. After we lose a handful of guineas to the man in the straw hat in several pretend rounds of vingt-et-un, he will kindly give us Renfield's address before bidding us good day. That is not a plan, your grace. That is a scene from *The Castle of Wolfenbach*. I am shocked Stephens proposed it."

Patiently, Kesgrave explained that Stephens had done nothing of the sort. "And he would be horrified at your attributing it to him. The plan is mine and based on information in the report, which describes the man in the straw hat as a dealer in intelligence. He makes it his business to know things, and although I cannot say how or where he gets his information, I have been assured he excels at his vocation. Even Hawes has used him upon occasion."

Despite this reasonable explanation, Bea remained skeptical, for it struck her as needlessly circuitous when they had a more direct route. "We can ask Hawes. As we are investigating the murder at his behest, he will make an effort to appear helpful even if he actually is not."

Kesgrave did not think it was to their advantage to alert the crime lord as to the direction of their inquiry. "We have no idea what he actually wants us to discover, and until we are able to discern his motive, it is in our best interest to keep him in the dark about our progress. That way he will not be able to interfere or point us where he wants us to go."

His reasoning made sense—of course it did—and yet a man with a straw hat!

It was all a little silly.

"And just you wait: We will walk into the tavern and every

man inside will be wearing a straw hat," she added with an irrepressible giggle.

Thankfully, her dire prediction did not come to pass. Upon entering the Crown & Kettle, whose sign bore the image of a zebra (equine indeed!), they spied only six patrons sporting the troublesome accessory.

"I apologize for being unduly pessimistic, your grace," she said softly as the door snapped shut behind them. "Half the room offers far more favorable odds. How do you suggest we proceed? Perhaps from oldest to youngest? What does the report say about the age of the intelligence broker?"

Kesgrave, revealing no dismay at the preponderance of options as he walked over to the barkeep, said their straw hat was in the back corner, next to the mirror. Taken aback, she studied the man in question while the duke ordered three ciders and belatedly noticed the set of playing cards by his elbow. Although the deck was easily spotted when you knew to look for it, it was an impressive observation.

The encounter with Mr. Book was just as easily managed, with the duke losing four guineas in the course of eight hands, and they left the tavern before Beatrice had a chance to even taste the cider.

To her surprise, Renfield did not live in Saffron Hill. He resided to the west of Hatton Garden, in a brick house with a green door and a pair of large maple trees in front obscuring the view of the upper floors. As it was early in the afternoon, Bea did not expect him to answer their knock. Surely, he was about in the neighborhood, flexing his muscles and flicking aside rivals. It would probably be better to call after six, when he returned for his evening meal. In the meantime, they could visit Higgins, the dealer who sold Mortimer's reliefs to collectors.

Bea was just about to propose this plan when the door was opened by a maid who greeted them with confusion.

"This is a private home, sir and madam. If yer looking for a lawyer's office, ye must continue along Holborn and turn left onto Chancery Lane," she said, glancing over their shoulders to where the carriage stood in the road. "Yer driver will figure it out."

The duke, thanking her for the information, explained that they were in the correct location. "We would like to speak to Mr. Renfield if he is available."

Making no attempt to conceal her befuddlement, the servant said, "Are ye sure ye aren't looking for the solicitors? Lincoln's Inn Fields is just around the corner and a bit."

Kesgrave assured her they were certain, which did little to lessen her concern, and she tightened her grip on the door frame, as if fortifying her stance. A voice inside the house, however, asked if there was a problem and she reluctantly stepped aside.

Responding to the query, she announced that they had visitors. "They seem all innocent and genteel, sir, but I don't trust them half an inch, let alone a whole country mile. Look at their carriage. It has a crest, an *elaborate* crest with garland and lions. It's a trick, sir. Larder McCoy scheming to get back at ye for breaking up his mill yesterday before he could take bets. Ye let them slither inside, and the gent will cut out ye guts, he will. He looks ruthless to me."

The comment amused Bea, who had likewise ascribed ruthlessness to the duke, although her understanding of the term centered on eviscerating set-downs, not disemboweling swords.

Renfield came into view then, filling the doorway with his frame, and Bea was startled by the sight of him, for he was an elegantly attired behemoth with an affable smile. His form was exactly as advertised—broad shoulders, barrel chest, thick neck, imposing height—but his tailoring defied expectation, delineating each limb with beautiful precision. It did not come cheaply, she thought, admiring the simplicity of his dark-colored tailcoat, which lay flat against his arms without any unsightly wrinkles despite the bulging muscles. His waistcoat was likewise subdued, lending him an air of solemnity, and she was reminded of Hawes. Like his employer, Renfield had kicked the mud off his shoes and styled himself as a gentleman.

The refined presentation worked to the lieutenant's advantage, lending him a veneer of sophistication that felt as thin as paper. Its flimsiness, the sense that it could tear at any moment, only added to his menace, and she could not imagine his being more frightening *without* his tailcoat.

Examining him further, she noticed that he was younger than Hawes by at least fifteen years. Not yet thirty, he must have been barely out of leading strings when he entered his first fight. That he had thrived in his chosen profession was evident in his visage, which bore few scars. His cheeks were wide and ruddy, his forehead was high and smooth, and his brown eyes gleamed with curiosity.

But his hands—oh, his hands.

They were meaty and thick, with fingers like miniature tree trunks, and now he put her in mind of another of Hawes's associates, Thomas "the Bludgeon" Trudgeon, who routinely pounded his victims to death with a club or a hammer or whatever was readily available.

As with Trudgeon, Bea could picture Renfield pummeling his victims to death, and bearing that image so clearly in her head, she wondered what it meant that Mortimer was stabbed with a chisel. Had Rennie Rumpus veered from his signature method to obscure his involvement in the murder or was he simply not involved in the murder?

Renfield, following his servant's command, examined the carriage before turning his benign gaze to his guests and inviting them inside with a wave of his hand.

The maid squeaked in protest.

"Calm yourself, Martha," he said mildly. "There is no cause for alarm. They are not associates of Larder McCoy, who won't dare set foot east of the Strand again after the drubbing I gave him. It is the Duke of Kesgrave and his wife. I have been anticipating this opportunity for an age and can only marvel that it took so long. We will discuss our business in the study. Please bring us some tea and include biscuits if we have any."

Despite these assurances, the maid's demeanor altered little, and as she spun on her heels to return to the kitchen, she muttered, "Wouldn't trust a dook as far as I could throw him. Feral beasties. The lot of them."

Amused, Renfield closed the door, bathing the corridor in darkness, and led them to his study, a small but graceful room that also bore traces of Hawes in its thistle-patterned paper on the walls and bright blue rug. A shelf hung opposite the door, displaying an assortment of pretty glass objects: a trio of coral-colored paperweights, a Cornish serpentine egg, a pair of candlesticks, a cut glass bud vase. A desk pressed against the wall, and although it had molded legs like the one in Hell and Fury's residence in Grape Street, it was fashioned from wood that was far less dear than mahogany.

The difference in quality struck her as fitting for a protégé.

Following them into the room, Renfield apologized for his servant. "She has an innate distrust of everyone, not just the aristocracy. And McCoy *did* threaten to strike back at me for ruining his illicit boxing match. But it was just bluster for the benefit of his chaps. He has already returned to Potsgrove with his tail between his legs," he said, urging his visitors to make themselves comfortable. "Martha will be here any minute with the tray, and she will find you less threatening if you're seated."

Puzzled by his manner, Bea complied.

That he was not yet cognizant of Mortimer's murder was evident in his relaxed pose. Hawes had not apprised his lieutenant of the development, which was hardly surprising in light of his decision to task her and the duke with the responsibility of finding the killer.

And yet what other business could Renfield have with them?

Oh, but he said he had been waiting an age for their visit.

That was even stranger.

Addressing the matter forthrightly as he lowered into the chair across from her, she said, "We are here, Mr. Renfield, because—"

"Edmund," he said, interrupting. "You must call me Edmund. All my friends do, and I think we are going to be fast friends, your grace. I know, I know, you are all out of sorts with me at the moment for leading Mr. Matlock down the garden path. You are going to demand that I release him from our arrangement at once. The family name is at stake, and it has already suffered enough, what with that tawdry business with the gin parlor. You are outraged by the attention, which is only right. There are no positive associations to be made with gin. Upon hearing the word, any decent citizen of our fair city immediately pictures Hogarth's print depicting its horrible effects: infanticide, starvation, insanity. The second I heard about Lord Myles's tragic fate, I knew you would soon learn the truth about Mr. Matlock as well and ultimately find your way here. That is why I have taken the time to prepare this proposal."

As he spoke, he opened a drawer and withdrew two pages. He laid them down gently before sliding them across the table to her and Kesgrave. Directing them to the top line, he said, "In a survey of cakes and pastries, rout cakes enjoyed an approval rating of ninety percent. Even those participants who do not prefer them to Shrewsberry cakes and profiteroles had nothing bad to say about them. In contrast to gin, rout cakes have only positive associations."

Other statistics followed, including the number of buns sold daily at the Old Chelsea Bun House, whose success Renfield aimed to replicate with Her Outrageousness's Rout Cake House.

"And that is where we will locate our shop," Renfield continued. "Near the bun house, in Grosvenor Row. My employer owns a building with large windows overlooking the street that is suitable for a baking concern. Ideally, we would place the first Her Outrageousness's Rout Cake House in Berkeley Square, next to Gunter's, but I realize that is a little too close to home."

He said it lightly, teasingly, and raising her eyes from the document to stare at her host, Bea felt her heart hammer at the absurdity of the predicament. Having earned a reputation for eccentricity, thanks almost entirely to Mr. Twaddle-Thum's embellishments, she was now a promising prospect to the criminal class. Renfield had in all likelihood discovered her acquisition of the *Bright Benny* and assumed she was on the prowl for other trade opportunities.

Renfield, perceiving in her silence a worrying judgment, suggested that perhaps the prospect of a dozen Her Outrageousness's Rout Cake Houses scattered throughout London and the surrounding countryside seemed a little too outrageous for her. "In that case, may I suggest an alternate plan that is smaller in scale and reach?" he asked, opening the drawer once again and retrieving more sheets of paper, which he also placed on the desk in front of her. "This version is simpler and draws less attention to the enterprise. We create a special Her Outrageousness rout cake to be available at only the most exclusive bakeshops in Mayfair. An order of twelve would come wrapped in ribbons in your signature colors, which, if you do not yet have, I would be delighted to help you select."

Unable to withstand her curiosity, she skimmed her eyes over the second proposal, which delineated the number of rout cakes to be prepared each day, the shops that would be allowed to sell them, the price of various orders based on their size, and a list of society members who would be barred from purchasing Her Outrageousness rout cakes as a way of increasing their exclusivity.

Prinny topped the list.

Utterly bemused, Bea could not fathom how the drab Miss Hyde-Clare had wound up there, in the study of a bare-knuckled brawler named Rennie Rumpus receiving an offer to establish a baking concern that would withhold its goods from the ruler of England.

The ruler of England!

It did not make sense.

Her life: decades of docility followed by months of madness.

Amused despite herself—and grateful that Kesgrave was beside her to witness the spectacle—she slid the proposal back across the desk and offered a firm no, thank you. Then she explained that they were there to question him in regards to Mortimer Matlock's murder, which had taken place sometime between eight and midnight on Tuesday.

Renfield, who, in the wake of her refusal, had opened the drawer again, possibly to present a third option, halted his movements and jerked his head up. Seemingly stunned by the news, he stared blankly at the duke as Martha crossed the threshold bearing a silver tray laden with biscuits and tea. Taking note of her employer's expression, she glared at Bea as she carried the refreshments across the room and placed them on the desk with a thud, causing the teacups to clatter against each other. Then she pressed one lip against the desk and folded her arms across her chest as she settled in.

She had no intention of leaving.

Renfield thanked her for executing her duty diligently and asked her to please close the door on her way out of the room, which the maid did not like at all. Her scowl deepened, and she muttered to Bea as she turned to leave, "I got my eye on ye, I do. Don't trust ye as far as I can throw ye."

The interlude with his servant restored Renfield's equanimity to some degree, and after apologizing for the interruption, he asked Beatrice to continue. "I believe you said Mr. Matlock was killed. Are you certain it was murder and not an accident?"

"There is no mistaking a chisel in the stomach," the duke replied mildly.

"No, there is not," Renfield said amiably, revealing no hint of squeamishness. "Well, this is highly concerning. Mr. Hawes will be disappointed when he finds out."

Kesgrave assured him he already knew.

Renfield, opening his eyes wide in surprise, admitted the development was unexpected. "I heard nothing about your visit."

"Does Hawes report all his callers to you?" the duke asked.

"No," he replied, mirth flitting across his features. "It is only that the last time you and your wife visited Mr. Hawes, you drew the entire neighborhood's notice."

Indeed, they had.

She and Kesgrave had assumed full ducal regalia precisely to ensure their presence was noticed. They had no idea what sort of welcome they would receive in Grape Street and hoped the widespread awareness would ensure their safety.

All she said in reply, however, was that the situations were different.

"Are they?" he asked curiously. "I assume you believe Mr. Matlock's ties with Mr. Hawes's organization are the reason he was murdered, which is what you believed the last time, and on that score, you were wrong. It had nothing to do with the Duke's Brother."

Well, *nothing* was overstating the case, as it was Lord Myles's association with the gin parlor that led to the lethal events of May. But the point was well taken, and she allowed that Mortimer's murder might be unrelated to his involvement in the counterfeit antiquities scheme. "We are just gathering information. Tell us about your dealings with him, Mr. Renfield."

Again, he urged her to call him Edmund before explaining that they had not been in regular contact for quite some time. "I worked closely with Mr. Matlock in the beginning, after he accepted Mr. Hawes's proposal. There were details to figure out and we needed to put a system in place. That took about six months. Now we speak every few months. I cannot remember the last time I saw him."

She exhorted him to try.

Obligingly, he said it was probably two months ago, when he encountered Mortimer by chance at Addison's. "It is a coffeehouse on Fleet Street."

Bea knew the place well, for it was where she had conducted research into her parents' murder. "You did not visit him in his studio?"

"Not for almost a year. There was no need. As I said, the system was in place and everyone knew their task. It did not require either my attention or interference. I trusted if Mr. Matlock needed something from me, he would send a message. He was as reliable as he was capable. I am sorry he is gone. He will be missed," he said, striking a lugubrious note with his downturned lips.

"And what is the system?" Bea asked.

Renfield appeared flabbergasted by the query. "The system?"

"Yes, the system," she said firmly. "The one you have in place, the one that runs smoothly without your constant oversight. Tell us about it."

Renfield looked at the duke, as though seeking his sympathy. "I cannot give you that information. It is confidential. Surely, you understand that that is the nature of an illicit enterprise even if your wife does not. Please, let us return to a more amiable subject: Her Outrageousness's Rout Cakes. You are reluctant—I understand that! The thought of being in trade does not sit well with you. If you will allow me, I have another idea, one that obscures the connection between you and the product."

Kesgrave, who appeared to share none of her delight at the outlandish proposition, reiterated her request, and Renfield stared stonily at him for several seconds before insisting there was very little to know. "Mr. Matlock was recruited in November 1813 and spent the first six months of his employment perfecting his technique. He told me what he required in a studio and what tools he would need. I organized everything. I found the house in Banner Street and arranged for regular deliveries of supplies. In April of the next year, the first sale was made, to a collector up north because it was generally agreed that collectors in the north were less sophisticated than in the south. A second sale followed the successful first one and for quite some time, Mr. Matlock has been making two reliefs per month. And *that* is the system."

But it was not, Bea thought, asking him to identify the collier.

Renfield goggled at her. "Good Lord, your grace, I consider myself a man of the people, but I do not know the name of every tradesman and laborer plying their trade in London!"

"Who calls at the studio twice a week," she said. "I assume he is not actually delivering coal that frequently. Who is he and what is he doing?"

Despite a stiffening obstinacy in his frame, he said, "Oliver Eckhart. He is my representative. He delivers stone slabs, picks up finished works, conveys relevant information, and generally makes sure Mr. Matlock has everything he needs."

Bea asked for his direction.

Renfield swore she did not need it. "Ollie no more killed Mr. Matlock than I did. Mr. Matlock was central to our scheme and cannot be replaced. I truly do not know what we will do without him."

"Hawes believes he can be replaced easily," Bea asserted.

He scoffed in disdain. "Mr. Hawes did not kill the duke's cousin."

"How do you know?" she asked.

"Because it was a stupid thing to do and Mr. Hawes does not do stupid things," he replied with a hint of exasperation, as though annoyed at having to explain a simple concept to a dull-minded child. "What is his motive? Why risk infuriating the Duke of Kesgrave now when he barely squeaked by last time?"

It was not how Bea would describe their previous interaction, which had cost the crime lord little in the end, and she wondered if the description was Hell and Fury's own or his lieutenant's. Perhaps there was a resentment there, nurtured by Renfield on his employer's behalf. "Where were you on Tuesday night from eight to twelve?"

Biting back the stinging reply that clearly rose to his lips, he said, "What is *my* motive?"

Bea shrugged and said that criminal enterprises were generally prone to violence. "I do not know your motive yet, but give me time. I will find it."

"You have no idea what you are talking about," he snapped, tugging open the top drawer, retrieving a round object, and tossing it onto the desk in front of Bea. "What is that?"

Baffled, she examined the medallion, which was old and worn, depicting a man in profile wearing a crown. Running her fingers over the surface, she realized it had been cast in a metal alloy, most likely lead. She picked it up—it was light but not without heft—and flipped it over to see the head of a helmeted knight. Below the image was the year: 1030.

"It is a forgery," she said softly, amazed to see the very thing Kerrich had been railing against in Renfield's study. "A cheap Roman trinket."

"You knew it at a glance," he said with almost accusatory vigor. "How?"

"The date," she replied as she handed the medallion to the duke to examine.

"The date!" he repeated with unnerving satisfaction. "England did not adopt Arabic numbers until the fifteenth century. Remarkably, I did not know that. My dear papa neglected to mention it while he was whipping me for not planting seeds fast enough. But Mr. Matlock knew it. He saw it in an instant just as you did, your grace, and it is one of the reasons why I am certain the counterfeit antiquities scheme will not continue long without him. He saved us. Not a single one of us had the least notion of the mistake, but Mr. Matlock caught it before we sent the first shipment out and insisted on taking the matter in hand even though the financial compensation was not huge. He accepted what we could give him and owned himself grateful for the opportunity. It goes without saying that the trade is not as lucrative as the reliefs, but it turns a steady profit."

The shabby baubles Kerrich had seen in Higgins's shop were made by Mortimer as well. Little wonder he had not abided by the antiquarian's request to have them removed. It would have cut into his own earnings. If Kerrich discovered the connection, it might have reignited his fury. Forced to endure one betrayal, he could not stomach another.

If nothing else, it would explain the viciousness of the attack.

Renfield clasped the trinket between his thumb and forefinger. "I keep this medallion as a reminder of all the things I do not know. It is a talisman of sorts, as was Mortimer. It would be fanciful to say I regarded him as a good luck charm, but it would also not be inaccurate. A reliable man is a blessing, especially in my line of work, and I genuinely do not know what I will do without him."

Although not particularly superstitious herself, Bea understood the impulse to attach meaning to an object. Life was chaotic, and a superstition allowed one to feel a measure of control over events.

As exonerating evidence to dispute a murder charge, however, it fell short.

Whatever purpose Mortimer served, whether practical or mystical, Renfield would not hesitate to remove him if it fixed a problem or averted an issue.

A man who went by the name Rennie Rumpus was not sentimental.

Bea prompted him again for his whereabouts during the time of the murder.

Having made his rousing plea, he regarded her with disappointment and said that he was at the Duke's Brother from seven until nine, keeping an eye on the patrons and enjoying the house's specialty. "Then I returned home, drank a glass of port, and retired to my room."

"We will need to confirm your alibi," she said.

"Naturally, you will. Martha can attest to my return sometime before ten, and I will write down the names and addresses of three customers at the Duke's Brother who were sober enough to recall my presence there," he offered easily, grasping a pen at once to compile the list.

Accepting the slip of paper, she asked what he and Mortimer had discussed during their meeting at the coffeehouse.

Renfield insisted again that it was not a meeting but a chance encounter. "We were both there to pass a quiet morning reading the newspaper. I had no idea he would be there as well."

Accepting the clarification, she asked what they talked about during their chance encounter.

He shrugged lightly. "The abominable weather. Croton's new filly. The regent's weight gain."

"Nothing about the reliefs?" she asked.

"Certainly not."

Bea could not believe it. "Even with the impending sale to the British Museum? The momentous achievement you had been working toward for more than two and a half years was finally within reach and neither of you said a word about it?"

If he was taken aback by just how much she and the duke had managed to discover about their illicit antiquities trade, he was too appalled by her profound lack of discretion to indulge it. "It is a public venue, your grace," he said with sweeping condescension. "One does not conduct business in a public venue. One makes wry observations about the increasing impudence of rabble rousers in the north or the latest dispatch from St. Helena. Furthermore, Mr. Matlock did not know we were close to achieving a long-held objective because he was never told of any of our objectives. The key to the success of Mr. Hawes's organization is its lack of centrality. Information is dispersed throughout the network; each participant's knowledge is limited to his particular field of interest. Mr. Matlock never knew where the reliefs went after Ollie picked them up from his studio. In turn, Ollie knew only that he was delivering them to Cowcross Street. The recipient in Cowcross Street does not know if the relief will end up in St. John's Wood or Portelet Road or Golden Square or the docks or a cellar in Knatchbull Road, and so on and so forth. In this way, the tree can continue to grow even if one branch sickens and dies."

Having failed to contemplate the intricacies of overseeing a vast criminal empire, Bea could make no recommendation regarding its operation. Hawes's system of isolation and dispersal, however, struck her as logical, and she wondered just how many details his second in command knew.

Eager to add suspects to her list, she asked for the address of the resident of Cowcross Street and received a blank stare for her efforts. "Very well, you may keep that secret," she said graciously. "Tell us about the docks instead. Do you load the reliefs onto ships before unloading them again to make their point of origin appear more legitimate or merely access the manifest?"

In an attempt to either tease her or simply change the topic of conversation, Renfield reached into his desk and pulled out another tightly scrawled document. "As I mentioned, my third proposal capitalizes on your connection to rout cakes but keeps your name out of it."

Kesgrave rose to his feet and announced they were done. "Summon your servant so that we may confirm your alibi and be on our way."

Although disconcerted by the abruptness of their departure, Bea stood as well and thanked Renfield for his time. Graciously, he owned himself delighted to make her acquaintance, reminded her he had been hoping for the opportunity for several weeks, and encouraged her to put the rout cake venture out of her mind for the present. "I can see you have more pressing concerns and can't give it proper consideration."

The maid appeared in the doorway, kitchen rag gripped tightly in her fingers, and the duke asked her when her employer returned home on Tuesday night. When Martha raised her eyes to catch Renfield's attention, he said sternly, "No, do not look at him before answering. Look at me."

Grumbling, Martha insisted she did not know the exact time. "I don't go around with me eye on the clock. I got too much work to do to look over every few minutes. I suppose it was after ten. Yes, it was a few minutes after ten and he was worse for drink. I had to help him over the threshold and got a bruise for me efforts. Here," she said, raising her sleeve and waving her arm meaningfully. "I don't know why it is any of ye business, but there is it!"

Bea barely had time to take note of a thumb-size purplish mark on the underside of the forearm before the maid stamped off mumbling about the intolerable presumption of Quality. "Demanding to see me limbs as if I was an animal in a menagerie. Next, they'll want to stare at me ankles. Disgraceful!"

Although, yes, Bea would have welcomed an opportunity to inspect the bruise properly, for it had been offered as exculpatory evidence, she let the woman dash off without further questioning. Ideally, she would have confirmed that Renfield had not only returned to his residence around ten but also remained inside it, but at least one pertinent piece of information had been verified.

She would return to probe deeper if it proved necessary.

Owning himself satisfied with their initial meeting, Renfield held out the set of proposals to Bea and suggested she take them with her so she would have them conveniently on hand when she was ready to give the business matter proper consideration. Confounded by the offer, she stared at him blankly and, returning them to his desk, he promised to hold on to them for her. "They will be here when you are ready," he said, escorting them to the front door.

Stepping onto the pavement, Bea turned to Kesgrave to apologize for exposing him to the crass materialism of bakery ownership. Before she could utter a word however, he said, "Sir Thomas Soames is a noted collector who lives in Golden Square. His reputation is impeccable. I assume he extended himself too far in his zeal to acquire antiquities and needed additional funds to settle his debts."

It was an excellent lead, she thought, climbing into the carriage, and as she settled onto the bench, she asked him what he knew about the residents of Cowcross Street.

Alas, his knowledge was regrettably slight.

Chapter Ten

◆◆◆

Sir Thomas Soames's townhouse was situated on the north side of Golden Square, its facade presented in the classical Grecian style with a trio of loggias on the second floor surrounded by terra-cotta caryatides copied from the portico of the Erechtheum at Athens. Attached to the piers between the galleries were four Gothic corbels.

"They came from the niches on the north front of Westminster Hall and date to the period of Richard II," Sir Thomas said, his expression lively as he pointed his slim ebony stick at each particular feature as he described it. Captured in vibrant oils by a skilled painter, his building stood against a bright blue sky, its neighbors elided for the sake of art and to provide a sense of isolation. "The triglyphs are fashioned on the ones found on the Temple of Zeus at Olympia."

Darting around his heels, its wagging tail brushing against the legs of the easel displaying the canvas, was a small black poodle. The giddy creature barked at sporadic intervals, as if to call attention to its favorite aspects of the exterior.

Sir Thomas regarded the dog tolerantly, alternatively

ignoring its antics and commending them, and when it rose on its hindlegs to try to take the pointer into its mouth, he chided it gently, "Not now, Aggie, we have visitors who wish to know all about our collection."

Aggie, whose full name was soon revealed to be Agamemnon, Commander of the Achaeans, obligingly dropped to all fours.

The baronet's steward, who was also trying to get his employer's attention, was not treated with the same consideration, and he stepped back as the collector waspishly replied, "Not now, Travers, we have visitors!"

Cautiously, the steward said that he had just one extremely small question regarding an item in the gallery. "It requires only a yes or no."

"No!" Sir Thomas yelled.

Travers darted from the room.

Aggie barked and followed the man out.

Sir Thomas apologized for the many interruptions. "It is rarely quiet here, but the situation has been particularly chaotic of late, owing in part to my injury," he said, holding up his right hand, which was dressed in a pristine white bandage. "It makes it difficult to sign documents. If anyone else had called asking to see my collection, I would have turned them away. But not the Duke and Duchess of Kesgrave. You are always welcome!"

In fact, the Duke and Duchess of Kesgrave had not asked to see his collection. Twenty minutes before, upon arriving at his home, they had asked to *discuss* it. Bea had very plainly said, "We have a few questions."

The distinction was lost on the baronet, who had led them to a small parlor with the painting of the home displayed in the front of the room. Klismoses, their legs splayed elegantly, faced the easel in two even rows, and taking a seat as she was instructed by her host, Bea realized they were in Sir Thomas's personal lecture hall.

A moment later, ebony pointer in hand, he launched into the story of his collection, which was really the tale of his grand tour, which was actually an account of his love of travel. It was all of a piece—his trip to Athens and the chairs on which they sat.

"It begins with my father," their host had announced portentously.

As Sir Thomas was well into his sixth decade, his thinning hair almost entirely gray, with only scattered strands of blond, and liver spots on his forehead, Bea thought going back a half century or more was taking things a bit too far. Nevertheless, she had listened politely because she'd had no wish to give offense. If they were to extract vital information from the baronet, he would have to be pliable.

Now, however, she seized the opportunity, rising to her feet and swearing she could not bear to take up more of his precious time. "As much as Kesgrave and I would both enjoy hearing about each and every object in your vast collection, we are most interested in the forged Assyrian reliefs. Let us discuss those so that you may return to your more pressing business."

At the statement, Sir Thomas's jaw clenched and he bobbled the stick, almost dropping it altogether as he stared at Bea with his wide eyes.

Then he said, "Ouch."

Aware that he had not imbued the interjection with an appropriate amount of pain or urgency, he tried again. "Ouch. My hand."

Curiously singsong, it was not a vast improvement, but Sir Thomas deemed it adequate and added that the pain was excruciating. "You must forgive me. I feel lightheaded," he said, leaning on the easel for support and realizing it was not equal to a podium when it toppled over. Horrified at the ill treatment of the painting, he frantically set it right, using the hurt hand without incident until he remembered he was suffering unendurable agony. He released the canvas, which dropped to the floor, and eked out another *ouch*. "I must go before I faint. Travers will show you out. Please wait here."

Bea, murmuring softly in sympathy for his terrible injury, urged him not to think twice about them. "You must take care of yourself. Get plenty of rest and apply pork jelly twice a day."

The baronet, settling into his performance, replied with convincing weakness that he would do precisely as she instructed. "Thank you, your grace. You are kindness itself."

Nodding, she watched him leave the room in a sort of hobble, as though the pain had migrated downward to his legs. It was, she supposed, his interpretation of general feebleness.

As soon as Sir Thomas disappeared, Bea strode to the entrance and peered out. Seeing nobody in the hallway, she gestured to Kesgrave to follow. "Come, let us find the gallery. If there are more forgeries, they are certain to be there."

Taking no issue with this plan, the duke followed her into the corridor, and when she paused for several seconds at the end of the passageway to decide between left or right, he took charge, deftly identifying the correct room with unerring swiftness, either following an unfailing instinct or trusting that all London townhouses were more or less the same.

"Here we are," he said, stepping aside with a flourish so that she could enter before him. "The gallery is usually the room on the first floor with the widest double doors."

Of course he had to explain his methodology!

Delighted, she brushed a kiss on his cheek as she slipped past him to inspect the large space, which was bedecked on all sides with artifacts. But Kesgrave, deciding perhaps that his accomplishment deserved greater fanfare, tugged her into his arms for a more thorough demonstration of appreciation.

Bea felt it at once, the familiar flash of desire, the welcoming awakening of her senses, and marveled that she could succumb to either in Sir Thomas's gallery.

Naturally, she would not.

Confident that Travers and Aggie would keep the baronet sufficiently occupied, she nevertheless believed trysting in a suspect's home was a gross violation of the investigator's behavioral code. Stealthily wandering the corridors after being expressly invited to leave was an impertinent transgression deserving of gravity, not vulgarity.

Furthermore, they *had* gone through all that trouble of locating the gallery and she was eager to have her suspicions confirmed.

They would find more forgeries.

She was sure of it.

Even with all her resolve, she allowed herself the pleasure of the duke's ardor for another moment, leaning into the kiss before pulling away. Softly, against his lips, she murmured, "You did not pick the lock."

Unable to see the relevance of the statement, he regarded her with amused bewilderment as he noted it was true, yes, for the door was open. "But I can secure it and then pick it if that is essential to the furtherance of the activity. I have the tool on my person, although I am not sure it is the best use of our time."

This display of preparedness was freshly provoking, for there were few things more appealing than a duke who stood ready to confront any situation, and she forced herself to take another step back. She swept her eyes around the room, noting it was almost as large as one of the galleries in Montague House, with glass boxes containing centuries-old vases, amphorae, bowls, and sections of broken pottery. Fragments of textiles hung on the wall to the left in a tight cluster, and statues, some remarkably well preserved, stood on pedestals throughout the room, with a concentration of busts along the perimeter. Small plaques detailing pertinent information about the artifacts were placed next to corresponding works.

Surveying the collection as a whole, she thought it was a dense and vast assortment of things bearing a sense of the infinite, as though there were far too many objects for them all to be known. It was little wonder Sir Thomas felt compelled to make his long-winded speech before allowing admittance. He knew the second a visitor stepped into the room, he would be forgotten.

Kesgrave, whose family's own vast trove of treasures would no doubt make the baronet's appear modest, did not pause in astoundment. He crossed the floor immediately, drawn to a counter on the left-hand side that was thick with antiquities.

Bea's gaze landed on Zeus's head.

It was massive and marble, rising at least five feet from the floor, with a vengeful glare beneath wildly curling hair, and she could not fathom how he had arrived there, in Golden Square, to sit in a room gathering dust when he belonged atop a temple in a far-off land.

Poor Zeus, king of the gods, relegated to ornamentation, less powerful than a small poodle with an affinity for ebony sticks.

"I think this is one of Mortimer's," Kesgrave called from the far side of the gallery. "It bears many of the elements found in the reliefs in the studio."

Bea stepped around the awe-inspiring statue, then weaved between glass cabinets and marble pedestals, to examine the sand-colored artifact. The slab, depicting a horse cart being pulled by a team of four, had a convincingly aged quality to it, with rough and uneven edges. The top corner was missing entirely, ruthlessly cutting off the heads of the first two horses.

"It is strange," she said, drawing closer to the reliefs. "Being surrounded by authentic antiquities has the paradoxical effect of making Mortimer's forgeries appear more genuine."

The duke agreed with her assessment and turned his attention to the next relief, which showed a king hailing his subjects. Bea rested her elbows on the counter to improve her vantage and admired the beauty of the primitively rendered horses. The angled tilt of their heads was so graceful and familiar.

Struck by the latter, she leaned closer, certain she had seen that image before.

And it was not just the arc of the neck.

The flow of the mane and the drape of the bridle were also known to her.

She had scarcely wondered how when she realized she was looking at the same horse as in the painting. Softly, almost to herself, she marveled, "It is *The Huntress*. Look at the manes and the way the horses hold their heads. Mortimer based these horses on his painting of Miss Brewer. Or he based the horse in the painting on these horses. Regardless, they are similar despite being different mediums."

"And bridle," Kesgrave said.

She nodded, pleased he saw it as well. "Yes, precisely, the bridle too."

But the duke rushed to clarify. "No, I mean the bridle is unchanged."

About to dismiss this particular bit of pedantry—yes, yes, your grace, Mortimer did not alter the bridle either—she suddenly understood what he was saying. Clutching his hand in excitement, she exclaimed, "It is modern! Mortimer put a contemporary bridle in an ancient relief. It is blatantly a forgery. There is no way the experts at Montague House would miss that detail. They are not dunderheads. If the one already purchased by the British Museum was as sloppy as this one, then Kerrich was right to be furious. The trail leads directly to his door. He would be drummed out of the society and possibly imprisoned for fraud. His motive is the strongest so far and the clearest."

When Kesgrave begged to disagree, she warned him against underestimating the primal satisfaction of revenge. "Mortimer not only lied and belittled him but also exposed him to ruination. Perhaps when he discovered his true employers were men infamous for their violence, he realized he could slay Mortimer in the most brutal way possible while incriminating them. And then he could tell whatever story he wanted about his participation in the scheme and Mortimer would not be able to refute it. He could claim, for example, that Mortimer coerced his cooperation by threatening his family's lives, and it would be plausible because of Hawes's and Renfield's involvement."

"I meant the bridle has no bearing on Kerrich's motive because he does not know it exists," he explained. "The fact that it is here means he never saw it. Outside of that one specific point, I find the case against him compelling. It does not help that he refused to provide an alibi for a significant portion of the murder interval."

It was, she allowed, an undeniable argument.

And yet she could not believe the anachronism was irrelevant. "What about Sir Thomas? Could he have known Mortimer was the forger and therefore the person responsible for the egregious mistake? The relief is in his possession, so he had the opportunity to notice it, and he stands to lose just as much as Kerrich if the scheme is exposed."

"More," Kesgrave amended. "His standing is greater and he prides himself on being a discerning collector. You heard his lecture. The truth would reveal him to be either a thief or a fool, both of which would turn him into a figure of fun. He craves the respect of society and considers it his due. It is not difficult to imagine him striking out in fury, though perhaps not with a chisel. He is more inclined to demand pistols at dawn, which is hardly a surreptitious way to get one's revenge. Regardless, your original question is a good one: Would Sir Thomas know whom to blame? According to Renfield, he would not, as he is an isolated branch."

It was true, yes, that in the second in command's formulation, none of the conspirators in the scheme knew anything beyond their own purview. But Kerrich knew about Higgins the dealer as well as the sale to the British Museum. "What if Hawes's tree is more like a climbing plant with intertwining vines?"

The idea appealed to the duke, who smiled faintly. "Trumpet creeper, not oak."

"A shrub at the ready and still you deny your knowledge of twigs is comprehensive," she said with a dazed shake of her head. "You are being unduly modest, your grace."

Sternly, he reminded her there were more than one thousand different types of trees and shrubs native to England. "You do not wish for me to enumerate the five dozen I happen to know by name just to prove the nine hundred and ninety-nine-plus I do not know."

Oh, but she did, of course, especially as the exercise would prove her point. Only an arborist could list sixty varieties.

Alas, as the exercise would bring them no closer to learning what Sir Thomas knew and rather than continue to debate the metaphorical configuration of Hawes's criminal organization, she strode across the room past the statue of

Zeus, to the door. Grasping the handle, she pushed it open, stuck her head into the corridor, and called for their host.

Kesgrave, following behind her at a more sedate pace, owned himself impressed with her audacity. "Summoning a man—and with a snap of impatience, no less—to attend to you in his own home is very duchess behavior, your grace. You will have no trouble ordering Carver to allow you to add notations to the visitant florilegium at Haverill Hall."

Although she blanched now as she always did at mention of their imminent departure from London, it was with a particular intensity because she had not known prior to his statement that the world contained such a thing as a visitant florilegium, let alone that she would be obliged to annotate it.

Seeing her response, the duke shook his head and said, "No, Bea, no, it will not stand anymore. I know you like to see yourself as the timid spinster who was so without power all she could do was imagine pelting me with eels *à la plancha* in the Lake District, but that is not who you are anymore. You have come so far that you are imperiously ordering baronets to appear before you in their own galleries."

Oh, but there were so many things wrong with his observation, she thought, her fingers tightening on the edge of the door as she peered into the hallway to avoid his gaze. It sounded auspicious—summoning, ordering—but the truth was she had acted without thinking. During her brisk march to the door, she had considered only the investigation and the frustrating gaps in their knowledge. Sir Thomas had scurried off during their first attempt to elicit answers, and she would not permit that evasive behavior to continue.

Furthermore, calling for the baronet was a singular action with a clearly defined goal: to get him to the room. That clarity of purpose did not apply to her earning the respect of the staff at Haverill Hall, a task that required something far less targeted and precise: to embody the essence of duchessness.

As an objective, it was as boundless as the sky.

Additionally, she took strong exception to his use of the word *like*: I know you like to think of yourself as the timid spinster.

Bea did not, no. There was not a single thing she *liked* about her perception of herself as an unwanted orphan too faint of heart to speak up for herself. The image undermined her at every turn, and there was nothing she would *like* more than to banish it to the farthest reaches of her mind.

But she knew how it would sound, quibbling over his language, as though the problem were the way he had expressed the idea rather than the idea itself. Consequently, she saved her breath and made only the most trivial correction. "It was eels *à la tartare*."

Grinning at the slight modification, Kesgrave said, "You better take caution, brat, or you will end up aping all my habits, a development to which I would not object. I find your boldness incredibly alluring. I am inclined to lock the door before Soames gets here and demonstrate just how much. As you know, I have my tool at the ready."

Bea blushed.

Having opened her mouth to explain why her amendment did not meet the criteria for pedantry, she shut it abruptly at his wicked double entendre.

Or maybe she had only heard it that way—in which case, it was she who had imbued his words with wickedness.

The flush rose in her cheeks, suffusing her with warmth, and she sought to hide her embarrassment by turning away to peer into the hallway again.

So much for her daring, she thought satirically, inhaling deeply to beckon Sir Thomas at the top of her lungs when suddenly he was there, next to her, gasping her name in horror. Then he screeched and lurched backward when he saw Kesgrave behind her, his eyes opening so wide, Bea feared they might pop out of his head.

Torn between anger and confusion and fear, he said, "You ... you... you cannot be here. You left a half hour ago. Travers showed you out. I am certain of it. And yet you returned to skulk about my house like thieves in the night. I cannot believe you would violate my privacy like this. The want of conduct is staggering. The disregard for the sanctity of home is breathtaking. If I were the vindictive sort, Kesgrave, I would send for the magistrate and you and your wife would be dragged off to prison and your behavior exposed to the world. The beau monde would be scandalized. Fortunately, for you, I abhor a scandal and simply want to put this ugly experience behind me. Leave now, and I will forget it ever happened."

Smoothly, her shoulder resting against the side of the door, Bea said, "Yes, Sir Thomas, let us talk about criminality and exposure. You have been quite naughty, have you not, defrauding the British government. I wonder what the beau monde would have to say to that, never mind Parliament."

He turned violet.

Chapter Eleven

E very inch of skin on the baronet's face assumed a purplish cast, and he inhaled so deeply, Bea feared he might swoon from lack of air. Scathingly, he screeched, "How dare you! How dare you come into my house and lodge baseless accusations against me! Never in my life have I encountered such wanton disregard for decency. You will leave now or I will instruct my staff to make you leave!"

Sir Thomas would not, no, for summoning his servants would only extend his humiliation. He knew how the table was set: He was guilty of fraud, and no amount of protesting or yelling would change that. When he was done with his tantrum, he would settle down and admit it.

To help him regain control of his temper, Bea suggested soothingly that they step inside the gallery. "So that you may discuss the matter without fear of being overheard."

But the notion that there was any topic he could not talk about in front of his servants incited another spate of affronted blather. Unfortunately, there were only so many ways to express indignation, and after he decried her unmitigated gall for the third time, he abruptly broke off, swore profanely, and punched the door in fury.

He used his bad hand, the one with the bandage, and he turned white in the same instant he howled, "*Ouch!*" and dropped to his knees. His eyes closed, he held his fist against his chest as he whimpered. Slowly, the color returned to his cheeks, and he rose unsteadily to his feet. "I bruised it quite dreadfully when I punched Zeus in the nose. Well, not the nose per se because the sculpture is missing that appendage, but that was where I was aiming, the middle of the face. I was so furious when I found out that a recent addition to my collection was a forgery that I felt compelled to strike out. And as is frequently the case, I did more harm to myself than anything else. You are right, your grace, we should discuss it inside, where nobody can hear. It has been a troubling couple of days, and I am still not thinking as clearly as I should."

"Very good," Bea said, stepping into the room.

Sir Thomas closed the door and, clutching his injured hand gingerly against his body, followed her across the floor to the counterfeit antiquity.

"You noticed the bridle, I suppose," he said equably as they came to a stop in front of the relief. "I did too. Once you know it is there, it is impossible not to see it. But in the moment before you realize it is too modern, you have no suspicion the piece is a forgery. And that is what happened to me. I am a fool, an overconfident fool who thought he knew so much that nobody would ever be able to deceive him. I was tricked, your graces, and the fact of it pains me deeply. That is why I lashed out. I am now twice mortified: once by my gullibility and once by my display of temper. I hope you can forgive me."

Sir Thomas's performance of remorse was significantly more convincing than his display of pain in the lecture room. There was an air of nuance to it that she suspected came from the fact that he was genuinely sorry that he could not avoid this conversation with the Duke and Duchess of Kesgrave. He tried so hard to get them to leave.

"We did notice the bridle," Bea replied, curious as to the direction he intended to go with his new approach.

"The blasted thing," he said without heat. "It will be the ruin of me. As soon as I realized this relief was a fraud, I feared the same was true of the one I had just sold to the British Museum. I have wrangled over what to do about it for days. Do I alert the chief librarian to the possibility of fraud, exposing myself as a fool, or do I trust the experts to know the genuine article when they see it? Every moment that passes I live in terror of a message arriving informing me that I cheated the museum. That is why I reacted as I did, your graces. My nerves are frayed."

As if to demonstrate just how desperate the situation was, he sighed and rounded his shoulders. "You know, it does feel good to make a clean breast of it. Thank you, your graces, for providing me with some relief. And now if you would be so kind, would you please explain how you even know of this dreadful business. Did you also buy a forged relief?"

"We're investigating a murder," Bea said.

Stunned, Sir Thomas dropped both arms to his side, knocking his wounded hand against the counter and crying out again. Cradling it gently, he looked at her with bafflement. "What do you mean you are investigating a murder? Why would you do that yourselves and not the Runners? I do not understand. Who is dead? Why seek me out?"

"Mortimer Matlock," Kesgrave said.

Well, that, at least, made sense to the collector. "He was family?"

The duke nodded. "My cousin."

"Your cousin was murdered. That is terrible. Please accept my condolences, your grace," he said, pursing his lips together in a show of compassion for several seconds before the sympathy was replaced by confusion. "I am not sure I understand what that has to do with me."

Kesgrave, gesturing at the relief, said, "Mortimer carved it."

Sir Thomas responded with another of his signature gasps of surprise. "Dear Lord, you had a forger in the family! Your poor grandmother! What will she do when she finds out? The shame and humiliation will be unbearable. The *ton* will devour her whole. This is a shocking revelation indeed, and you may trust me not to repeat it to anyone. You have my word."

The duke's lips twisted with impatience as he told the baronet to cut line. "You are deceiving nobody. We learned of the scheme from Hawes himself."

And yet another sharp inhale. "You and the duchess are in league with the King of Saffron Hill! That is sure to set tongues. ..."

But the baronet trailed off with a shake of his head and confessed that he did not have the vigor to affect more outrage. It was exhausting, and his hand genuinely pained him. "Very well, your graces, I give up. I admit it. *I* am the one who is in league with the King of Saffron Hill. He approached me in Hyde Park, as brash as you please, and quoted the exact amount I owed to my creditors. Then he told me the debt would vanish if I did one small favor for him. Naturally, I refused! I might have my bills, but I also have my honor! But then he told me what it was and I realized it was a harmless little pas de deux. The British Museum would acquire Assyrian reliefs, of which its collection is sadly lacking, and Hawes would make a tidy profit. The forgeries were so well done, I figured nobody would know the truth and I could move forward without that crippling debt hanging over me. Harmless, as I said. And everything would have gone splendidly if not for the damnable bridle!"

Sir Thomas rested an elbow on the counter, as if unable to hold himself upright as he lamented at length the damnable anachronism. He could not fathom how the counterfeiter had made such a fundamental mistake. "He is an imbecile!" he cried before recalling the victim was cousin to the duke and apologizing tersely for maligning his slain relative. "But you must understand how upsetting this is for me. I sold the forgery to the British Museum in good faith and would never dream of insulting the artist by questioning the quality of his work. And now when I think about the chief librarian examining this relief, my knees grow weak beneath me. He was supposed to come to inspect it *this week*. I thank God that he had to cancel due to a complication with the Elgin marble display. Can you imagine what would have happened if he spotted the bridle? Or one of the trustees? I would be driven out of London in shame."

Having admired the giant head of Zeus in the middle of the room, Bea was unsurprised to find the duke's speculation regarding Sir Thomas's debts was accurate. She could not conceive how many thousands of pounds it had cost to purchase and transport the colossal statue.

Kesgrave, displaying a distinct lack of sympathy for the baronet's predicament, asked what else he knew about the scheme of which he was a prime player.

Sir Thomas took umbrage at the use of the word *prime*, for he was a minor player. "Minor! I am only tangentially involved and know nothing more than my part. You say your cousin Mr. Matlock produced the forgeries. Well, that is news to me. You are more informed than I am, your grace. *I* should be asking *you* questions!"

But of course he did not.

Their host wanted to preserve his ignorance.

Bea, recalling Renfield's disclosures, asked about the baronet's association with Oliver Eckhart and received a blank stare in return. She repeated the name and identified him as the collier who picked up the finished reliefs from Mortimer's studio and brought them to Cowcross Street.

Awareness flicked across his face at the mention of the road, and although he continued to deny any familiarity with the scheme, he avoided her gaze, tilting his head down to affect intense fascination with his own fingernails. The evasion was revealing, and she pressed for the name and address of the resident in Cowcross Street.

Frustrated, he swore he did not know anything about Kirks. "He is a stranger! You must believe me when I say I am barely a participant. There have been three shipments. That is all! Three shipments in total, and they are brought by this man Samson Kirks of 82 Cowcross Street. I have never met him or exchanged a single word with him or know anything about a collier who calls himself Oliver Eckhart. I know his name and address only because I had one of the stable boys follow him. I wanted to find out more about the men with whom I was in business and hoped Robbie would uncover something useful. But all he discovered was a name. You must believe me. I am ignorant of everything else."

Bea said they would have to speak to the stable boy next.

Sir Thomas gasped. "You cannot! You know how it is with servants. They love to gossip. The moment you start asking question, they will think I am involved in something extremely unsavory and tell the neighbors about it and then the whole square will be whispering about me. It is better all around if we keep this little contretemps to ourselves. Think of the chief librarian at Montague House! Goddard will be summarily dismissed. You do not wish to have that poor man's misery on your conscience, do you, Kesgrave, especially as it was your own cousin who placed him in this predicament? His involvement is a black mark against your family honor, and there is already that nastiness with your uncle's tavern. A gin parlor, was it?"

If Kesgrave took issue with this description, he made no mention of it as he said they would also have to speak to the footmen who received the deliveries from Kirks.

"Oh, but you don't *have* to talk to them," the baronet protested hotly. "You *want* to because you are determined to ruin me for making one bad decision. Yes, I agree! I should never have consented to sell the reliefs to the British Museum. There, are you satisfied? It is so easy for you to sit in judgment, but you have no idea what it is like to be crushed by debts. And I have already been punished for my part in it. There is the injury to my hand and all the lack of sleep. I have barely had one night of satisfying rest since I saw that blasted bridle, expecting Goddard to show up at any moment and accuse me of fraud. It became so unbearable, I broke down and called a specialist from the antiquarian society to examine the third relief for signs of fakery. Thank God he found nothing. Now I can proceed with the sale."

Scarcely believing her own ears, Bea stared at him in astonishment. "With all that has already happened, you still intend to proceed with the scheme? The likelihood of exposure increases with every forgery you sell."

"Yes, your grace, I am cognizant of the risks," he replied with a waspish snap before insisting that he had no choice. He could not renege on his deal with the King of Saffron Hill. "I gave my word! I will not sell the one with the glaring anachronism—that would be unhinged—but the third relief is as perfect as the first and I cannot continue with this wretched debt. One more sale and I shall be free of it all."

Although the promise of significant financial reward had the ability to dull the greatest intellect, she was still taken aback by his inability to fully comprehend the situation. He was openly discussing the sale of forged antiquities with the Duke and Duchess of Kesgrave.

He was no longer operating in secret.

And yet Sir Thomas remained sanguine, adding that the third relief was perfect. "Holly could not point to a single thing that was wrong or off. He did note that the cut lines were a little sharper than usual, but that only means that it had been preserved well, possibly in a cave where it did not have to endure the elements. He declared it an exceptional piece and suggested it was worth nine hundred pounds, which is actually more than Goddard is offering. It was a comfort. I had known the workmanship on the forgeries was excellent, but watching an accomplished antiquarian unable to tell the difference was hugely reassuring. The museum will never know—that is, if nobody tells them. I trust I can rely on your discretion, Kesgrave."

A bold maneuver, it had little chance of prospering, and while the duke regarded him with his imperious, ant-at-the-picnic disdain, Bea reminded him that a man was dead. "We will pursue every avenue of investigation until we have identified Mortimer's killer and brought him to justice. That will require a trial, at which point the whole story will come out. And even if for some reason it did not, decency demands that we tell Goddard the truth. It is over, Sir Thomas. Resign yourself to it."

Alas, the baronet could not.

The prospect of his disgrace was too unsettling to accept without argument, and he made increasingly desperate appeals to what he called "her soft woman heart," which all proved futile. He turned then to the duke and petitioned for leniency.

It was only what one man of honor owed to another!

This contention also fell short of achieving its objective and Sir Thomas lapsed into sullen silence.

Bea allowed him to wallow for a few moments before asking about the specialist's visit. "What reason did you give for your concern about the relief's legitimacy?"

A morose obstinacy overtook his features and he appeared determined to withhold the information, but it passed quickly. "An indistinct sense that something about it was not quite right. It was the best I could do in the circumstance, and given my long history as a collector, I thought it was a valid observation. Holly was unimpressed and mocked me for thinking experience had honed my instincts for authenticity. There was no substitute for learned expertise, he said, and then he pointed out that there *were* forgeries in my collection, just ones I never suspected. He thought it was funny, damn his eyes!"

It must cut deep indeed, the irony of being duped yourself while in the process of duping others, Bea thought, sweeping her eyes around the room. Given the size of the collection, the sham artifacts were most likely among the larger works. Otherwise, the antiquarian would not have noticed them as he crossed the room to the relief. That meant the statuary.

She asked if Zeus was a fraud.

Curtly, he sneered at the suggestion. "I will have you know, missy, that I oversaw the removal of that head from a temple in Smyna in 1789 and personally accompanied it to London. It is the crowning glory of my collection. The pieces he identified as counterfeit were minor works among my medieval hoard, an assortment of pilgrim badges, medallions, ampullae, statuettes, coins, and ornamental spearheads. They are in the cabinet to the right of the entrance, and although they are not significant archaeological finds or excessively valuable, I think they are charming and display them prominently. Holly called them amateurish attempts and ridiculed me for not knowing the difference. It required every iota of my self-control not to deride him in turn for his own gullibility."

Fascinated, Bea strode to the display case to look at the artifacts, presumably the very ones that had infuriated Kerrich when he saw them in the same shop where he had spotted one of Mortimer's reliefs. Arranged in a jumble on a trio of shelves, they made an appealing set, and comparing them to the medallion Renfield had shown them two hours ago, she allowed that the quality of the pieces was better. The hand that had carved the molds was far more deft.

She asked if he bought the artifacts from a dealer called Higgins in Marylebone.

Sir Thomas glared at her for several seconds before complaining about her seeming omniscience, which he called exceedingly rude. "It is the height of discourtesy to know everything, your grace. But yes, yes, I did buy them from Higgins, from whom I have been purchasing antiquities for years. I thought he was a trusted source! I still cannot credit it. How dare he gull me—*me!*—a patron who has been loyal for more than a decade. I will have his head for this! That is why I contacted Hawes right away to inform him that his associate had cheated the wrong customer. And to have to endure that betrayal on top of the anachronistic horse's bridle in a relief bound for the British Museum, it was unacceptable. I accused him of running a shabby outfit and demanded prompt action."

"And did you get it?" Bea asked.

"I did!" he replied with the haughty confidence of the entitled. That he was deserving of fair treatment while depriving it of others was an irony that did not occur to him. "Hawes was at my door within two hours. He apologized for the muddle, swore it was all a misunderstanding, and reimbursed me for the worthless artifacts. He was not stingy about it either, giving me ten percent above the purchase price to compensate me for my distress. He even took the forgeries away so that I would not be offended by the sight of them."

Clever Hawes, smoothing the baronet's feathers to avoid a fuss. He knew the damage a wounded baronet could do to his scheme and would not allow him to withdraw his support in a fit of pique. In its simplest form, overlord of the underworld was a management position. Like a housekeeper or foreman, he was tasked with overseeing a large staff, which required him to wield his power wisely. Sometimes that meant suppressing his own ego to placate the wounded vanity of an underling.

"That must have been gratifying," Bea observed.

"To a certain extent, yes, very much so because it showed that he perceived the gravity of the offense," he replied evenly. "Did I relish playing host to a man of his unsavory reputation and worry that the neighbors would recognize him? I would rather he had sent a note. But he took reasonable precautions, such as wearing a nondescript suit and arriving without a carriage. Even so, I was anxious the whole time he was here."

"How long was that?" she asked.

"Forty-one painstaking minutes," Sir Thomas revealed, then flashed a smile as he admitted he had kept an eye on his pocket watch. "It was longer than I hoped, and because I did not expect him to linger, I did not ask my housekeeper to prepare a tray. And then I was fretful he would be affronted at my not offering him refreshments and decided I *should* request the tray, but by that time he had already been here for a half hour and I did not want him to extend his visit only to drink tea. So in the end I did not offer tea, and if he *was* insulted, he concealed it well. His manners are excellent."

They are, yes, Bea thought, the better to hide his monstrousness.

"From the newspaper reports, one imagines a brute with the shoulders and ferocity of a bull, but he is actually elegant and soft-spoken," he added. "He was admiring of my collection and made many lovely and considered observations about several of my favorite pieces. He was taken with the head of Zeus. He marveled at its size and exclaimed in wonder when I told him it was the only one of its kind."

It would not be for long, she thought with cynical amusement, assuming Hawes could find a replacement for Mortimer as easily as he had claimed. Then there would be a dozen mammoth Zeus heads for sale by the end of the year. "What did he say when you showed him the relief?"

"He apologized," he replied simply before adding that the crime lord took responsibility for the wretched blunder without trying to wiggle off the hook. "It was his organization, so it was his fault. I railed at him about the sloppiness and how it went against everything I had been promised when I agreed to lend my consequence to the scheme. He did not make a single excuse. As I said, his manners are impeccable."

"How did he seem?" she asked.

Sir Thomas professed not to understand the query.

"Did he appear upset by it?"

When he inserted the modern bridle in the supposedly ancient artifact, Mortimer had imperiled an operation that had taken three years to come into fruition. The plan had finally arrived at its pinnacle, and his error would have brought it all crashing down.

It was a motive.

"He was startled more than anything else," the baronet said. "He did not see it at first, which is a comfort. At least it is not blatant, and there was a slim possibility nobody at the museum would have noticed it. Regardless, it is a relief that it did not get that far."

The fact that Sir Thomas's keen eye for detail averted disaster did nothing to lessen the severity of the mistake. If anything, it worsened it by revealing the scheme's fragility.

They squeaked by only through luck.

Hawes had every right to be furious and vent his rage where he saw fit.

There was, after all, little point in being a ruthless crime lord if you could not swiftly and efficiently eliminate the bungling artists who imperiled your grand schemes.

And yet she could not make the theory align with the reality of the situation.

Hell and Fury recruited them.

If he had not called on Kesgrave House to request their expertise, she and the duke would have no knowledge of Mortimer's death, let alone his brutal slaying.

Furthermore, the killing was not in proportion to the crime.

The lapse required accountability, to be sure. Mortimer deserved punishment of some sort.

But retribution—it was excessive.

Hawes's role as housekeeper required him to maintain order. Dispensing penalties that exceeded the offense risked not only leaving him without a sufficient number of servants to ensure the smooth running of the establishment but also demoralizing the staff.

An even hand was necessary.

She was certain Hawes knew that.

And yet the day of the visit was Tuesday.

A coincidence perhaps but still a damning one that required further investigation.

Although not particularly eager to question Hell and Fury about his motive for wishing to harm his prized forger, she was nevertheless determined to get answers and drew the current interrogation to a close by asking Sir Thomas to recount his movements during the time of the murder.

He stiffened in insult but replied without quibbling and rattled off a list of easily verifiable activities: cards at his club, dinner at home, a play at Drury Lane. He offered to arrange interviews for them so they could confirm the information quickly, and declining the assistance, Bea reminded him that they wished to speak to the footmen and the stable boy who had spied on Kirks for several days.

"Not several," the baronet corrected sourly. "A few! It was no more than three, and as I said, he learned nothing of note. Kirks rarely left his home and received few visitors. Robbie cannot tell you anything, so there is no reason to take him from his duties."

Bea assured him there was every reason.

"But my reputation!" the baronet cried. "You are determined to ruin it!"

Coolly, Kesgrave reminded the baronet that the pleasure of his ruination belonged solely to him. "I did not hold a gun to your head and compel you to defraud the British government. You chose that freely. Now, to mitigate the harm that is about to befall you, I would advise you to confess all to Goddard before he learns the truth from either myself or the authorities. You may claim you had a crisis of conscience and wish to undo as much damage as possible."

As practical as this course of action was, it appalled Sir Thomas, who could not conceive of doing anything without the King of Saffron Hill's sanction, lest it be construed as a betrayal of their bargain. "Freeing myself of the debt is essential, of course, but I also do not want to get on the wrong side of a man of his ilk. But I thank you for the warning, Kesgrave. I appreciate your candor and will steel myself for my pending disgrace."

So saying, he made the requested staff available for interview in the parlor, where Sir Thomas sequestered himself in a corner while the footmen answered queries regarding the deliveries. As the baronet had indicated, the servants had gleaned nothing useful in their interactions with Kirks. Robbie from the stable likewise reported that he had little to share, as he had failed to find out where the reliefs originated.

Casting a sidelong glance at Sir Thomas, who had the grace to look abashed, Bea said, "That was part of your assignment? Finding out where they originated?"

The stable boy nodded avidly, adding that the master had said the reliefs were top quality. "He could buy more if he got them from the source rather than from Samson Kirks. So I tried real hard. I watched and watched, but Kirks didn't go anywhere except the tavern on the next street. After the third day, the master told me to return to my duties in the stables."

Curtly, Sir Thomas dismissed the servants from the room and announced that he had hoped to make a little side bargain with the counterfeiter to sell reliefs to other collectors. "Given the current popularity of ancient artifacts, it seemed wrong to limit my scope to the British Museum. I could sell them all across England, thereby ensuring fewer antiquities are taken from their place of origin. I think what Elgin did to the Parthenon is criminal!"

Of course he did.

And if sparing other treasures helped refill his coffers, it was only what he deserved for being so selfless.

Chapter Twelve

It seemed inconceivable to Bea that a man with Mortimer's attention to detail could make such an egregious mistake as carving a modern bridle into a two-thousand-year-old Assyrian relief. Having recognized at a glance that Arabic numerals on a medieval medallion were wildly inaccurate, he would have noticed the anachronism in his own work—something he had stared at for hours.

"The horse itself was based on *The Huntress,* which was his focus," Kesgrave pointed out as he wiped his hands on a serviette. Upon returning to Berkeley Square, they had discovered that the chef had prepared a variety of tartlets. The lovely assortment, which was laid out in the library, included asparagus with bacon and puffs of potato sprinkled with Parmesan cheese. "He did dozens of drawings in preparation for the painting and copied the horse for the relief. He might have copied the bridle without thinking."

Unconvinced, Bea selected an olive tart as she shook her head. "He was too meticulous. The swirls in the king's beard are identical. You cannot distinguish one from the other because he painstakingly matched them. The toes on his feet are perfectly proportional. He paid attention to everything. The idea that he simply forgot to tailor the bridle in the carving is too implausible. Presumably, he did a separate drawing for the carving. It is not as though he got to the horse, looked around his studio for an example, and inserted the first one he spotted. It was deliberate."

The duke, who had offered the explanation only to satisfy her request to play devil's advocate, readily agreed with her conclusion. His cousin was too scrupulous to make a sloppy blunder, especially after two years of producing reliefs. He would have a procedure in place that he followed for each new work. "The notion that he would come up with the design as he carved it is patently absurd."

At this reasoned reply, Bea frowned and reminded him he was supposed to make a compelling case against her theory. "I know you do not excel at taking instruction, but you did agree to the request."

Deeming the criticism fair as he selected another asparagus and bacon tart, he swore he had made a sincere effort to uphold the other side. "But the assignment defies my own considerable powers of persuasion, and I think it is more useful for us to move on to the equally confounding question of why. Why did he insert the bridle? What did he hope to accomplish by making the piece obviously fake?"

Bea questioned the accuracy of the premise, uncertain that the mistake was in fact glaring. "We spied it immediately because we were familiar with *The Huntress*. But it evaded Sir Thomas's notice for so long he invited the chief librarian of the British Museum to inspect it."

"Goddard," the duke said mildly.

Although the name of the librarian did not seem relevant to the conversation, she allowed that it was the nature of the pedant to add excess information. "Mr. Goddard, yes."

Kesgrave's lips twitched as he informed her she was

acquainted with the functionary in question, which caused her to draw her brows together as she struggled to recall how or when she had met a librarian at the British Museum. When was the last time she had visited Montague—

Goodness gracious, the Fazeley affair!

Recalling him now—a man about her uncle's age with the tall, wiry frame of a giraffe—she said, "He is the preening windbag who denied me access to the archives because I am female."

"Yes, well, no serious patron is," he replied, his eyes glittering with mirth as he repeated the pompous librarian's judgment of women, which he had overheard after following her to the museum. He had arrived at Portman Square to offer his condolences on the tragic death of Mr. Davies in time to see her leave without the company of her maid and had been compelled by curiosity to discover her destination.

He had hardly blinked an eye when he learned she was conducting a second murder investigation and refused all her attempts to discourage his participation.

That Bea had required his assistance to secure Sir Walter's papers from the archive still infuriated her, and remembering how eagerly Goddard had prostrated himself before Kesgrave's title, she revised her assessment of the mistake's subtlety. A baronet was several rungs below duke, but it still possessed the reflected glory of rank and status. The librarian, seeking to curry Sir Thomas's favor, would have barely glanced at the relief as he hailed its perfection.

Bea was certain of it.

Even if Goddard were not a sycophantic ninny, he was still an insufferable prig with an overly developed sense of his own importance. Assured of the correctness of all his opinions, he could never conceive of himself as the victim of a swindle.

He was far too clever!

Swallowing the last of the olive tart, she washed it down

with barley water, rose to her feet, and announced there was no time to waste. "A terrible fraud has been perpetrated upon the English people, and I, for one, cannot sit idly by while their pockets are picked by unscrupulous actors."

Rather than stand, Kesgrave took the last asparagus and bacon tart—before she could have a second one!—and leaned back against the cushion. "It is after six, which means Mr. Goddard is gone for the day."

Bea brushed this minor detail aside by insisting Stephens could quickly locate the librarian's home address. "One missive to his network of brothers and he will have the information in hand in a matter of seconds."

"I am reasonably certain it does not work like that," he observed, crossing his left leg over the right as she reached for the bell pull to summon the steward. "Composing the note itself will take upwards of ten minutes."

She shook her head in disgust at his appalling lack of urgency. "Our fellow countrymen, Damien. The good people of England! You may be able to sit here and enjoy asparagus tartlets while the salt of the earth are bamboozled out of thousands of pounds. I cannot!"

"What you cannot do is wait to eviscerate Goddard," he observed mildly.

Bea made no attempt to deny it. "Obviously, yes, for he is a pompous bore who disdains women, and I would delight in puncturing his ego. At the same time, I genuinely believe that a little humility will help him perform his duties better."

"How public spirited of you," he said.

Acknowledging the comment with a dip of her head, she returned to the settee without pulling the cord. His point regarding the efficiency of the Stephens network was well taken, and it was unduly late in the day for her to assign the poor steward a new task. Calling on Montague House could wait until morning.

Indeed, it was the better course.

If job improvement through humiliation was the goal, then informing Goddard of his egregious error in judgment in front of members of his staff was the most charitable way to break the news.

As she sat down again on the sofa, she wondered what Mortimer's intention had been. "Did he assume a man of Sir Thomas's reputation and experience would identify the problem and halt the sale before any damage could be done or did he expect one of the experts at the museum to spot it?"

"That depends," Kesgrave replied evenly. "Did he know Sir Thomas was the destination? According to Renfield, he was an isolated branch. But we know that is nonsense because Sir Thomas knows about Samson Kirks and Kerrich knows about Higgins. According to the trumpet creeper theory, Mortimer could have known any variety of details. So let us say for the sake of discussion that he did know the relief would be sold to the museum via an expert of Hawes's choosing. He would be within his rights to assume that expert would detect the imperfection, and detecting it, contact Hawes in a high dudgeon."

"Which is precisely what happened. So what did your cousin have to gain by provoking Hawes's ire? At best, he would earn his mistrust and at worst he would incite a reprisal," she said thoughtfully, then sat up straight, for the answer was right there in the relief.

Mortimer had made no effort to be subtle.

"The freedom to pursue his passion for art unencumbered by an association with Hawes's criminal network," she said excitedly. "That is what he hoped to achieve. He craved recognition and respectability and was convinced *The Huntress* would confer both. There was not a doubt in his mind that it would be accepted in the annual exhibition. As his confidence grew, so did his ambition, and he was no longer satisfied with producing work to which he could not affix his name."

Kesgrave conceded the logic—Hawes *would* be more inclined to release Mortimer from their agreement if he believed it was his idea—but the gambit was risky. "He could not know that Hawes would calmly suggest they go their separate ways. He might have responded with violence."

"Well, yes, but Hawes is the housekeeper," she stated confidently.

Amused by the assertion, the duke murmured, "Is he?"

"Consider it: As the overseer of a large organization, he assigns responsibilities, maintains order, adjudicates disputes, buoys spirits, soothes egos, allocates funds, and metes out punishment—all while keeping a cool head. How is Mrs. Wallace's position any different?"

Seemingly struck by the cogency of the argument, he allowed the premise had merit. "Very well, Hawes is the housekeeper, and as such he must keep an even hand."

"Driving a chisel into the stomach of one's underling for making a blunder is the opposite of an even hand," she added. "It's an overly vehement response, and an overly vehement response in a leader is an indication of weakness, not strength."

"Because it is perceived as emotional," he said.

She nodded. "If Mortimer reasoned all of this for himself, then he might have decided the risk of a violent reprisal was not great enough to outweigh the potential reward. That said, there is no way to get around the fact that Hell and Fury lied to us by omission. He should have mentioned the uproar caused by the error in the relief, given he found out about it on the same day as the murder, which makes me wonder if Hawes knew there was more to the mistake than the obvious. What if he realized Mortimer had ruined it on purpose and considered it an act of sabotage and personal betrayal? Then the brutality of the murder would be more in line with the crime, would it not?"

His lips twitched again. "And now you are playing devil's advocate for yourself."

Ruefully, she admitted it was a frequent occurrence. "In my head, I am always making both sides of an argument. But it occurs to me that a man who rises to Hawes's level of success becomes the target of other men's ambitions. There is always someone younger, faster, smarter, stronger ready and willing to prove their worth at his expense. Knowing that could have a corrosive effect on Hawes's peace of mind. If he felt a general sense of persecution, he might have suspected the anachronism was not an honest mistake. He *did* call on Mortimer immediately after his conversation with Sir Thomas."

Ah, but no.

As the duke was compelled to point out, cooling one's heels for eighteen hours did not satisfy the requirements of an immediate reaction. "He waited until nine the next morning, which implies that he considered the matter important but not pressing. If he believed Mortimer had deliberately betrayed him, I think he would have run him to ground at his lodgings if not the studio."

It was true.

Allowing almost a full day to pass did not qualify as striking while the iron was hot.

But Hell and Fury was too calculating to succumb to impetuosity. First, he would settle on a course of action, then he would call on Mortimer at his studio.

Except he would not call on Mortimer at his studio at nine yesterday morning. At that hour, any proper Corinthian would still be exercising his horse in the park or getting dressed or attending to his correspondence. Even while working on *The Huntress,* he still never appeared in Banner Street before eleven.

Would Hawes know that?

Probably not.

Would he have surmised it?

Yes, absolutely.

Twisting to look at the duke more clearly, she said, "Hawes's story does not make sense. He had no reason to believe Mortimer would be in his studio at nine in the morning. Hawes is not intimately acquainted with the schedule of all his underlings—he is not *that* kind of housekeeper—but he knows Mortimer maintained a reputation as a top of the tree Corinthian. A man of that cut would not begin work until later in the morning, and having already waited eighteen hours, Hawes would have waited a few more. But he did neither. He found Mortimer's body on Tuesday night."

Kesgrave considered her hypothesis silently for several seconds before asking what the crime lord had to gain by saying he waited a day.

"Other than obscuring his involvement, I have no idea," she replied with a frustrated shrug.

"Do you think he did it?" the duke asked.

"I believe he is capable of it," she replied with thoughtful measuredness. "I believe he has rammed a variety of sharp and blunt implements into numerous stomachs. But he came to our home and asked us to investigate. That is the implacable truth. If he had not, Mortimer would have vanished like a puff of smoke."

It was so logical.

And yet the logic felt oppressive, as if it existed solely to defeat her.

"I cannot decide if it is as simple as it seems or if the seeming simplicity is the trick," she added quietly, letting her shoulders drop to the soft back cushion of the settee. "I worry that he is controlling me like a marionette puppet and I cannot see the strings."

"Us," Kesgrave said with meaningful emphasis as he grasped her hand in his. "Either he is controlling *us* and *we* cannot see the strings, or you are giving him too much credit. You may trust it is the latter, as I have not been susceptible to manipulation since I was thirteen and was caught stealing the headmaster's toothbrush."

It was, Bea thought, a tantalizing tidbit, and desiring to know more, she tilted her head to the left to solicit details. No words passed her lips, however, for they were suddenly engulfed in a searing kiss, and as the duke's fingers fluttered tenderly against the nape of her neck, she purred in delight even as she pulled away.

"You are just trying to distract me," she murmured chidingly.

He regarded her with gentle amusement. "Am I?"

"From dashing to Grape Street and questioning Hawes."

"Tomorrow is soon enough, and I would like to look in on my grandmother before we sit down to dinner. But there is no *just* about it," he said, his voice deepening. "There is never any *just.* It is always *and*—I am trying to distract you *and* give you pleasure."

Although her heart quivered in reply, she felt instantly contrite. She should have suggested the visit herself, as she had been there when he read the note from his cousin and frowned at its contents.

"She is emptying *all* the chests in the attics?" she said now, recalling his description of the missive.

"Emptying the chests, making huge piles of everything inside, and then putting it all back. Maria is unable to determine how worried she should be. My grandmother is occupied, which is good, but is wearing herself to the bone, which is not."

The poor dowager, Bea thought, picturing the frail septu-agenarian in a dust-filled garret surrounded by mounds of powdered wigs, paniers, and bum rolls. Her consuming urge to clean was not entirely inexplicable, as keeping oneself busy with useless tasks was a time-honored method to stave off the crippling despair of grief. But it was not a durable solution. Sooner or later, she would have to stop moving and be alone with her thoughts.

Not yet, of course.

"For the moment, I think the only harm is in a moth infestation if those chests are stuffed with woolens," she said, rising to her feet. "But you're right. We should go over there right away, and I am ashamed that I did not think of it earlier. Hawes *and* Goddard can wait. Maria is probably exhausted as well if she has also been in the attic all day and could use our help."

Kesgrave replied that the greater danger was from silver-fish, as the trunks were chiefly filled with the insect's favorite treats: journals, diaries, calendars ledgers, novels, family bibles. "And reams of letters. My grandfather never conducted a correspondence he did not deem historically significant. I read several of his notes to his bailiff, and they addressed crops, soil conditions, cow excrement, and the number of grouse on the property in great detail."

"Fascinating," she murmured.

"Yes, brat, I come by my pedantry naturally," he said, tugging her into arms to press a kiss against her forehead before leading her to the door.

They had taken barely a dozen steps before the dowager duchess entered the room carrying a valise. Crossly, she chas-tised them for being at home. "I could not believe it when Marlow told me you were here. You are supposed to be looking for Mortimer's killer, not relaxing by a cozy fire enjoying rout cakes, though I know you require sustenance in your condition, Bea, and do not begrudge you any meals. I just wonder at the necessity of taking them here, in the library. Oh, but I must say, Damien, the room is looking wonderful. It has been several years since I have been in here and I am so glad you finally took down that ghastly paper your mother hung. Black and gold are the two most inhospitable colors by which to read. Red is warmer and inviting. The settee is a nice touch. Those heavy wood chairs were atrocious and all the proof anyone needed that your mother was illiterate. She liked the Windsor style because it forced her to sit up straight, which accentuated her breasts. All her design decisions could be reduced to that single criterion: breast accentuation. But truly, my dears, why are you not out and about London finding my grandson's murderer? I know Bea can eat in the carriage for I have seen the rout cake crumbs on her skirts."

The dowager's manner was frantic, a bit fevered, and she took long breathy pauses between her sentences in which she seemed to almost gulp the air. It was disquieting to behold, and if Maria had not warned them of the grieving woman's state of high agitation, Bea would have been hugely alarmed.

Revealing none of her concern, she hailed her grace's timing as impeccable as she strode forward to greet her, gently removing the leather case from her grip. "We were just on our way to Clarges Street to apprise you of our progress. Here, do sit down and have one of the wonderful olive tarts and potato puffs chef prepared. I would also offer you asparagus spears wrapped in bacon, but your grandson devoured every last one."

"It is true," the duke admitted easily as he escorted the dowager to the settee. "I did not want André to be insulted."

"I am not sure if this is a trait he shares with his ducal predecessors, but Kesgrave has an absolute terror of hurting the servants' feelings," Bea said. "It is endearing, to be sure, but also baffling. I am not certain he understands that they work for him."

"I understand that showing a little consideration costs me nothing," he replied.

Shrugging off the duke's attempt to help lower her to the settee, the dowager snapped, "You are trying to lull me with your nonsense. Maria has been doing it all day and I will tell you what I told her: The staircase sags to the left."

"Of course it does," Kesgrave replied soothingly.

Her grace scowled as she leaned against the cushion and testily explained that she had ejected Maria from the attics. "She was fussing like a maiden aunt, and I ordered her to go back downstairs, where she could not bother me. And now you are hovering, Damien, and I do not like it. I am a grown woman in full possession of my faculties and do not need to be lulled or cajoled or coddled. Tell me what is happening with the investigation. Do you have suspects?"

Kesgrave assured her they did. "Several, in fact. And we will tell you all about them just as soon as I ascertain if you have eaten anything today. Yes, you are going to be coddled, so you may as well resign yourself to it."

Despite the ornery expression that washed over her face, the dowager submitted to this treatment without protest, conceding after an extended moment of petulance that she had not eaten since breakfast. Upon further examination, the meal in question was revealed to have been half a slice of toast, and as the duke sat down next to his grandmother, Bea left the room to arrange a tray with Mrs. Wallace. She could have just as easily summoned the housekeeper to the library, but she wanted to give Kesgrave some time alone with his elderly relative.

Returning fifteen minutes later, Bea found them with their heads close together examining a watercolor. Bathed in gentle pinks and yellows, it depicted the sun setting over a wide swath of green. The hand that had rendered the scene was deft and assured, knowing how to use gradation to great effect.

"It is the field behind the gardens at Haverill Hall," the dowager said, patting the seat next to her invitingly. "Mortimer painted it when he was eight. It was the earliest work I could find despite searching for half the day. I know I have drawings from when he was younger. He did one of his governess, and the proportions were wrong—her head was the size of a pumpkin and her neck as thin as a tulip stem—but the expression on her face was perfect. Miss Josephine always looked as though she had just eaten a lemon, and he flawlessly captured that bitterness. It might be in the dower house or even the hall."

As Bea sat down next to her grace, she promised to help her look for the drawing when they retired to the country in a few weeks, an offer her grace gratefully accepted. Then she reached into the valise she had brought with her and withdrew another work, which she placed on her lap. It was a landscape as well, also of the park at the ancient estate but a different aspect and medium. A respectable effort, it represented one of Mortimer's first forays into oils.

In all, the case contained five paintings and a small ivory sculpture of a cow whom Mortimer called Josie in honor of his sour governess.

"What a wonderful little figurine," Bea said, turning the little statuette over in her hands and marveling at its detail. "How old was he when he made it?"

"Fourteen and already so skilled," she replied softly. "Myles called it whittling to be mean. He always knew the precise thing to say to be as nasty as possible. It was his talent, and he crushed Mortimer. Over and over, he crushed the boy and then the man. I was sad for Mortimer when he gave up his art, but I was also relieved because it meant he would no longer be tormented for it. Goodness, what a horrible thing to say."

Tears trickled down her cheeks, which the dowager steadfastly ignored as she unrolled the last canvas. It was a sumptuous still life conceived in the same rich strokes as *The Huntress*—roses and carnations and tulips and narcissi and irises and love-in-a-mist and larkspur all spilling out of a wicker basket with a butterfly and a cricket crawling amid the petals.

It was glorious.

Bea asked if she could have it. "I would like to frame it and put it in my office for rout cake enjoyment, so that I may see its gorgeousness every time I look up from my book."

The tears intensified, falling with such frequency and velocity that her grace was compelled to acknowledge them by brushing them away. She pressed her lips together tightly as though to hold something in and started guiltily when Mrs. Wallace entered with James carrying the tray. She promptly looked down again.

Silently, the housekeeper cleared the old plates before laying the new ones, an exchange that did not take long, barely two minutes. Even so, it was enough time for her grace to regain control of herself. After Mrs. Wallace left, she acceded to Bea's request, adding that she thought it was a lovely idea that would have pleased Mortimer.

"This is the painting that broke his heart," she murmured as she swept her hand over the image, her fingers lingering over a translucent pink peony blossom. "This is the one he thought would finally earn the Royal Academy's approval. He was so certain of it. He had run into a member of the selection committee in Hyde Park during the Fashionable Hour, and Charles Vandermash had been effusive in his praise of the work. Each successive word he uttered convinced Mortimer he would be accepted. Then the next week he got the familiar rejection from the president of the academy. You know him, I am sure, Samuel Sandby-Smith—he is invited everywhere. His grandfather was an earl, and although he did not inherit the lands or title, his mother left him the London townhouse."

In fact, Bea was acquainted only with Sandby-Smith's work: brooding historical portrayals of advancing armies and vibrant depictions of biblical stories. His mastery was undisputed, and as she had contemplated one of his paintings in Somerset House, she had felt the immensity of the scene and even found the grandiosity of his signature—a trio of swirling S's stacked on top of each other—somehow fitting to the moment.

"Sandby-Smith damned the painting with faint praise, calling it an admirable effort," the dowager continued, her tone rousing to anger as she repeated the remark. "This sumptuous work—an admirable effort. I will never forgive him for that. It destroyed Mortimer, who decided it was better not to try at all than to live with the devastation of hope. When I arrived to console him, he was about to destroy the canvas. He had a knife in his hand and planned to cut it to shreds and feed it to the fire. I convinced him to allow me to take it instead."

Bea, who did not want to overstep her position by making physical contact where it was not invited, curled her fingers into a fist rather than lay her hand on the septuagenarian's shoulder and said the intervention must have meant something to Mortimer. "With his father's relentless malice, he would have been doubly appreciative of your kindness."

The dowager nodded mutely, as tears hovered again on her lashes, and Kesgrave gently removed the canvas from her lap so that she could eat the roast joint of mutton in a white wine sauce accompanied with carrots and peas the chef had prepared. Pulling the table closer, he assured her that seeing to her nourishment was not in fact coddling.

Indeed, it was the very opposite, for he was about to abuse her horribly by sharing every detail of their investigation. "And for that you will require sustenance."

The dowager scoffed at this minor rhetorical distinction, insisting that it made no meaningful difference, and Bea said, "There, you see, your grace! That is precisely the sort of pedantry I am forced to endure hourly."

Kesgrave insisted that inexact language was a heavier burden to bear, and his grandmother accused them of trying to lull her again. With a regretful shake of his head, he wished Bea's blatant display of disrespect for his consequence was only for her benefit.

"Alas, it is constant," he said.

The dowager eyed him doubtfully—and so she should, the imperious Duke of Kesgrave looking down at his hands woefully—but did not reply to the obvious plumper. Instead, she spread the serviette on her lap, picked up the fork, and speared a carrot.

Chapter Thirteen

❧❧❧

Having never convened a gathering of servants at Kesgrave House to allocate assignments before, preferring instead to leave all domestic matters in the hands of the capable Mrs. Wallace, Bea failed to consider the awkwardness of inviting members of the staff to sit down in the drawing room.

Treating the footmen like guests in the house they served —it was the height of thoughtlessness, and upon receiving the order, all three momentarily froze as they tried to make sense of the command.

Sit down—as in on one of the chairs they routinely dusted and rearranged?

It was madness!

Naturally, Bea perceived the problem right away.

She did not need to see their vaguely distraught looks to comprehend the gravity of the misstep.

Even so, the damage had been done and changing course now would only deepen their self-consciousness by calling attention to it.

There was nothing to do but barrel through the unease with an airy confidence.

Clutching the notebook in her grasp, she resisted the urge to thank them for coming and announced that she had numerous alibis from three suspects that required confirming. "I have the list here. There are twelve in total, and I have sorted them into groups by geographic location. I would appreciate if you could speak to the men on your list and verify the information provided."

The *appreciate* was questionable.

On one hand, it made it sound as though she were asking for their help rather than issuing a directive. On the other, there was nothing to be lost in treating one's servants with consideration and respect. She said *please* and *thank you* all the time even though they were not required by her position.

Or perhaps it was the other way around and her standing as mistress of the house obligated her to act with an excess of courtesy to the staff.

Noblesse oblige, as it were.

Regardless, these ruminations did little to mitigate the discomfiture of the situation, and Bea pushed them aside as she removed a slip of paper from her book. She handed it to Edward, who professed himself greatly honored to be entrusted with the task while at the same time expressing disappointment by its lack of complexity.

Was her grace absolutely certain he did not need to assume a disguise or concoct a story to hide his interest? It seemed a little too bold of him to simply ask his targets if they had been in the company of Mr. Renfield at the stated time.

Joseph, who had been honing his French accent for just such an opportunity, also expressed his concern that they were not being subtle enough. If the suspect decided to flee, it would undermine their entire investigation.

And, yes, he used the plural possessive pronoun to assert partial ownership.

Bea, smothering a smile, felt profound relief that Lord Colson had ceased reporting her every move to the readership of the *London Daily Gazette,* as she could all too easily imagine how absurdly he would render the scene in the drawing room, making it seem as though she were overseeing an ancillary rotation office in Berkeley Square.

As she had been the one to assign them disguises and stories for previous outings, she acknowledged their concerns as valid and explained that each case required a tailored approach. "The suspects gave his grace and me the information on the understanding that we would be confirming it, so you may be forthcoming and honest with the men on your lists."

Reassured, Joseph nodded solemnly. Edward remained doubtful, but before he could ask another question, Marlow appeared in the doorway to announce a caller. Seeing the footmen arrayed on the furniture, he winced in horror.

Well, no, he did not wince or flinch or in any other way reveal his disgust. His unremittingly black brows remained as implacable as ever, but Bea still felt it keenly and it required all her self-control not to offer an explanation. Instead, she grimaced with embarrassment and asked the visitor's name.

It was not the gravitas for which Flora advocated but at least she had managed to restrain her blushes.

"Mrs. Palmer," the butler replied.

As Bea had expected the society hostess to respond to her request for help with a missive of her own, she did not know if she should be reassured by her sudden appearance or unnerved by it.

Either way, it indicated that her friend comprehended the severity of the problem, which was to the good. There were few things more irritating than a person who could not see what all the bother was about.

On a firm nod, she instructed Marlow to show Mrs. Palmer in, then returned her attention to the trio of footmen and thanked them for their assistance. "If you need more information than is provided on your sheet, please apply to Mr. Stephens. He will be happy to help."

It was a flagrant falsehood.

The steward, who wanted only to mind the business of the estate, had not agreed to be an auxiliary member of her ancillary rotation office. But he was too professional to protest, which made the offense even greater, for she was taking shameless advantage of his decency.

And yet she could conceive of no other option.

It was not as though she could hire a manager of investigations.

Well aware that she could in fact hire for any position she wished, however absurd, she handed James a missive to her aunt and asked him to ensure its swift delivery to Portman Square. Then she requested a tray for her guest just as Mrs. Palmer swept into the room in an excited flurry. She embraced Bea briskly, stepped back several steps, and announced with bracing confidence that a solution was at hand.

"It won't be pretty, but it will be effective," she added, slipping her reticule off her wrist and untying the cords that bound it closed. She withdraw a small diary and flipped through it as she sat down. "It is a remarkable predicament, and before we begin discussing my ideas, I have to commend you on entangling yourself in unprecedented quandary. Her Outrageousness indeed!"

Taking no offense at this remark, Bea nevertheless begged her to direct her admiration toward Lady Abercrombie, for it was she who had created the quandary without precedent.

Mrs. Palmer, however, ardently disagreed, for as the new Duchess of Kesgrave, Bea should have organized a country party well before the countess got a bee in her bonnet over it.

"But that is neither here nor there," she said with stern dismissiveness. "You do not want to have a party and so you shall not have a party. The reason for your reluctance is irrelevant, although I assume you are taking a stand against her ladyship's high-handedness. You do not have to say another word about it to me, for I do it all the time. Just last month, Palmer's mother clucked over the state of the drapes in the dining room, and even though I had already ordered new curtains in a lovely light blue damask from Argyle Smith & Co., I canceled them and intend to keep the old ones until they are too threadbare to be of any use whatsoever."

Although it was impossible to hear these remarks without feeling a frisson of defensiveness, for it made her sound quite childish, Bea knew her friend's outlook was in large part the reason Lady Abercrombie was so set on having the party: It was what society expected.

Bea's preferences were beside the point.

Mrs. Palmer, reading something of her hostess's emotions on her face, immediately apologized for broaching the subject after foreswearing it. "As I said, it is immaterial, so let us not waste another moment and jump headfirst into the thicket. We shall start by reviewing the guest list, which is impeccable. Lady Abercrombie was selective and did not invite anyone who would create a commotion. As you know, it is I and Palmer, my brother, Hartlepool and his wife—not his scapegrace nephew, I am relieved to report—Lord and Lady Leland, and Mr. Cuthbert, of course, for the countess's private entertainment. You see, unassailable. There is not a featherbrain among them, which is why the gossips are not yet nattering about it."

It was worse than Bea had expected.

The Palmers, Nuneaton, even the Lelands were innocuous.

No doubt the viscount would grumble at regular intervals about the discomforts he was made to endure such as the upsetting lack of symmetry in his poached eggs, but there was no harm in it. His lordship would be teasing, making as much fun of himself as he was of her.

But Hartlepool found her investigative pretensions off-putting and could only regret that his oldest friend had not possessed the good sense to take a more conventional woman to wife. It was really not so difficult to find an insipid beauty who kept her notions to herself.

Indeed, a duke had to go out of his way to wed an aspiring lady Runner.

Hartlepool's inclusion meant she could not simply rescind the invitation, for he already considered her a ridiculous nuisance and the clumsy maneuver would only feed his contempt.

"Well, no featherbrains excluding Mrs. Hyde-Clare, who is not officially on the list but is presumably invited," Mrs. Palmer amended with a prompt apology for maligning her host's aunt.

"Accurate statements do not count as aspersions," Bea assured her as Mrs. Wallace appeared with the tea service and delivered it to the table. She thanked the housekeeper for the lovely tray and waited until she had left the room before noting that Lady Abercrombie had withheld invitations from her relatives. "That is why part of me thinks she is just toying with me. She knows there is no way I can host Hartlepool and Lord and Lady Leland while excluding my family. But the invitations are real."

And yet her tone tipped up at the end, as though nurturing a sliver of hope that they were merely a collective figment.

"As real as this teacup," Mrs. Palmer affirmed, raising the brew to her lips and sipping delicately. "I want to say that I am surprised by her audacity, but it is in perfect keeping with what I know about her. She has always been singularly focused on her own goals, and I am simultaneously relieved and disappointed that she never turned her attention to politics. With her skills she could do so much good and so much bad. At any rate, this time she will be thwarted. And it is the easiest thing in the world. All we need is a fire."

Alas, the simplicity escaped Bea, who regarded her friend blankly.

Mrs. Palmer smiled and explained that it did not have to be a large one. "A small blaze in an unused part of the house will do. It is only a token or a gesture—a burnt offering, if you will."

Bea could not believe she understood it correctly. "You want me to start a fire at Haverill Hall?"

"A small one," Mrs. Palmer reiterated. "It is an old stone manor, and you are clever. I am sure you will find the right place to create a modest conflagration that will do only minimal damage. Then you can cancel the house party on account of the house partially burning to the ground. Nobody would question it, not even Lady Abercrombie. It is the perfect plan."

"You are teasing me," Bea said.

Her guest swore it was a proven tactic. "Two weekend parties I was meant to attend in the past five years were canceled at the last minute because of fires. I cannot believe both were coincidences."

It was deranged folly, Bea thought, unable to conceive of anyone trusting a fire to constrain itself to a prescribed amount of destruction.

They raged out of control.

That was what fires did.

And even if she deemed the plan feasible, she could never bring herself to set any portion of the duke's ancestral home ablaze.

It just seemed like a gross betrayal of trust.

Mrs. Palmer, sensing her resistance, reminded her that Haverill Hall was several centuries old, which meant it had seen dozens of fires during its existence. "I wager whole sections have burned down two or three times. All these old piles of stones are being endlessly rebuilt. Still, I see the prospect does not appeal to you. No matter. I have other ideas," she said, waving her diary in the air between them. "Let us proceed to the next one: illness. It is more daunting than fire because there is no burned husk to which you can point as proof, and merely swooning during tea and lying in bed for a few days will not do the trick. Your ailment has to linger for at least a week—ideally, with a terrible, racking cough and a debilitating headache—or the servants will know are pretending and word will spread, and then the vicar is at your door insisting on giving you weekly Bible lessons to preserve your mortal soul. I promise you, one little inferno, thoughtfully placed, is a pleasure in comparison."

Given the odd specificity of the account, Bea assumed her friend spoke from firsthand experience, a supposition immediately confirmed by Mrs. Palmer, who readily acknowledged going to the extreme to avoid her mother-in-law. "It worked in that she and her husband canceled their visit out of fear of catching my illness. They are both of delicate temperaments. The fact that the vicar still follows me around waving his Bible six years later might indicate that success came at a very high cost. But do not let my negative outcome persuade you because I did not have the benefit of my wise counsel and you do. I will teach you how to cough with so much urgency you sound as though you are on the verge of expelling a lung. It is a very useful skill. I launch into one of my fits whenever a man decides to lecture me on a topic of which I know more than he."

Bea laughed and said, "Ah, so once a week?"

"At least," Mrs. Palmer replied. "Well, what do you think? You are with child, which means you are vulnerable to difficulties, and nobody would gasp in astonishment if you had to cancel the house party because you were consigned to bed out of an excess of concern for the Matlock heir."

Despite her visitor's caution, Bea thought feigning an illness was a practical recourse for evading an unwanted situation. Flora had pretended to have food poisoning twice in order to escape her mother's watchful gaze and investigate Mr. Davies's murder. It could work if not for the fact that she would have to tell Kesgrave the truth, for she could not allow him to worry about either her or the cherub.

What a humiliating admission that would be!

Yes, your grace, I am so terrified of hosting our friends at Haverill Hall that I have chosen to affect a grave disease. Please bear with me while I collapse from a mild case of consumption from which I shall recover in eight to ten days. Please have Mrs. Wallace prepare a vat of thin gruel.

He would shake his head sadly at her determination to see herself as a timid spinster.

Perceiving that this second suggestion had no more chance of prospering than the first, Mrs. Palmer closed her diary and said she did not think Bea would welcome any of her ideas. "Next on my list is a highly contagious disease of cloven-hoofed animals. It would keep away Lady Abercrombie's guests as well as a significant contingent of locals. The recovery time for pustules on the mouth and foot is several weeks, which makes it another extreme measure. Instead, I have this radical proposal: Proceed with the party as though it were your own idea. Other than a reflexive opposition with which I have already expressed full-throated sympathy I cannot fathom what objection you may have. Planning a country party requires skill and organization, and one never stops worrying about the weather, but you are an intelligent woman. It is nothing you cannot handle, especially in light of the highly competent staff at Haverill Hall. Your role would be supervisory at best. You would provide the general pattern for how you would like the week to proceed and guidance."

It was a compliment, Mrs. Palmer's persistent belief that Bea's lone objection was to Lady Abercrombie's overbearing presumption, and if she had any hope of making her friend understand, she would have to explain how alien and terrifying she found the prospect of taking on a supervisory role at the centuries-old estate. It was a simple enough idea to articulate, as it swam through her head constantly, and yet the words stuck in her throat.

Mrs. Palmer knew only *this* Bea—the brave Bea, the brazen Bea, Her Outrageousness—and the thought of introducing her to the other Bea created a knot in the pit of her stomach.

Seeming to intuit some fragment of this sweeping insecurity, Mrs. Palmer placed her teacup on the table and laid a gentle hand on her hostess's arm. Softly, kindly, she said, "I did not know you before the events of this spring. I have racked my brain for some scrap of Miss Hyde-Clare because it seems inconceivable to me that we attended the same affairs for years and never met. Usually, when someone I do not expect becomes the *on-dit,* I have a vague sense of them. I think, Oh, yes, *them*. But I have nothing of you, which is strange because you are vibrant and capable and I keep an ongoing list of all the vibrant and capable women in society. That can mean only one thing: You hid your vibrancy under a bushel. I do now know why you hid it, but I do know it was there, your grace, the whole time. And I think you are used to either hiding it or hiding from it, and I hope you realize you do not have to do that anymore. You can be just as vibrant and capable in Cambridgeshire as you are in London. It is not nearly as hard as you suppose."

Horrified, Bea felt the heat rise in her cheeks. To think she presented as such a desperate creature she required an admiring speech to rouse her spirits!

Consumed by a desire to squirm, she forced herself to remain still and meet Mrs. Palmer's distressingly earnest gaze head on.

"Give it some thought," Mrs. Palmer said, her manner brisk now as she rose to her feet in anticipation of taking her leave. "I know it may seem as though I am mocking you with these suggestions, but I assure you they are sincere. The situation calls for extreme measures, and it is my dearest hope that I never shrink from an extreme measure. To that end, if you decide you still want to thwart Lady Abercrombie's machinations, we can return to the list. Number four involves ancient papyri, Anubis, and an Egyptian curse. A bothersome number of your silk gowns will be ruined with linseed oil, but it yields results."

Bea eked out a smile, and although it felt natural enough to her, she feared it resembled the ghastly grin she had aimed recently at the duke, the one he had described as stiff and ghostly as a Grödnertal doll. "I shall bear it in mind, as it indeed sounds promising. My maid would gasp in dismay to hear me say it, but I have silk gowns to spare."

Mrs. Palmer, nodding in approval, lauded her practical attitude toward her clothing, as so many schoolroom misses developed a sentimental attachment to what was ultimately just fabric and thread arranged in an appealing fashion. "But I should not reserve my scorn to young girls as Nuneaton is the worst offender. He frets and sighs over every waistcoat. If a button falls off, he raises the hue and cry and launches an investigation to find out if the stitch was at fault or the tailor."

The cheerful reply was a thing of beauty, breezing blithely past her host's gruesome smile, flushed features, and ill-disguised agitation to make a teasing bon mot about her dandy brother.

Vibrant and capable—surely, Mrs. Palmer topped her own list.

Bea responded to the frippery in kind, recounting the viscount's urgent early-morning visit to inform her of Mrs. Flimmer-Flam's interest and noting that despite claims to the opposite, his appearance was remarkably kempt. "Not a hair out of place."

"That is his gambit: swear he looks like a rag-muffin to obligate you to assure him he does not," Mrs. Palmer said as they reached the entrance. "He has been playing that game since he was in leading strings, which, you may believe, I was compelled to observe made his spine appear strong and noble."

Bea laughed at this sally and bid her friend goodbye in a more tranquil frame of mind. Obviously, Mrs. Palmer had meant only to be encouraging with her stirring speech, and Bea's humiliation was merely an unfortunate secondary effect.

But that was the problem in a nutshell, was it not?

Anything could discompose her.

One vaguely unkind word—or in this case a kind one—untethered her from sense and she wound up stammering nonsense in reply.

It had happened repeatedly during her six seasons.

Clearly, there was nothing to be done but to cancel the party outright.

No ruses, no ploys, just rescinded invitations.

Kesgrave would stand by her, for he would be infuriated by Lady Abercrombie's wanton disregard of his authority.

She would tell him at once.

And yet when he appeared in the entry hall to marvel over Stephens' newfound popularity with the footmen, she only asked if he was ready to visit Hawes.

Chapter Fourteen

✻

Hell and Fury was waiting for them.

Well, not *waiting* in the traditional sense of marking time in expectation of their imminent arrival.

He was not even home when they called at ten, but his housekeeper—a rail of a woman in a white mobcap—scowled upon seeing them and said, "His nibs is never wrong, not ever."

Then she shook her head wearily and stepped back, bidding them to enter with a wave of her arm. "I'm to bring ye to the office and let his nibs know ye are here. Come along, then. Don't jest stand there. I don't want the neighbors to see. A dook in Grape Street—it ain't natural. Who be next? The prime minister himself?"

Despite his ascension to local royalty, the King of Saffron Hill lived more or less modestly, in a four-story row house with freshly painted windows and a graceful pediment over the front door. The interior was equally neat and restrained without lavish flourishes, and the room to which they were shown was decorated in red paper patterned with thistles and wide windows that admitted bright streams of daylight. A sapphire rug partially obscured the floor, which was painted a rich ebony. In the center was a stout table with molded corners to anchor the room.

The last time they visited, Hawes had been sitting at the table amid a flurry of papers, hard at work attending to his empire, when they entered the room.

Now they were instructed to take a seat while the housekeeper sent Danny with the message. "I have some coffee if ye want it. It's from this morning, so it's cold. But I ain't making tea. His nibs said nothing about providing refreshments."

Kesgrave declined this gracious offer.

The elderly woman was visibly relieved. "Good, then, ye sit and wait. He didn't go far, just to the house on the corner to talk to Mrs. MacBain about her son. He got into the gin again and he's only thirteen. Ye wouldn't know it, but his nibs takes an interest in the young lads in the neighborhood. He wants them to grow up bright and strong."

In fact, Bea would know it. She assumed it was in the crime lord's interest for his subjects to mature into sturdy men with the courage and cunning to flaunt the law.

Having fulfilled her duty, the housekeeper left them alone in the office long enough for her to reach the end of the hallway and turn around. Although she did not reenter the room, she hovered awkwardly on the threshold, as though simultaneously worried and not worried that the guests might steal the silver.

Examining the room with amusement, Bea noted there was very little of value that could be easily transported. The cast-bronze candlesticks with cut-crystal teardrop ornaments flanking the fireplace mantel looked dear but were too large for her to discreetly slip into her pockets. Their foliate luster ring would surely snag the silk, causing a fuss.

Curious if something of significant worth was on the table, she raised her chin.

The housekeeper took a step into the office.

To ease the other woman's anxiety, Bea leaned back in her chair and then immediately darted to her feet when Hawes swept into the room.

His broad cheeks were swathed in smiles as he came to stand before them and apologize for not being present to greet them properly. "I had a niggling sense you would want to talk to me again after examining the crime scene, but I could not sit around and twiddle my thumbs. I have responsibilities requiring my attention. But I did make a point of staying close to home for when you did eventually call. And now here you are. It has been two days. I trust you have made progress and intend to apprise me of significant developments in our investigation."

His eyes sparkled as he said it—our investigation—and Bea had the unsettling feeling that she was being toyed with again. Unwilling to allow him to direct the conversation, she announced without preamble that they knew he had lied to them. "You found Mortimer's body—*if* he was in fact already dead—on Tuesday night, not Wednesday morning as you claimed in order to obscure the urgency of the visit. Mortimer had endangered your scheme and you were angry."

In the act of retrieving a sheet of paper from his desk, he let it flutter to the surface as he said with an air of appreciation, "Jumping straight to it, I see. No signing caricatures, then. Duly noted!"

Striding across the sapphirine rug, he urged them to sit down. "Please make yourselves comfortable. I cannot allow her grace to make a murder accusation while she is stiff on her feet. There, very good, thank you. Now you may proceed with all the righteous anger you can muster, and I shall endeavor to be as coherent as possible as I grapple with my disappointment at this disheartening display of a coarse mind. I had thought better of you, duchess!"

Bea regarded him blandly.

"And now you are pinning me with your penetrating stare," he added with an exaggerated tremble. "Have mercy on me, your grace, for I am only human. I told you a trivial falsehood because the time of my visit has no bearing on your investigation and I feared you would imbue it with undo meaning if you knew it had occurred late at night. I wanted to spare you the embarrassment of your suspicion because we both know I would never have sought your assistance if I were the guilty party. And you cannot blame me for not dashing from the murder to Kesgrave House. I am not given to impulse or rash action and required some time to decide whether your expertise as an investigator outweighed the cost of inviting you to scrutinize my organization."

And yet Bea *did* blame him, for his lie had led them astray. "The bearing the time of your visit has on our investigation is it allows us to narrow the window during which the murder took place."

Hawes, appearing amused by the notion, apologized for inadvertently keeping the murder window open wider than necessary. "My only intention was to avoid this precise conversation because your supposition regarding my motive is not wrong. It is not right either, but I will concede that I was displeased with Mr. Matlock's sloppiness and planned to make my unhappiness known. When I arrived at his studio and looked around, I recognized the source of the problem as a troubling lack of focus. I had not realized he had returned to painting. If I had, I would have discouraged the interest."

"And what time was that?" Bea asked.

"After ten, about a quarter past," he replied smoothly, the customary mockery momentarily gone from his tone. "I had sent word to his rooms requesting that Mr. Matlock attend to me here, but he was not at home and the porter had no idea when to expect him, as he kept an erratic schedule and sometimes did not return home to change for dinner. I thought it was possible he was still at the studio and went to look for him there."

"Why did you wait so long to express your displeasure?" she pressed.

"*Did* I wait long?" he murmured softly. "I dispatched the message to Mr. Matlock's lodging as soon as I returned from Golden Square, then devoted myself to other business. I had appointments to keep and issues to resolve. I did not wait until after ten. That was the earliest opportunity I had to make my expectations known to Mr. Matlock."

At this mild reply, Bea eyed him doubtfully. "That was all you were going to do: take him to task? Mortimer's mistake threatened to destroy everything you had worked for at the worst possible time, and your only response was to chastise him?"

Amused by her skepticism, he chuckled and asked what she imagined he did all day. "I oversee a large concern employing hundreds of people who are all fallible in one way or another. If I drove a sharp implement into the stomach of every one of them who made a mistake, Saffron Hill would be thick with corpses. I might take some personal satisfaction in primal retribution as I am only human, but it is a terrible way to run a business—and not only because it would bring Her Outrageousness to my door. I find that expressing my disappointment is a highly effective stratagem for getting the best out of my associates, especially when I remain calm. Apparently, my composure is more alarming than my fury."

It was the first thing he had said that she had no trouble believing.

"I know it does not sit well with you, duchess, but we are allies," he added with gentle understanding. "We both want the same thing."

"Justice," she replied archly, not at all swayed by his repeated insistence.

"Justice," Hawes agreed. "And that is why you can trust me when I tell you I had nothing to do with this murder. I did not order it or sanction it or commit it myself. Was I peeved by the mistake? I admit it, yes. I have little patience for carelessness. But it was a rare misstep in an otherwise flawless career, and I was determined to be forgiving, as I still required his services. The Assyrian trade continues to flourish, and I have begun to look ahead to our next venture. The Elgin marbles have spurred a renewed interest in Grecian statuary that I find particularly auspicious."

He did not, no, Bea thought.

Or at least he did not find it auspicious in the way he wanted her to believe.

Hell and Fury was merely taunting them again because it amused him to flaunt his power. All three of them knew the counterfeit trade involving Assyrian reliefs was dead. It had ceased to exist the moment he had told them about Mortimer. But something new would take its place as soon as the fuss over the museum's credulity died down, which could be as soon as a fortnight. He knew their options were limited. Aside from publicizing the current scheme, there was little she or the duke could do to stop the next one.

And that was what he enjoyed—contemplating their help-lessness.

It was, she assumed, a familiar experience for him, as he was accustomed to thinking of himself as the smartest person in the room, especially among the aristocracy, whom wealth and privilege had rendered effete. His dealings with Lord Myles had only reaffirmed the judgment, for his lordship was everything a cynic would expect from a member of the pampered elite: greedy, entitled, leaden-minded. Hawes had easily manipulated him, allowing him to think he had outwitted his nefarious business partner while effectively consigning the peer to a sandpit like a small child building mounds with a shovel.

Hawes had been in control the entire time.

As he was in control now.

Or so he thought.

The truth was, he understood little about his own current predicament.

It was unavoidable, of course.

As he himself had just noted, Hell and Fury was in charge of a massive enterprise with hundreds of people in its employ. He could not know all the minor dramas that unfolded in the many darkened corners of his empire. By necessity, he had to employ lieutenants to take care of the everyday issues that arose, and in entrusting men like Renfield to competently handle the seemingly endless details, he effectively removed himself from its daily operation.

That was why Hawes did not know about the mistake Rennie Rumpus had almost made.

If he had even an inkling of an Arabic number on a Roman artifact, he would have approached his conversation with Mortimer in a different frame of mind.

As his feeling of superiority was to their benefit, Bea made no effort to pierce his ego. Overly confident men were more inclined to make costly blunders, and there was no reason to put him on his guard. She had yet to figure out how to ensure that the fuss over the fraudulent sale to the British Museum did not subside after a few weeks, but she had a niggling idea concerning Mr. Twaddle-Thum's scurrilous pen.

Knowing how much hay Lord Colson had made over a few granules of sugar, she was certain he could stretch the story over several months to ensure that every collector in England knew to keep an eye out for counterfeit antiquities. If she could not halt the supply of the forgeries, then she would do what she could to reduce the demand for them.

When she did not immediately respond to his provoking comment, Hawes made another, adding that he would never use a carving instrument. He preferred his murder weapons to be neat and reliable from ten paces away. "My aim is impeccable. Whatever I point at, I hit," he said, needlessly underscoring his boast by directing his thumb and forefinger at Bea and pulling the imaginary trigger.

She ignored these dramatics as well. "Was Mortimer still warm to the touch?"

"Quite," Hell and Fury answered, delighted by the question. "And you are correct in your deduction. Judging by the temperature of the body and the liquidity of the blood, I would say I missed encountering our murderer by less than an hour. That narrows your window even more, does it not?"

It did, yes—if he was to be believed.

In accordance with testimony provided by Foster and Miss Brewer, Hawes's information meant that the murder most likely took place between nine-fifteen and ten-fifteen.

A narrower window indeed.

Kesgrave asked Hawes to detail his movements on Tuesday, starting with his meeting with Sir Thomas. "Where did you go when you left Golden Square?"

The crime lord received the request with a vicious smile and insisted that nobody was interested in the dreary minutia of his business. "It is just one boring meeting after another. I lead nothing like the exciting life of a duke and duchess. I cannot remember the last time I was pelted with a bucket of vomit during an ambush."

Relatively banal, the comment nevertheless revealed how closely he was watching them, as the story of how they apprehended Miss Lloyd's killer had not been widely circulated. The event happened after Twaddle bowed to his friend Miss Lark's request that he cease tormenting her half brother's wife.

"Your movements," Kesgrave said.

Begrudgingly, Hawes complied.

Well, rather, he partially complied, giving the times of all his appointments but adamantly refusing to divulge the names of the associates with whom he met. "You already know about my antiquities venture and will presumably take an interest in the Duke's Brother now that you have inherited your cousin's share. You must allow me to keep some aspect of my business private."

Bea, weighing the relative advantage of pressing for the information, decided to leave the matter unresolved for now. They could always raise it again if it proved relevant. "What did you do after finding the body?"

"Why, come directly home of course," he replied with that familiar mocking lilt. "Deeply unsettled, I attended to my correspondence and entered some figures into a ledger before tucking myself into bed. I was asleep by midnight."

As was frequently the case, she looked at him dubiously. "You found one of your associates brutally slain and your response was to come home and devote yourself to paperwork?"

"Well, yes," Hell and Fury said matter-of-factly. "What do you do, duchess?"

With a look at Bea, Kesgrave rose to his feet, and Hawes, expressing surprise that they were leaving so soon, consoled them as he escorted them to the hallway. "You must not be too crushed! It was a very good motive, I am sure, and most men might have considered Mr. Matlock's sloppiness sufficient cause for violence. But as a pragmatist, I appreciate a useful mistake—in this case, providing Sir Thomas with the opportunity to demonstrate his acumen. He has a reputation for being a discerning collector, but it was reassuring to witness it firsthand. Having said that, I do not like that he sought Mr. Addleton's expertise, as the request for a second opinion implies a lack of confidence in the first."

It was on the tip of Bea's tongue to point out the inaccuracy of this statement, as Sir Thomas had been gulled by amateurish Roman artifacts, but the name of the specialist distracted her.

The baronet's friend Holly was Hollis Addleton, the Royal Antiquarian Society's resident gossip?

Given Addle the Prattle's compulsion, she was willing to bet he had broadcast the details of his visit to the baronet's house to half the membership of the organization.

Kerrich, hearing the tale, would have been extremely cross.

Those cursed trinkets would be the ruin of them all!

In a frenzy of anxiety, he might have called in Banner Street to tell Mortimer that the worst had come to pass: A renowned collector had been duped by the shabby medieval artifacts in Higgins's shop and now Addle the Prattle would visit the store and discover that Higgins peddled many false treasures, causing their brilliant scheme to unravel and ruining his brilliant career along with it.

If Mortimer dismissed his concern or responded with contempt or irritation, Kerrich's anger at the repeated betrayals might have overcome him.

Another visit to the society was necessary at once.

Arriving at the front door, Bea bid their host a curt good day and waited patiently as Kesgrave informed him that a solicitor from Grundy and Furst would be in touch regarding the dissolution of their partnership in the gin parlor. Owning himself deeply disappointed, Hell and Fury begged him to reconsider: He had just received delivery of the new sign—The Duke's Own—and could not fathom banishing it to the cellar before it was even hung.

"It bears your family crest and motto," he added.

The duke told him to expect word within the week.

Chapter Fifteen

A s a shy spinster with little countenance, Bea had routinely drawn disappointed frowns from men who had hoped to be seated next to an heiress or an Incomparable or at the very least a young lady with enough address to respond to polite sallies with coherent replies.

Maintaining a blank expression, she would cringe inwardly and chew thoughtfully and count the minutes until she would be released from the obligation of making stilted dinner conversation.

But that was a social scowl.

The glare Kerrich aimed at her now was a different sort altogether—an investigative glower—which had long since lost the power to cow her into silence. Ignoring his curled lips and seething eyes, she greeted him calmly while he stared daggers and swore he had told her everything he knew. His gaze darted around the room to see who else was present. As it was noon, the coffee parlor was relatively quiet, with only a pair of tables occupied in the far corner with six antiquarians having a lively discussion regarding the origin of Stonehenge, with the most ardent voice advocating for William Stukeley's Druid theory.

Lowering his voice, he leaned forward and said, "I have endeavored to be helpful, as I think gutting a human being like a trout is repellant. I still cannot grasp how that happened to Mr. Matlock. But I do not know what else you wish for me to say. As much as I respect you both for trying to find out the truth, you must comprehend how an association with you can only hurt me. People will talk!"

A rumble of laughter filled the room, causing Kerrich to recoil, and Kesgrave suggested they retreat to the secretary's office upstairs to continue their discussion.

The notion that his callers had so many questions they constituted a conversation further unnerved him, and he seemed on the verge of refusing when Couch strode through the door. Recognizing the duke and duchess from their visit the day before, he marveled at their returning so soon and asked if they were thinking of joining the society. The organization could always use more devoted members of noble descent.

"It would burnish our reputation, would it not?" Couch asked with a half smile. "We are perceived as being fusty-dusty, obsessed with history when we are actually in the vanguard, trying to understand the future by making sense of the past."

Before Bea could reply to this erudite remark, Kerrich exclaimed that he was interviewing for a position. "With the duke! He is seeking an antiquarian to catalogue his family's collection of gold coins. Vikings, he thinks, and he is reviewing my qualifications to see if I am suitable. He is most eager to know my opinion of the ... of the ... Stukeley method. Yes, the Stukeley method. He is a strict adherent!"

Fascinated, Couch noted that he was unfamiliar with the methodology and begged Kesgrave to tell him more.

"No!" Kerrich screeched wildly, then sought to moderate his response so as not to draw even more interest. "Their graces have to be on their way soon. They keep busy schedules! So they do not have time to educate you. But I will explain later. We shall have a cup of coffee together, shall we? Very good. All right, then, goodbye!"

If Kerrich could have grabbed the callers by the wrists and dragged them out of the room without raising a single eyebrow, he would have done it in a heartbeat. His arms rose at his side as if to reach out, and he forcefully pushed them down as he swirled on his heel and strode to the door.

Couch, confused but not alarmed, watched them leave with a calm expression and owned himself eager to hear more at his colleague's earliest opportunity.

Kerrich stomped up the stairs to the secretary's office and almost slammed the door before thinking better of it. Instead, he closed it with a satisfying snap while thanking them for not correcting his minor fabrication. "I am very sorry that Mr. Matlock was murdered, but I do not think the tragedy should upend my entire existence."

"I am sure Mortimer would regret the inconvenience," Bea murmured as she sat down across from the grimy window overlooking the alley.

The antiquarian flinched.

Smoothly, she explained that they had discovered information that seemed pertinent to the case. "Mr. Addleton inspected Sir Thomas's collection and found it contained several Roman artifacts from Higgins's shop, the ones you like to call medieval trinkets."

Kerrich, smiling tightly, took exception to her words. "Yes, I know all about the visit and would have happily discussed it if you had asked. I made no attempt to hide it!"

"Of course you did not," she replied reassuringly. "As you had expressed your concern about those very forgeries to

Mortimer, we are curious how you reacted when you learned Addleton visited Golden Square to look for counterfeit antiquities."

"I was beside myself with apprehension," Kerrich said as if explaining the obvious. "Addle the Prattle was summoned by Soames to look at an Assyrian relief that the collector said 'felt off.' Naturally, I thought the whole thing was about to come crashing down! Amazingly, it was not one of Mortimer's. I cannot tell you how relieved I was about that! But as you already noted, the Roman artifacts were the very same cheap trinkets I had repeatedly warned Mortimer about, and so I have done little else in the past few days but imagine the opposite series of events: Sir Thomas summoning Addle to look at the Roman artifacts because something about them 'felt off' and Addle finding a counterfeit relief with my signature on the authentication certificate. It was a narrow escape. Too narrow! I could not risk it happening again."

"So you called on Mortimer," she said.

On the verge of agreeing, he suddenly halted his speech and lifted his chin. "Good God, no! I had wasted enough time trying to reason with him. I went to Rennie Rumpus."

"You did?" Bea asked, startled into darting a look at Kesgrave.

"My entreaties to Matlock had fallen on deaf ears and now I knew why: He was not in charge," Kerrich said. "Having presented himself as the architect of the scheme, he was only a minion like myself and not making the important decisions. So I called on Mr. Rumpus, whose address I recalled from when Matlock taunted me with it during our argument on Friday, and explained that the trinkets risked undermining everything Mr. Hawes had built."

"How did Renfield respond to the news?" she asked.

"Gratefully," he replied, the relief he had felt at the positive reception keen in his voice. "He thanked me for alerting him to the problem. He had been unaware that the display in Higgins's shop could endanger the reliefs. He thought of the two schemes as unrelated."

"But you made him see how they were connected," she prompted.

"He need look no further than Sir Thomas!" he exclaimed. "A noted collector who fell prey to a dealer's rapaciousness! Higgins could have just as easily sold Sir Thomas one of the fake reliefs, and then Addleton's inspection would have turned out very differently. Unlike Mortimer, Mr. Rumpus did not dismiss me out of hand and asked me to explain. The artifacts looked authentic to him, and he was taken aback by my describing them as shabby. Seeking to soften the critique, I explained the issue was presenting them in volume. Each medallion and pilgrim badge and statuette on its own looked authentic, but that many together in one place, all looking so similar, makes a collector think."

"Think what?" Kesgrave asked when the antiquarian did not immediately elaborate.

Kerrich's demeanor changed as he moved to stand behind the desk, as if taking the podium in a lecture hall, and he crossed his arms before his chest. "Where they are coming from. A supply that large has to have a source, which any collector worth his salt knows. Establishing provenance of an object should be his largest concern. In this case, a collector must wonder if Higgins has access to a secret Roman hoard or does he employ dozens of mudlarks to search the Thames at low tide? Either option is possible but also not very likely because it would be more widely known. If scavengers were finding Roman badges daily under the dock at Wapping, then the area would be crawling with mudlarks. There is no way to keep something like that quiet! Abundance invites scrutiny, which Mr. Hawes seemed to understand because he has made sure the flow of reliefs has been steady and slow. He never overwhelmed the market. But with these small treasures, Mr. Hawes is determined to make as much money as quickly as possible, to hell with the consequences, and that is dangerous."

Bea, who could not refute the logic, wondered how Renfield had felt listening to what amounted to a critique of his methods. Unlike Kerrich, he knew the part Sir Thomas played in Hawes's grand scheme and might have felt a tremor of alarm at having given unintended offense to someone essential to his employer's ambition. For all Renfield knew, the baronet renounced his support, leaving the King of Saffron Kill scrambling to find another easily corrupted, well-respected collector with flexible morals.

"Did Mr. Renfield consent to address your concern?" Bea asked.

"He is a reasonable man and agreed to take it up with Higgins," he replied with satisfaction. "I cannot conceive why Mortimer was frightened to mention it to him, for his conduct does not match his reputation. It was a pleasant surprise to find myself in league with someone so sensible and receptive to criticism. Matlock had led me to expect the opposite. Mr. Rumpus was amused by that."

"You told him that Mortimer refused to convey your concerns?" she asked.

Kerrich's lips broadened in a patronizing smile. "When dealing with the criminal class, it behooves one to stay on their good side by placing blame with others. It is a fundamental principle."

Ah, so Renfield knew that it was Mortimer's reticence that had exposed him to Hawes's disapproval. Perhaps he had confronted the forger, the two men quarreled, and the chisel was driven into the victim's belly in the heat of the argument. Or maybe Mortimer accepted the rebuke without a word, then invited Kerrich to his studio to take *him* to task for running to Renfield with tales about him, they clashed, and a furious Kerrich fatally stabbed Mortimer.

"I am sure Matlock would not have hesitated to do the same thing to me, if given the opportunity. We are all fighting to survive," he added defensively, then flinched slightly as he recalled the other man had failed in that endeavor. "I meant that remark in a figurative sense, not as a literal reference to Mr. Rumpus. Please do not tell Mr. Rumpus that I implied he murdered Matlock. I do not believe that for a second. Well, for *more* than a second! It did occur to me fleetingly. How could it not? The man is notorious for pummeling people to death. It is right there in his name!"

The art of redirection was a subtle one, and Bea could not decide if Kerrich was a skillful practitioner or a slightly buffoonish man trembling sincerely in fear. Frustrated, she pressed him again for his alibi, adding that they had narrowed the time of the murder to a one-hour window between nine and ten, which was precisely the interval for which he refused to answer.

Kerrich remained adamant. He had been with a young lady of high character and standing, engaging in a perfectly chaste activity of which nobody of decency and breeding could take issue, and he would not have her exposed to the harsh condemnation of coarser minds.

He would sooner go to Newgate!

In truth, he would not.

He had a family to support, and there were school fees and governess's salaries and all the sundry items a wife and mother required to turn herself out in style.

But he would not relent without the threat of imprisonment.

"I really have told you everything I know," Kerrich said on a plaintive whine. "Any further information on the topic can be had only from Mr. Rumpus or Higgins. So may I please be excused? My afternoon was already stuffed with more tasks than I had time for and now I must invent the Stukeley method out of whole cloth to placate Couch, who will ask for citations. He always asks for citations, which means I will have to create supporting materials as well. It will take me hours, and I would like to get started right away if you do not mind, your graces."

They did not.

Bidding him good day, Bea thanked him for his time and wished him luck in devising the new methodology. Already engrossed in his project, he acknowledged her remarks absently and wondered if the Stukeley method could be a variation on the Hoare technique, which took one's local landscape as the starting point for one's academic exploration.

They left him staring out the window, muttering encouragingly to himself.

Jenkins, hailing them as they approached the carriage, frowned when he learned of their next destination, and although he asked if they intended to visit every disreputable resident of London or only the most violent ones, he compliantly took up the reins.

As the wheels clattered into motion, Bea wondered if Kerrich had indeed shared everything or if they would be compelled to question him a third time. "For someone whose role in the scheme is marginal, he is certainly in possession of a lot of information that exceeds his purview. He connected Higgins to Mortimer and knows about the sale to the museum. His alibi is nonexistent as far as we know, he has the best motive, the timing works out, and by consenting to participate in the scheme he has demonstrated a flagrant disregard for morality and legality. And then there is the murder itself, which was messy and poorly planned.

Renfield and Hawes would have made a much cleaner job of it."

"Unless they knew better than to make a clean job of it," Kesgrave pointed out.

The truth could not be denied: Bearing a signature method of attack behooved the killer to vary his technique to escape detection. It was elementary avoidance.

"We have yet to find a persuasive motive for Renfield," she said, proposing the only idea that had occurred to her. "Maybe there is something in the trinkets and the fact that Mortimer did not pass on Kerrich's warning, thereby exposing him to Hell and Fury's harsh disapproval. If Renfield called on Mortimer to chastise him, the exchange might have turned violent. Or perhaps he saw something in the studio that made him realize Mortimer wanted to withdraw from the scheme. If Renfield was as an infrequent visitor as he claimed, then he would not know Mortimer had taken up painting again."

"The second he saw *The Huntress,* Hawes knew Mortimer's renewed interest in painting presented a threat to the scheme," the duke said pensively, adding that it seemed likely Renfield would draw the same conclusion. "If he told Mortimer that the painting must stop, an argument would been inevitable. Convinced that his long-sought goal was within reach, my cousin would never have agreed."

"We know from the incident with the Arabic numbers on the medallion that Renfield does not report minor issues to Hawes," she pointed out. "He might have considered the distractive painting an issue he should address before it became a problem for his employer. Concern for his own welfare might have led him to respond with too much force."

"That is true, yes, but if Renfield feared Hell and Fury's reaction to his prized forger being distracted by painting, then what does killing Mortimer accomplish other than making his predicament a thousand times worse?" Kesgrave asked.

Incapable of providing a cogent response, Bea shrugged and wondered if it was the nature of the beast. "Renfield is a brawler, and brawlers brawl."

It was highly unsatisfying and returned her to her original observation: They did not have a persuasive motive for Renfield.

Arriving at the chief lieutenant's residence, they were greeted by Martha, who opened the door little more than a crack and eyed them balefully. Ignoring the hostile welcome, Bea greeted her cheerfully and asked to see her employer. As much as she wanted to turn them away, the maid recalled her duty, opened the door wide to admit them to the dim hallway, and told them to remain there.

"Don't go wandering about neither!" she snapped.

Reassuringly, Bea murmured, "Of course not."

The obliging response further ruffled the servant's feathers by implying the sullen directive was unnecessary, and Renfield's willingness to receive them did little to improve her temper. Begrudgingly, she led them to his study, where he rose from his desk to greet them amiably. As the day before, he was dressed beautifully, in a well-fitting tailcoat that hugged his broad chest and a loosely tied cravat that emphasized the width of his neck. Taken together, the garments created a refined nonchalance.

In every way, he had adopted Hawes's image of the gentleman thief.

"Two visits in two days," Renfield said, his voice lilting with incredulity. "I suppose it is too much to hope you are here to discuss my proposed business venture?"

"It is," Kesgrave said as they crossed the room.

Sitting down, Bea regarded Renfield across the swath of his desk, which was strewn with papers, and wondered if he had written yet another proposal for their joint venture. Intrigued, she tilted forward as she looked over the assortment, observing that it contained several newspaper articles, a playbill, an envelope with a torn corner, *The Morning Chronicle,* a bill of sale with a lavishly scrawled signature, a shopping list containing six pantry items, a calling card from—

Sharply, she drew her eyes back to the bill of sale, stuck by a humming sense of familiarity. That extravagant swirl—she had seen it before.

Where had she seen it before?

Transfixed by the question, she pressed forward to try to read the name just as Renfield neatened the desk, gathering the various sheets into two messy piles. As he straightened their edges, he said, "Naturally, I am disappointed, but I hold out hope that you will change your mind."

Bea leaned back in her seat as the bill of sale disappeared into the middle of the stack and she forced herself to focus on the conversation.

What had Renfield said?

Something about changing their minds after they had had more time to consider the proposition.

Dampeningly, she explained that they had further questions about Mortimer's death.

If he was disappointed by this turn, Renfield hid it well, noting only that it was correct and proper that the investigation would be uppermost in their minds.

Bea responded with a bland smile and explained that they had acquired new information since their last visit and sought to understand how it pertained to the murder. "We know that Hawes recruited Sir Thomas to make the sale to the British Museum and Sir Thomas, worried that one of the forgeries was not convincing enough, asked Mr. Addleton from the Royal Antiquaries Society to examine it. Mr. Addleton validated the relief but discovered the collection contained other forgeries."

Nodding, Renfield owned himself familiar with the episode and added that he had not been surprised to learn Mortimer's relief had withstood scrutiny. "It underscores how vital his talents were to the success of the enterprise. As I said, Mr. Matlock will be sorely missed."

Although tempted to ask if he knew about the bridle, she decided it was better to proceed in the proper order. First, she wanted to ask about his conversation with Kerrich, who did not know about it. Next, she would ask about how Hawes had actually felt about the egregious mistake.

The crime boss's calm acceptance simply did not sit right with her.

"We spoke to Mr. Kerrich, who is also a member of the society, and he told us he called on you following his colleague's visit to Golden Square to share his concerns regarding the display of Roman artifacts in the shop in Upper Chiltern Street," she said, her eyes drifting toward the stack of papers with the sheet containing the whirling signature.

It was so familiar.

Renfield recalled the meeting. "He was waiting for me on the doorstep and was practically quivering with anxiety. He was very upset about what had happened. He said he knew Higgins was arranging the sale of Mr. Matlock's reliefs to collectors and as such his shop had to be above reproach, which it could not be with Higgins selling his shabby medieval trinkets. When I informed him that they were *my* shabby medieval trinkets, his face lost all color and he apologized and said they were admirable efforts that could withstand a slight improvement. He was happy to advise the forger."

On the phrase *admirable effort,* something snapped into place, for it was precisely the phrase the dowager had used in describing Mortimer's last rejection from the Royal Academy. Samuel Sandby-Smith, damning the sumptuous still life with faint praise, had called it an admirable effort.

That coil of looping letters was his pile of S's.

Why the devil was the esteemed president of the Royal Academy writing bills of sale to Hell and Fury Hawes's chief lieutenant? What business could they have between them?

More to the point: What possible item could Sandby-Smith possess that Rennie Rumpus would not only seek to buy but also could afford?

Perplexed by the connection, she felt certain it somehow related to the murder, which meant she needed to get a better look at the document.

Well, obviously, yes.

But how to manage it?

As Bea considered her options, she asked Renfield how he had responded to Kerrich's offer.

"I assured him Mr. Matlock would welcome his input, as his goal was to make the artifacts as believable as possible," he replied.

Bea stiffened. "You told him Mortimer made the artifacts?"

Renfield smiled thinly and admitted it was shocking, as it violated the isolated branch practice to which Hawes ardently adhered. "But it seemed like the easiest way to address the problem and I appreciated Mr. Kerrich's honesty. When he realized removing all the artifacts from Higgins's shop was untenable, he suggested a more spare display, which seemed reasonable to me. I thanked him for his candor and sent him on his way."

Tuesday, she thought.

Kerrich found out that Mortimer was responsible for the shabby trinkets on the day of the murder, something he had failed to disclose during their two conversations.

Neither fact was without meaning.

And yet she could not dash off to push the antiquarian for the truth until she had a chance to examine the document bearing Sandby-Smith's signature.

That bill of sale was meaningful too.

"What did Hawes say when you discussed it with him?" she asked, wondering if the best approach was to leave the slip of paper for now and return after dark to steal it. With Kesgrave's lockpicking skills, they could break into the house without creating too much of a fuss. Renfield did not appear to employ a large household staff, although the prospect of getting caught by Martha was daunting. And coming back later when they were already in the room struck her as needlessly complicated. At that very moment, she was less than two feet from the desired item.

All she required was a distraction.

An abashed look descended over Renfield's features as he admitted that he had not raised the matter with his employer as he felt implicated by Kerrich's critique. "Everything he said regarding the display made intuitive sense, which meant I should have realized the problem myself. That failure does not reflect well on me, and I called on Higgins immediately to have him remove some pieces. I also advised him to stop selling the Roman artifacts to well-known collectors."

What about the medallion?

Could she ask to see it again or maybe one of the proposals?

They were in the drawer next to his elbow, which meant he would look away for only a few seconds. To find the slip, read it, and return it to the stack would take at least a minute.

Renfield had to leave the room.

That required a pretext.

She could claim intolerable thirst and beg a refreshment.

He would oblige, yes, but most likely by ringing for Martha.

As she contemplated the value of affecting a coughing fit to give her request urgency, she asked if it was unusual for Hawes not to discuss a major development such as one participant in their counterfeit antiquities scheme swindling another participant in their counterfeit antiquities scheme.

"Nothing is unusual for Mr. Hawes," Renfield replied. "He tells us what he thinks we should know, and that varies depending on the circumstance."

"So you are just another branch on the tree," she observed pensively.

Although his lips tightened churlishly at the description, he granted it was accurate. "But one of the thickest branches."

"Of course," she murmured consolingly.

Renfield glared at her and said that developments that seemed significant to her were in fact minor in the context of Hell and Fury's enormous organization, such as Mortimer's murder. With an apologetic look at the duke, he noted that the King of Saffron Hill employed hundreds of men and women who performed scores of vital tasks each day. "It is a regrettable consequence of Mr. Hawes's success that the slaying of a single man cannot make a huge impression on him. For all we know, Mr. Matlock's death was one of several to take place on Tuesday."

Bea, who had hoped to get a sense of Hawes's true feelings about Sir Thomas's drubbing or Higgins's rapaciousness or Mortimer's mistake, was frustrated by the prospect of leaving Renfield's study without acquiring the information she had expressly sought. Learning that Kerrich knew Mortimer was responsible for the Roman forgeries was helpful because it bolstered his motive, but it told her nothing about the crime lord.

Irritated, she resolved to snatch the bill of sale from the pile and stuff it into her pocket.

It was too intriguing to leave behind, and he was unlikely to notice its absence immediately.

In anticipation of nabbing it, she brushed her hand against the side of her gown to confirm the pocket was easily accessible and as her hand brushed her stomach she realized she had the perfect distraction: the cherub.

Unmarried men were often stupefied by breeding females. Consequently, she gurgled.

Well, it was more accurate to say she attempted to gurgle.

In reality, the delicate burble came out as a guttural rumble.

Nonetheless, it served its purpose.

Renfield turned to her abruptly as she pressed an arm meaningfully to her belly.

"I am fine, Mr. Renfield," she said bravely, then winced and grunted again. "It is just a little pressure, a strange sensation, to be sure, but not unheard of given my condition. Do not trouble yourself. I am fine. I was going to ask about your conversation with Higgins."

Understanding flitted across her host's features only to be supplanted at once by confusion and concern. He glanced from Bea to the duke, as if expecting him to instruct him on a suitable reply. Kesgrave, however, was looking at her with an almost identical expression, and wishing to calm his anxiety, she added soothingly, "I get these twinges all the time. There is nothing to worry about, I am sure."

Alas, she did not *sound* sure.

And jolting forward in her chair did little to persuade Renfield she meant it.

Kesgrave, who knew the cherub had caused her no significant physical discomfort, only mental, pressed a hand gently to her shoulder and suggested a drink. Trying to figure out her game, he asked, "Do you think barley water might ease the pressure?"

Clever man.

"Yes, I think that would help," she said, gasping as though in pain. "Please, Mr. Renfield, would you mind getting me a glass?"

Then she inhaled sharply again.

Her host rose unresistingly to his feet and said he would call for Martha right away.

Bea, squealing now, begged him to hurry.

"If you fetch it yourself, it will be faster," Kesgrave said before turning to Bea and directing her to take a deep breath and picture a calming scene, such as a babbling brook or a field at daybreak—just as the physician had advised.

Renfield strode across the room, and as he reached the door, Bea gesticulated wildly, indicating that the duke should follow their host out of the room. Failing to comprehend, he stared at her with a what-the-devil scowl as Renfield turned around to assure her he would not be a minute. She smacked a flailing hand against her forehead and announced that she did not have a fever.

"That is a relief," Kesgrave said, his eyes still baffled by her actions.

Bea jerked up her chin meaningfully.

Illumination struck!

"Let me help you, Renfield," he said, rising to his feet.

Their host demurred, but the duke insisted, and Bea did her best to look pale and weak as she waited for them to step into the hallway. When they finally did, she jumped up and lurched forward, all but throwing her torso onto the desk, and sifting through the pile on the right.

There it was—the bill of sale.

She glanced from the top to the bottom, located the signature, and confirmed it was from Samuel Sandby-Smith.

He had sold Renfield a crystal decanter for two hundred pounds, an astronomical amount for the item. Confounded by the expense, she swept her gaze around the room, as if expecting the glass vessel to immediately make itself known. Something that exorbitant would inevitably stand out.

It did not.

The room contained a few ornamental glass pieces on the shelf to her right and a cabinet next to the window displayed books and clay pipes.

Perhaps it was tucked away in a drawer.

Even as she had the thought, she knew it was immaterial.

A two-hundred-pound decanter did not look like a two-hundred-pound decanter.

Obviously, it was a cloak concealing something quite different.

"... is very comfortable," said Kesgrave, his voice unduly loud and drawing closer as he asked Renfield how long he had resided in Doddington Lane.

They were almost back.

Devil it!

Springing into action, Bea folded the bill of sale, shoved it into her pocket, neatened the edges of the pile, and flung herself back in the seat just as the door swung open. Feeling the rush of anxiety through her body, she waved a hand across her face and announced that she was hot.

"Is it the room or is it me?" she asked.

As Kesgrave handed her the glass of barley water, Renfield generously allowed that the room was a trifle warm.

Bea took a large gulp, then laughed awkwardly as she suggested her embarrassment was responsible for the sudden suffusion of heat coursing through her. "What you must think of me, Mr. Renfield! I style myself as a sort of lady Runner and then succumb to a mortifying female ailment. I cannot thank you enough for your patience!"

He swore it was the least he could do.

She raised the glass to her lips again and sipped deeply, closing her eyes as if actually imagining the meadow as Kesgrave suggested. Then she sighed and announced she felt much better. "The barley water was precisely what I needed. Thank you again, Mr. Renfield, for being so gracious with what I know is an annoyance and inconvenience."

Renfield swore he did not mind her questions in the least. "You want to find out what happened to your relative, and I am happy to help. Where did we leave off?"

"Your conversation with Higgins," she said. "Did you have any concern that your warning against well-known collectors might alert him to Sir Thomas's participation in this scheme?"

His tone rife with condescension, he said, "Your grace, if Sir Thomas were the only well-known collector with whom Higgins consorted on a regular basis, then we would not have secured his assistance. It is because he works with so many of them across the country that he has any value to us."

"I see," Bea murmured, placing the glass on the desk.

Soberly, Renfield said, "I hope you do. Mr. Matlock's murderer is still at large, and from what I can gather, you are more focused on understanding the inner workings of Mr. Hawes's antiquities trade than finding the killer."

It was a fair point—not accurate but fair. She *was* fascinated by the audacity of the enterprise.

Thanking him again for the ready supply of barley water, she rose to her feet. Next to her, Kesgrave hovered anxiously, urging her to proceed with caution in case she felt faint.

"Steady, my love, steady," he murmured, taking hold of her arm suddenly, as though she had been on the verge of tipping over.

Was he doing it a bit brown?

Almost certainly, yes, and as he warned her not to trip

over the threshold, she wondered if her performance had been equally histrionic.

Taking his cue from the duke, Renfield exhorted her to get plenty of rest and have codfish oil at least once a week. "My own mother swore by it!"

Bea received this advice warmly, thanking him yet again for the way he had responded with equanimity to her freakish start. "I cannot say what strange thing came over me, but it has passed now and I feel so much better."

Renfield owned himself relieved to hear it as he stepped back to allow them to slip out of his house. Kesgrave, his grip firmly on Bea's elbow, dipped his head in gratitude at their host and escorted her to the carriage, where Jenkins, noting the excessive concern for the duchess, immediately asked if Bea had swooned.

"She looks pale," he said.

Obviously, no, she did not.

If anything, her complexion was unduly flushed from her exertions, but rather than quibble over his assessment, she said they would called on Samuel Sandby-Smith next as soon as they ascertained his direction. To do that, she assumed they would have to consult either Lady Abercrombie or Stephens, but by a stroke of luck, Kesgrave rattled off his address, much to his groom's disgust.

Jenkins, casting a reproachful glare at his employer, muttered about increasing females keeping punishing paces as he slammed the door to the conveyance shut.

Highly diverted, she warned the duke that he would suffer for his extravagant knowledgeability. "If only you feigned ignorance every once in a while! Now you shall have to take extreme measures to get back into your driver's good graces. May I suggest a new chaise? Just yesterday, Jenkins was complaining to Michael that the suspension on the current one is dashed."

Kesgrave replied that she would have to adjust her understanding of extravagance if his supplying an address qualified. "And rather than mocking me, it would have been more helpful if you reassured him of your continued good health. By morning, the entire staff will be looking daggers at me."

Soberly, she noted that a new oven would not go amiss in the kitchens.

Ignoring this provoking comment, he asked to see what she had stolen from Renfield's desk, and she extracted the bill of sale from her pocket. He studied it silently for several moments, his brow furrowing as the carriage clattered into the road, then stated that he found it difficult to believe the esteemed painter and president of the Royal Academy of Art was corrupt.

"Really?" she asked mildly. "I find it incredibly easy, considering he accepted payments from Lord Myles to keep your cousin out of the annual exhibition."

Fascinated, he said, "Is that what he did?"

"It is what your grandmother intimated last night when she implicated Sandby-Smith in the rejection of Mortimer's gorgeous still life," she said, allowing that her interpretation might be inaccurate. "Previously, she had insisted that Lord Myles was responsible for his son's repeated rejection, although she could not fathom how, and then the president snubbed an acknowledged masterwork. The only explanation that makes sense is that Lord Myles paid Sandby-Smith to reject Mortimer's paintings regardless of their quality. It would certainly fall under his purview as president of the academy."

"Indeed, it would," the duke murmured. "And if he was willing to thwart an artist's lifelong dream in order to line his pockets, then he would not cavil at hawking fake antiquities to unsuspecting collectors. He would need the money, of course, as paintings of historical scenes are not as popular as portraits, which in themselves are not hugely lucrative. Lawrence can charge up to three hundred pounds but most of his contemporaries earn closer to one hundred. As my grandmother mentioned, he inherited a townhouse but not the funds to support it."

Amused by his ability to cite the price of various genres of painting, she nevertheless did not linger on it as she lamented their failure to surmise the existence of other collectors in Hell and Fury's scheme. "Given the scale of his ambition, he is probably working with half a dozen."

"In that case, the bill of sale is a reliable method for delivering a payment without raising suspicions," he said.

"Precisely," she said approvingly, then wondered if she should approach her next conclusion delicately out of concern for Kesgrave's feelings or state it plainly. Finding out that his cousin was a blackmailer on top of a forger might be a disquieting discovery.

Was there nothing decent about his cousin?

The hesitation, however, was unnecessary, for the duke had arrived at the same conclusion, noting that Mortimer's renewed confidence in his work being accepted by the famous institution suggested only one thing: extortion. "He threatened to expose Sandby-Smith's participation in Hawes's scheme if the president did not grant him entry to the annual exhibition."

"Sandby-Smith did," she said.

"And then he began to fear what Mortimer would ask for next?" Kesgrave replied pensively. "Is that what you think his motive is? Having given in to the first demand, he feared the next and the next, and rather than wait for Mortimer to ask for something he could not satisfy, such as making him an academician, he decided it was better to nip the problem in the bud."

"People have their patterns," she observed. "The Wraithe

did not just blackmail one supervisor; she blackmailed them all. I assume Sandby-Smith frequently takes bribes to allow or deny admission. A vast network of malfeasance spanning a decade might have ultimately been exposed, which he could not risk. He would be would be well motived to keep Mortimer silent, and Mortimer would be more determined than ever to free himself from the stigma of Hawes's counterfeit scheme—hence the bridle."

It was another promising lead, and as the carriage turned sharply onto the wider thoroughfare, she felt confident they would have news for the dowager soon.

Chapter Sixteen

Finding Sandby-Smith away from home, Kesgrave left his card and directed Jenkins to take them to Upper Chiltern Street. Twenty minutes later, they entered the antiquities shop, which displayed only a fraction of the artifacts found in Sir Thomas's gallery. Wide and airy, with a high ceiling and parquet floor, the space exuded peace and quiet comfort, with the owner, Arnold Higgins, sitting at a table to the right of the door. Making a notation in his ledger, he looked up serenely to welcome his guests, then gently laid the writing utensil down and rose to his feet. He was a portly man with bushy eyebrows and a crooked nose, about forty years of age and in no rush to show off his wares. Instead, he asked about the weather, if they had traveled very far, and what period of history intrigued them the most.

Kesgrave answered the questions politely as Bea surveyed the wares, noting that the garish assortment of trinkets against which Kerrich had railed were neatly arranged on a black velvet field under a pane of glass. Presumably, the appealing display was in response to Kerrich's critique as delivered by Renfield.

Satisfied with pleasantries, Higgins gestured to a trio of delicate porcelain vases that he identified as being from the Ming dynasty and explained that he had more stock than what they saw in the shop. "I have a warehouse where I store the balance of my offerings, and I have excellent contacts in London and throughout Europe, making it possible for me to fulfil any request. I also support several archaeological digs in far-off regions, which means I have access to new discoveries. I believe nothing is beyond my reach, and I invite you to challenge me with a request, the more esoteric the better."

As he spoke, Bea drifted toward the medieval display and studied the pieces with a critical eye. Knowing they were modern reproductions cast in a plaster mold and aged with acid gave them an arch appearance, as though they were children's toys trying to present as more solemn versions of themselves, a tin monkey endeavoring to look like a gold ape.

"You have excellent taste," Higgins said with approval as he opened the showcase and withdrew the appealing array. He placed the black velvet board on a nearby table and encouraged her to examine the artifacts. "You may pick them up. Do not be shy. As you can see, some are remarkably well preserved. This ampulla, for example"—he held up a small round vessel designed to hold holy water—"is almost in its original condition. I have been lucky in the mudlarks whom I employ. They discovered this piece just last week."

He was an excellent salesman, to be sure, and if Bea had not known any better, she might have been inclined to inquire as to the price of the item.

Declining the invitation, she announced that they were forgeries.

Untroubled by the accusation, the dealer smiled and replied that her cynicism was in no way unique. "People who are new to collecting, as I assume you are, frequently harbor a deep suspicion and assume anything that has been preserved to a reasonable degree is not authentic. I call it the dithers—new collector dithers. You are eager and excited but also anxious and worried about investing funds to grow your collection. If you are not assuaged by my assurances, then I advise you to seek assistance from a trusted source. Do allow me to suggest the Royal Antiquaries Society. They are consummate professionals who will provide you with the necessary education to help you overcome your dithers. And when you do, I hope you will return to my shop."

At the conclusion of this reassuring speech, Bea apologized for failing to introduce themselves properly. "I am the Duchess of Kesgrave and this is my husband, who is cousin to the man who produced these artifacts."

It startled him, the announcement, for his eyes widened to an almost intolerable degree as he shifted his gaze to the door. In every other way, he remained calm, displaying no hint of anxiety.

After a moment during which he drew a deep breath that he exhaled slowly, he said, "Oh, I see. Then there is no point in my offering to show you a certificate of authenticity from the London Guild of Antiquarians. It is very convincing. It bears a crest and a seal. I designed both myself. I am skilled at drawing."

Kesgrave agreed there was little value in providing them with documentation from an organization that did not exist.

Although he had anticipated the refusal, Higgins was nevertheless disappointed by it, and he rounded his shoulders as he returned the artifacts to their case. "I suppose you are inclined to take a hard stance against fraudulence, but I hope you will consider the good that I do by giving patrons who could not ordinarily afford to buy such precious objects the opportunity. You may call it fraud. I call it *thrill and frill*—that is, the thrill of owning a meaningful frill. The problem with the antiquities market is scarcity, as a man of your estimable reputation knows well. Scarcity is what keeps prices high. As a corrective, I provide abundance, so a less prosperous collector can gather together enough guineas to purchase one. That is how I believe it should be. These medallions, coins, ampullae, and badges are a part of English history, which belongs to all of us. If you believe it is a crime for the people of a country to own their own history, then I must insist that you arrest me at once, your graces. I am prepared to go to prison in support of my principles. I just ask that you allow me to lock up my shop so that everything does not get stolen during my imprisonment. Upper Chiltern Street is not the safest in London."

As this high-minded protestation rang hollow to Bea, she was tempted to accept his challenge and cart him off to Bow Street. She resisted the impulse only because it would waste her and the duke's time. "We do not *intend* to arrest you," she said with pointed emphasis, leaving open the possibility that their plans could change.

In an instant, the dealer's demeanor altered as he seemed to dissolve into a puddle of relief. "Oh, thank goodness! I am not prepared to go to jail at all, especially for a principle that I know is errant nonsense. I was just trying to appear brave. Inside I was trembling in terror. Indeed, I still am. It is like the dithers but much worse," he said, laying a hand flat on the display cabinet, as if to hold himself up. "But you do want to *ask* me about the forgeries, don't you? There really is not much I can tell you, as evidence by the fact I had no idea who makes them. You say it is your cousin, your grace? That is remarkable and may I also add shocking."

Kesgrave invited him to tell them what he did know, as limited as it was.

A hunted look washed over the dealer as he again glanced at the front door before reiterating that it was almost nothing. "I get a delivery every other week, usually on a Monday."

"And?" Bea said coaxingly.

Higgins shrugged. "And nothing. I get a delivery every other Monday morning, although twice it has come on a Tuesday."

Annoyed by his deliberate obtuseness, she asked who brought the shipment, how it arrived, what it typically contained, and when the deliveries began.

"Six months ago," he said, answering out of order. "I got the first delivery in January. They come in a valise. It is brown leather, well oiled with brass buckles and tight stitches. Each delivery contains a dozen, but the assortment varies. Sometimes it is a dozen medallions and a few of the others, or it's an equal number of each. They are brought by a man called Underhill, John Underhill. He helps me unpack the valise in the storeroom and then joins me in a cup of tea and then leaves. We talk about the events of the day, usually what absurd thing Boney is trying to do. That is truly all I know."

"What about Renfield?" she asked.

He regarded her blankly. "I'm sorry, who?"

"Edmund Renfield," she clarified. "He is Hell and Fury Hawes's second in command."

"You mean Rennie Rumpus!" he exclaimed.

"I do, yes," she confirmed flatly. "How often are you in contact with him?"

"Never! Whyever would I be in contact with a ruthless brute like that?" he asked.

Bea gestured to the display of medieval trinkets. "He represents Hawes, with whom you have partnered in a counterfeit antiquities scheme."

The dealer whirled his head to the right, to look at the duke, and begged him to deny her grace's claim. "Rennie Rumpus can't have anything to do with it. Neither he nor Hawes. As I said, it is Underhill. He and his friends came up with the idea while they were looking for artifacts under the dock near Wapping. They realized it would be an easy way to make money and to spread the joy of collecting to people who could not ordinarily afford it. They make the baubles themselves!"

Bea tsked softly and lamented how ill-suited Higgins was for illegal activity if he could not keep his information coherent for more than a few minutes. "Previously, you told us that you had no idea who made the artifacts and now you are saying it was Underhill and his friends."

Although he acknowledged the inconsistency with a wince, he adopted an aggressive pose, snarling with testy impatience that he would say anything to escape the conversation without causing harm to himself. "And you are not helping, your grace! It is as though you *want* to get me in trouble with my business associates. Well, I happen to like having all my fingers and toes, and if that makes me eccentric, so be it! Now please leave me in peace."

Kesgrave said they could not do that, for his cousin was dead and they were investigating his murder, an explanation that caused the dealer to rear forward in terror. "Good God! And now you are here, trying to get me killed? I say, your grace, that is poorly done of you. Very poorly done."

"No one is trying to kill you," Bea said soothingly.

The assurance had no effect on the dealer, who begged them to leave. "You may take the ampulla as a gift in parting. If it is not to your taste, then please give it to your housekeeper or groom. I am sure they would be grateful. Now good day!"

Kesgrave insisted they would not leave until they had the information they sought. "We have questions about the scheme and your place in it."

"You are determined to persecute me over nothing!" Higgins cried in distress. "All I have done is provide my customers with lovely baubles. They do not care if a medallion was made four centuries ago or four days as long as it looks authentic. I would not have agreed to sell them if I did not believe they would bring people pleasure. Thrill and frill, your grace. Thrill and frill!"

As there was nothing to be gained from alienating him further, Bea allowed him this fiction, noting that pleasure was a lovely thing to bestow. Then she asked him again about his relationship with Renfield. Horrified, the dealer took passionate issue with her describing a few brief encounters as a relationship.

They were barely acquaintances!

When it became clear to him, however, that their graces would not leave until he told them everything he knew about Renfield and Hawes, he invited them to sit down at his table. He would make some tea. He just had to fetch the kettle from the storeroom. "I won't be a minute," he said brightly, a pledge that seemed at odds with the fact that he closed the door behind him and then promptly locked it.

Calling to them through the wood panel, he apologized for changing the plan so abruptly, but he just remembered he had pressing work to do with his inventory. "Please take a vase on your way out for your trouble. Any one at all!"

Coolly, Kesgrave withdrew a slim device from his pocket and made quick work of the lock. Stepping inside the room, which was stacked from floor to ceiling with wooden shelves holding everything from statuettes to candlesticks, they found Higgins with a ledger in his grasp, furiously scrawling on the page. Looking up, he affected surprise and said with unconvincing sincerity, "Oh, was there something else you wanted?"

Bea responded in kind, making no reference to his desperate attempt to escape their interest by burrowing in the narrow back room like a rabbit. "Yes, we were waiting for you to tell us about your acquaintanceship with Mr. Renfield."

Utterly despondent, he sighed heavily as he closed the book and placed it on a shelf next to a clock with gold trim. "Do you want a drink, your graces? No, no, it's not another trick. I keep whiskey back here. If you do not object, I will pour myself a glass. Dutch courage, as they say."

Although she made no objection, Bea did observe that the dealer's reaction seemed excessive in light of the situation. "As the duke said, we are only seeking information. Even if you are conspiring to bring down Hawes's empire from the stockroom of your shop, it is no business of ours. We are investigating Mortimer's murder. You may start with the reliefs, as we know about them as well."

The smile elicited by the notion of anyone overthrowing the King of Saffron Hill, let alone an antiquities dealer with a faint heart, was immediately supplanted by a grimace. "You know about that as well, do you? I suppose the reliefs were also your cousin's handiwork?"

Kesgrave confirmed that they were.

"A talented fellow," Higgins said before finishing the fiery liquid in a single gulp. "If I did not say so before, I am sorry for your loss."

The duke received his condolences with a nod.

Higgins refilled his glass and said, "Three—that is the total number of times I have met Renfield, and each subsequent meeting has been shorter than the last. The first was right after Hawes approached me about selling the reliefs in December of 1813. He said he had been watching me for a few weeks and knew I was too clever to refuse an opportunity with so much earning potential. When I expressed interest in hearing more, he introduced me to Renfield, who supplied the details of the arrangement, complete with rates and commissions. Finding the terms satisfactory, I agreed to move forward on the condition that we proceed cautiously on account of the limited nature of the market for Assyrian reliefs. Unlike Roman artifacts, which sell as soon as I place them on display, the reliefs are collected by a particular sort of buyer. So I said I would sell one to a collector in the north with whom I had done business in the past and then wait a few weeks to see if he grew suspicious. No alarm was raised, so we decided it was safe to move forward with another sale, waiting less time to see if the forgery was detected. After that, we communicated through Underhill, who delivers the reliefs as well as the artifacts. Slowly, we expanded the territory, drawing closer to London, but still keeping a safe distance from the capital. I must say, it has been far easier to pull the wool over collectors' eyes than I had anticipated. At first, I was all dithers, but they slowly subsided as time passed."

Bea assumed it was the dealer's sterling reputation, accrued over the decades he had been in business, that made the process so effortless. Trust could not be purchased. "And the medieval artifacts? When did your apprehension about them recede?"

The dealer waved his hand in vague dismissal. "Oh, those trifles! They have never given me a moment of anxiety. The customer for that sort of thing lacks discernment. Nobody looks closely at a badge or an ornamental sword hilt when it costs them only four or five pounds. When Renfield showed me the medallions, I said I would be happy to display them in my store. That was the second time we met, by the way. It was in December of last year, and he called on me here. The third was just a few days ago, when he advised me to trim my display of the medieval artifacts. It had occurred to him that perhaps having so many in the case made them seem a little too abundant. I explained that was part of their appeal, but he was adamant, so I obliged."

As this aligned with the information provided by Renfield and Kerrich, she nodded and asked what else Renfield had discussed with him during his visit on Tuesday.

Higgins tilted his eyes down to examine the liquid in his glass as his cheeks turned a bright shade of red. "He told me to stop selling forgeries to Sir Thomas."

"Did he?" she asked, surprised by the forthright request, which differed from Renfield's account.

"Not in so many words," the dealer hastened to add. "But I know my clientele and he is the only collector of any repute to whom I have sold Roman artifacts. I knew I was courting danger, as he is famous for his acumen, but it was irresistible. He was so smug about them, buying several at once because he thought I had undervalued them in my pricing. As he believed he was exploiting my ignorance, I was compelled to exploit his."

Sir Thomas's shrewdness and gullibility were a curious combination, and she wondered again if Mortimer had known the identity of the collector to whom the erroneous relief would be given.

"In light of Renfield's request, I have to think Sir Thomas realized he had been hoodwinked," he continued, a glimmer of amusement in his eyes as the whiskey worked its effects. "I would have liked to witness that moment. He must have been beside himself with fury."

"Do you know why Renfield is interested in Sir Thomas?" she asked.

Higgins claimed he did not, although he assumed Hawes planned to soak him for a lot of money and did not want him worrying about forgeries. "The other possibility is Sir Thomas is also involved in the trade, but I would never presume to speculate about something that is none of my business."

The answer implied the dealer knew nothing of the sale to

the British Museum—or that he was clever enough not to provide information that was not explicitly sought.

"Have you sold anything to Samuel Sandby-Smith?" she asked.

"He does not buy. He sells," Higgins replied. "Primarily antiquities from the collection his mother left to him. He works exclusively with Joseph Dagnall, who earns a tidy commission on the sales. I have tried to lure Sandby-Smith away by promising a higher return, but he has as yet been unreceptive. I will have no chance at all if he discovers I am in league with Hawes."

It was amusing, the notion that Higgins was too corrupt for Sandby-Smith.

"I suppose he will find out," the dealer added, staring morosely into the glass. "You will have to mention it to someone, won't you, as you are trying to identify your cousin's killer. How long before I am ruined? A couple of weeks or a few days? I should like to move as much stock as possible before it is too late and perhaps even sell the shop to a competitor. Dagnall made an offer for it years ago."

Bea ventured it would probably be a few days, noting that it was impossible to say how events would unfold. For the most part, it depended on how quickly they identified Mortimer's murderer and surrendered him to the authorities. As soon as the charges were laid against the killer, the newspapers would have the story and delight in the scandal.

It was not every day that the Duke of Kesgrave's first cousin was slain in an illicit forgeries scheme involving the King of Saffron Hill and the British Museum.

Resigned, Higgins sighed and, raising his glass to drink more whiskey, realized he had already finished it. Rather than pour another refill, he drank straight from the bottle. "I cannot imagine Mr. Hawes is delighted with any of this. Do you think he will hold me responsible for the demise of his business in some way? I have done everything he has asked, but Renfield *was* displeased with the Roman display. Maybe Hawes is upset by it too?"

Although nothing can account for the whims of an all-powerful crime lord, Bea believed the arrangement of two dozen medieval trinkets was not foremost in his mind.

The dealer appeared relieved by her opinion.

Bea announced that they would get out of his way as soon as he provided his whereabouts on Tuesday between nine-fifteen and ten-fifteen, and although he readily cited his wife, he flinched when he realized they would have to confirm. There would be no hiding the truth about his descent into iniquity with Her Outrageousness seeking confirmation of his alibi.

The thought agitated him again and he slumped over in his seat, knocking over the bottle of whiskey, which Kesgrave caught before it shattered on the floor. Higgins thanked him for his assistance, then bid them goodbye.

Leaving the dealer to his misery, they returned to their carriage, where the duke instructed Jenkins to take them to his grandmother's house. Once they were on their way, Bea said they could eliminate Higgins from their list. "We will confirm his alibi as a matter of course, but he does not seem to know enough about the scheme to target Mortimer. Nor does he appear to have a motive. I think Kerrich is our best suspect, followed by Sandby-Smith. I do wish he had been home when we called. The fact that he is known for selling pieces from his personal collection makes him an ideal conspirator because the provenance is undisputable. I do not suppose we can try again?" she asked as the academician's residence was not far from the dowager's. "He might have returned."

Kesgrave noted it had been barely an hour and a half since their first attempt.

Annoyed by how little time had passed, Bea frowned and suggested Kerrich as an alternative. "We have to question him again now that we know Renfield told him Mortimer made the trinkets."

The duke suggested the interview could wait until morning, as he wanted to call on his grandmother before it grew much later. "I do not want her to feel obligated to serve us a meal."

"You are right, of course," she replied instantly, mortified that she had not thought of that herself. "We shall keep the visit brief, then, and allow her to have a quiet evening."

Entering the drawing room in Clarges Street, however, she revised the duration of their stay to mere seconds when she spotted her aunt standing before the fireplace with the *Cheapside Advertiser* in hand, reading aloud from Mrs. Flimmer-Flam's most recent report. Russell was there, on the settee next to the dowager, and Flora occupied an armchair to their left. Across from her sat Uncle Horace.

Dear lord, it was all of them, every Hyde-Clare.

Her instinct was to turn tail and run.

Kesgrave, perhaps sensing the impulse toward cowardice, laid a reassuring hand on her back.

Or was he pushing her forward?

Flora spotted them in the doorway first and ran to welcome her cousin, throwing her arms around Bea in an overly enthusiastic welcome that served as a ruse for her to convey secret information. "You are running out of time to dissuade Lady Abercrombie from her course. Mrs. Ralston was coming to tea today and would have surely asked Mama about the house party at Haverill Hall. That is why we are here. I had to propose an outing that would take precedence," she said in a breathless spurt before pulling away and apologizing to the duke for allowing her concern to get the better of her. "You must brace yourself for disheartening news, my dear. Your admirer Mrs. Flimmer-Flam uttered her first critique of you in this morning's paper."

Briefly, Bea squeezed Flora's hand in gratitude as she imagined the combination of outrage, self-pity, and moral certitude with which Aunt Vera would react if she discovered she had been excluded from the event at the duke's estate. Her relative would ardently insist she understood, for someone like her had no business attending an august country gathering of the beau monde, despite standing as a parent to one of the hosts. She would just be a nuisance, saying all the wrong things and embarrassing her niece, whom she had already forgiven for choosing social advancement over familial affection.

She would not have invited herself either!

Picturing the scene, Bea shuddered with dread, which drew a curious glance from Kesgrave, and Flora continued as though her cloying behavior were in no way unusual. "Mama was sharing the story with her grace because she knows how much she enjoys gossip. We are here to pay our condolences and are doing our best to distract her from her grief. I think we are succeeding because after listening to Russell and me bicker over his boring lessons with Gentleman Jackson—"

"They are dashed interesting!" her brother insisted.

Flora rolled her eyes. "To you maybe because you are a puppy who enjoys fisticuffs. But her grace is fantastically old and not only had sons who took instruction but is also grand-mother to arguably the finest Corinthian in London. I am certain she knows all about boxing."

Although Aunt Vera flinched at her daughter's tactless description of their host, she left it to her husband to chastise the girl for her rudeness, which he did with snappish impa-tience. Then he apologized to the dowager for subjecting her to his heathen offspring and explained to Bea and the duke that it was the third such mea culpa he had been compelled to offer. "Her grace has been tireless in her patience, merely noting that Flora and Russell's squabbling affirmed for her the wisdom of having children farther apart in years, which your hen-witted cousin took as a compliment," he added in disgust.

"All affirmations are positive," Flora replied matter-of-factly, as though stating a well-known aphorism.

Uncle Horace sighed as he rose to his feet and announced that they should be on their way. "We have been here for more than an hour."

But his progeny would hear none of it.

Flora argued that her mother must be allowed to finish her dramatic reading of Mrs. Flimmer-Flam's column, as she captured the author's faintly disapproving tone so beautifully.

And Russell—he could not possibly deprive her grace of a demonstration of the pugilistic maneuver he had just mastered. "It is called the block-hand."

"More like the blockhead," Flora murmured.

Uncle Horace, keenly aware that he had lost control of the situation, looked at his wife beseechingly, as if pleading with her to intervene.

Amused, Bea thought it was the first time the Hyde-Clare patriarch had ever sought his spouse's assistance, and to his frustration, it fell well short of achieving its objective. Aunt Vera, still preening at her daughter's compliment, concentrated exclusively on the newspaper article, her lips moving silently as she practiced her lines.

The dowager, taking pity on the beleaguered man, begged him not to rush off on her account. "I am grateful to your children, as their quarreling has chased off Maria, which is a considerable accomplishment as she is hard of hearing. Furthermore, Miss Hyde-Clare is correct. I do like gossip and wish to hear what else Mrs. Flimmer-Flam has to say about my granddaughter. Her wit is not as biting or sharp as Mr. Twaddle-Thum's, but beggars cannot be choosers."

"More affirmation!" Flora said with a triumphant sparkle.

Defeated, Uncle Horace lowered slowly to his chair.

That will teach him to leave the house in the company of his family, Bea thought humorously as she stepped farther into the room, Kesgrave's hand still warm on her back. Together, they crossed to the settee to greet the dowager, who shifted in her seat as though determined to rise. At the duke's directive, however, she ceased her efforts and allowed them to lean over to place a brisk kiss on her cheek. Russell stood to make room for them on the sofa as her grace noted that Bea must be tired, for she looked a little pale.

Even with her attention focused elsewhere, Aunt Vera heard the comment and said that her niece had always been an unsettlingly wan child.

Bea smothered a smile at the familiar lament as the dowager prescribed tea as a curative, and just as her grace asked Russell to pull the cord to summon the housekeeper, Sutton appeared on the threshold with a tray. She instructed the butler to place the teapot and cups on the table and to inform the housekeeper that they would be seven for dinner. Although Horace swore it would be wrong to stay, she told him it would be wicked to leave. "As I said, the clamor keeps Maria away and I will not allow you to abandon me to a meal alone with her. Of course, if you have made other arrangements for the evening, then you must go. I have no intention of holding you hostage."

Aunt Vera, folding the newspaper in her hand, accepted the invitation, adding that they had nothing planned. "Only whist with Mr. and Mrs. Venicombe."

As the female half of the couple was in fact cousins with one of the hostesses at Almack's, the description did not apply, as cards with her was actually quite something, and Bea waited for her relative to give the Venicombes their proper due before clarifying that she did not mean to imply that they were something more than the Dowager Duchess of Kesgrave. Then she would expend several sentences exalting her grace before falling into an awkward silence.

However, she did not.

Aunt Vera, grasping the *Cheapside Advertiser* in one hand, walked to an empty chair, sat down smoothly, and laid the paper on her lap. "I am sure my children will oblige you with endless sniping, but if they succumb to an unprecedented fit of amiability with each other, I shall ask for a demonstration of the block-hand."

Was that a sally?

Did Vera Hyde-Clare make a joke about her own cantankerous children while sitting in the dowager's impossibly opulent drawing room, the veins of its elegant marble from Livorno, Italy, matched perfectly under her feet?

Was that actually what had just happened?

Apparently, so, yes, for her grace tittered in appreciation and said she was relying on Vera to ensure a proper cacophony. And then Russell stiffly replied that the maneuver was meant to be performed in silence, for that was part of its advantage—it took its target unaware—and Flora called him a blockhead again for not following the direction of the conversation.

Pleased, Vera turned to the dowager and said, "There, you see, I am fulfilling my function already. Now if my niece and your grandson do not object, I think we should return to Mrs. Flimmer-Flam's examination of Bea's astrological chart. It is informative and explains so much about her erraticism."

Bea was so stunned by Aunt Vera's concision, by the way she neither rambled nor rattled, that she paid no heed to the subject of the gossip's article. She was trying to fathom how the very thing that discomfited everyone else in the world—

untimely death and the particular grief that accompanied untimely death—somehow calmed her relative. At the moment when other people lost their composure, Vera Hyde-Clare gained hers.

It was bewildering.

And it had happened before, when the dowager had needed a companion to escort her to the Cambridgeshire estate to oversee the burial of Lord Myles. Vera had volunteered for the task even though she was a wretched traveler, grumbling constantly about the holes in the road, and easily awed by consequence.

Bea had assumed she would make the journey miserable for herself and her grace.

Instead, she had comported herself handsomely, providing the dowager with both the material and emotional support she had required to lay her son to rest.

Disconcerted by Aunt Vera's bizarre equanimity, Bea also found it oddly comforting. If her relative was able to exceed the limitations of her character, then the possibility existed for everyone. Temperaments were not fixed like buildings but mutable like trees.

On this encouraging thought, she accepted a cup of tea from the dowager and sipped at it gently as her aunt read through an assortment of traits applicable to people born under the zodiac sign of Leo.

Passionate, loyal, vivacious, theatrical, fiery, creative, dominant—one by one, Mrs. Flimmer-Flam described these qualities and ascribed them to Bea.

The praise was fulsome and flattering, for the murder duchess was capable of great feats, but Bea could see what Flora meant about the hint of criticism. There was something slightly ominous about her grace's tenacity. What if she *was* actually capable of anything?

What horrors would she propagate?

In truth, Bea was not surprised the gossip had adopted the vaguely menacing tone. As Mr. Twaddle-Thum had ably demonstrated, Her Outrageousness was always a noteworthy subject, and if Mrs. Flimmer-Flam did not have the elaborate network of spies available to a former agent of the Alien Office, then she would have to rely on whatever nonsense was at her fingertips.

Bea's correct zodiac sign, alas, was not among the items within the gossip's reach, for she had misjudged her subject's sign. Born on July 10, Bea was a Cancer.

Reassured by the sloppiness, she listened quietly and joined the dowager in lauding Aunt Vera's performance. Russell, impatient with the triviality—for goodness sake, who had even ever heard of the newspaper from Cheapside—asked if he could demonstrate the block-hand *now*.

Before Flora could issue yet another cutting set-down, Sutton appeared to invite them to the dining room for dinner.

Chapter Seventeen

As her fencing instruction was both physically and mentally grueling, Bea was not able to present herself to the drawing room until well after nine-thirty. Lily, troubled by the flush of exertion in her employer's cheeks, which she considered as excessively unducal, insisted she sit by the window for ten minutes to return her complexion to its usual pristineness.

Only then would she consent to dress her.

As she was allowed to enjoy tea along with a book during the prescribed interlude, Bea did not object to expending the time. Indeed, she was a little warm from her lesson and appreciated the brush of chilly air against her heated skin.

Her hair, of course, took a little longer than usual to arrange because its curls had escaped their pins in all that parrying and thrusting, and by the time she arrived down-stairs to greet her guest, Samuel Sandby-Smith had been cooling his heels in the drawing room for almost thirty minutes.

He did not mind at all.

Of course he did not!

He had presented himself to the residence without warning, admitting not even the slightest courtesy such as a missive or the gallantry of an invitation.

It was the height of presumption, and yet how could he have acted otherwise?

He had been seeking an excuse to set foot inside Kesgrave House for years.

"The awful truth is, any pretext would have done," he said, waiting for Bea to make herself comfortable on the settee before sitting down himself. "If I could have come up with a reason that had the faint whiff of legitimacy, I would have intruded years ago. Alas, I could never think of anything, and being a creature who is not without shame, I would never be so brazen as to simply knock and request entry. That is why I am here now. When my butler informed me of your visit, I knew it was a golden opportunity. I hope you are not offended by my candor. I find I have no patience for subterfuge."

"Not at all," Bea said smoothly. "I tend toward directness myself."

"Oh, yes, I know," he replied, his green, deep-set eyes twinkling with amusement as he admitted he had read all of Mr. Twaddle-Thum's reports. He was a handsome man, with graying auburn hair sweeping over his ears and a sharp nose. "When you and the duke wed, I hoped he would host a ball in your honor and that would allow me entry, but it quickly became apparent to me and the *ton* that you had more important things to occupy your time. I find your investigative spirit fascinating, your grace. It is unlike a young woman to be interested in grisly things. And yet you are so lovely as well. I would not know by looking at you that you enjoy staring at beheaded corpses."

As this charge had been laid against her at least a dozen times, most frequently by her own family, she felt no impulse to protest and simply accepted it as fact. Instead, she asked him about his interest in the house. She did not want to begin the interrogation until Kesgrave returned from his ride in Hyde Park.

His eyes sparkled brightly as he tilted his head up and looked at the frescoes decorating the ceiling. "You sit beneath these glorious works by Zick and ask me what my interest in your home is. Despite your pledge to speak frankly, you are being disingenuous, your grace. Everything in this house is a wonder. This room alone is a trove. I have spent the past half hour exploring it, and while I am delighted to not only make your acquaintance but also get to know you, I do wish you had taken a little longer to attend to me. Are you absolutely certain you do not have one more pressing matter to see to? Perhaps a letter you have been meaning to write?"

Bea knew she was supposed to find him charming.

His open demeanor, his unrestrained enthusiasm, his willingness to poke fun at himself—these behaviors were meant to endear him to her.

She imagined most people, women mainly, found him irresistible.

Perhaps she would have too if she did not know him to be corrupt. Even if it turned out that he did not kill Mortimer, he had conspired with Lord Myles to thwart a young man's most cherished desire, and that was enough to earn her disgust.

Nevertheless, she smiled politely and dangled the possibility of a tour. "Marlow would be happy to show you a few more of the public rooms if there is time."

His eyes glowed even as he made a pretense of declining. "I could not possibly, not after imposing on your hospitality without warning. I flirted with sending a note beforehand, but I feared you would refuse. So you must not reward me."

"Very well," Bea said with a glance at the clock. It was

almost ten o'clock, which meant Kesgrave should appear soon. He usually returned from the park at around now. "I rescind the offer."

Chuckling, Sandby-Smith said, "Now I am the one being disingenuous. Of course I should like nothing more and am grateful to you for making the offer. As I said, I do not deserve it but am happy to take advantage of your kindness, so much so that I am going to ask about La Reina. Is she here?"

Startled, she stared at him blankly, uncertain she had heard him correctly.

He rushed to explain. "Reynolds's painting of the duke's mother. Is it hanging in the London house or at Haverill Hall? As he held my position at the Royal Academy before me, I take a particular interest in his work. I wish I could say I had an opportunity to get to know him well, but we overlapped only briefly. His portrait of La Reina is reported to be a thing of wonder. If it is here—and in a public space—then I would love to see it. To be candid, it was one of the reasons I called rather than reply with a note with my availability, as you and the duke had requested."

Bea, who knew the painting well, for she passed it daily on the first-floor landing, was further taken aback by the work's repute. To be fair, Reynolds had rendered his subject expertly, his skilled hand seeming to capture the fine detail of each hair in the mane of the large black steed next to which La Reina stood. And the silk of her vibrant red dress shimmered with inviting warmth.

Your hand itched to touch it.

But the composition itself—the tiny woman in the shadow of the great beast—was grandiose and silly, and she had often marveled at Reynolds's willingness to gratify La Reina's ego at the expense of his own artistic integrity. That inclination no doubt explained his success as a society portraitist.

"The painting is here, yes," she confirmed just as Kesgrave strode into the room.

Sandby-Smith darted to his feet to bid the duke an apologetic hello, his voice brimming with self-deprecation as he announced his overweening enthusiasm to see the many treasures contained within the house for himself. "Do not blame my parents for my appalling manners. They raised me better!"

As he made the deprecating remark, his eyes drifted upward to admire the fresco on the ceiling and he lowered his chin purposefully, as if yanking his gaze away from the scene overhead. "I hope you will be generous and overlook my faux pas. But that is neither here nor there! Your grace wishes to speak to me about a particular subject and I am at your disposal. What can I tell you?"

Before the duke could reply, Marlow entered with a tray of rout cakes and strawberries, and Bea felt the rebuke keenly. She had barely put anything in her mouth all morning, only a slice of toast before her fencing lesson and half a glass of milk following it. Sandby-Smith's sudden appearance had pushed all thoughts of breakfast from her mind.

Well, that, and Lily's churlishness over the state of her curls, for the fifteen minutes the maid had been allotted to return her employer's locks to their usual neatness was not sufficient to accomplish-the task to her high standards.

Bea's stomach rumbled in anticipation as the butler placed the plate of cakes on the table before her, and she thanked him for his consideration. She leaned forward to examine the strawberries as Kesgrave offered their guest tea.

Sandby-Smith accepted gratefully, noting it was more than he deserved for his intolerable impertinence of calling without even a by your leave. "I must say, Kesgrave, that the charity with which I have been received by you and your lovely wife has convinced me I could have appeased my curiosity years ago by simply requesting admission to your home. Once again, the frank approach wins out," he said before turning his attention to the porcelain and observing its quality. "Even your teaware is magnificent. It is Meissen, is it not? The rose pattern is a classic. I am fond of it myself. Thank you. The tea is also exquisite. I do believe I could sit in this chair all day—the damask is superb; it is Italian, I suppose—and stare at your ceiling while drinking your tea. But I am mindful of your time and have no wish to try your patience. Please tell me what the purpose of your call was yesterday, so I can be helpful to you and justify my visit."

Kesgrave, returning the teapot to the salver, replied that they wanted to know more about his relationship with Renfield, an explanation that elicited only a confused frown. Helpfully, the duke provided the subject's full name, but that did little to shed light on the matter for Sandby-Smith, who swore he did not know anyone called Edmund Renfield.

Impatient with his subterfuge, Bea said, "Rennie Rumpus."

Now Sandby-Smith brushed his right middle finger across his eyebrow and owned himself most intrigued. "He sounds like an intriguing character. Do say more."

Obligingly, Kesgrave added that he was Hell and Fury Hawes's chief lieutenant, which drew another blank stare from the painter as he wondered whom the duke meant. Then he shook his head promptly and confessed he was teasing.

"I do know who Hawes is," he asserted confidently. "I keep abreast of the news and have several friends with dealings in Saffron Hill. None of them have encountered Hawes personally, but they report his presence is felt everywhere. A finger in every pie, as the saying goes. But I cannot conceive why you would think I know any of his associates. I am an artist and an academician, respected in my field and by the wider society in which I live. I do not consort with thieves."

As denials were commonplace in an investigation, she did not waste her breath refuting the fabrication, preferring instead to lay the proof of his flagrantly false claim on the table before him. Sandby-Smith did not immediately recognize the bill of sale and bent his head to the side as he tilted forward to get a better look at the slip of paper. His unkempt hair fell forward, momentarily shielding his face from view. Then he leaned back and said with sudden comprehension, "Oh, you mean Eddie!"

It was, to his credit, a convincing enough performance. The artist appeared genuinely surprised to learn the subject of the conversation. His amusement upon discovering it was a particularly effective touch.

Even so, Bea was not fooled.

Sandby-Smith was a thoroughly dishonest customer, and curious to see what sort of defense he would mount, she replied with deceptive amiability, "Yes, we mean Eddie."

"You should have made that clear from the beginning," he said chidingly, looping a finger though the delicate handle of the teacup. "I forgot that he is called Edmund Renfield or that he goes by that horrible appellation Rennie Rumpus. I only know him as Eddie. But you are right to question me about the sale because I took shameless advantage of him."

Intrigued, she replied, "Did you?"

"Quite, quite shameless," Sandby-Smith replied, nodding fervently as he returned the teacup to its saucer and brushed his brow yet again. "He knows nothing about cut glass. He could not tell a decanter from a pitcher, let alone the work of Perrin, Gedes and Company from Peter Seaman and Company. But he is so eager to assume the trappings of wealth, it was a little thing to persuade him that three hundred pounds was a fair price for the piece, which he was happy to pay because he believed he was getting a bargain. I allowed myself to be swayed by his superior intellect into accepting fifty pounds less than I originally asked. Mine was not the most gentlemanly behavior, but all parties were satisfied, so I do not see the value in kicking up a fuss."

"How clever," she said admiringly.

He accepted her praise as his due. "I am an artist and frequently engage in protracted negotiations to sell my work."

"And is that how you met Mr. Renfield?"

Having failed to anticipate the query, Sandby-Smith looked momentarily nonplussed before seizing onto the explanation she had provided. "We wrangled over one of my paintings. As I said, he craves the trappings of wealth. But in the end he could not afford it, and *Scenes from the Life of Saint John the Baptist* went to Plunkett instead."

"Fascinating," Bea murmured.

"Is it?" Sandby-Smith replied with a self-conscious chuckle.

"Well, Eddie, as you call him, could easily spend three hundred pounds on a decanter and yet one hundred pounds for one of your paintings was beyond his means," she noted thoughtfully. "It makes me question his understanding of ostentation. In terms of displaying his wealth—the trappings, that is—an artwork by the great Samuel Sandby-Smith would draw more attention than a decanter regardless of how pretty it is."

The artist, who firmly agreed, observed that it was impossible to account for the vicissitudes of personal preference. "At the risk of seeming immodest, I would also consider one of my paintings a better investment. But everyone is different!"

"That is so true, Mr. Sandby-Smith, so true," she said with a marveling shake of her head. "Remind me how you met

Eddie? Was it at the annual exhibition? He mentioned that he attends regularly."

As happenstance would have it, it was indeed the annual exhibition!

"I approached him in my capacity as president," he explained, holding the teacup lightly as he settled into his story. "I would do that from time to time to stay abreast of the public's interests, which I felt was my responsibility as head of the institution. My successor does not take the same approach to cultivating a wider audience for our work. But as we just said, everyone is different."

"I suppose it was during that conversation when he indicated he wanted to increase his status by acquiring impressive objects of significant value, such as the decanter," she replied as though the reasoning were impeccable. "Was he interested in buying one of the paintings on display and the topic progressed from there?"

Remarkably, this speculation also proved accurate, with Sandby-Smith asserting that was precisely what had happened. "It was not unusual, as many of those who attend the exhibition are hoping to find works to adorn their drawing rooms."

"And it is a short step from paintings to glassware," Bea said knowledgeably.

Before Sandby-Smith could endorse this account as well, Kesgrave said her name with a hint of exasperation, then informed the artist that he was being led down the garden path. "My wife is deliberately supplying you with answers she knows to be false to prove you are lying. She finds it entertaining and could no doubt do it all day. But I do not share her patience. Now, we know you are in league with Renfield in a forged antiquities scheme. No, do not try my patience further by denying it," he added with a faint snap when the artist opened his mouth to protest.

Sandby-Smith swore he would do no such thing. "How can I deny what I do not understand? Forged antiquities? I do not even know what those words mean."

Despite his warning, the duke received the other man's protestations of innocence calmly and helpfully defined the term to remove the possibility of further incomprehension. "It refers to the artifacts given to you by Renfield or his associates to sell to other collectors at a profit to yourself. They were made by Mortimer Matlock. You remember Mortimer, do you not? You dashed his hopes of being accepted into the Royal Academy's exhibition in exchange for a payment from my uncle. How much does it cost to dash the hopes of an aspiring artist? I trust it is at least as much as a Perrin, Gedes decanter."

An ornery expression overtook Sandby-Smith's features as he listened to the accusation of malfeasance, and Bea expected him to mount a highly outraged defense. Instead, his face lightened and exclaimed, "Oh, you mean antiquities that were forged! I am being very stupid. Of course I know all about that. But it is only a small thing, a mere peccadillo. I am making hardly any money at all. As you surmised, your grace, admitting and barring artists from the academy's exhi-bition was more lucrative, and for the most part, I was paid to do the former. Lord Myles was unique in his aim—usually, fathers buy entry for their sons to puff up their consequence —and the pity was, I had to charge him more and more each time because Mortimer's skill was improving at a dizzying pace. That last year, Vandermash and I almost came to fisticuffs when I described the quality of Mortimer's brush-strokes as middling to mediocre. It is amazing to discover it is he who has been making the vases. They are very good. I would not know the difference if I did not already know the difference."

Startled, Bea said curtly, "Vases?"

"Well, some are urns, others are amphorae," he rushed to clarify before adding that regardless of its particular classification, each piece was beautifully rendered. "I must confess, I am surprised to learn they were done by Mortimer. He did not appear to have any facility with clay, although I know he liked to sculpt. Regardless, it is remarkable. Tell me, how is the old boy?"

Although astonished to discover there was yet another prong to Hawes's counterfeit scheme, she knew she should have anticipated it. Assyrian reliefs, Roman medallions, Grecian pottery—it was all of a piece. Anything that could be faithfully reproduced would be faithfully reproduced at a profit.

The King of Saffron Hill did not ascend to his throne by allowing opportunities to remain unexploited.

Addressing Sandby-Smith's question, Kesgrave said, "He is dead."

Disconcerted by the stark statement, Sandby-Smith bobbled the teacup, causing it to clatter as he returned it to its saucer, and tilted his head in concern. "I am sorry. I had not heard. Was it sudden?"

The duke confirmed that it was very sudden. "He was stabbed in the stomach with a chisel."

Revulsion supplanted sympathy as Sandby-Smith cried, "That is horrible!"

Readily, Kesgrave agreed.

Seeming to struggle for composure, the artist announced that he did not understand. "Who would do such an atrocious thing?"

"We do not know," Bea replied.

Once again, Sandby-Smith drew a finger across his brow in what she recognized as a habit spurred by apprehension. "And you ... you are the lady Runner. You are investigating because that is what you do. Everyone knows it. If you called on my home to discuss it, it is because you mean to interrogate me about Mortimer's murder. You mean to interrogate me because you think I can shed light on the horrible events, which you would only think if you believed I had something to do with them," he observed softly, almost under his breath, as he followed the progression of thought. Then he stiffened and glowered fiercely. "You believe *I* had something to do with it?"

Bea permitted that the idea had occurred to them, yes.

More angry than alarmed, he sneered at her for being obtuse and misguided. "Why would I hurt Mortimer? And with a chisel of all things! That sounds ghastly. Where in God's name would I even *get* a chisel? I own several knives and a dagger that is so sharp I accidentally cut my thumb while returning it to its drawer. But a chisel—I would not know where to start!"

The improbability of the device was part of its appeal, allowing the suspect to make precisely the argument he was making. But Bea elided that from her reply, simply stating that he had acted impulsively. "You called on Mortimer to discuss his blackmail threat because you did not want your connection to Hawes's criminal empire exposed, and when he proved intractable, you seized the first implement you could find to settle your differences in a more permanent way."

Sandby-Smith refused to consider it.

Even in the most desperate of circumstances, he would not gut someone with a chisel.

"I am a painter!" he announced hotly, as though his artistic bent precluded all acts of violence. "All your chatter is nonsense. I bore Matlock no ill will. I always thought he was an excellent artist and am delighted to know he had a chance to put his talents to good use before his unfortunate demise. The vases he made are impeccable. As I said, even I cannot tell which one is real."

His words rang hollow to Bea, who found his repeated rejection of Mortimer even more egregious in light of his admiration for the victim's work. "You are corrupt in every way."

Sandby-Smith seethed at the insult. "In twelve years as president of the Royal Academy, I have never done a single thing that exceeds the moral authority of my office. Art depends on patronage, and the disbursements I accept from hopeful artists are a type of sponsorship. I think it reflects poorly on your own morality that you would distort something ordinary and decent. Shame on you, your grace."

Bea smiled at this high-minded defense and asked if that was the artist's final argument or if he planned to refine it before presenting it to London society. "Because I must warn you it is not at all persuasive, which I suspect you already know. Corrupt is corrupt, and you rightfully feared that the whole truth would come out if Mortimer revealed your participation in the counterfeit Grecian vase trade. In exchange for his silence, he demanded you arrange his acceptance to next year's exhibition, and then you killed him because you could not risk exposure."

Amused, Sandby-Smith curved his lips into a condescending smirk and told her she had veered wildly off the path and driven herself into a ditch. "Why in God's name would Matlock have to coerce me into doing something I had already consented to? It was in my agreement with Eddie, which I struck with him months ago, in April. He insisted upon it! I did not know why but nor did I care, just as I did not care why Lord Myles was determined to thwart his son's career. It was an insignificant detail, and I resent your attempt to cast it as meaningful. In fact, I resent this entire conversation. I am sorry the duke's cousin has been killed in a gruesome way, but it has nothing to do with me. My bargain with Eddie is not a nefarious or disreputable affair. It is only a jape—a great lark if you will. I have been selling faux vases for six weeks and it is great fun, and if Haysbert gets his ego tweaked, so much the better!"

"Haysbert?" Bea said sharply, struck by the name because Hawes had mentioned the noted expert as well. "What does he have to do with your scheme?"

"It is not a scheme," he snapped, his impatience rising even as he struggled to retain a courteous disposition. "It is a prank, which you would know if you would just listen to the words I am saying rather than concocting machinations in your head."

Duly, she apologized and asked him to clarify the difference between a scheme and a prank, a request that caused him to pinch his lips in annoyance. Nonetheless, he complied, explaining that the latter caused amusement for some and harm to none.

"Not even Haysbert?" she said, her thoughts racing as she tried to make sense of the unexpected turn. Hawes had been unequivocal: He would sell no forgeries to Haysbert.

"Especially not Haysbert," Sandby-Smith said with an affronted grimace. "It is a little tomfoolery and no less than he deserves for stealing a march on me. *A Collection of Artifacts of Roman, Grecian, and Etruscan Origin Found by Viscount Haysbert and Displayed in his Cabinet for the Benefit and Elucidation of All Mankind* was my idea! Obviously, I would have chosen a more wieldy title and inserted my own name, not his, but the notion of a book featuring the wonders of a private antiquities collection was mine. I told Hayes that a publisher was willing to pay me to write about my mother's collection, and he knew I needed the money. I inherited the house in London without any funds to support it. He congratulated me on my good fortune and then proceeded to undercut me! He hired an engraver to make drawings of his collection, commissioned a historian of antiquities to compose the text, and published the first volume in only a few months. London was instantly enamored! Suddenly, every drawing room in Mayfair was graced with an ancient vase with elegant cameo glass engravings. *The Times* dubbed it the Hayes Vase Craze, but it should have been named after me!"

His fury over the twenty-year-old injustice made him an inexplicable recruit for the crime lord, who knew better than to allow personal resentments to undermine his business, especially as it was as plain as day to Beatrice that Sandby-Smith intended for his nemesis to know he had been duped.

If she could see that from one brief conversation, then it had been equally obvious to Hawes.

And yet he proceeded with the recruitment.

Unless he had not.

Simmering with suspicion, she asked how many vases he planned to sell to Haysbert before telling his lordship the truth about his purchases.

Sandby-Smith delighted in the query, for it was just the sort of thing he enjoyed contemplating. "Originally, I thought just the one, as that was all that I needed to humiliate him. But he was so condescending in his willingness to help me out of a fix by purchasing the vase, which I had told him was my mother's favorite. He could tell it pained me greatly to have to sell it and promised to give it pride of place in his dining room. I sold him a second one, earlier in June, and he made an insultingly low offer for what he believed the piece was. I pushed back and managed to squeeze a few more pounds out of him, but even as I pleaded with him to pay a fair price to help me settle with the grocer, he refused. So now I think I shall wait until after the fourth or fifth vase. Knowing I hood-winked him repeatedly will make the cut deeper."

It was precisely the answer she had expected.

Confident now that Hell and Fury knew nothing about Sandby-Smith, Bea strode to the entrance of the room and called for Marlow, who presented himself immediately. "Our visitor would like to see Reynolds's portrait of the duchess. Would you be so kind as to show it to him?"

If the abrupt change in topic disconcerted the academician, he was too excited to dwell on it as he lurched forward to return the teacup to the table. "Of all things wonderful, your grace! Thank you so much for this opportunity. I promise I will not stare at it overly long."

Bea assured him there was no need to rush on their account. "You must take all the time you need to soak up Reynolds's genius. The work is indeed majestic."

Sandby-Smith flushed with pleasure as he nodded giddily and asked if *The Triumph of Death* by Brueghel was en route to La Reina. If so, he would not object to pausing briefly before it in awed appreciation. Marlow responded to this remark with his customarily blank stare, causing the artist to lose a little of his enthusiasm, and Bea called to his departing back to admire anything that took his fancy—even the wainscoting if he was thusly inclined. "The balustrade is Inigo Jones."

In fact, it was not.

The ironwork on the staircase had been done by one of Jean Tijou's apprentices, but she thought the name of the famous architect would impress the academician more.

Sandby-Smith all but skipped down the hallway, and Bea waited until he had rounded the corner before closing the drawing room door. Then she turned to Kesgrave and announced that it was Renfield who oversaw the counterfeit Grecian vase trade. "It has nothing to do with Hawes. Hawes said during our initial conversation that he would not sell one of his forgeries to noted experts and gave Haysbert as the example. He explicitly said he would never sell to the viscount and now the viscount is the one person to whom his latest conspirator wants to sell? I do not believe it. Renfield is scheming behind his employer's back. He has set up his own network of forgeries."

The duke, who had not recalled the statement without prompting, allowed that some aspects of her theory seemed accurate. "Sandby-Smith did not meet with Hawes—that much is clear. But assuming Renfield is cheating his boss rather than carrying out a task at his request is rather a large leap in logic."

She darted an amused glance at him as she crossed to the hearth. "You understand little of my investigative process, your grace, if you do not know it entails regularly making galloping leaps in logic."

His own lips twitched as he assured her he was quite familiar with the finer points of her practice, which also included reading much into oversights and making mountains out of molehills.

"As if I would ever have the temerity to mount the great height of a mountain," she said with modest fervor, conceding at most to a slightly higher-than-average hill. "Regardless, Hawes is the housekeeper. He manages all staffing decisions. He would never leave the business of enlisting an esteemed member of the *ton* and the president of the prestigious Royal Academy to the man he relies on to intimidate rivals with physical violence. He would do it himself as he did with Sir Thomas and Higgins. We know that Mortimer was not making the vases, as there was no evidence of them in his studio, and Hawes taunted us about moving into Grecian antiquities. He would never have done that if he had already moved into Grecian antiquities."

"That is true," Kesgrave murmured. "But Renfield had made Mortimer's inclusion in the annual exhibition part of his bargain with Sandby-Smith. Why would he do that? What is the connection to Mortimer if he had nothing to do with the vase trade?"

Yes, that was the question.

"Perhaps it was an inducement?" she proposed.

He allowed it was likely, then immediately added that a quid pro quo required an even exchange. "What did Renfield need from Mortimer?"

Bea resumed her pacing, striding across the rug to the hearth as she wondered if he had the same idea as Sir Thomas and wanted Mortimer to make extra reliefs that he could sell on his own. "If he recruited Sandby-Smith to sell Grecian vases, then he might have found someone to sell reliefs."

Kesgrave insisted it was too risky. "Renfield would know better than to be in the same market as his employer. He would find something different, which is what he did."

Ancient vases were a sensible choice, she thought, for they were not as rare or as difficult to transport as reliefs. As Sandby-Smith had noted, most families in London already owned one or two and considered them lovely ornamentation for their homes. As familiar adornment, they were subjected to far less scrutiny than a stone slab from Assyria. No doubt that was their appeal to Renfield, who had looked at Lord Elgin's ordeal and learned the opposite lesson from his employer.

Except that was not quite accurate, as Hawes had entered the Roman artifacts trade, which had also earned him a fair penny. Those trinkets had come no farther than Wapping.

Reconsidering the medieval baubles in light of recent discoveries, she stopped in the middle of the room as she realized something. "Hawes never mentioned the Roman artifacts."

He furrowed his brow into a curious frown. "He did not?"

"In our two conversations with him, he provided significant details about his forged antiquities operation. He discussed the reliefs in depth, extolling the success of the scheme, but he did not reference the trinkets once. If

Mortimer made them as well, why did Hawes not mention them?"

Perceiving the implication at once, he said, "Renfield started small, testing the waters."

"And finding them favorable, launched phase two," she confirmed.

"The vases."

"It explains the gross disparity in their distribution," she added softly as she grasped her hands behind her back and contemplated how the reliefs had been offered discreetly to maintain the appearance of scarcity while the trinkets were displayed in abundance. "Hawes would never be meticulous with one artifact and careless with the other."

Of course he would not.

But Renfield—younger, bolder, hungrier—did not share his employer's qualms. He had probably been impatient with Hawes's caution from the very beginning. No doubt it was one of the things that spurred him to establish his own trade.

"He knew Roman artifacts sold briskly because Higgins told him he could not keep them in stock. He mentioned that very thing to us when we questioned him about the display," she said, closing her eyes as she tried to recall when Mortimer's interest in painting was revived.

He hired Miss Brewer in March.

And that was after several weeks of auditioning models.

That meant late January or early February, which corresponded with the beginning of the Roman artifacts trade. Mortimer's earnings increased, providing him with the blunt to hire a muse.

And then eight weeks or so later, in May, he began to work with Miss Brewer in earnest, adding two more weekly sessions because he knew his work would be accepted into the exhibition.

Enter *The Huntress*.

Sandby-Smith would accept any work, but Mortimer wanted to create something spectacular.

Yes, but that connection did not explain what Renfield hoped to gain with Mortimer's compli—

Oh, but it was right there, leaning against in the center of the wall: *The Huntress!*

"It was the bridle!" she said, spinning on her heels as she realized how immensely she had misunderstood everything. "That was what Renfield wanted from Mortimer! His plan is not just to set up his own counterfeit antiquities trade under Hawes's nose; it is to depose him as King of Saffron Hill. The bridle is merely one aspect in a far-reaching, labyrinthine scheme to assume the throne."

Regarding her with a mixture of admiration and amusement, he said, "You deduced all that from a single anachronism?"

"Deliberately inserted!" she reminded him avidly. "We thought Mortimer had done it to free himself from his obligation to Hawes, but that was a risky proposition with an uncertain outcome. In all likelihood he would have been forced to continue with the reliefs only with greater supervision. You heard Hawes—he would never have allowed his prized forger to be distracted by his painting ambitions. But if he did it at Renfield's behest in exchange for admittance in the annual exhibition, then Mortimer's motive is clear. And the timing aligns because Mortimer began to work in earnest on *The Huntress* in May, which was a few weeks after Sandby-Smith agreed to Renfield's condition. Renfield needed Mortimer to insert a mistake that was just subtle enough to escape detection until the experts at Montague House examined the relief. A respected baronet daring to sell a blatant forgery to Parliament would cause a massive scandal with Sir Thomas cast as a fraud or a dupe. Either way, his ties to Hawes would inevitably be exposed—Renfield would see to that—and the bumbling attempt to defraud the British government would humiliate Hawes while exposing the limits of his power."

"Labyrinthine indeed," he murmured appreciatively. "You think Renfield has been doing this for a while, arranging a small but steady trickle of seemingly minor mishaps to signal to his followers that Hawes's grip on his empire is slipping. The king is in decline."

"And there is Renfield—younger, bolder, stronger."

"His army at the ready," Kesgrave added.

He meant it figuratively, extending the metaphor she herself had introduced, and yet something about the statement struck a chord.

An army at the ready.

"Warning off rivals is one of Renfield's primary duties as second in command—you said that, did you not?" she asked, her brows darting upward. "What if he consolidated them instead? If they were all brawlers like Larder McCoy, then he would have a formidable army indeed."

Bea shook her head, marveling at how obvious it was in retrospect, for Renfield had made no effort to disguise how ardently he wanted to be Hell and Fury Hawes. He had aped not only his manner and dress but also his decorating style down to the red thistle paper on the walls of his study.

"His plan was not without its merits," the duke allowed. "Hinging a humiliating public revelation on Sir Thomas's buffoonery was a reasonable decision."

"He *does* seem too busy posturing as a great collector to actually be a great collector," she agreed. "I, too, would not have expected him to catch the mistake. But because he is not quite as buffoonish as he appears, he did notice it and took the precaution of summoning an expert to examine the remaining relief. That Addleton just happened to notice the Roman forgeries was a stroke of bad luck for Renfield. The moment Sir Thomas sent the note to Hawes, Mortimer's fate was sealed. Renfield could not allow him to speak to Hawes under any circumstance."

"It was the artifacts all along, not the bridle," the duke said.

Bea shook her head and clarified that it was not *only* the bridle. "Taken in consideration with the artifacts, the anachronism was quite damning. That is why Hawes sought out Mortimer, not Higgins. Someone had given the forger specific instructions, and he wanted to know who. And he was measured about it. He did not rush to Banner Street to press for answers. Instead, he kept all his meetings so that nobody would realize something was amiss. He assumed he had time."

"That Addle the Prattle was the expert Soames consulted was a stroke of *good* luck for Renfield, which he wasted no time in exploiting," he observed. "But he underestimated Hawes."

"Oh, indeed he did," she replied with wry amazement that a man could be just cunning enough to damn himself. "In all his plotting, he failed to account for the impact of his previous successes. They put Hawes on notice, so that when he saw Mortimer lying there, surrounded by blood, the deadly implement protruding from his belly, he knew it was all related. That is why he was willing to do the unthinkable and seek our help. Renfield should have taken the time to make the death look like an accident."

"He did not have the time. For all we know, Hawes missed him by minutes. He had to make quick work of it. And that puts us in a devil of a position, does it not?" he asked with a regretful shake of the head. "In identifying the killer, we are finding the traitor for him."

She did not like it any more than he did, but there was no way around it.

Hell and Fury outmaneuvered them just as she had feared.

And still they had to finish the job by apprehending the killer.

But how to prove to the authorities that Renfield was the culprit?

All they had were theories and a bill of sale.

Kesgrave insisted it was not as little as she thought. "And only we know that is all we have. Renfield has no idea what evidence we have uncovered, and you may be sure his servant can be persuaded to recant her testimony when threatened with legal action. She will not want to be arraigned as an accomplice to murder. We also have Sandby-Smith's testimony. And then, of course, there is Renfield's confession, which we will attain presently."

"Oh, we will, will we?" she asked archly, annoyed by his confidence but also fascinated by it. "And how will we manage that? By asking him nicely?"

"Precisely, yes," he said cryptically before excusing himself to send a missive to the Runners requesting their presence in Doddington Lane. "While I am taking care of that minor business, you may show Sandby-Smith out."

Oh, but she would not.

The prospect of being further subjected to the artist's insincere apologies and lavish musings held little appeal, and she instead requested a breakfast tray be delivered to her office of rout cake enjoyment, leaving Marlow free to dispense with their visitor as soon as his patience was at an end.

Presumably, that would be any minute now.

Chapter Eighteen

❦

I f Renfield was startled to see the Duke and Duchess of Kesgrave enter his home yet again, Bea gave him no opportunity to express it, insisting instead that he thank them for saving him from a dire fate.

Bewildered by the demand, he echoed it blankly.

"Dire fate, yes," she repeated firmly as she strode down the hallway to the study, where she paused on the threshold to regard her host with patient understanding. "I know your instinct is to object to my high-handedness. This is your home! How dare I march into it and begin barking orders!"

Indeed, Renfield's eyes glowed fiercely at this raillery, and as he drew a breath to protest, she waved him off, urging him to sit down so they could discuss the matter calmly. "You, too, Martha," she said to the servant, who stood by the front door, one hand clutching the frame as she tried to decide how to respond to the invitation. "Yes, yes, my impudence is appalling. But it does not signify, and you were only going to listen at the door anyway, as you did the other day. This way you can hear everything clearly and contribute your thoughts, which will help us determine your complicity."

At this ominous statement, the maid's expression remained stony, but she darted her eyes at Renfield, whose glower deepened as he told Bea not to address his staff.

Blithely, Bea shook her head, as if baffled by his decision, but she agreed to abide by his preference. "No doubt you are accustomed to her hovering by the door and having her in the room feels strange or even a little wrong. May I ask her to close the drapes or is that impertinent as well?"

Even as she posed the question, Kesgrave walked to the windows and drew the curtains. "It is probably unnecessary, but there is no harm in being overly cautious."

Oh, but Renfield, who still had no idea what was happening, vehemently disagreed and tugged the fabric back, exposing the room to full sunlight.

Bea, wincing visibly at the action, lauded his bravery. "And to stand by the window where just anybody can see you—truly, Mr. Renfield, your fearlessness knows no bounds. If I had devised a scheme to undermine and ultimately destroy Hell and Fury Hawes, I would not have the nerve to go about my business in broad daylight. I suppose that daring is what led you to formulate your cabal in the first place. You are not the sort of man to skulk in the shadows. But that is all over. You made your bold play for Hawes's empire and fell short. Now the duke and I are here to rescue you from your own folly. Let us begin."

If Renfield felt anxiety at being confronted with the broad outlines of his plan, he revealed none of it, regarding her instead with fierce impatience.

Martha, however, goggled in astonishment.

Whatever devious plot Renfield had hatched with his coterie of conspirators he did so away from the prying interest of his staff, and Bea sought to exploit the servant's shock by promising her the die was not yet cast. "You can still save yourself. All you have to do is tell us the truth regarding your employer's whereabouts on Tuesday night, and we will make sure Hell and Fury knows you had nothing to do with the scheme to dethrone him."

The maid did not budge. She remained frozen in the doorway, which was not an auspicious beginning to Kesgrave's four-step plan.

Naturally, yes, the duke had numbered the components, the first of which entailed convincing Martha that it was in her best interest to tell them the truth about her employer's alibi. Her admission would lead to the next step: unsettling Renfield further with Sandby-Smith's testimony, thereby encouraging him to confess to Mortimer's murder rather than face Hawes's wrath (step 3) and to enjoy a more lenient sentence—exile, not death—in exchange for sparing the dowager the spectacle of a trial (step 4).

Gesturing to a chair, Bea urged the maid to sit down, and when Martha refused to comply, Renfield lauded her good sense in resisting the duchess's manipulations. "She thinks so little of your intelligence that she believes you can be swayed by a show of confidence. She and her husband are putting on this performance for your benefit, although the reason for it escapes me at present. Fortunately, she is champing at the bit to tell us."

Bea affirmed that she was indeed eager to resolve the matter quickly, as allowing it to persist for an undue amount of time risked endangering them all. "Your safety, Martha, is our number one concern, followed by Mr. Renfield's. So in the interest of expediency, let us place our cards on the table, as it were, and deal candidly with each other. You, Mr. Renfield, have been slyly undercutting Hawes for months in order to weaken his position among his own associates and ultimately take over his criminal enterprise. As you are not without intelligence, you knew there was always a chance Hawes would realize he harbored a traitor in his midst—and that is precisely what has happened. Aware that someone is undermining him from within, he asked the duke and me to investigate Mortimer's death. He knows it is another act of sabotage, and in iden-tifying the killer for him, we would provide him with the name of his betrayer."

Renfield's expression remained placid as he listened to these revelations.

An impressive accomplishment, Bea thought, as he had to feel some tinge of alarm at discovering the lengths to which Hawes was willing to go to learn his identity.

Seeking the assistance of the Duke of Kesgrave—it was unthinkable.

Renfield dismissed Martha on the grounds that it would take all morning to untangle her grace's snarled thoughts and the maid had better things to do. Scowling furiously, the servant left the room, and Bea wondered if the other woman would actually return to the kitchen or remain by the door to listen.

Apparently, Martha's employer shared this concern, for when he warned Bea that she was digging in the wrong field, it was in a noticeably softer voice. "Now, I cannot stop you if you want to waste your time making baseless claims, but I *can* stop you from wasting my time. As I have no intention of dignifying your accusations with a denial, I think it is best that you leave now. Good day!"

Kesgrave, regarding the other man with pity, advised him to restrain his posturing, for it had no bearing on reality. "Bluster for your maid's benefit, if you must, but please spare us the theatrics. We know everything and must decide how to move forward if we are to save you from unnecessary suffer-ing. Hawes is not a stupid man. He will figure out the truth soon enough. The fact that he was willing to swallow his pride and request my wife's help should give you some indication of his determination. He will not rest until he knows who the traitor is."

"And once he does know, he will exact a terrible price," Bea added with an urgency commensurate with step three. "That is the last thing Kesgrave and I want. We did not agree to lend Hawes our assistance only to become instruments of his vengeance. All that can be avoided if you will consent to go with us to the magistrate and confess. Whatever the crown has in store for you will be mild compared with Hawes's revenge. Our carriage is waiting outside."

Renfield chuckled heartily and sincerely, completely forgetting his intention to keep his voice low, and said the duchess's thinking was far more mangled than he had ever imagined if she honestly believed he would toddle off to Bow Street and plead guilty to a murder he had not committed. "Or even one that I had! You have been reading too many tales of King Arthur's court if you think I would incriminate myself out of a sense of honor or gallantry."

Bea assured him she harbored no such illusions. "You will do it out of a sense of self-preservation, as I just explained. The moment Hawes finds out you killed Mortimer, he will know you are the traitor and seek retribution. The only way to ensure your survival is to come with us. I am no admirer of yours, Mr. Renfield, but I have no desire to see your limbs scattered among the fields on Hampstead Heath. The magistrate will deal with you humanely."

And still he regarded her with amused condescension, owning himself amazed at her gross misapprehension. "I have taken no action against Mr. Hawes. I would never dream of taking action against the man who gave me the opportunity to better myself. If not for Mr. Hawes, I would still be boxing in dingy cellars in Long Crandon. Only a fool would repay that kindness with betrayal. I am neither. I am a loyal soldier, and Mr. Hawes would not take kindly to your attempt to sow discord among his people with these outrageous lies. But let us say for the sake of argument that you *are* digging in the right field. You still have no proof. It would be your word against mine, and I am the trusted lieutenant who has served him faithfully for a decade. And you are … what? A status-seeking dilettante who would stand on a pile of corpses to rise higher in society. I do not care if Mr. Hawes asked you to find Mr. Matlock's killer. If you try to serve me up as the answer, he will laugh you out of the room."

It was an excellent defense, precisely the sort she would expect from a bare-knuckle brawler, for it was sharp and aggressive, aiming punches squarely at her face as a way to protect his own.

Even so, it would not prosper.

"Oh, but we do have proof," she replied mildly, withdrawing the bill of sale from her pocket and holding it up for his inspection.

Renfield was surprised.

Although he controlled his reaction quickly enough, she saw utter befuddlement flash across his face. His tone was snide as he complimented her on uncovering irrefutable evidence that he enjoyed collecting cut glass by Perrin, Gedes. "Hawes will be rightly horrified by my profligate spending, for he knows I am ordinarily too sensible to allow my enthusiasm to overcome my frugality. But the decanter was too beautiful to resist, and the appraiser said it was worth three-quarters of what I paid, so Sandby-Smith did not squeeze me for as much as he thinks. The fact that you saw something nefarious in a man of my temperament appreciating a crystal decanter for its beauty reveals your prejudices."

"We spoke to Sandby-Smith," she said, ignoring the provocation.

"Did you?" he asked curiously. "I suppose he bragged about taking advantage of the provincial rube who does not know a Ravenscroft from a raven's claw. He is an insufferable prig but knowledgeable and happy to sell any number of deeply personal family heirlooms as long as the price is high enough. I could have had his grandmother's wedding ring if I nurtured a fondness for garish diamonds."

He was, Bea thought, an excellent dissembler, capable of skillfully piling on particulars as though the only thing separating a lie from the truth was an unspecified number of details. Listening to him prevaricate now, she realized his business proposal for duchess-branded rout cakes was merely another form of chatter. From the moment he had thrust the chisel into Mortimer's stomach, he had anticipated a visit from them and wanted a distraction on hand.

No, not a distraction.

A disguise.

The dogged man of business, negotiating deals while Rome burned.

Rousingly, Bea congratulated him on his performance and assured him that Sandby-Smith had kept to the script as well. "In fact, he did mention how easy you were to gull. But after we applied a little pressure, he admitted that he was working with you to sell copies of ancient Grecian vases, and from there it was not difficult to deduce that the entire operation was unfolding in secret. You would have done well to show some of the discretion and caution of your employer, but that is how you brash young rebels are—loud and impatient and so certain you are smarter than everyone else. But once Hawes sees the bill of sale, he will figure it out as quickly as we did, which is why Kesgrave and I are here. We do not wish for you to be boiled alive and dissolved in a bath of lye."

Renfield's smile dimmed.

He remained as determined as ever to affect disinterest, but the repeated references to a ghastly death had begun to weigh on him.

Even so, he continued to deny the bill of sale was anything but what it appeared: proof that he allowed himself to be led astray by his passion for cut glass. "Regardless, it is a moot point, for you would never throw me to the wolves. The fact that you are here to coerce me into confessing proves that you have no intention of showing the document to Hawes."

Bea conceded his assessment was more or less accurate. "As reluctant as I am to subject you to a slow slicing death— and you must know that I am adamantly opposed to any torture devised by China in the tenth century—I cannot allow Mortimer's killer to evade justice. If you will not agree to surrender to the magistrate and confess to the murder, then you leave us with no choice other than to tell Hell and Fury Hawes everything."

Although daunted by the prospect of bleeding to death from a thousand little cuts, Renfield managed a shrug. "That is your prerogative, of course, but you will only wind up looking foolish and deluded. Mr. Hawes would never doubt my loyalty. He knows me well and you know little."

"Oh, but do we?" Bea asked with menacing softness. "We know you are helming your own counterfeit antiquities ring and making a tidy profit that you are using to amass your own small army of thieves and thugs, which I trust Mr. Larder McCoy will be happy to confirm. We know you bribed Mortimer into carving a modern bridle into one of the reliefs bound for the British Museum by promising him inclusion in the Royal Academy's annual exhibition. We know you panicked when Kerrich told you his colleague had discovered a dozen fake medieval artifacts among Sir Thomas's collection because you knew Hawes would recognize Mortimer's handiwork and demand answers and ultimately figure out that you are responsible for the spate of minor failures that have bedeviled his businesses as of late. We know that you knew the only way to ensure Mortimer's silence was by murdering him, so you did—swiftly and sloppily. We know you are in over your head and are offering you a way out."

Renfield scoffed.

A way out!

A noose or a knife—he was dead either way.

And then that hateful smirk danced at the edges of his lips again as he flatly stated his disbelief. "You do not have the stomach for handing me over to Hawes and allowing him to desecrate my body in retribution. Your sense of right and wrong is too highly evolved to subject me to gratuitous cruelty. That is why you are here pleading with me. It is your only maneuver. If I do not confess, you have nothing."

"You are right but also wrong," she replied. "I do not wish to aid Hawes in his project of revenge, but I must balance my natural revulsion with a need for justice. That is why we are prepared to offer you leniency. If you confess to the murder, Kesgrave will ensure that you go to a penal colony rather than the gallows. You will not have your freedom, but you will have your life, which I assume is worth something to you. It is a fair bargain, and I advise you to accept it."

But a cunning grin spread slowly across Renfield's face as the tension seemed to lift from his body. "You have over-played your hand, duchess. Offering an inducement to convince me to surrender reveals how desperate you are. We all know your threats are empty. You would never hand me over to Hawes. As I said, you don't have the stomach for brutality, and the duke is no errand boy to jump obediently when the powerful crime lord crooks his fingers. You have nothing. It is over. Now I invite you to leave—unless you would like to discuss our joint business venture. I remain as eager as ever to capitalize on Her Outrageousness's notoriety and believe we would make a small fortune if you could just overcome your squeamishness about being in trade. As I am not one to allow an opportunity to go to waste, I took the liberty of drawing up another prospectus."

He added that the document was in his desk—the top drawer—as he stepped around the pair of bergères to retrieve it, and Bea, marveling at his commitment to the tenacious character he had created, could not believe he had drawn up a fourth proposal in anticipation of yet another visit from them.

His foresight was incredible.

And then she thought, Oh, but it *was* incredible.

Also difficult to credit: his blithe indifference to the threat they posed. He could speak as confidently as he wished about Bea's morality and Kesgrave's egoism, but as long as they were in possession of the bill of sale from Sandby-Smith, he was vulnerable to their whims. Surely, the prospect of their having physical evidence of his treachery did not sit as easily with him as he sought to project and had something else in mind.

Acting on instinct, allowing no consideration at all, she grabbed one of the glass pieces from the shelf—the Cornish serpentine egg—and flung it at Renfield, hitting him squarely on the forehead. The blow knocked him backward, causing him to teeter unsteadily, and as he cried out in pain, Kesgrave ran to the drawer to examine its contents, his utter bafflement immediately supplanted by comprehension as he withdrew a pistol.

As he adjusted his grip on the weapon, she asked the duke if he had noticed how perfectly she had aimed the paperweight. "I hit my target dead center, and that was without practice. Now imagine what I could do with a flintlock."

Coolly, a voice in the doorway said, "You would be invincible, your grace, a prospect I find utterly terrifying."

Hawes!

It was Hawes, standing on the threshold in an impeccably

tailored waistcoat and silk hat, his manner unhurried as he sauntered into the room. He glanced at Renfield, whose glassy eyes seemed incapable of taking in the whole scene, and observed that the marble egg would leave a nasty bruise. "But do not worry: It won't bother you for long."

A cryptic remark, its meaning was nevertheless clear, and Renfield darted a baleful glare at Beatrice before staring impassively at his employer.

As he strolled deeper into the room, Hell and Fury thanked them for finding Mortimer's killer. "I knew it was someone in my organization but could not lay my finger on who. I had a list of suspects in mind, and I must confess that Rennie was not on it. He was always an obedient lad. Or so he appeared. Do not trouble yourselves with explaining all the whys and wherefores. I shall find them out myself soon enough."

Bea could not fathom how he was there.

They had made a great show of fearing his sudden appearance in the study, but it had been a performance. Drawing the curtains was stagecraft.

"You have been following us," Kesgrave said flatly.

Hawes dipped his head in acknowledgment but rushed to clarify that he had not personally engaged in the activity. Rather, a few of his associates had made it their business to know where the Duke and Duchess of Kesgrave were at every moment. "As a way of staying abreast of your investigation. I knew it was only a matter of time before you identified the culprit, and I wanted to spare you the inconvenience of having to keep me informed of your progress. As you can see, it worked out beautifully. I will take Mr. Matlock's killer into custody, and you can return to providing the dowager with the comfort she needs at this wretched time. Please convey to her my condolences and assure her that the villain who

murdered her grandson will suffer the appropriate consequences for his actions."

A chill danced up Bea's spine.

To think that his henchmen had been watching them for
days and neither she nor the duke had any idea!

Their obliviousness was horrifying.

And yet how could it be otherwise?

They were not spies engaged in secret government work
or seasoned criminals accustomed to stalking their prey on
the streets of London. It would have required an unprecedented level of suspicion and distrust to even glance behind
them, let alone scrutinize the landscape for signs of Hawes's
minions trailing after them.

The more astounding turn would have been if they *had*
noticed.

Even so, the information to which Hawes's men had
access was limited. All they could compile was a list of
addresses; the actual exchanges that occurred inside the
buildings were unknown to them.

But somehow that was enough.

Unable to squelch her curiosity, Bea asked Hawes why he
was certain of Renfield's guilt. "We have paid almost a dozen
calls in the past few days. What about this one was decisive
for you?"

Gratified by her bewilderment, he explained that it was her
third visit to the Doddington Lane residence. "That in itself was
notable because Rennie has little to do with the counterfeit
trade. He was instrumental in the beginning, setting Matlock up
in the studio and arranging for regular delivery of supplies, but
other men oversee the day-to-day operation. The initial conversation made sense, as Rennie is familiar with the general para-
meters of the scheme and knows useful details. The second
interview was questionable because he would not have much to

add. The third was damning, signaling that he was far more embroiled in Mr. Matlock's business than I was aware and the only reason I would not be aware was if Rennie was hiding it from me. I trust you can follow my logic from there, your grace."

Indeed, she could.

In killing Mortimer to hide his perfidy, Renfield had led Hawes literally to his door.

"Now that I have appeased your curiosity, I trust you will step aside and allow me to take Rennie in hand," Hawes continued smoothly. "You have done all that I asked."

Galled by the complacency of his command, as though she and Kesgrave were in fact his hirelings sent to perform a service for him, she replied that his observation was not quite accurate. "You asked us to bring the murderer to justice, which is why we will surrender Renfield to the magistrate at Bow Street."

Hawes's demeanor did not change—it remained affable and interested—but his tone was icy as he assured her he would dispense justice.

"Rough justice," she snapped.

Unable to argue, the crime lord shrugged. "Justice is justice."

It was not, no, and she and Kesgrave had not solved his cousin's murder as a favor to Hell and Fury or to help him reinforce his position in his organization. Despite how he perceived them, they were not his errand boys and had no intention of blithely handing over Renfield to be vengefully tortured.

At least, Bea did not think they did.

Kesgrave might have an entirely different perspective on the matter, and she slid her gaze from Hawes to the duke to assess his thoughts. Alas, his expression was blank as he trained the pistol on Renfield, whose complexion had turned a waxy shade of white.

Patently, they would not endanger their own lives to spare Mortimer's killer from torture and a horrendous death. Despite his attempts to style himself as a man of taste and refinement, Renfield was savagery personified. He had not only ruthlessly driven a chisel into his victim's stomach and allowed him to die from his wound but also meted out violence as a matter of course.

Rennie Rumpus, ready to thump us.

If there was a principle at stake, it was the importance of maintaining law and order in a fair and free society, and she could not discern what defending it was worth.

Injury, no.

Infuriating the King of Saffron Hill, possibly.

Although Hawes had not drawn a weapon, she knew he had one, either in a pocket or in a holster or tucked into the waistband of his trousers. Presumably, he never left the safety of his domain without some means of defense, and his restraint indicated that he did not wish to exchange gunfire with a high-ranking member of the English aristocracy. His criminal enterprise had been allowed to flourish because the crown had little interest in defending the territory, and as long as the violence held to the rookery, they would continue to look away.

But killing a duke—that would obligate the government to care.

Hawes, who knew it as well as she, would ultimately agree to leave without his quarry rather than wake a sleeping beast. He was too sensible not to.

But the capitulation could come at a cost to his vanity, in which case he might feel compelled by the humiliating loss to arrange a reprisal that would not draw the notice of the authorities—an accident on a dark road, for example, or a robbery gone horribly wrong.

Her deep misgivings about tacitly condoning the intentional infliction of mental and physical pain on any man, even a murderous scoundrel such as Renfield, faltered at the prospect of eternal vigilance. If Hawes set his sights on harming either her or Kesgrave, then they would have to be constantly on their guard.

And then there was the cherub.

Scarcely larger than a strawberry, little more than a flurry of wonder in her heart and already a source of trepidation.

Infants were so helpless.

Newborn ducklings could feed themselves and even foals could walk within a few hours of birth, but human babies had no resources at all.

They required everything.

It was terrifying.

Halting this line of thought before she sent herself into a paroxysm of apprehension, she reminded herself of Hawes's pragmatism. He had not built an empire by responding to every minor sling and arrow that pierced his skin.

Tyrants and despots held on to petty resentments.

Hell and Fury Hawes was a businessman.

As such, he might be receptive to compromise.

The question was, what did she have to offer.

As she contemplated the answer, Kesgrave told Renfield to sit down, an indication that he did not see the matter resolving itself within the next few minutes. "No, not there, on the other side of the desk," he added when the other man took a step toward the leather armchair. "One of the bergères, and you will keep your hands flat on the desktop, where I can see them. A man of your proclivities must have a dozen weapons scattered throughout the room, and I will not allow you to avail yourself of any—for your own safety, you understand. Your former employer is waiting for the right moment to draw his gun, and I would rather you not give him an excuse. We have several points to discuss, and we will start with the most problematic," he said before turning to Hawes and addressing him directly. "You are not taking custody of Renfield. He will be tried for the murder of Mortimer Matlock and suffer whatever punishment the state deems appropriate."

Pleasantly, Hawes said no.

Renfield flinched.

The crime lord continued, "In light of the egregious nature of Rennie's offenses, I cannot agree to your condition, your grace, no matter how much it pains me to argue with you and the duchess. As I said, I am grateful for the service you have performed for me and consider myself in your debt, but I cannot allow sentiment to interfere with the management of my organization. It would be irresponsible of me not to discover the extent of his betrayal and the names of his conspirators. And of course I must make an example of him. As personally repugnant as I might find it to mount his head on a pike, it is what I must do to make it clear what will happen to the next person who trifles with me."

"Head on a pike!" Bea exclaimed with an air of satisfaction. "You see, now *that* is an image that is properly gruesome. Dissolving a corpse in lye is too immaculate. Oh, but where would you put it? In front of your residence on Grape Street strikes me as the most logical spot, perhaps next to the lamp post, but traditionally bodies are displayed at crossroads. In that case, where Farringdon meets Clerkenwell is more suitable because it gets a lot of traffic. Although that corner *is* home to the King's Head tavern, which makes it either ideally suited or in bad taste. I am afraid I have no idea which. *Mrs. Yeamond's Book of Etiquette: A Sensible Guide to Good Breeding and Comprehensive Directory to the Adherences of Society* does not address the proper placement of heads on pikes."

Solemnly, without a hint of the pique she knew him to be feeling, Hawes explained that the courtyard of the Red Lion on Bernard Road was ideally suited. "It is public but not frequented by small children, it has a central porch, and I conduct business in the holstery's public rooms several times a week. But I will take Farrington and Clerkenwell under advisement. Thank you for suggesting it. Now regarding Rennie, you will cede custody to me, or our genial discussion will turn heated. As you have probably already surmised, I am not alone. Three of my most trusted associates are waiting outside and will enter the house as soon as I give the signal. Your objections are noted, you have made a respectable effort to assert the rule of law, and you may rest firmly on the higher ground. Now please put that pistol away, your grace, before someone gets hurt—and by 'someone' I mean the duchess," he said, pressing his lips together in a moue of concern, as though the notion troubled him as well.

Kesgrave showed no response to the provocation. His grip on the gun remained steady and he continued to regard the crime lord with bland interest.

But Renfield stiffened.

Clenching his hands on the table, he tightened his shoulders and lowered his head.

He knew it was the end of the negotiation.

The duke would never defend the killer's life at the expense of his wife's safety.

Except it was not over.

Chidingly, Kesgrave urged Hawes to refrain from making threats he would regret. "Your exasperation is understandable, as this frustrating impasse is of your own making and you know it. If you had not insisted on embroiling us in this affair, then you would be free to torment Renfield as you see fit—only you would not have cause to torment him because he would still be among your most trusted lieutenants. Now you have the truth and the identity of the traitor, and your position as the supremely powerful King of Saffron Hill is secure once again. All in all, a fine outcome for you. It is a win. Accept it and be satisfied."

It was not what Hawes wanted to hear, and with a shake of his head, he murmured, "So be it then," drew the gun from the holster, and aimed the firearm at Bea.

The movement was gorgeous, smooth and swift, and even as her heart thudded with painful vigor at the sinister length of the weapon, she craved the exquisite fluidity.

That was what she wanted Prosser to teach her.

Imagine doing everything with such agility, she thought as she slowly, cautiously, raised her chin to look Hawes dead in the eyes.

And they *were* dead, she noticed with alarm.

Under thick lashes, the gold-colored eyes had none of their usual liveliness.

They were flat and focused.

He would do it.

To gain possession of Renfield, Hell and Fury would pull the trigger.

And yet as a shiver of terror raced through her, she knew it did not make sense. A man of his intelligence inciting a duke of the realm to vindictive fury over a neutralized threat —it defied logic.

"On your feet, Rennie," Hawes said coolly, his lifeless eyes trained on Bea as he took a step toward her, the gun lifting upward one inch, then two, then three, until it was pointed at her forehead. "We are leaving."

Another tremor coursed through her as she contemplated stepping in front of Renfield and ordering Hawes to stand down. In her head, she pictured her body crumbled on the floor in a heap, blood seeping onto the rug from the hole in her temple.

Hawes saw it too, the fear she could not hide, the uncertainty she could not smother, and he smiled faintly as he drew closer, the menace of his presence increasing with every step.

It took everything Bea had to remain fixed to the spot, for it was frightening the way he loomed, the way her own breath caught in her throat, the way the barrel came into focus, and she marveled at his determination to cow her up close when he was utterly petrifying from ten paces away.

Oh, and then it whispered in her ears, the echo of Hell and Fury's own voice as he declared his preference for murder weapons that were reliable from ten paces away, and she realized it was all a hum.

The dead eyes and the ominous stance were tactics designed to make her yield, thereby relieving him of the obligation of sparing her.

Because he *was* too clever to rouse a sleeping beast.

The trembling in her limbs subsided as she crossed the few remaining two feet to Hawes and told him to put the gun away before someone got hurt. "And by 'someone' I mean me because I know you do not want to live with the consequences of harming a hair on my head. You are too clever not to appreciate the difference between being a wanted man and being a *wanted* man. The latter would not know a moment's peace before being hounded to an early grave, while the former could continue as he was with the added benefit of knowing who had betrayed him. As Kesgrave said, you got from us exactly what you asked for: the identity of Mortimer's killer. With that, our business is concluded."

Hawes's lips tightened and for one humming second Bea feared she had grossly misjudged the situation, and her throat went dry with terror. But then the light reentered his eyes and laughing he said, "When you are right, duchess, you are right. I do appreciate the difference and dutifully bow to your wishes. It is with heavy regret, as I was genuinely looking forward to a public tribunal. We were going to put on quite a show, Rennie and I, but I will have access to him in Newgate and he is here now."

And then boom!

Bea pitched backward as gunfire roared in her ears followed by a high-piercing shriek, which she knew was the discharge of the bullet, but it aligned so perfectly with Renfield's cry of distress it felt as though it was emitted from the depth of his soul. He heaved forward to clutch his shoe, already soaked with blood, as Kesgrave leaped with preternatural speed to propel Hawes against the nearest surface, which happened to be a cabinet with a glass window that shattered from the crash of bodies.

Amused despite the forearm pressed against his throat, Hawes said, "Not a hair harmed—I believe that was the only condition. Duchess, please confirm for your husband that you are unhurt."

She heard the request dimly over the ringing in her ear, and even as the noise began to subside, the throbbing in her head intensified.

And her knees—they were unsettling weak.

She wanted nothing more than to sink to the floor but comprehended on a visceral level the importance of remaining upright.

To show any ill effects from the shot would be to further enrage Kesgrave, which would take them further and further away from a resolution.

Testing her voice, Bea said, "I am fine."

It did not quiver or shake.

Emboldened, she continued, "I have suffered no damage."

"You see—as fit as a fiddle," the crime lord said approvingly as Renfield shrugged off his coat to wrap it around the wound. Then he lauded his former lieutenant's capability, predicting that he would thrive in Newgate, even with the bullet wound. "I am sure there is no reason to worry overly much that it will turn gangrenous amid the squalor on the ward. And I had to shoot something, didn't I, because the predicament was so vexing and Her Outrageousness was not a viable option."

How reasonable he sounded as he matter-of-factly justified discharging his weapon a few inches from the Duchess of Kesgrave's head, and the duke, not sharing this assessment, informed the crime lord he would never draw on Beatrice again. Then he swung his fist, striking Hawes in the eye with a clean slice, economical and neat, and as the victim's head flew back, she wondered if she could learn how to deliver a blow like that as well.

Probably, yes, as her brawling instructor was less prim and prejudiced than Prosser.

Bea no sooner had the thought than its cool appraisal struck her as an inexplicable thing. Seconds ago, she had stared down an infamous killer training a gun at her head and now, even as a desperate ringing sounded in her ears, she was weighing the likelihood of acquiring a new pugilism skill.

Kesgrave was right: She *had* come a long way.

Whoever she had been—the stammering wallflower hiding behind a ficus, the timid spinster cowering in expectation of her own bludgeoning—she no longer was. It had been months since she had sputtered incoherently, mortified by attention, humiliated by her own insufficiency. Now she routinely confronted murderers and issued strange assignments to her staff.

She had even asked Marlow to accompany her to Newgate!

Truly, she could not think of any action more chilling, and yet it had proceeded without incident, with the butler readily acceding to her request and keeping whatever private distaste he felt at her appalling conduct carefully concealed.

Of course he did.

She was his employer.

The vibrant and capable Duchess of Kesgrave.

Well, no, she would not go so far as to allow *vibrant,* but on the whole the sentiment fit, and as she stood in the study of one murderer while bidding farewell to another, it seemed incomprehensible that the thought of removing to Haverill Hall turned her bones to jelly. She had stared down London's most notorious criminal, and yet the mean-spirited snickers of a few servants or villagers terrified her.

Let them snicker, she thought now in defiant contempt, unable to conceive of what anyone could do or say that would be more ruinous than Miss Brougham's snide designation of her as drab.

The worst thing had already happened.

Hawes tugged the hem of his tailcoat as the duke stepped back, and whatever anger smoldered at the rough treatment, he hid it behind a mask of good humor. "And on that note, I will bid you farewell. I cannot say I am satisfied with the way our business has turned out, but I have learned my lesson well: The next time I make a deal with the devil, I will secure more favorable terms," he drawled, brushing a speck of dust from his lapel as he reached for the door handle and smiled fleetingly at Bea. "If I see a glimmer of my humiliating capitulation in the window of Hannah Humphrey's shop, your grace, then our agreement is null and void and you are fair game."

Before Bea could respond to his stipulation, Martha flew into the room and announced the arrival of Runners. "There are three, sir," she said to Hawes, for whom she had apparently been keeping watch. "They've nabbed Chester, and one is giving chase to John. It might be simpler if you go out the back way, sir, if the noise I heard earlier was a shot. The garden leads to an alley."

"You are a wise and cautious woman, Martha, which I

appreciate. Thank you for your warning," Hawes said kindly before scowling at Kesgrave. "Bringing in the Runners was an especially low blow, even for you, duke."

Kesgrave shrugged and reminded him that he had imposed himself on a private discussion. "You were neither invited nor expected. I cannot be responsible for your poor decisions."

If Hell and Fury took issue with this rebuke, he did not linger to voice it, sending one last disgusted look at Renfield before crossing the threshold. As he turned into the corridor, he looked back and said, "Remember, duchess, not a whisper in St. James."

The warning amused her, for standing off against the notorious criminal was hardly the sort of thing that would burnish her reputation, and she could readily imagine the caricature of a frail Hawes quivering before a monstrous murder duchess.

It was all just fodder, Bea thought, deciding that she would allow the house party.

Short of burning the ancient home to the ground, per Mrs. Palmer's helpful suggestion, she could not conceive what irreparable harm she could do.

Martha waited for Hawes to disappear into the far room at the end of the corridor, then opened the front door and yelled at the Runners to stop making a spectacle for the neighbors. "We are a respectable establishment!"

In fact, they were not, no, as evidenced by the trail of blood Renfield left as he tottered to the other side of the desk and opened the top drawer. He withdrew a cheroot, which he lit on the wall sconce, and lowered himself gingerly to the armchair. On a hefty sigh, he said, "It is not the way I would have chosen to resolve the matter, but it will do. I am sorry if you are disappointed, your graces. You may console yourselves with knowing you did everything you could to get me to damn myself. Sometimes the villain is too wily for the authorities. As soon as I finish my puff, I shall take myself off to parts unknown. The wounded foot will slow me down, but I reckon I can get myself clear of London before Phinny realizes I slipped the noose."

"But you have not," Kesgrave replied silkily. "When the Runners are done gathering up your former associates, they will arrest you for Mortimer's murder."

Renfield smirked as his lips closed around the cigar and he inhaled the elegant, bitter taste. Expelling the smoke, he begged the duke to recall that he never admitted to the crime. "Without my confession, you have nothing. You said it yourself. The only sway you had over me was the threat of revealing my dark secret to Phinny, and that is gone. You are without power, your grace."

Now he was tough, Bea noted in cynical amusement. The second his former employer left the premises, Renfield felt free to express his contempt lavishly.

"The confession was for the dowager," she said.

"Hmm?" he said vaguely, examining the smoldering tip of his cheroot.

"We wanted to avoid the scandal and difficulty of a trial to spare the dowager duchess further grief," she explained. "That is why we sought a confession. But we have enough evidence without it, especially now that Martha is so eager to please Hawes. Your alibi is gone, and that coupled with testimony from Sandby-Smith, Kerrich, Soames, and Higgins will be enough to close the box nice and tight. Hawes will not like having his dirty business aired in the courtroom, but I suppose he will not let it get that far."

Ash spilled onto his white sleeve as he seemed to forget about the cigar. Suspiciously, he asked, "What do you mean 'not *let* it get that far'?"

"Hawes will orchestrate your execution well before the

trial begins," she replied mildly, as though stating an obvious fact to a small child. "Is that not what he was implying when he said he would have access to you in Newgate? Kesgrave, how did you interpret that remark? Am I being unduly pessimistic?"

On the contrary, he believed she was being needlessly optimistic. "Before arranging Renfield's murder, Hawes will have him tortured, initially to extract information about his plot and then simply to inflict pain. His intentions were crystal-clear to me."

"Yes, that sounds right," she agreed with a nod. "And as someone who recently bribed her way into Newgate, I can say with one hundred percent certainty that Phinny will have no trouble arranging it. Anything can be had there for a price."

Dropping the cheroot on the desk, Renfield cried out, "I did it!"

Bea, tilting her head to the side with curiosity, asked if he intended for his exclamation to stand as a confession.

"It depends," he said evasively. "Is the original offer still available? In exchange for sparing Mortimer's grandmother the pain and agony of a public trial, I am exiled to a penal colony in New South Wales."

"It is," Kesgrave replied.

"Then it was me," he stated forthrightly. "I did it. Your theory is correct. When Kerrich told me about his colleague's visit to Soames's collection, I knew Hawes would find out about the medieval forgeries and question Matlock about them. It was only a matter of time, so I had to act quickly. That night, I snuck into his studio after dark—he was still at his worktable—and did not hesitate or waste time with explanations. I was gone within minutes, leaving behind a murder scene that bore none of my usual hallmarks. It was bloody and chaotic, as though Matlock had put up a good struggle. In reality, he had no opportunity to understand what was happening. It was a risk but a minor one, I thought. None of the neighbors could identify me because I wore a disguise, and they would not have recognized me regardless because I had not been to the studio since September. I assumed I was safe, and so I should have been. Phinny asking the murder duchess to investigate was beyond my wildest imaginings. I still can't believe he exposed his business dealings to you. He was more suspicious than I realized."

"He was the Duke of Kesgrave's cousin," Bea pointed out. "You must have known we would take an interest in his relative's death."

"But I didn't!" he exclaimed with an air of self-disgust. "The *Gazette* hasn't mentioned Her Outrageousness in weeks, and the assumption was she had stopped investigating because she carried the Matlock heir. I trusted that I had nothing to fear from that quarter, for even if the duke was inclined to take an interest in his cousin's murder, it was unlikely he would find out about it. Matlock's real name was not on the lease, and the neighbors knew him as Louis Rousseau. If anything, I figured it would be at least a week before Ollie realized something was wrong. The idea that Phinny confided in you astonishes me. When I heard it was your own groom who fetched the coroner, I cursed my rotten luck, came home to write business prospectuses for our joint enterprise, and waited for you to call."

A Runner appeared in the doorway to take custody of Renfield, who asked for a few minutes to finish his cheroot, as he doubted his new situation would provide many opportunities to enjoy fine Indian tobacco. Then he puffed several times on the cigar, blew a cloud, and advised the duchess not to dismiss the rout cake venture out of hand. "I was facetious in my proposals, but the more I think about it, the more I warm to the idea. If you play your cards well, you could have a thriving concern for decades to come. You could have a rout cake empire. Yes, I know that is properly horrifying to you. Quality and their abiding contempt for trade! It can't last. At some point greed will overcome disdain."

Exile to a penal colony in the tropics had put the bare-knuckled brawler in a philosophical mood, and as Kesgrave informed the Runner of his prisoner's injured foot, Renfield expounded on the inevitable changes time would bring to society. Despite his dire prospects, the notion of a future dominated by crass financial incentives seemed to cheer him considerably.

Stepping outside, Bea observed that Renfield appeared to regard his forthcoming incarceration as an intriguing invest-ment opportunity. "It is probably for the best. Considering the conditions to which he will be subjected, Hawes's comment regarding gangrene was not wide of the mark. I suppose that is why he shot him. If he could not torment in close proximity, then he would do it remotely."

To her surprise, Kesgrave agreed with this verdict.

She had expected his first words once they left the house to be a condemnation of her recklessness. Instead, he noted that necrosis was an especially painful way to die, then asked Jenkins to take them to Clarges Street. He wanted to inform the dowager of the apprehension and conviction of her grandson's murderer right away.

"It will give her some peace, I think," she said softly as she settled onto the carriage bench. Relieved to have escaped excoriation, she contemplated the best way to tell him about the house party Lady Abercrombie had arranged in direct defiance of his command.

She could simply announce it.

Or she could ask him to explain again how his dear friend Tilly had too much respect for his authority to flout his wishes and *then* announce it.

Obviously, she wanted to gloat.

But only a little.

She would never be so gauche as to cross the line into exuberant preening.

What was its opposite?

Subdued preening?

Restrained preening?

Preening inflected with a hint of morosity?

Amused by the quandary, she turned to Kesgrave to put the question to him and realized he was glowering at her. "Evade my gaze all you want, Bea, but it will not dissuade me from grasping you by the shoulders, shaking you violently, and asking what in the devil's name were you thinking, *arguing* with a man pointing a gun at your head?"

But it was not a shake, violent or otherwise.

It was a single jostle followed by caressing strokes.

Despite the gentleness, he was furious, and his cerulean eyes glittered with wrath. "I know what you are going to say. You are going to point to your continued good health as proof that you were never in danger, as though the outcome were predetermined. It was not! Despite the great faith you have in your judgment, you know nothing of the heart and mind of a man like Hawes. You cannot assume he will act rationally—and what does *rational* even mean for a criminal of his magnitude? Silencing a harpy who will not get out of his way might have been the rational response!"

Even as his voice deepened with rage, his touch remained soft, and she mustered a smile at the description. "A harpy, really? Are you sure you do not wish to go with a creature a little less vicious and predatory, such as a fishwife?"

His brow creased fiercely as he warned, "You will not cajole me out of my temper."

"Or a virago," she suggested, not willing yet to abandon the tactic.

"Bea!" he said threateningly.

Clearly, he would not allow himself to be teased out of his dark mood.

Very well, then, she thought, announcing that she had just been following his lead. "Hawes threatened me, and you replied with bland pedantry. When you did not express concern or respond in kind, I assumed that meant you did not perceive him as a threat, which struck me as logical because he is too clever to make an enemy of you without a benefit for himself. I briefly questioned that conclusion when I met his dead-eyed stare over the barrel of the gun, but then he took a step toward me and I knew there was no danger. If he actually intended to hurt me, then he would not have made an effort to convince me he intended to hurt me—if that makes sense. He was like a gambler putting more money on the table to bolster a weak hand."

Far from mollifying him, her answer only enraged him further, for he had not replied with *bland pedantry*! "It was cold calculation. I knew revealing even a hint of fear would give him control of the situation and he would stroll out with Renfield in tow. The Runners could not have been more than a few minutes from arriving and I wanted to distract him while keeping the focus off you. I did not expect him to pull out a gun and aim it at your head or for you to march toward the firearm and start issuing orders. You took ten years off my life, Bea."

But that was nonsense, was it not, for she had seen the way he had assailed Hawes, hauling the crime lord against the cabinet before she had even drawn a breath and planting a facer with dizzying speed.

Those agile maneuvers were not the actions of a man rendered ineffectual by fear.

No, his years of sparring with Gentleman Jackson had served him well, and recalling the punishing blow now, she marveled over his impressive dexterity and enviable fluidity.

"Zimmer is doing a commendable job, to be sure, for he equipped me with the trick that allowed me to overcome Waltham, but nothing I have learned compares with your remarkable abilities. I am envious and in awe."

Rather than accept the praise, he raised an eyebrow cynically and announced with stern disapproval that nor would he be flattered out of his temper. "Your conduct was reckless, and we will discuss it."

"You are right, of course," she said firmly, filing away all thoughts of the house party as a more interesting way to pass the drive to Clarges Street occurred to her. "We must examine every detail of the encounter with diligence and care to ensure I comprehend just how egregiously I behaved. To that end, I shall endeavor to quell my deep admiration for your form and say nothing of how watching you move with the beauty and grace of a dancer created a highly disconcerting sensation in my belly."

Regarding her severely, he was nevertheless gentle as the fingers grasping her shoulders began to entice upward, along her neck, eliciting a shiver of pleasure. His tone was grim and censorious as he said, "And now you are trying to seduce me out of my anger."

"I am not, no," she murmured, shifting forward to draw closer to his heat before adding with an impish smile, "I am angling for lessons with the great Jackson himself."

Either the quip or the grin had the desired effect, for his grip tightened as he pulled her against his chest and claimed her lips in a consuming kiss that immediately muddled her thoughts. She made no word of protest when his hand slipped beneath the edge of her gown or when he said softly in her ear, the wisp of breath a seductive titter, "We are not done talking about this, brat."

Oh, but they were.

**BEA AND THE DUKE RETURN WITH
ANOTHER MYSTERY SOON!**

In the meantime, look for Verity Lark's latest adventure, in
which Bea ***FINALLY*** gets her shooting lesson!

A Lark's Regret.

Available for preorder now

My Gracious Thanks

Pen a letter to the editor!

Dearest Reader,

A writer's fortune has ever been wracked with peril - and wholly dependent on the benevolence of the reading public.

Reward an intrepid author's valiant toil!

Please let me know what you think of *A Pernicious Fabrication* on Amazon or Goodreads!

About the Author

Mistress Lynn Messina is the author of 14 novels of questionable morality, including the *Beatrice Hyde-Clare Mysteries* series and the *Love Takes Root* series of lurid romances.

Aside from writing scandalous fiction to corrupt well-behaved young ladies, Mistress Messina hosts a Socials page where a certain dubious gentleman by the name of Mr. Twaddle-Thum regularly shares scurrilous and certainly false gossip.

Mr. Twaddle-Thum is likewise the author of a worthless little news sheet known as *The Beakeeper.* It prides itself on being filled with nothing but utter tripe and nonsense. It can, however, serve as a remedy for a spot of Sunday afternoon ennui.

Mistress Messina resides in the uppity colonial city of New York with her sons.

The Fellingham Minx

The Bolingbroke Chit

The Impertinent Miss Templeton

Stand Alones

Prejudice and Pride

The Girls' Guide to Dating Zombies

Savvy Girl

Winner Takes All

Little Vampire Women

Never on a Sundae

Troublemaker

Fashionista (Spanish Edition)

Violet Venom's Rules for Life

Henry and the Incredibly Incorrigible, Inconveniently Smart
Human

Welcome to the Bea Hive

FUN STUFF FOR BEATRICE HYDE-CLARE FANS

NEW DESIGN ALERT!!

Office of Rout Cake Enjoyment tee

The Bea Tee

Beatrice's favorite three warships not only in the wrong order but also from the wrong time period. (Take that, maritime tradition *and* historical accuracy!)

The Kesgrave Shirt

A tee bearing the Duke of Kesgrave's favorite warships in the
order in which they appeared in the Battle of the Nile

Available in mugs too!

See all the options in Lynn's Store.

Printed in Great Britain
by Amazon